# *Arthur's Ashes*

Reg Elliot

**COVE PRESS**

Published by Cove Press 2006

Copyright © 2006 Reg Elliot

The moral right of the author has been asserted

Cove Press,  Bristol, UK

British Library Cataloguing in Publication Data.

A catalogue record for this book is available from
the British Library

ISBN   0-9551714-0-7

For Orders, Inquiries & Feedback :

Arthursashes@hotmail.com

*'That so few dare to be eccentric marks the chief danger of our times.'*

Frank Stewart Mills - 1938

*Somewhere in the not too distant future.*

*Dark days have befallen England's greatest game. If one were to liken the state of English cricket to the weather, one would be very wet. If one were asked to forecast the weather it would be a gloomy forecast for the foreseeable future. But one could be wrong! For way off, in a distant part of the land, the clouds have parted. The sun is given a brief chance to shine. Just how much sunshine we are allowed is in the hands of the gods, and Arthur Jenkins!*

# Part One

# The Second Chance

# 1

In the rainforests of Madagascar lives a possum-like creature named the aye-aye. In order to identify the whereabouts of its next meal, the aye-aye taps upon tree trunks to locate larvae within. Having done so, the animal gnaws and scrapes a hole in the trunk and sends in a long, spindly finger to extract a squirming snack.

At first glance Arthur Jenkins appeared to be the human equivalent of the aye-aye. Not that he had a spindly finger – it was more to do with his behaviour as he shuffled around trains, tapping on walls or listening against floors. Unlike the aye-aye, having located what it was he was after, he didn't rip out an offending corroded bolt or stripped screw and pop it in his mouth; he just jotted it down on a report card and went in search of the next defect.

Arthur glanced at his watch before rushing to a window on the opposite side of the carriage as if he'd forgotten something important. He wiped the condensation from the window pane, pressed his face against the glass and peered outwards. A fellow worker appeared by his side and nudged him in the ribs.

'Fiver says he misses,' said a voice.

'You're on,' replied Arthur, not taking his eye off a distant figure on an sports field adjacent to the train tracks. The other man hurriedly cleaned the pane next to Arthur and looked outside as well.

It was raining. Squinting slightly, the men could make out the figure of a lone boy near some sodden cricket nets. Holding a red ball in his hand, the boy walked away from the nets before turning to face them again. Performing a bird-like hop, he lunged forward and broke into a stride that quickly became a canter. His shoulders rose and his chest deepened, his arms seemingly entangled. Finally, he arched backwards as he leapt high in the air, his body turning side-on. The boy appeared to float for a moment before crashing back to earth. His arms finally unfolded and the red ball shot from his hand down the wicket.

Arthur squinted, straining to see the ball's destination as the train bulged outwards around a bend. The picture had almost become obscured as the ball sailed harmlessly wide of three stumps stabbed into the ground at the end of the pitch.

'What happened?' cried the fellow worker. 'I couldn't see.'

Arthur was already reaching into his back pocket for his wallet.

'Not again. I don't believe it.' said the man. 'Over a year we've been watching him and he still ain't hit em.'

Taking five pounds from Arthur the fellow smiled, stuffed the note in his top pocket, and turned away.

'Cheers, Arthur.'

'Next time,' warned Arthur keenly. 'Middle stump!'

Arthur slid his wallet back into his pocket and shook his head in disbelief.

The cumbersome train continued to bully its way up the Northern line towards Alemead Station. Eventually there was a surging motion followed by a shudder as the train came to a standstill. Arthur, as was his custom, was always the last off the train, shuffling towards the guard's compartment where he removed his navy cap. In the corner sat a shrivelled-looking man with a toothless grin, fumbling with a chart on his lap. His knees bounced up and down like a child's. His name was Eric.

'What do you make of her, Arthur? Her time up?' Eric asked expectantly. Arthur carefully placed his cap on a hook and put the clipboard on his desk, as Eric winced and sucked his teeth.

'Bearings and bushes,' said Arthur. 'She's not going anywhere just yet. Running smoother than you!' Arthur joked as he pulled a wad of paperwork from a rack of wooden shelves and sat down.

'Not much *don't* run smoother 'an me,' reflected Eric.

Arthur reached up towards an old radio perched on a shelf above his head and flicked it on. Always set to the same station, it sparked to life. A sports round-up was in progress.

Arthur listened as he completed his forms methodically.

'*It was a massive run chase for an out-of-form England side and with the wicket turning their hopes looked slim from the start.*'

'Oh blimey!' cried Arthur turning the set off instantly. Eric looked quizzically across the room as Arthur went on, 'Don't want to know the score.'

Eric mumbled. 'I don't either but I'll tell you who . . .'

'Ah!' said Arthur irritably.

4

'What you bothering for?' asked Eric confused. 'We lost the series two weeks ago!'

Arthur continued doggedly with his paperwork.

'Yes but we can win the last Test!' he informed Eric.

'Don't know why you bother. They're a dead loss.' moaned Eric.

Arthur completed a page, ripped it from the pad, stamped it, and exclaimed across the musty room, 'Well, that's something then, Eric!'

'What's that?' the little man asked.

'English cricket don't run as smooth as you!' Eric smiled, feeling better.

The land was drenched by sheets of rain falling from a blanket of cloud. Among the houses and cottages of Wielding Willow, Arthur's home village, were the perfect lines of a rectangular hedge, broken only by a wooden gate bearing the name 'Lord's'. The shoulder-high hedges, like a massive inverted moat, protected a single-storey cottage, on top of which, a prominent weathervane was mounted. The weathervane was in the form of a batsman playing a stylish straight drive. At the front of the cottage, jonquils sagged under the weight of swollen raindrops.

A figure ambled towards the gate. It was Arthur. Wearing a hat and a heavy coat, but carrying no umbrella, he walked in the rain at a measured pace with his head tilted forward, deep in thought. Most men's heads would have been full of much the same things: unpaid bills, the latest world news, which team won at what sport. But not Arthur Jenkins – his head was invariably crammed full of thoughts relating to all things cricket. In fact that afternoon, as he walked home, he had had only one non-cricketing thought as he struggled to recall the name of the man with the jellied eel stand outside the Fat Lady's Arms, a pub of his youth. He eventually gave up, knowing full well he'd remember sometime later, probably when it didn't really matter anymore. As he approached the gate he had another non-cricketing thought: would Shirley, his wife's best friend, be visiting again? As it turned out, this thought did have something to do with cricket, for, if Shirley *were* visiting, Arthur would be able to go to his local cricket club for a pint and watch the day's play in Australia.

Spotting a familiar car parked up the road, a smile spread across his face. He would get his pint after all.

Arthur's wife, Jean, was standing just inside the doorway talking to Shirley as Arthur went in.

'Hello,' he chirped as he kissed his wife on the cheek.

'Hello,' he said more formally turning to Shirley. Rather than kiss her, he extended his hand.

Jean rolled her eyes, sighing. 'Arthur, you've known Shirley thirty-five years.'

'Just don't want her getting the wrong idea!' he replied jokingly.

'I wouldn't kiss you anyway, Arthur Jenkins. Not even if you were George Clooney,' said Shirley.

'And if I were George Clooney–' Arthur said before being interrupted by Jean.

'Arthur!' she exclaimed. 'I've asked Shirley round so you can go to the club and watch the cricket, so don't be cheeky!'

His behaviour improved immediately.

'Ted called and asked if he'd see you there. So off you go.'

Arthur looked wide-eyed at Jean. Then he looked at Shirley. Then back at Jean again. 'Right. Home about nine then,' he told her.

'If you want dinner,' she suggested with a nod.

'Nine*ish*,' Arthur replied hopefully. He gave Jean an appreciative smile, grabbed his cricket jumper, tied it in a knot around his waist and flicked a waterproof jacket over his shoulders. After checking he had money and the house keys, he turned to go.

'Cheerio, Shirley,' he called, giving her a regulation smile this time.

'You're not expecting us to win are you?' said Shirley quite to Arthur's surprise. 'They don't seem too good to me.'

Arthur stopped, slightly shocked. 'Is that what you think?' he asked her.

Shirley said nothing as Arthur continued, 'There's a wonderful old saying, you know: We live in hope! And you know what? I do.'

With that, Arthur blinked and bustled out of the front door. Then, just as quickly as he'd gone, he reappeared, having forgotten something. He grabbed his hat, and again disappeared backwards out of the door, flashing another grin at Shirley.

'Nineish,' he shouted to Jean.

# 2

The once white walls inside the Good Walloping Cricket Club had seen better days. Occasional sunlight and the tannin of a thousand cigarettes had seen to that. The small clubhouse bar ran almost the entire length of its back wall, while opposite the bar, large glass windows extended the length of the space, which resembled a comfortable games room. On cricketing days, most patrons could be found perched on a small deck outside the clubhouse, cheering on their team as they watched the wickets tumble. This particular evening, the dormant wicket was surrounded by stakes and plastic tape to keep bicycling children and non-cricketers off the hallowed square. It was plainly the off-season and the clubhouse was open only because the Test series was being played.

Most of the patrons at the club sat at tables, facing away from the ground and craning their necks up at the ancient television set and VCR mounted above the bar. Being a small club, and therefore very thrifty, there was no live coverage. The committee had decided to record the previous day's play and re-run it from 4.00 p.m. until close. Although this was illegal, most felt it better than getting up at midnight to watch it alone. Bar takings had skyrocketed and the end-of-season trip to Scotland was looking likely to be scrapped for the Caribbean. Those viewing gripped their pints and listened as the commentators set the scene for the day's play.

As he waited for Ted, Arthur stood with his beloved Good Walloping cricket jumper pulled down over his paunch, and sipped his ale as he stared out the window towards the dormant pitch.

A loud voice from behind him called, 'Thinking about all your ducks, are you, Arthur?' A roar of laughter went up from a small group to Arthur's rear. A tall, well-built man in his late twenties stood facing Arthur with his hands on his hips. His hair was short at the back but long and unruly at the front; a jet-black curl hung down, almost touching a cruel, hooked nose set between two full-length sideburns. His eyes were beady and unflinching. He was Jim Singleton, the fastest bowler at Good Walloping, and a right prat in Arthur's opinion. Not looking the least bit perturbed, Arthur turned round to face Singleton, who went on,

'You'd be counting for a while.' claimed Singleton as a table full of his cronies continued to giggle.

'If you put more effort into your bowling than your piss-taking, Jim, you'd be a good bowler.' Arthur's composure wasn't what the man had expected.

'Listen to the Svengali of Good Walloping, master coach Arthur Jenkins,' Singleton continued to taunt, moving closer to Arthur before leaning towards him in a menacing manner. 'Mate, I'm already the best in the club, in case you weren't aware.'

'Could be better,' Arthur informed him. 'If you wanted,' he added challengingly.

Singleton was silent for a moment.

'You should listen to him, Jim!' shouted Reg Foster, the barman and an ex-chairman of the club. Singleton glanced over his shoulder. Foster was stationed at the end of the bar. 'Arthur was a shite cricketer, but a bloody handy coach!' he went on, provoking more laughter. He pointed to an honours board on the wall close by. 'Remember these?' Foster asked, tapping where four consecutive entries indicated championships for Good Walloping. 'He coached them all!' Foster nodded in Arthur's direction. 'Our longest run as champions,' he announced as Arthur appeared to grow a foot taller. 'And the last time we won the cup!'

Singleton was outgunned. But like most big mouths with a belly full of booze, didn't know when to quit.

'Heard it all before, Reg,' he sighed. 'Maybe you should be coaching the national side.' Singleton prodded Arthur in the chest. 'Seeing as they're such rubbish! Maybe you could save English cricket . . . supercoach.' Arthur was about to turn away when Singleton continued. 'We heard all about your ideas Arthur,' he announced to the room at large. 'Them maaaad ideas. All those years ago,' Singleton teased.

There was another round of laughter and applause from his mates as Singleton swallowed thirstily from his pint and thumped the empty glass down on the bar, looking satisfied with himself.

Arthur's response was a cold stare.

At that moment a man slipped into the bar unnoticed. It was Ted Doyle, Arthur's best mate.

'Cheers,' said Ted, greeting Arthur.

'All right, Ted?' replied Arthur.

Ted saw Singleton scowling in their direction, but thought little of it as Singleton always scowled.

'All right, Jim?' asked Ted in a friendly manner.

Singleton burped and nodded.

'Pint of Pride?' Ted asked Arthur, already making his way over to the bar.

'Yep,' said Arthur, 'a pint of *Pride*,' he added loudly. 'Thanks, Ted. Why don't you get Jim one as well?' Arthur looked at the brooding shape of Singleton. 'He could do with some,' he went on, staring the man down. As his friends returned to their beers, Singleton realised he had been beaten by a better man and kept his trap shut.

Arthur moved towards a table as Ted approached with the drinks. 'What was all that about?' Ted asked as he handed Arthur his beer.

'No matter,' Arthur told him. 'Let's just say it was a spirited discussion between cricket lovers.' Arthur sipped his pint then placed it on a soggy beer mat, rubbed his cheeks and sat upright.

'Right!' he exclaimed, turning his attention to the reason he was at the club. 'It's fine in Sydney. We need 489 runs to save the Test. The pitch is playing a little slow and we're at full strength. What do you think?'

Ted wiped beer from his upper lip before answering. 'We'll be out of here in two hours,' he observed dryly before asking, 'What do *you* think?'

Arthur thought long and hard then pulled his chair closer to Ted's and locked eyes on him. 'I think it's going to be our day, Ted.' Arthur rarely seemed so earnest. 'We could do this,' he said, slamming his fist on the table. 'Sooner or later the drought must break!' He shook his fist vigorously at Ted, who was sitting bolt upright now. 'It won't be long now – we can teach these Aussies a lesson, you know. We just have to find the old *fighting spirit*!' Arthur said with feeling, before sitting back and grabbing his pint. 'Come on England!' he shouted. They charged their glasses.

'I love watching cricket with you, Jenkins,' he told Arthur. 'You even have *me* believing we can win!'

Arthur motioned to the TV set as play began for the day. The two men watched as the ball was delivered.

'Bowled him!' the commentator almost shouted. 'First ball of the day and England lose their first wicket with the score at nought. Well . . . this is a disaster.' The voice was drowned out by the mutual groans of the crowd.

'Hell's bells,' sighed Ted.

Later that evening Arthur's eyes had lost a little of their sparkle. Perhaps it was the smoky room or the ale, for his optimism rarely deserted him. He managed to hold his chin up defiantly, but his bottom lip gave him away this particular evening, hanging limply beneath his freshly trimmed moustache. While everyone had hoped for quick runs in the chase for victory, the only thing happening on this particular evening was the toppling of English wickets.

As the last of the beer slid down his throat, the world around Arthur appeared to be slowing down, the voices around him seeming to mock him. His thoughts hit a melancholy patch and he had to force the gloom from his mind.

'I'd buy you a pint, Arthur, but it'll all be over shortly,' said Ted sadly to his mate.

'Nonsense,' blurted Arthur. 'Buy a jug. We're not done yet!' Ted somehow managed to get to his feet, swaying a little as he pushed his seat back.

'Bowled him!' came the cry from the television commentator. 'Evans is clean bowled by Rogers to end the sorry tale for England this summer.'

Ted slumped back in a heap.

'You're not getting out of a shout that easy,' Arthur informed him sternly. 'One for the road,' he instructed, adding at the last moment in a more subdued tone, 'A half!'

Ted knew Arthur was bitterly disappointed. 'We'll get them next time, mate,' he said and gave Arthur a slap on the back.

'Aye. Two and a half more years. How many more *next times* do we have left, Ted?' Arthur reflected as his friend made for the bar. 'Maybe there's some good young 'uns coming up,' he mumbled optimistically.

For a moment a shadow of doubt crossed his mind as he looked down at the floor disconsolately. His head bobbed causing him to sway a little then, catching himself quickly, he propped himself upright again. Arthur was tight and he knew it! Half a pint later he wasn't much better.

'Time gentlemen,' Ted said to Arthur. Arthur smiled as he hauled himself out of his chair.

'Reckon so,' he conceded.

Behind them Singleton and his mob still carried on, but when Singleton spotted Arthur and Ted getting to their feet, he shouted, 'The supercoach is leaving the building!' laughing at his own joke. Arthur couldn't be bothered to reply. 'I told you they were shite, Jenkins!' taunted Singleton, who seemingly wouldn't give up until he had got a response. He stood up and tried again. 'We need you, Arthur,' Singleton called as he staggered towards them. 'You're our only hope,' he slurred.

'What's he on about?' Ted asked, having missed the earlier exchange.

Singleton jumped in to answer. 'He's a SUPERCOACH!' Singleton told Ted as if he were the last on the planet to find out.

Arthur had had enough and went to retrieve his sweater from the back of his chair, but Singleton was quicker than he, and placed his hand over the top of the sweater and chair. 'Those who can't do . . . Coach,' Singleton hissed.

'You know, I meant what I said earlier,' said Arthur. Singleton was too drunk to remember, so Arthur reminded him. 'You really could be a good bowler.' With that Arthur yanked his sweater out from under Singleton's hand, causing the big man to crash to the ground in a heap.

As Arthur and Ted moved towards the door, Singleton staggered to his feet and stumbled after Arthur. Just as he was about to reach him, Reg Foster stepped in and restrained Singleton. 'It'll be the last thing you do in this club if you do, Jim.'

Singleton was fuming but kept his distance as he faced Arthur. 'You're no supercoach, Jenkins. You're nothing,' Singleton spat angrily. 'I been told they were the best team ever,' he slurred, pointing at the honours board. 'They would have won anyway. With or without you! Singleton was laughing again. 'They lost faith in you old man.'

Arthur stopped in his tracks – it seemed as if Singleton had finally hit a nerve.

'Crazy coach!' Singleton shouted as Arthur finally left the room.

Reg Foster spun Singleton around and pushed him towards his mates. 'That's you for the night, Jim.'

Singleton murmured incoherently under his breath and slumped back into his seat with a heavy thud, his friends still sniggering amongst themselves.

Arthur and Ted sat in the back of the minicab they had ordered earlier, Ted having pulled Arthur's jumper sleeves down past his hands and tied each one in a knot.

'Hope you don't need a leak,' he joked.

'Look, I've had my tubes tied,' Arthur announced, waving the knots at Ted. The cab pulled over.

'This is you, Arthur,' Ted said.

Arthur tried to open the door but of course struggled so that Ted had to open it for him.

'How much do I owe you, Roger?' Arthur asked, trying to shove his knotted hands into his pockets. Ted was in fits of laughter and even the cabbie was amused.

'Think Mr Doyle 'ere will be getting this one, Arthur,' said the cab driver as Ted pulled the door shut still laughing. 'Night, Arthur,' he called, ramming the cab into gear and moving off. Arthur waved his knotted hands at Ted who was peering through the rear window at his daft friend; he watched the lights grow smaller until they popped and were no more.

Fumbling with his twisted jumper, Arthur eventually released his hands as he ambled in a slightly crooked line towards his house, speeding up a little when he saw that his watch read 9.48 p.m. As he approached his house he peered up at the weathervane.

'Shot!' he called up to it, reflecting after a moment. 'Must be an Australian.'

A feeling of emptiness washed over Arthur as he reflected on the day, the season and life in general. Singleton's words still festered.

'*They lost faith in you, old man.*' They hurt him to the core and yet he was strangely grateful that Singleton had been so hard on him. The man's unpleasantness had exposed a void that Arthur could not shut his eyes to.

He pushed past the gate and shuffled up the front path. Leaving the cold night air behind him, he opened the door, muttering, 'You've not done enough.'

## 3

Arthur had fond memories of his coaching days, and although they had finished over twenty years earlier, his recollections remained vivid. Having coached Good Walloping to its fourth consecutive championship, Arthur had promised himself it would *not* be his last. The most recent one under his guidance had been a narrow victory to say the least, whereas the three previous finals had been comfortable wins. Arthur had sensed the other teams were improving rapidly. The next year the opposition would be well and truly out to get them.

Arthur had realised that if he and his players kept using the same methods on the field it would ultimately be Good Walloping's undoing; he had sensed that any team bold enough to attempt something different would take the prize. So he set about devising a new strategy. Watching his team practising one day, Arthur decided he would start by focusing on a regime of strength and fitness – after all, most senior members of the team were always promising Arthur (and themselves) that they would be fully fit 'next year'. The trouble was there had been four 'next years', and the only thing they had developed was their girths.

Arthur began learning all he could about the human body and how to condition it from books, but he felt he needed expert guidance. Enrolling on a simple physical fitness course, he spent ten nights over five weeks in a dim room at the local university. He then went on a course that concentrated solely on the anatomical workings of the human body, pestering the lecturer in between classes with an endless stream of questions. As he dug deeper and deeper, Arthur worked his way down to the finest detail of the muscular-skeletal system, and by the time the course ended he had already embarked upon another: biomechanical fundamentals. Jean thought Arthur had found a new love. She was right.

It had never occurred to Arthur to combine his engineering background with his newly acquired anatomical knowledge. However, one day, whilst picnicking with friends, the two streams of unrelated thought clashed, causing a collision of gargantuan proportions. Arthur sat bolt upright in the long grass to ponder his discovery. Struck by the force of this great idea, Arthur immediately made his apologies to Jean and his friends, and raced off home to document his revelation.

Some days later, when the idea was further developed, Arthur called a meeting of the Good Walloping team. He outlined his bizarre-sounding plan in detail to the total disbelief of the players. Unlike anything they had ever heard of, it was far too radical and overly complex for mere cricketers to grasp. Adopting Arthur's plan would require an enormous amount of sustained physical effort and, being a lazy team at heart meant he had a battle on his hands from the start. Lacking Arthur's imagination and passion both the committee and players ridiculed him terribly.

Normally such an episode would have been laughed off as a moment of madness and quickly forgotten, but an undercurrent of support had recently been growing for another potential coach. Arthur lost the confidence of both the committee and players, and soon after he was ousted from the coaching role.

The next season Good Walloping finished fifth in the league and went in search of yet another coach, not even considering Arthur. The following year Arthur had once more tried to convince the board of his ideas, which were now fully developed. But again he was rejected and labelled a crackpot thereafter.

With his coaching days over, Arthur had lost something. Were it not for Ted Doyle's encouragement, he might never have set foot in the clubhouse again. Where once he'd been popular with the players, they came to avoid him, and in time he became filled with self-doubt. Though not obsessed or completely consumed by thoughts of his bold plan, try as he may, Arthur could not put it to rest over the years. It would forever be the great unanswered question in his life.

# 4

Arthur woke early despite the fact he'd had several pints the night before. '*You have not done enough.*' Did *I* say that? he wondered as he lay in bed pondering the previous evening's events. And why? Because it was true, he admitted to himself, sensing a familiar warmth course through his veins. It was as if something lost had returned. Feeling energised Arthur leapt out of bed and went downstairs to his desk. Opening the top drawer in a hurry, he looked under a small stack of loose papers and removed a thick brown folder. Flicking on the desk lamp, he sat down, opened the folder and withdrew its contents.

Jean had seen Arthur like this before. Busying himself around the house while singing and whistling wasn't necessarily a new thing, but it had been a while since she had seen such a spring in his step. There was definitely something strange about his mood that day. It was not so much his behaviour that worried her but the timing of it. Normally the day after England lost a Test match, let alone a Test series, he was downtrodden and grumpy. Then she worked it out: England must have won!

'You'll be rushing out to buy all the papers then, I expect,' she said, handing him a cup of tea and placing a kiss on his left cheek.

'Why?' he asked.

'The cricket?' she said.

'Why would I want to buy *all* the papers when one will tell me how badly we lost?' Arthur asked her, taking a sip of tea.

Now it was Jean's turn to be confused. 'And why then are you in such a good mood?'

'I had a very insightful chat with a lad at the club last night,' Arthur stated in an upbeat tone. 'He'd had a little too much to drink, but he's given me something to think about.' Arthur said.

'Oh yes?' inquired Jean as she fished inside a cupboard for Arthur's jacket which she handed to him as he went on.

'Yes. In fact, I feel as though I may be about to embark upon one of my industrious periods,' he announced as he pulled on his cricket jumper instead of the jacket which he placed upon a peg by the door.

17

'A long one or short one?' asked Jean.

'God willing, a long one.' he said fishing an apple from his pocket, he took a bite from it and opened the front door. Turning to face Jean he told her, 'I'll be late today. They're working on the lines. I'll get off at Bairsdow and walk home.'

The Bairsdow station announcer politely informed passengers that the train on platform one would be terminating due to track work and that buses had been laid on for those with valid tickets to continue their journey. Dozens of commuters streamed out of the train and headed for the buses. As the last of them bustled along the platform Arthur tottered out of a carriage, scribbling on his trusty clipboard as he went. He checked his watch and looked up at the sky – the weather forecast had been right, the sun was pouring through a break in the clouds and bathing the countryside beyond the platform. Carrying a bag no bigger than a school satchel, Arthur passed the crowded buses and headed down an unkempt lane flanked by a sprawling hedge. Finding himself approaching a deserted station, he turned left and followed the disused track in the direction of Alemead Station and home.

As he walked the weather changed and a large black cloud appeared; there came the roll of thunder in the distance and a light rain began to fall. Arthur scurried to the side of the track heading for a gap in the hedge that he'd spotted. Forcing his way through, he eventually emerged beside a large cricket ground, quickly recognising it as the one he'd viewed many times from the train. Through the rain there was another familiar sight – on the far side of the ground, he could make out the solitary figure of the boy bowler in the nets.

Arthur made for the cover of the old scoreboard as the rain came down harder. Luckily his flask had enough hot tea for one more cup. Adding three lumps of sugar to the tea, he stirred it while taking in his surroundings, then settled down to watch the bowler.

The boy ran in and sent down a delivery that pitched short of a length, just missing off stump and hitting the net behind. The boy seemed disappointed and shook his head. Arthur noted he was a left-hander. Arthur quietly sipped his tea and continued to watch unnoticed. At that moment his glasses steamed up from the tea and he missed the next delivery which took middle stump. It seemed that the boy was consistently accurate, but to Arthur's trained eye, he could see that he lacked the ingredients essential to success for any fast bowler – speed and aggression!

When the rain finished some fifteen minutes later, Arthur put his thermos away in his bag and turned towards the gap in the hedge. Just as he was about to duck into it, he seemed to hear a strange voice. 'Still time to do more.'

He stopped dead in his tracks a little shocked that the voice had been his. Arthur knew he had only two choices: keep walking, or go over and talk to the boy.

A man's voice from behind the boy announced confidently, 'I'd say you play for Fraser College under 18As.'

The boy turned to see the smiling figure of Arthur, hands clasped neatly behind his back.

'17Bs actually.' replied the boy.

Arthur was a little taken aback so he tried again.

'The 17Bs! Ahhhhh. Second only to the As though.'

'The Bs are the bottom team,' the boy informed Arthur.

'I thought Fraser's had more teams?' replied Arthur, confused. 'I remember watching a 17D team some years back.'

'Probably, but people don't play cricket any more,' explained the boy.

Arthur was aghast.

'I'm Tim Gibson,' the boy said as he walked over to Arthur and extended his hand.

'Arthur Jenkins.' They shook hands. 'Nice to meet you. Finally!'

The boy was perplexed by the 'finally' bit.

Seeing his confusion, Arthur turned and pointed in the direction of the railway line, explaining, 'The train I work on passes most days and I . . .' He was a little embarrassed. 'I can see the ground and well . . . you're always here. At least, I assume it's you.'

The boy smiled and nodded. 'Yeah . . . probably me. I'm here quite a bit,' he admitted, slightly embarrassed. 'I'm trying to make the As.'

There was a long pause. Then Arthur piped up, 'Well,

today's your lucky day.' The boy looked amused as he went on, 'I happen to be . . .' Arthur moved closer and whispered, 'a supercoach!'

Tim began to think that Arthur might be some kind of nutter. There was a moment's awkward silence.

'Go on then. Let's see what you can do,' Arthur told him. The boy regarded Arthur curiously but after a moment's hesitation turned and trudged towards his mark. No sooner had he set off than he heard, 'That how you hold the ball?'

The boy looked at his hand and nodded.

'Well, here's the first thing.' Arthur said and walked over to the boy. He moved the ball out of the back of Tim's hand and placed it closer to his fingertips, so that it touched just three of his fingers instead of four. 'Now that's given you more height, therefore more speed and bounce. Those couple of inches in additional height represent approximately . . . mmm . . .' Arthur scrutinised the boy's height, '. . . say, five per cent of your total height. How many wickets did you take last season?' Arthur asked.

'About twenty,' the boy replied sheepishly.

'Well now, we've just increased that to twenty-two without taking any other factors of the Arthur Jenkins theory into consideration. What do you think?' he asked. The boy looked as if he still thought Arthur was a complete nutter, but set off on his run and let one go which pitched short, sailed over the stumps and through a hole in the back of the net. The boy looked surprised.

Arthur asked him, 'How did that feel? A bit different?'

'They don't normally get up so high,' the boy admitted uncertainly. Arthur beamed with pleasure.

Tim never actually accepted Arthur's proposition to coach him – Arthur just assumed the role, arriving dutifully every Monday, Wednesday and Friday afternoon to put the boy through his paces. Tim even moved his session times to tie in with Arthur's availability.

About three weeks into training Arthur brought with him a large canvas bag.

'What's in that?' asked Tim.

'Tools of the fast bowling trade,' replied Arthur

mysteriously. 'This is what I've been working on. It's a cut-down version but if I'm right, what's in here could change the game.'

For two avid cricket fans Arthur and Tim discussed the game itself surprisingly seldom – there were too many things to do. Tim had never received so much attention and grew to like having someone actually interested in his progress. Arthur almost always referred to Tim as 'boy' and if he did use his name, Tim thought it sounded awkward.

Arthur didn't hold back and put Tim through some strenuous routines employing the techniques once ridiculed at Good Walloping. Already there was a pleasing increase in Tim's bowling speeds. It was the perfect time in his development to introduce him to this type of training as he was growing stronger naturally, which complemented their efforts.

One day Tim brought some kit to the nets and had Arthur pad up just for fun. Arthur found putting the pads on a bit awkward after twenty-five years, but once he'd taken strike and peered down the pitch his hands seemed to melt into the handle of the bat and the comfort of his old stance returned to him, even though he was rather more stooped these days. His bat tapped out a familiar sound on the toe of his boot as Tim ran in. Tim needn't have bowled a ball – Arthur was in heaven. It even felt wonderful being beaten all ends up by an in-swinging yorker that took middle stump. Arthur played carefully. Although Tim was winding him up by pitching the ball where he could hit it, Arthur still couldn't quite middle it. Finally, his frustration led to a rush of blood. With a small skip he brought the bat down on a half volley and there was a crack followed by a warm buzz that travelled from the blade to his hands.

'Shot!' cried Tim.

Arthur watched the ball shoot into the net then skid out of the end and past Tim. As Tim ran to fetch the ball he noticed Arthur twirling his bat in the air proudly – only to fumble and drop it.

The off-season gave Tim lots of time to improve his game, and he and Arthur still met at the ground at least three times a week. When Arthur was not there, Tim would go alone and perform his exercise routine with great diligence.

Time passed and with the new season fast approaching, Tim had a rapid succession of exams and Arthur a wedding in Scotland, forcing the two of them to take a brief break from the training schedule prior to Tim's first game of the season. Arthur returned from Scotland with a nasty dose of flu but nevertheless arrived punctually for their Monday catch-up session. Tim felt he shouldn't have bothered but as usual Arthur's commitment was faultless.

'Two more weekends, boy. How do you feel?' said Arthur coughing into his hands.

'Better than you by the looks of it,' said Tim. 'How did you get a cold in spring anyway?'

'Present from Scotland,' replied Arthur.

That Saturday Jean confined Arthur to domestic duties only – all indoors – even though he was over the worst and hoping to be one hundred per cent better in time for Tim's big day the following week. As he sat by the fireside pouring over the papers there came a loud knock at the front door.

Arthur, sports section of the paper tucked under his arm, opened the door to a stranger in his early thirties. The man had a serious expression and thin rimmed spectacles. He held a small notepad in one hand. Slightly agitated, he introduced himself. 'Carl Thompson from the *Standard*, Mr Jenkins.' Arthur found himself shaking the man's hand firmly. 'May I come in?'

There was a pause as Arthur pondered the man's request.

'What's it about?' asked Arthur.

'Cricket,' replied Thompson.

'Ah! Why didn't you say so?' huffed Arthur, holding the door open as Thompson moved past him. 'Pleased to . . .' he went on as Thompson interrupted him.

'Just seen an interesting cricket match, Mr Jenkins. Thought you might like to know!' he said raising an eyebrow. Thompson rubbed his chin. He possessed an air of smugness.

'Yes, well, I do like cricket,' Arthur admitted earnestly.

'Indeed,' snapped Thompson.

'Would you like a cup of tea?' asked Arthur. 'You can tell me *all* about it.' He moved towards the kitchen without waiting for an answer. 'Just make yourself at home.'

'Know a boy named Gibson, Mr Jenkins?' Thompson called after him, causing him to turn round.

'Tim. Yes,' said Arthur. 'But he's not playing until . . .'

There was a sound from the front door and Tim appeared in his whites completely out of breath.

'You've played!' Arthur said in amazement.

Breathing heavily, Tim replied, 'They moved the game ahead a week. Mrs Jenkins and I though it best not to tell you because you were poorly.'

'Well?' said Arthur eagerly. 'Come in. Tell me how it went. Any wickets?' Arthur ushered him inside.

At that moment Tim spotted the reporter and paused. The three looked at each other awkwardly for a moment until Arthur calmly enquired, looking straight at Tim, 'How about one of you telling me what's going on then?'

'He was asking me all these questions after the match,' said Tim hesitantly, nodding at the journalist. Thompson's eyes flicked to Arthur.

'I saw him bowl today!' he said. Arthur twitched a little and waited for the reporter to continue. 'And I saw him bowl last year as well!' he added. Arthur was still none the wiser. 'No one improves that fast, Mr Jenkins.' Now it was Thompson's turn to wait.

Arthur, proud as punch, said excitedly, 'Created a bit of a storm, did you, boy?'

Tim said nothing.

Thompson urged him on, 'Go on, tell him.'

'Yes, spill the beans, lad,' Arthur added.

'Nine for five,' Tim blurted out. As Arthur let this sink in, Tim still did not allow himself a smile.

'Did you win?' asked Arthur, deadpan. Then he smiled and shook Tim's hand proudly. 'Excellent. Well done, boy! Marvellous!' he said. 'My God, nine wickets, eh!'

'They bloody won all right!' erupted Thompson. 'Four of the runs came from a dropped catch that went straight through the slips!'

'Oh bad luck,' Arthur remarked.

'Opposition's chasing 157 runs. He comes on at 146 for

one.' Thompson paused again for maximum effect. 'They were all out for 156!' His tone was decidedly accusatory now. 'I know what's going on here. I heard you talking to one of your mates before the match,' he said looking at Tim, 'saying how you had a new coach . . . a supercoach.' Thompson was on a roll. 'You're playing with fire here, Jenkins.' he told Arthur. 'I'm on to you,' he warned with a mad gleam in his eye.

Arthur looked at Tim, whispering, 'And you thought *I* was a nutter!' Tim laughed. 'Nine for five! Well done, Tim.' He furiously shook Tim's hand again then turned back to Thompson.

'This is the sort of thing that scandals are made of, Jenkins,' Thompson said in a low voice.

Arthur was utterly confused now. He squinted at Thompson who was all agitated. 'You're coming across quite strange now, Mr Thompson. I'll see to the tea, then you can tell me what's on your mind.'

'Illegal use of a prohibited substance, as if you didn't know,' Thompson blurted out.

'What, Earl Grey?' asked Arthur.

Thompson had now lost his cool. 'I'm talking about your protégé,' he said, pointing to Tim.

Arthur got the drift but Tim had heard enough from the reporter and let fly. 'Mr Jenkins has been coaching me – that's all.'

'No one improves that fast from just training.' He told Tim who moved nearer as things got slightly tense. Arthur stepped between them, then calmly spoke to Thompson from close range. 'There's no such story here, Mr Thompson,' he said, 'but you're welcome to stay for tea.' He paused for a moment and stood back. 'I'm sure Tim will be more than happy to tell us about his fantastic haul, if you're looking for a proper story.' With that, Arthur retired to the kitchen, from where he called back, 'Mind you, I've got a bucket Tim can use if you want. You can take a sample when you leave. Carry out some tests.'

Thompson appeared to be the one with doubts now as Tim sat down on the edge of a chair rubbing a muddy elbow. Thompson turned away from him towards the open fire, warming his hands. When he turned back he found Tim staring straight at him. He folded his arms and bit his top lip.

Meanwhile Arthur was dancing a jig in the kitchen, slapping his thighs and singing, 'Nine for five . . . nine for FIVE!'


On leaving the house, Thompson stood at Arthur's front gate for a moment looking thoughtful. He finally pulled the gate closed behind him and turned around still looking confounded by the day's events. He could see Arthur through the lounge window, with both his hands on Tim's shoulders, shaking him wildly in celebration. Thompson turned away from the scene and with long purposeful strides returned to his car.

## 5

Arthur's health was much improved as he and Jean settled into their folding chairs the following week to watch Tim play his second game of the season. Arthur had read the *Standard* that week from cover to cover searching for an article by Thompson but found nothing.

The boys in their whites drifted like sleepwalkers onto the flat green surface of the ground. Some chatted softly; one boy polished a ball vigorously on his trousers, and the two opening batsmen, looking every bit the white knights they were, strolled out to the middle exuding an air of confidence. Everyone observed the obligatory cricketing rituals. The bowler – Tim in this case – marked out his run and did a practice run-up. The batsmen scratched out their markings on the crease with their spikes while observing the positions of the fielders. Meanwhile, one of the umpires appeared to have fallen asleep with his left arm outstretched. Tim's captain shook the old man who, without so much as a blink, wink or nod, woke immediately shouting, 'Play!'

Tim's first ball was a classic yorker and, like a tracer bullet, it homed in on the batsman's crease, hitting his front ankle at breakneck speed, forcing his feet backwards as if someone had pulled a rug from under him. As the batsman crashed to the ground, the ball dribbled towards the stumps, hitting them with enough force to dislodge the bails. It was a sensational ball, though some might have felt that the batsman had been unlucky. But not Arthur; nor another spectator that day.

From a hidden vantage point, Tim was being watched.

The felled batsman dragged himself to his feet, stunned by the speed of the ball and the end result. Tim was congratulated by his team-mates enthusiastically. Some of them held their hands high for the obligatory high five, which never came easy for Tim who was a handshaker – cricket wasn't the only thing Arthur had taught him.

Arthur turned to Jean. 'Supercoach!' he said proudly, nudging her. Just then, he spotted a man far off in the bushes behind the bowler's mark, watching the game through binoculars. It was Thompson!

'I'll be back shortly,' Arthur told Jean.

He wasted no time in skirting the edge of the ground and working his way towards Thompson. Using the cover of a large tree, Arthur moved to within a few feet of him and then announced in a loud voice, 'Looking for banned substances, Mr Thompson?'

Thompson lowered his binoculars to face Arthur, looking strangely pleased to see him. Smiling, he said, 'Mr Jenkins! I thought I might find you here,' and he moved towards Arthur with hand outstretched. As he did so Arthur noticed another man who had been standing beside Thompson. He too held a pair of binoculars and was following the proceedings so keenly that he ignored both of them, his glasses fixed on the action in the middle.

There was a loud cry from the small crowd as Tim's latest delivery caught an edge and flew past the wicketkeeper to the boundary.

'Wow!' exclaimed the stranger.

'He's bowling every bit as well as last week,' remarked Thompson over his shoulder to the stranger. 'All thanks to this man,' he added, slapping Arthur on the shoulder.

Arthur peered suspiciously at the stranger as Thompson continued, 'This is the chap I was telling you about, Bob.' The man managed to tear himself away from the game and lowered his binoculars. Arthur stared at him as Thompson went on, 'Arthur, this is Bob Fryer, the coach of the England cricket team.'

The man approached and grasped Arthur's hand shaking it firmly.

'Pleased to meet you, Arthur.' came his greeting. Strangely, it seemed very formal to Arthur.

'Bob's got a property not far from here.' offered Thompson before Fryer chipped in. 'I like to meet up with Carl before the season starts . . . get in some grass roots stuff.'

'Very good. Yes. Nice to meet you,' replied Arthur.

'Essential to see the game played with such passion,' Fryer said enthusiastically.

'Quite,' Arthur replied, not altogether understanding what was happening.

Meanwhile Thompson had raised his glasses again to watch the play and called across to Fryer as if Arthur wasn't there. 'I chatted to Tim's coach from last year as you asked.'

'Good,' said Fryer.

'He claimed the boy was pedestrian at best, as I said.'

Fryer nodded, watching another ball.

'I hear you've done some out-of-season coaching with the boy bowling now,' he said.

Arthur struggled for an appropriate response. 'Well—' Arthur began.

'Another one!' Thompson exclaimed as the crowd applauded another wicket. Fryer and Arthur watched as the batsman turned towards the pavilion, his stumps shattered. The fielding side crowded round Tim, who once more was causing havoc. Arthur felt in a better position to answer Fryer's question.

'Yes,' he said earnestly.

'What's your secret then, Arthur?  Don't be shy,' Fryer prompted eagerly.

'Bit of elbow grease,' Arthur replied cautiously.

'Elbow grease!' laughed Fryer as he looked at Thompson before turning back to Arthur. 'I think you're being modest, Arthur,' he went on. 'Either that or you're keeping your cards very close to your chest.'

'Maybe,' said Arthur.

They watched the new batsman take strike. No sooner had he done so than the spectators let out a cheer as the next delivery whistled past the batsman's head.

'Bloody hell, he's headed for another haul,' cried Thompson.

All three men watched as the ball was returned to the bowler.

'Why are you here, Mr Fryer?' Arthur asked.

Fryer smiled and looked at him. 'Well, since you ask.' He paused. 'Tim looks like something very special. His speed is quite incredible for someone his age.' Arthur's expression gradually altered as he listened to Fryer. 'But he's not the sole reason for my being here – I've come to see you as well!'

'Me.' Arthur asked stunned.

'You've achieved something . ,' Fryer searched for the right words. ' . out of the ordinary I feel.'

Arthur was overcome with surprise but tried to maintain his composure. In the end all he could was mutter an excuse to get away.

'My wife will be wondering where I am,' he told Fryer.

Unfazed by his strange reaction, Fryer politely inquired, 'Will you at least join us for a pint later?'

'How about the Twelfth Man at five o'clock?' Thompson suggested.

'Yes. Why not,' Arthur replied as he set off to rejoin Jean. 'Twelve o'clock at the fifth man,' he said, giving a feeble wave. Fryer watched Arthur stumble off like a tipsy old badger.

'Strange, or what!' he said to Thompson.

Jean teased Arthur about his mysterious engagement that evening, threatening to drive him to the pub to ensure there was no woman involved – after all, he hadn't brushed his hair in front of a mirror for a good fifteen years.

Arthur managed two non-cricketing thoughts on the way to the pub. The first was that he almost wished he *was* going to meet a mysterious woman; the second was that he was glad he was not! His walk gave him time to think things through, and soon he was contemplating his first meeting with Thompson, wondering if he actually had trained Tim illegally. Were there new guidelines to bowling that he needed to be aware of? Could it be he was actually in trouble?

So wrapped up in thought was he that he very nearly passed his favourite part of the walk into town: a break between two hedges on top of Man-Cad Hill. Some considerate person had placed a single seat in a gap from where one could take a final look back at the rolling hills that surrounded Wielding Willow. Arthur stood on the seat in order to gain the height required to see the bedroom window of his cottage in the distance. As usual Jean was keeping an eye out and waved.

Arthur spotted Fryer and Thompson propping up the bar, each with a pint. As Fryer greeted him warmly, he wished he was only meeting the England cricket coach, for he had not yet made up his mind about Thompson.

'What'll it be, Arthur?' Fryer shouted above the din of afternoon drinkers.

'That'll be fine thanks!' Arthur hollered, motioning to their pints. Fryer nodded and signalled to the barman to pour another three.

'Well, your lad did it again, Arthur. First week in the A's and he's taken seven for,' Fryer remarked. 'Sixteen wickets in two matches. Impressive.'

'Amazing what a few banned substances will do,' Arthur remarked dryly. Thompson's eyes narrowed momentarily.

'Look, I'll get right to the point, Arthur,' Fryer said, as the barman pulled the pints. 'I've done a lot of work with Carl. He keeps his eye out for good young 'uns coming through the ranks. We follow their progress and from time to time steer them in the right direction, put them in touch with the right sort of team, that sort of thing.' He paused as Thompson carried on.

'As I told you, I saw Tim last year when I came to see another boy at Fraser College and I remembered Tim. Mainly because he was quite ordinary.' Thompson paused for maximum effect. 'But now! Well . . . I've never seen such a turnaround.'

Fryer picked up the conversation again as the pints arrived. 'Carl here overheard your boy telling his mates after the game about his coach and some unique training method he'd undertaken in the off-season. There's no doubting Tim's a very good bowler now, but what I'm more interested in is how you improved him so considerably?'

Arthur pretended to be lost for words – but he wasn't. He could have revealed all, but was not about to spill the beans. He took a deep breath to buy more time.

Thompson butted in, unable to stop himself. 'One of the boys mentioned some exercises.'

'Well . . .' Arthur began then appeared to lose his train of thought. Fryer and Thompson were all ears as he took a long swig and put his beer down. 'I think I'd best start at the beginning.'

Starting with his playing days he then told of his coaching successes, his seemingly brilliant idea, the ridicule, his sacking from the coaching role and the fallow years that followed. He went on to tell of his clash with Singleton and explained how it became a turning point. He explained the chance meeting with Tim and the hours spent improving his speed and control. He spared almost no detail – except the detail Fryer was after. When Arthur had finished he was faced with two blank faces and two empty pints. 'And that's it in a nutshell!' he concluded. It had taken him twenty-five minutes.

'And?' asked Fryer.

'And what?' said Arthur.

Fryer looked disappointed but he was not about to embarrass himself.

'Never mind,' he sighed.

Arthur let the remains of his pint slip down his throat before gently placing the empty glass on the bar. 'I've always thought my methods could revolutionise the game of cricket,' he told them, 'but I never had the chance to test my theory until now. And you know what – it works. It works with just basic equipment. If I could build exactly what I need, the results would be–' he waved his hands, lost for words '–incredible!'

'Look, Arthur,' Fryer said slowly, 'I know we've only just met but we—'

'No!' said Arthur holding up his hands. 'I know what you're going to say. I can't tell you what you want to know, gentlemen. I can't *tell* you.' Fryer and Thompson looked downcast as Arthur spoke. 'But I can *show* you.'

## 6

The following day Arthur and Fryer arrived at the nets around 10.00 a.m. Arthur had called Tim the night before asking him to be there for a short session. Although Tim thought it unusual the day after a match, he was happy to oblige having just read an article in a cricketing magazine about good bounce being a key ingredient to a pace bowler's success. The first ball he bowled pitched short and hit the back net below a red marker tape he'd set up.

'Damn it!' he cursed.

'If you'd stop clenching the fist of your leading arm, you might notice a difference.' Tim spun round to see Arthur accompanied by Fryer striding in his direction. He retrieved the ball and jogged towards the two men.

'Supercoach,' Tim greeted Arthur, causing him great embarrassment. Red-faced, he introduced the stranger. 'Tim, I'd like you to meet Bob Fryer.'

'Pleased to meet you, Tim,' Fryer said politely.

'And you, sir,' replied Tim respectfully.

'I have something for you,' Tim told Arthur. He crouched next to his kit bag and dug out a brown box. 'It's for you!' he said, presenting the box to a surprised Arthur.

'Oh!' he exclaimed. 'It's not often I get given something,' and he pulled the lid off to reveal the game ball from Tim's first week mounted on a small stand. There was a small engraving.

'They do this at Fraser if you get a five for,' Tim informed him.

'Yes, quite,' Arthur reflected, quite moved by Tim's gesture.

'It's for all our hard work,' said Tim.

Arthur took a deep breath as he regarded his charge, before exhaling with the words, 'Not over yet, boy!' Tim only half heard the remark and wondered if it had come from Fryer rather than Arthur.

Eager to get on with things, Fryer picked up a ball and tossed it to Tim. As he caught the ball, there was a flicker of recognition in his eye.

'Mind if we watch a couple?' asked Fryer as the penny

dropped for Tim.

'*The* Bob Fryer?' Tim asked incredulously.

Arthur didn't want Tim jumping to conclusions and was about to explain the nature of Fryer's interest in him, but Tim was one step ahead.

'Tim—' Arthur started.

'I know, Arthur,' said Tim before turning to Fryer. 'There's a thousand other bowlers like me–' he paused '–but there's only one Arthur.'

With that he strode to his mark, turned and started his run-up. Fryer and Arthur watched as Tim wound up and let go of a ball that streaked down the wicket, before hitting the top of the off stump and flying into the rear of the net with a thud. Fryer was impressed.

Deep in thought, he watched a couple more deliveries. His mood seemed to harden as he ignored Arthur and focused on Tim. Finally he asked, 'So come on, Arthur, how exactly did this metamorphosis come about?'

With his arms folded Arthur looked at Tim, who had heard Fryer's question, and pointed at a large olive canvas bag sitting next to his own kitbag.

'What's that?' asked Fryer incredulously, wandering over to the innocuous bag.

'Hang on,' Arthur told him with a smile. 'Tim, have you bowled full pace today?' Tim shook his head. 'Right, you need to see some really fast balls in that case,' Arthur told Fryer who raised his eyebrows at the prospect.

'Tim, would you be so good as to warm up using the equipment? We'll be back in fifteen minutes to watch a little more.'

Tim nodded and rotated his shoulders.

Arthur led Fryer away from the nets in the direction of the scoreboard on the far side of the ground.

He appeared to be confused. 'You're saying he can bowl faster?'

'Oh yes,' replied Arthur proudly. 'I've taught him never to bowl at more than ninety per cent when not fully warm.'

Having had a good chat on cricket in general, the two men found themselves back at the nets in no time. Arthur issued instructions to Tim not to bowl at full speed until he said so, then put him through his paces, calling out reminders as the boy ran in.

'Plant your back foot firmer, more side-on,' he shouted. 'Keep that ninety degrees in the front elbow until it's past your waist.'

Eventually Arthur called a halt, Tim had a drink, did some side stretches, before picking up a ball and making towards his marker.

'Is this the one?' Fryer asked, eager as a ten year old. Arthur nodded, motioned towards the rear of the wicket and both men took up a position behind the stumps outside the back net.

Tim paused, took a deep breath and focused on the stumps at the end of the pitch. He came steaming in, looking more powerful than ever before. Gone was the gentle approach of the previous year as he raced in to bowl and hurled the ball down the pitch like a lightning bolt. As it tore into the rear net Fryer's head snapped back in disbelief.

'Good Lord!' he exclaimed loudly, reeling back a few paces.

Arthur put his mouth near Fryer's ear and whispered, 'You give me the resources and I'll give you bowlers who can rip right through that net!' Any traces of self-doubt within Arthur had completely vanished.

Fryer didn't hesitate in asking. 'How long would it take?' he asked.

'A shade under two years!'

Tim saw the two men shake hands, although what they had agreed on was anyone's guess. Fryer's mobile phone rang; he looked at the number on the screen. It was Thompson.

'Excuse me,' Fryer said, walking a short distance away from Arthur.

'Hello . . . yes,' he said, 'I'm starting to get an idea,' he told Thompson, at the same time watching as another thunderbolt scattered the stumps. 'Yes, I'm sure I'll get what we want.' Fryer watched Arthur chatting to Tim about the last ball. 'No. No. I don't think we'll need him around very long.'

## 7

A week later the two men met in London at Fryer's request, the venue another busy pub, tantalisingly close to Lord's. Looking like two stuffy generals planning an attack, Arthur and Fryer were hunkered down in a smoky side room. Fryer leant into Arthur.

'Look, Arthur, it's all good news. But please, picture this: *"Bob Fryer, National Coach, involved in a radical speed-bowling programme"*. Fryer appealed to Arthur, his hands outstretched. 'For a start the ECB would simply not allow it. My current commitments would be jeopardised. And on top of that,' he emphasised, 'I couldn't ask the current players to change from our set programme at a whim.'

'Of course you can't,' Arthur agreed.

'Right. This is the plan,' Fryer said firmly. Arthur sat back and folded his arms as Fryer continued. 'There are an awful lot of people in this country who'd give almost anything to have a powerful Test side again. Not having one is very bad for business and this *is* a business, Arthur. So this is what's been decided. What I . . . *we*, have is the support of a consortium I've formed. Quite simply, on my say so, they have already made an initial contribution to our programme. Funds will be released as you need them. When we last met we noted down certain phases of the programme. Yes?'

'Correct,' replied Arthur, slowly producing a piece of paper and sliding it across the table to Fryer. On it were a few simple lines:

### Phase One

i) Recruit 6 bowlers
ii) Secure training facility
iii) Book accommodation
iv) Set up facilities

'That's the one,' said Fryer, taking an envelope from his pocket he handed it to Arthur who withdrew a cheque from within. 'Book the accommodation and training facilities, for six months only for now.'

Arthur looked first at the amount written on the cheque and raised an eyebrow. He then pulled another folded piece of paper from the envelope and put his glasses on.

'That is a list of all the bowlers I want you to look at. And a schedule of their matches,' Fryer informed Arthur.

'Any details of their vital statistics?' asked Arthur.

Fryer paused looking perplexed. 'Vital statistics?' he asked.

Arthur looked up at Fryer. It was as if they were suddenly on a completely different wavelength. Eventually he broke the silence. 'As I mentioned in our initial discussions, Bob, my theory is only bullet-proof if I am to work with bowlers of, how shall I put it . . . *oversized* proportions.' Fryer remained silent as Arthur went on. 'In order to fully maximise the effect of my training.' Still, Fryer appeared not to comprehend.

'There's no point in training midgets!' Arthur snapped.

'Well, I'm sure there's some fairly tall chaps in there,' Fryer suggested.

'I don't want *fairly* tall. I want giants,' growled Arthur, getting frustrated. 'Oh, and by the way, it may be a business to you but not to me. Look, Bob, there's no point mucking around. We'll only get one shot at this.' Arthur shifted his rump in his chair and focused hard on Fryer. 'Just imagine being able to do what I did for Tim, to someone six-foot-six or more. The result would be incredible. Devastating! I don't want a bunch of county hacks that I can squeeze another two or three per cent out of,' he said shaking the list at Fryer.

Fryer didn't seem to be totally convinced.

'Bob, you *did* listen to some of what I said last week, didn't you?'

'Yes, of course, but I feel where we need to start is this list. It will give us experience. I mean, sure, you could go to Africa and get an eight-foot-tall Zulu, but it would be a wasted exercise because he's never played the bloody game

. . . if you get my point.' Arthur remained silent. 'Let's just start with the list, can we?' Fryer pleaded. 'There's some real talent in there, Arthur. I mean, you still have the final say. Having seen what you did for the boy, I'm sure we'll see the desired results. Which brings me to . . . a small detail.' Fryer had Arthur's attention again. 'No one is to know what's going on. The ECB has nothing to do with this, remember,' he warned. 'If anyone in your squad appears up to scratch, and *only* if they are up to scratch, then I'll bring them into my squad. The players I – sorry – *you* select will have to observe strict confidentiality throughout the process. Understood?'

'Naturally,' agreed Arthur with a single nod. He had listened intently but he was not happy with Fryer's overbearing manner. 'Can I just ask?' he interrupted, appearing confused. 'The Ashes—'

'Arthur, this is not a fairytale. It's business, remember. The objective here is to build a strong team,' Fryer insists. 'We're grown men. Not twelve year olds. Now, have you had any thoughts on physios or trainers?'

Arthur said nothing for a few moments as he considered the question. Eventually he pushed his empty pint towards Fryer's half-full pint, saying, 'I'll need to have talks with a biomechanics boffin and a mechanical engineer, but yes, a trainer will be a big help.'

Fryer's mobile phone rang. He peered at its screen.

'Right, that needs sorting,' he said getting to his feet. 'That will have to do for today, Arthur. You OK with all that? We seem to have it all covered.' He smiled. 'Start the selection process. We'll aim for a middle of June kick-off.'

Fryer held out his hand and they shook. 'You know, you're going to have to do a lot of this yourself, old boy,' he told Arthur, adding, 'you'll probably need an assistant – someone cheap.' He waited for a reaction from Arthur. 'Any ideas?'

'I know one good girl,' Arthur said deadpan.

'A girl!' Fryer exclaimed. 'Excellent thinking. Should keep the place interesting.' He winked at Arthur.

'Not this one,' he responded dryly.

Arthur wasted no time planning a schedule for the first two weeks of the recruitment phase. It boiled down to watching an awful lot of cricket.

Later that evening Arthur drafted his resignation letter. Jean was initially unsure but as Arthur explained, he had a decent pension and was due to go in another two years anyway. Jean was concerned that their plan for a retirement cottage in Dorset might be derailed – but stopping Arthur in full flight wouldn't have been fair, or easy for that matter!

Arthur sealed the envelope and placed it upright on the dining-room table, then doodled on a sheet of paper for a while. He scribbled six words:

### HEAD, HEART, GUILE, BOUNCE, WORKHORSE & FEAR

His stage was set; now for the performers.

Embarking upon his arduous journey, Arthur travelled around the country with gusto. After twenty-four days he had seen ninety-two bowlers, most of whom were on Fryer's list. In order to keep a record of the players he'd seen, Arthur designed player profile sheets on which he identified ten key areas and awarded scores out of ten for each area, giving a maximum mark of 100.

The highest scorer was Ken Eccles from Northants who scored 81 out of 100, but he was only 6 ft 'short', as Arthur noted, and getting on a bit at thirty-two years old. James Feutrell was taller at 6 ft 5 in. but unfortunately he was contracted to play in New Zealand after the English summer. Another high scorer, with 79, was a Gloucestershire bowler, Mark Bell, who was 6ft 1 in., aged twenty-nine and quite nippy. His greatest asset was a wicked late swing; he was also a personal favourite of Fryer's. However, Arthur thought him far too heavily built, he had a history of injuries and due to his size it wasn't as if he could slim down. If he bulked up any further, he'd be far too heavy and that would spell more injuries. Alan Fletcher from Durham was very tall at 6ft 4 in., but he was renowned for his fiery temperament and trouble seemed to follow him – there had been several suspensions from his club following on-field disputes with his own captain. On the day Arthur watched him turn out for Durham, Fletcher had one particularly spiteful spell in which Arthur counted eight bouncers in three overs to one batsman. While Fletcher was fielding, Arthur felt sure he had not aimed directly at the wicket as the ball thumped the rump of one of the batsmen as he scuttled between the wickets. Fletcher made no attempt to hide his delight for which he was given a warning. When he bowled a beamer in his next over, his captain removed him from the attack on the umpire's recommendation. Arthur scrubbed him.

At last Arthur was down to the final names on Fryer's list of candidates, which included Mathew French of Surrey. Fryer had scribbled 'great hope of English cricket' next to his name. To Arthur the 'great hope of English cricket' seemed to be a bit on the young side and very green. He watched closely as the young man mingled awkwardly with his team-mates. He was quiet, seemed uncomplicated and had a flop of blond hair that flicked around as he carried out his warm-ups. He was of above average height and had a friendly demeanour for a fast bowler. Eager to please his coach in the drills, he appeared very focused. Arthur could see raw talent and the boy looked at home with the tag 'most likely' therefore Arthur was obliged to stay and watch. Sure enough, French showed glimpses of everything: pace, maturity, bounce, accuracy, movement and commitment to his team's cause, not to mention a heightened level of self-assuredness. In French's case, he'd come from a long line of fast bowlers. His Grandfather and two uncles had played for their counties with distinction. His father even had the honour of playing international cricket for New Zealand in two Tests though very late in his career. Nevertheless, French had been raised to believe that passage to the England team was his birthright as long as he went through the motions. He was also the tallest French ever at nearly 6 ft 4in. But there was something amiss.

Arthur watched two spells by French and could find no reason to either select him or leave him out, so he decided to move on. After all, he could return if he changed his mind. As he was leaving, he watched one final ball.

The young man's final delivery came after a dropped catch, which would have ended the innings of the opposing team. Showing more petulance than determination, French nevertheless demonstrated that when he really wanted a wicket he knew how to get one. Bowling a no-nonsense, in-swinging yorker, the ball flew under the bat of the No. 11 to end the innings. Food for thought, thought Arthur.

He had seen almost every bowler on Fryer's list but none had been close to what he had in mind when he began his search. Fryer would not have been pleased with what Arthur did next. Pulling out a list of his own making, he surveyed a record of names he had compiled over the years from reading scorecards and articles in local papers and magazines. Though they weren't county teams he was going to see, the standard was comparable. Arthur knew what he must do. Drawing up another schedule, he set off North in search of one George Samuels.

## 9

Struggling up-country, Arthur took a train and cab to reach the Dead Ball Oval in Yorkshire. The weather looked sour for the entire journey, but it came good by the time he reached the ground. He wandered around the clubhouse reading about records set by players he'd never heard of. Not renowned for his peripheral hearing, Arthur nevertheless couldn't help overhearing two men talking about George Samuels, the very bowler he'd come to see. He was 'bloody slippery' according to one of them. Any time an old hand says someone is 'slippery' it's a pretty good sign there's a fair bit of pace involved. 'Slippery' with a 'bloody' placed in front of it means they're even faster! Arthur's spirits were raised until he heard the next man speak. 'Damn shame he's given it away.'

Arthur was brought down to earth with a crash. Having keenly followed the career of Samuels for some years, Arthur had been looking forward to finally seeing him in action – the man was often written about by journalists in glowing terms. Of West Indian origins and over 6 ft 5 in. tall, Samuels was said to possess equal parts brain and brawn. Arthur unfolded a newspaper cutting of a regional final several years ago, showing Samuels holding up the silverware after taking 7 for 36. He looked down at the cutting.

'Bollocks!' he said angrily out loud. His Joel Garner . . . gone!

At that moment there were voices and as he looked up a group of players entered the clubhouse. He recognised Samuels from the cuttings as he held the door open for his mates, also noticing that he was carrying a kit bag as if he was going to play. Arthur was confused. Turning again to one of the men near him, he asked, 'So sorry. Couldn't help hearing you earlier. George Samuels,' he inquired, 'has he finished playing?'

'Last game today,' replied one man in a friendly tone.

'Ahhh,' Arthur replied, nodding and smiling. 'Many thanks.'

Samuels and his mates filled past en route to the changing rooms.

'Where's Lloyd? Not watching today?' a player asked

Samuels.

'Dad! No fear. I ain't even told him I'm stopping. I don't want the pressure. You guys can do all the hard work today. I might just bowl some spin!'

A sly smile broke out on Arthur's face as he walked over to a man in the clubhouse opening a cash till.

'I'm sorry to interrupt you,' he said, at the same time patting his trousers and feeling inside his pockets. 'I'm meant to be meeting a friend here and I can't find his number anywhere. Lloyd Samuels?'

'Oh Lloyd, yes. Call him at his garage. Or I may have his home number if you wait a moment,' he told him helpfully.

'All the time in the world,' said Arthur smiling broadly. 'Could you tell me where the phone is?'

Some thirty five minutes later the players were ready to go out onto the ground. Arthur stood by the gates chatting to the umpires who both laughed as they moved away and with a wave headed for the middle, followed by the players on the fielding side. Arthur spotted Samuels among them as they trotted out. As Samuels jogged past him, Arthur called out, 'George Samuels?'

Samuels, slightly startled, pulled up in mid-stride and turned round to see Arthur beaming back at him.

'That's me,' replied Samuels. Arthur smiled and held a small note out to him.

'From your father,' said Arthur pointing to the other side of the field where a man sat. Samuels's jaw dropped.

'What the—'

'Best of luck,' said Arthur as he turned in the direction of Samuel's father. Samuels, totally perplexed, unfolded the note which simply read: *'Bowl fast! Very proud. Dad.'*

Samuels looked over at his father, who shook a fist of encouragement in the air. Meanwhile Arthur strolled round the boundary to join the man, introduced himself and started talking as if they'd known each other twenty years or more.

Out in the middle George Samuels had been offered the new ball and had taken it. Arthur and Lloyd Samuels settled down to watch.

Samuels junior opened the day's proceedings with a tidy

maiden over, impressing Arthur with his pace, though he noticed something seemed wrong with his action. Something that he couldn't quite put his finger on. Excusing himself from Lloyd's company, Arthur went and stood behind Samuels's run-up for his second over. It quickly became obvious watching the first two balls that Samuels's thick Afro hairstyle was getting in the way when he delivered the ball at maximum speed – his right arm was not vertical as it passed over his shoulder. Not only that, it didn't allow him to have a smooth run-up, all of which would impact negatively on the pace of his deliveries. He also noticed that Samuels's fifth ball was the fastest of the over and nearly caught an edge. The last ball was a half-volley and the batsman dispatched it like a bullet towards the boundary. Samuels wasn't happy.

Arthur went back and sat with Lloyd for his son's third over. Samuels was tossed the ball by his skipper, who shouted some inaudible words of encouragement. Samuels seemed to withdraw into himself as he marked out his run-up again, and measured out six extra strides before putting down his marker. Rolling his shoulder, he rubbed an invisible mark off the ball, then polished it a bit as he gave the batsman on strike a hooded glare. Motioning for the field to come in, he set one man very close to the bat on the on side, took a breath and began his run-up. It was much faster and more balanced than in the first two overs and his leap into the air higher. His arm came over in a blur as the ball pitched short and reared up into the batsman, who rocked quickly onto his back foot, but didn't move fast enough as the ball spat up from the turf and whacked him on the underside of his elbow. There was a loud 'crack' and the bat hit the ground as its owner staggered away from the wicket grimacing and holding his arm.

As a bone in the arm might have been broken or chipped, the batsman was assisted from the field and eventually carted off for an X-ray. His replacement stood confidently at the crease, checking the fielding positions and twirling his bat. He took guard as Samuels glared down the pitch and walked two paces towards the batsman, before gesturing to another two men to close in on the off side. This was a confident move and overtly aggressive. It appeared Samuels was intent on another short-pitched delivery, which raised a few eyebrows even amongst the fielders.

'Yorker?' Arthur asked Lloyd after a moment's consideration.

'Mmmm. Another short one if I know George,' replied Lloyd as Samuels thundered in. Leaping high, he unleashed a vicious ball. It shot down the wicket but pitched neither short, nor full – a perfect leg-cutter that pitched middle stump, demanding a forward defensive shot. The batsman pushed forward hurriedly but before he could counter its deviation, the ball had moved off the seam towards the slips, just catching the edge of the bat as it flashed past, giving second slip a straightforward catch. As all the fielders appealed, Samuels jumped for joy, nearly punching a hole in the sky; Arthur and Lloyd were on their feet as well. As the batsman trudged off, Arthur watched Samuels who still appeared fully focused. He took the ball from the wicketkeeper and immediately went back to his mark.

'Both wrong,' Arthur observed.

Normally congratulations would still have going on amongst the players as the new batsman made his way out to the middle, but the fielders had quickly resumed their positions, and were ready and waiting when the batsman arrived at the crease. Taking a deep breath he confidently took guard – just as Samuels kept up the pressure by sending all the close-in fielders back again. As this usually meant the next ball would be of a fuller length, the two batsmen came together mid-pitch a quick chat.

'Watch him. He's nippy, and a smart-arse. Could still be a short one!' said the non-striker. The new batsman nodded solemnly and glanced at Samuels who was patiently waiting at the beginning of his run-up. The two men returned to their respective ends – and moments later the middle stump was cart wheeling towards the wicketkeeper. This time all the fielders went wild and rushed to congratulate Samuels as the batsman marched slowly back to the pavilion, where he later told his team-mates that he didn't even 'see' the ball.

'I've never seen him so . . . hell bent!' remarked Lloyd to Arthur. 'He's always had this in him . . . but not often enough,' he lamented.

At the completion of his third over Samuels had figures of 3 for 7, taking one more wicket with his last ball of the over (although including the injured opener, he had actually removed four batsmen). Only now did Samuels afford himself a glance at his father, who gave him a quick clap and a nod. By the end of the innings, Samuels had plundered 6 wickets as the opposition were bundled out for 124, which Samuels's team passed with 4 wickets down.

Standing outside the clubhouse at the end of the match, Samuels approached Arthur who was talking to the umpires again.

'Just been chatting with Dad,' he said.

'He's a very nice man, your dear old dad.' Arthur told him. 'Well bowled, by the way.'

'Tell me what's going on, will you? My old man gets a mystery phone call and can't remember writing me a note.'

Arthur handed him an envelope.

'Got another one for you,' he said. 'I very much hope you can make it.' Arthur drank the rest of his pint. 'It's possible your father hasn't seen your last game after all.' So saying Arthur handed a bemused Samuels his empty pint glass. 'See you soon,' he said and turned to leave.


A call to Jean told Arthur that not only had she started work on locating premises as a base of operations, but had already received details of houses for rent in the Somerset region – mainly because she'd always wanted to live near Bath. She couldn't believe her luck when she discovered that one of these was within the confines of a wartime fighter aerodrome near Bath, named Charmy Down. The house was an old B&B that was currently on the market and in very good condition. She read the property details to Arthur and described the pictures, in particular one showing an enormous disused hangar.

'Rent it!' Arthur said firmly, startling Jean a bit.

Upon contacting the owner, the woman jumped at six months' rent, and Jean even negotiated a 'long-term discount'.

Arthur was happy about the premises and the selection of his first player. Things were moving. He took a list from his pocket and put a solid line through the word '**HEAD**'.

## 10

Arthur travelled to Kent to see the opening pair of Jason Bingwell and Tosh Henry playing for the county second XI, noticing on the way that the train had some minor defects. He had just enough time to fill out a makeshift report and file it with a bewildered stationmaster at Copman's Corner.

Arthur was surprised to find a ten-pound note in the back of the taxi. He'd been hoping for some good luck, but not in this form! Arriving at the ground, he noticed a volunteer worker collecting for Second World War veterans and popped the note in the man's collection tin.

As usual Arthur headed for the clubhouse to have a look round. Chatting at the bar, he got the low-down on the team from an ex-club player named Bernie How. It seemed the two opening bowlers, Henry and Bingwell, didn't really like each other, which was one reason why the team was doing so well this year as both were constantly trying to outdo the other. Unfortunately their first-change bowler had an injury and was to be replaced by a bowler on the ground staff, Edwin Roberts, who had been in and out of the second XI for most of his playing career due to erratic form.

At that moment there was a loud barking from outside and Arthur watched as a young man rode into the car park on a rickety old bicycle. He wore a faded navy fighter pilot's jacket and mounted on the rear of the bike was a sturdy basket in which sat a black Staffordshire terrier.

'Here's Edwin now,' Bernie informed Arthur. 'That boy's twenty-five going on sixty, so he is.'

On seeing the veteran with his collection tin, Roberts stopped and emptied the contents of his pockets, a handful of change, into it.

'What's he like?' Arthur asked. Bernie squinted as Roberts dismounted and leant his bike against a wall as his dog leapt out of the basket.

'Wayward, but gets good bounce.'

Noticing that the young man was tremendously tall and painfully thin, Arthur felt a tingle run down his spine. Roberts hauled the bag he had mounted next to the basket onto his shoulder and headed for the changing rooms, his dog swaggering after him.

As a result of the toss, Arthur was delighted that Kent were to field first and it wasn't long before they were out on the grass rolling their shoulders, flicking an old ball amongst themselves, hitting catches and doing some light fielding drills. Arthur noticed that Roberts looked a little groggy.

'That Roberts looks a bit sluggish,' he observed, trying to prise more from his new-found friend.

'Therein lies the problem. It's very hard to motivate that chap. He's not lazy, mind. Just a wee bit dozy,' Bernie replied. 'Care for another?'

'Please,' replied Arthur eagerly, and with that Bernie wheeled around and made for the bar.

The batsmen strode out full of purpose – when they returned for lunch undefeated Arthur had seen enough. Henry and Bingham had both appeared to be bowling without purpose, while Roberts had bowled a useful, brisk over just before the break and looked likely to continue afterwards. Arthur and Bernie ventured down to the boundary fence to get some fresh air.

As the players made their way back out after the break, Arthur remarked loudly to Bernie, 'Not sure the visitors deserve to bat so well after their comments about our war veterans.'

Bernie had no idea what he was getting at, but the comment had the desired effect for it was overheard by Edwin Roberts as he made his way out of the pavilion. He stopped and listened as Arthur went on speaking to Bernie. 'Fancy their batsmen turning away a volunteer like that *and* telling him to push off. It's disgraceful!' Roberts had heard enough and continued on his way to the middle with a bit more purpose in his stride.

'What *are* you talking about?' Bernie asked Arthur. 'I saw them all make a contribution.'

'Edwin Roberts doesn't know that.' Arthur winked and tapped his nose before pointing to Roberts who stormed up to his captain, snatched the ball from him and made for his mark.

Bernie was amazed at Roberts's behaviour. 'Never seen 'im angry before,' he said. 'This should be good!'

And good it was! Just two hours later, Edwin Roberts had taken 7 for 51; after being 89 for nought at lunch the visitors were all out for 199. Edwin had achieved his best figures for the club and stormed off the ground after the innings had ended.

'Bowls better fired up,' reflected Bernie.

Having said his goodbyes to Bernie, Arthur found Roberts throwing a stick for his dog in the car park as the team prepared to bat. After a brief conversation, Arthur handed Roberts an envelope, telling him that if he turned up at the enclosed address, he could live at a disused wartime aerodrome and play cricket till the cows came home. Roberts was unsure – for a start he thought Arthur either slightly tipsy or a bit odd, just like everyone else did. And yet Arthur's eyes appeared to convey nothing but promise.

As Arthur left the ground, he stopped, took out his notepad and pen, and crossed the word '**BOUNCE**' from his list.

## 11

Although Middlesex proved fruitless, Oxford had a surprise packet waiting for Arthur in the shape of a 25-year-old rake named Will O'Hearn, the last of the bowlers on Fryer's list that Arthur had to see having missed him the first time around. Fryer had told him that O'Hearn was incredibly quick and Arthur was completely engrossed as he watched the willowy speedster work his way through a lively first spell that yielded two good wickets. He had a slow, deceptive run-up and a whippy action, which made him effective, if a little erratic. However, as Arthur was not fully convinced by his opening spell he stayed a while longer to watch the remainder of the game. It was during the lunch break that Arthur overheard a group of quite vocal Oxford supporters extolling the virtues of their speedster.

'Fastest in the land on a good day,' remarked one fellow as he tapped an unlit cigarette on the bar. There was a general murmuring of agreement on the matter.

'What about Cranley from Durham?' another asked.

'Not sure I've seen him play,' someone else said.

'I have!' exclaimed a confident-sounding man at the rear of the group, slightly obscured by a haze of grey cigar smoke. 'He isn't as quick as our man Will. No problem there!' He winked at the others. Everyone seemed happy with his answer.

Another stepped and announced, 'My eyesight may not be what it used to, but I seen 'em all this year, and mark my words, our Will beats the lot of them . . hands down.' His pale blue eyes flickered beneath a thatch of overgrown eyebrows. Everyone present mumbled in agreement. Happy to have finally all decided that their club had the quickest bowler in the land, the debate seemed over. Until a booming voice announced: 'There is one faster!'

The group turned their attention to a beefy looking man with bursting red cheeks. He was known in the club as 'the Major'. Arthur hovered about the fringe of the group, listening with interest, while the Major stood defiantly as if waiting to tackle anyone challenging his statement, his imposing figure revelling in the fact that he held his audience captive. Slowly and deliberately he tipped the remains of his glass down his gullet.

'Well?' inquired a rotund man with thick spectacles. 'Let's hear it, Major.'

Again there was a silence. The Major held his empty glass up to the audience and smiled. 'A story told dry, too quick flies by!' he informed them.

The men groaned as someone pushed forward with a refill and topped up his glass. The Major rocked from the balls of his feet to his toes and back as his drink was replenished. Arthur moved a little closer to the group as the Major cleared his throat.

'I told you all this last year!' he reminded the assembled group. 'But you still don't believe me, do you?'

'Which story was that, Major?' called someone drawing a laugh from all.

'The chap from Plymouth who played for Northants,' came his answer.

'Oh yes, I remember that one now,' one of them recalled.

'Blackbeard, wasn't it?'

'Bowled with a parrot on his shoulder!'

'Chap with the wooden stump?'

Obviously an extremely patient individual, the Major waited for the merry mood to subside before continuing as if nothing had happened. 'When you're all quite finished, my friends,' he said drawing a breath. 'He was no "Peg Leg" or the like, you idiots! It was Frank Arnold. Built like a steam train! Six foot seven if he was an inch. First time I saw him play it was his first county game.' He punctuated the end of his sentence by aggressively stabbing an index finger the size of a pork sausage in the crowd's general direction. 'He bowled nineteen wides and twenty no-balls, but he took seven wickets. He ended up playing just fourteen games for Northants and never took less than five wickets in an innings.' His index finger was now held aloft. 'A county record not many people know of.' He paused once more for effect and to lubricate his vocal cords once more. 'When he hit the bat it jarred your fingers *and* your toes. So fast was he that he split three bats in one day. Once, in Manchester, he broke four ribs of one batsman – and that chap has not picked up a bat since. On two occasions there were captains who refused to let their tail-end batsmen face him.' The Major's glass was topped up again. 'He was a champion in the making.'

'So what happened to him?' someone asked.

'It was a woman!' replied the Major. 'That's all I heard. He just disappeared.'

The men were silent. Finally, one man asked, 'Where is he now?'

'Plymouth apparently. Expelling drunken sailors from one of Union Street's finest,' said the Major with a hint of remorse. 'Such a waste.'

'Well, if he ain't playing no more, then Will's the fastest!' Someone pointed out to murmurs of general agreement.

When the noise had subsided the Major smiled. 'Perhaps,' he said making short work of his drink and turning back to the bar holding his glass up to the barman.

The crowd at the bar began to break up as Arthur headed back to his seat for the last session. He took out his notebook, scribbling in it: 'Frank Arnold, Plymouth'.

Had O'Hearn known what he was bowling for that day he might have tried a little bit harder. After being hit to the boundary twice, his head dropped and there was an unsightly altercation with a batsman who had reached a tidy fifty. It left Arthur with a bad taste in his mouth. O'Hearn was good but at just under 6 ft 2 in. he was not for Arthur.

Sitting in the stand after the match Arthur thumbed through a crumpled map of the UK. He jumped as his phone rang. It was Jean.

'Hello,' said Arthur, 'fancy a trip to Plymouth?'

## 12

Arthur and Jean arrived in Cornwall on a Wednesday and spent two days with relatives, during which Arthur went to watch in a match at Truro, but as expected he found no noteworthy bowlers. He held Fryer at bay with details of the selection process and certainly didn't reveal that he had journeyed to the South-West to recruit a nightclub bouncer. He had even asked himself why he was there. Instinct, he told himself.

The downside to their trip to Cornwall was the gastronomic feats of cousin Grace, who'd lost her sense of taste aged twenty-seven after a run-in with a batch of rancid clotted cream. A fine cook before the unfortunate episode, she was still under the misapprehension that she'd retained her culinary skills. Her awful cooking being her passion, she regularly proclaimed she delighted in 'filling others with the joy of food'. Or as Arthur put it '*killing* others with the joy of food'. After a week's slim pickings and much walking on the moors, Arthur stepped on the bathroom scales to notice a decline in his weight to the tune of 2 kilos. Happy with this result and in need of a decent meal, Arthur and Jean bid farewell to cousin Grace and made for Plymouth.

After checking in to a B&B in Plymouth, they went for a drive until some grey weather rolled in past Drake's Island and hovered over the city. An overwhelming urge to sit by a fire and drink tea overcame them and they were soon back at the B&B, where Jean was able to read up on the latest high fashion in London as Arthur practised his snoring. When he woke he was aware the day had slipped away and that it was evening already. As usual these days he had a map with him and studied it as he looked for Union Street in relation to their B&B.

When Mrs Bellamy, the owner, came in to inquire about the evening's dining arrangements, Arthur asked how long it would take to walk to Union Street.

She looked at him in horror. 'You'll not being going there, Mr Jenkins!' she responded emphatically.

'Yes I will,' replied Arthur.

'Whatever for? It's a horrible rough place, not for the likes of you . . . honestly.'

'Please don't worry, Mrs Bellamy,' he told her. 'I used to

work for British Rail!'

As Mrs Bellamy bustled out of the room, Arthur avoided meeting Jean's gaze by returning to his map.

If Brixton and Las Vegas had a child it was Union Street, Plymouth – 150 yards worth of neon, drunken sailors, short skirts, kebab shops and a strong police presence. Somewhere a violent row was taking place; screams and shouts were eventually followed by sirens. Two policemen went sprinting across the road and disappeared down an alleyway. As he walked past what seemed to be an overcrowded nightclub, Arthur spotted a huge man standing at the entrance door, reminiscent of a piece of stone with arms folded. Arthur knew he had found his man and tentatively approached his quarry, who fixed a stern eye on him.

Arthur stopped dead in front of the big man and boldly announced, 'Frank Arnold, I presume.'

The big man looked down at him. 'You need to keep going that way,' he said pointing down the street. Arthur was a bit disappointed that this behemoth was not his future Test bowler.

'Oh, sorry,' he apologised. 'How far exactly?'

'Just keep to this side,' replied the man. 'You'll know when you see Frank.'

'Right, thanks very much.' He waved feebly and trotted off as a group of sailors brushed past him, almost knocking him off his feet. He stumbled sideways and tripped into the arms of a solidly built woman.

'All right, me luvver!' she crowed.

'Terribly sorry, madam,' Arthur muttered, straightening his jacket before setting off purposely once more. Flustered from his recent encounter, he smoothed down his jacket, and tie and took in some deep breaths. He walked at a brisk pace until the street seemed to come to an end, just after he had passed by a rough-looking establishment called The Belfry. Judging by the queue outside, it seemed no less popular despite its ramshackle appearance.

Suddenly there was an almighty row inside. The crowd awaiting entry edged away from the club hurriedly. The light escaping the club was suddenly blotted out by something enormous emerging, which quickly became a man who towered above everyone as he lumbered forward. He had a massive chest and the broadest shoulders Arthur had ever seen. His arms were as thick as small oak trees and under each he carried an unconscious sailor, with two more held by their belts in his huge hands. Once clear of the crowd he dropped all four men in a heap on the ground, then turned slowly and trudged back inside. Arthur had a dull pain in the pit of his stomach – fear was a feeling he'd not felt in a long time, a fantastic feeling considering what he had in mind. He reached inside the pocket of his jacket once more and, fingering the single white envelope tucked away inside, he walked towards The Belfry.

With the third member selected Arthur slept soundly that night. Moonlight filtered through the window shedding light upon the bedside table where his notes lay open. **'FEAR'** had found an owner.

## 13

Arthur spent the journey from Devon to Somerset ignoring a bag of pasties on the back seat as he and Jean made a beeline to their home for the foreseeable future. Though he was prepared for Charmy Down to be somewhat neglected, Arthur still hoped that, of all the buildings, the hanger was at least intact. As they drew nearer, he felt a strong sense of anticipation and excitement which pleased Jean. At last, by early afternoon, they pulled up outside the former B&B, which thankfully was as the brochures had depicted it. As he scrambled from the car, Arthur succumbed to the lure of the pasties and took one with him on a tour of the airfield. Jean watched him stroll over to the control tower and peer through one of its broken windows. Then, spotting the hangar, he sauntered towards it, his pace increasing as he got nearer. He tried unsuccessfully to prise open the two huge doors at one end, but had better luck with a smaller side entrance. Disappearing inside, he reappeared a minute later to give Jean two thumbs up. Finally he climbed a small hillock covered in lush grass on one side of the hangar in order to command a better view of the entire area.

'Bloody marvellous!' he cried out just as his mobile phone began to ring. It was Fryer.

'Hello . . . what?' Arthur moved a little to improve the reception. 'Is that better?' he shouted down the line.

'Yes, fine,' came the distant voice of Fryer. 'How many do we have now? Is it four or five?' he asked.

'Three!' Arthur shouted.

'Who are they?'

Arthur's face contorted as he wondered if telling Fryer about the nightclub doorman was such a good idea.

'Come on, Bob, I can't give the game away. You'll see soon enough,' Arthur said defensively. 'Let's just say the last chap is a cross between Jonah Lomu and Curtly Ambrose.'

'You chose Alan Fletcher!' Fryer replied excitedly.

'Maybe,' Arthur said nervously.

'I'm coming down on the twenty-seventh of June. Correct?' Fryer's words crackled slightly but Arthur was not really paying attention any more. 'Arthur. The twenty-seventh. Yes?'

Arthur was mesmerised by what lay around of him. The

disused runway lay dormant like an ancient relic, potholes and expansion cracks making it look every bit its age. The vast area was covered in weeds and fissures giving it a Van Winkle like appearance.

'Arthur. Can you hear me?' Fryer insisted.

Arthur, still lost in the wonder of it all, replied, 'Bob, sorry. The twenty-seventh it is.' He was still gazing down the old runway in awe.

'Looking forward to it. We have much to do,' Fryer announced.

'Indeed,' Arthur agreed.

'Oh. Just one more thing. Did you see the score from the weekend?' Fryer asked.

'Of course!' Arthur said, stating the obvious.

'Well, it's about the tail,' Fryer admitted to him.

'Oh!' he sighed. 'Well, if you're wondering if any of them can bat, it's a bit early. I've seen one chap's handiwork on a car bonnet.'

'I'm thinking more of build-an-innings type players, actually.' Fryer said searchingly.

'I'll see what I can do. See you the twenty-seventh,' said Arthur, hitting the red button on his mobile. Still peering down the runway, he lingered a while before strolling off.

Jean was chatting to a middle-aged woman of stern appearance when Arthur arrived and planted himself next to the two women. Waiting politely for them to let him join their conversation, he rolled back and forth on his heels. Jean finally introduced the pair.

'This is my husband Arthur,' she said. He tipped his hat as Jean continued, 'This is Mrs Cheshire, who owns and runs Charmy Down.' He gave her one of his best smiles. The hard-looking woman's narrow, pursed lips and beady eyes presented an unfriendly demeanour – not the type of woman who would take kindly to odd remarks.

'Like the cat!' Arthur observed.

'Excuse me?' the woman spat back at Arthur who was totally unmoved. Jean closed her eyes tight and looked away.

'The Cheshire cat!' Arthur explained enthusiastically. 'The cat with the big smile!' he said flashing a huge grin. The woman, feeling insulted, turned and stormed off in a huff.

'Arthur,' Jean groaned.

'What?' asked Arthur bewildered.

Having completed their move into the house, Arthur and Jean set about preparing for their six guests. Each man was to share with another in bunk-style accommodation. They would all share a common bathroom and two lavatories. Mrs Cheshire was to perform all the normal duties that she would for any paying guest in occupation of the rooms; Jean had agreed to assist her if things became too busy. Arthur meanwhile had had some confidentiality agreements prepared by a solicitor in London, one of which he asked Mrs Cheshire to sign, even though she thought it odd for she never really spoke to anybody. But she signed anyway, grumbling to herself as she scribbled her name.

Arthur collapsed into bed at 2.37 a.m that night – any other night he'd have nodded off in front of the television by ten! But that evening he'd been busy contemplating the selection of the final three bowlers, and all the pieces of the jigsaw he had to fit together in coming days. Checking his well-worn, standard issue British Rail diary, he was surprised to see his list of 'Things to do' only had two things noted down:

- **Find more bowlers**
- **Drink more water**

He drank a glass of water next to his bed and turned out the light, his eyelids closing faster than the defences of Geoffrey Boycott last ball before lunch. But as he drifted off to sleep, he was still thinking of his next fast bowler – little knowing what fate had in store for him in Taunton the next day.

## 14

Arthur and Jean familiarised themselves with the place before Arthur began his task for the day, which was attending two more matches. The fixture at Taunton held the promise of a young quick by the name of Clatworthy. He was apparently under close scrutiny from Somerset Country Cricket Club and came recommended by one of Fryer's scouts. Having dropped Jean back at the house, Arthur made his way to the game in Mrs Cheshire's old Renault as she'd asked him to give it a run.

Unfortunately, Clatworthy proved to be unsuitable as his action was far too front-on, which could prove difficult in training, not to mention the fact that, having seen Frank Arnold, Arthur suspected someone of his build could well be front-on too, and didn't want two bowlers with similar actions.

Clatworthy's partner looked more promising, but unfortunately it turned out that he was from Australia, a fact that Fryer's scouts had failed to pick up on. All of which meant that it was a frustrating day for Arthur, made slightly more bearable by the appearance of a thoroughly entertaining spinner, who came on to bowl towards the end of the home side's innings.

Obviously of Indian descent he appeared an engaging character from the moment he was tossed the ball. Arthur had never seen anyone chat so incessantly whilst playing. It was positively non-stop. In fact it was hard to tell who he was annoying most – the opposition or his own team-mates as he barked instructions to his fielders and made a series of curious hand gestures to position them perfectly. At one point, while the spinner was fielding at close mid-on, the umpire at the non-striker's end halted proceedings to wander over and wag a finger at him in a recriminating fashion. The final straw for this particular umpire came at the beginning of the Indian's opening over when, rather than handing a hat or pullover to the umpire, he unwound his very long turban and handed the bundle to the umpire. It was promptly handed back to him and he was instructed to take it to the boundary. Having handed it over the white fence to a club official, he ran back to commence his over. His team-mates, umpire and batsmen all had a bit of a laugh as he strode to his mark, just as Arthur glanced at his watch, which told him it was 6.27 p.m., and remembered he'd told Jean he would try to be back at a reasonable hour. The score being 187 for 2, Arthur felt there was little point in staying. His thoughts were now turning to Leicestershire the following week, and a teenage whirlwind named Tommy Nutter. He hoped the lad was made of the right stuff as he found the name amusing.

Rising stiffly from his warm seat, Arthur gathered up his blanket and flask, before permitting himself a final glimpse of the day's proceedings as the little spinner hopped in for his first delivery, at which point Arthur rubbed his tired eyes. When he opened them he saw the little spinner jumping for joy and running down the pitch. Arthur scratched his head, realising he'd missed something. He wasn't the only one for the batsman didn't seem to know what had happened either. Bewildered, he turned to survey the shattered stumps and scattered bails. None the wiser he eventually trudged off. The cricketing gods were surely smiling down on Arthur that day. He resumed his seat and watched the next two balls of well-flighted spin – although it was hard to see the amount of turn sitting side-on to the proceedings.

As Arthur settled back into his seat, he could hear the little spinner reminding the new batsman that the score was 13 short of the 200 mark and that it was a very unlucky number. He also told him to be careful of the next ball as it was the fourth of the over and that 4 was his lucky number. All this in one mouthful! Arthur smiled – as did the batsmen. The bowler turned, bounded in again and over came his arm. This time Arthur didn't blink, but it made no difference as he lost sight of the ball. The cunning little bowler's fast ball – which by spin bowling standards was unbelievably quick – had zipped past the batsman's defences and again knocked back the stumps.

'Thirteen. I warned you. Cheerio!' he called out mockingly as the batsman began his trek back to the pavilion.

Arthur now knew he was watching a wily performer. The spinner was not just a fine bowler, but an intelligent reader of the game and his opposition, two of which he'd just outwitted. Like a snake hypnotises a rabbit, he'd put his opposition at ease then struck quickly. His fast ball was potent indeed. Arthur's mind was working overtime. Suddenly he was thinking all manner of things. Could he include a spinner in his Super Six? Could his methods be applied to increase spin as they could to increase speed?

The opposing captain arrived at the crease and was greeted by a brief round of applause. The expression on his face showed that he was determined to steady the innings. He took guard and waited, but this time the little Indian kept quiet and didn't make any offensive remarks. Batsman and bowler stood glaring at each other for what seemed an eternity. The umpire eventually grew impatient and half-turned to see if play was about to resume. But the two just stared at each other.

He's putting him on the defensive, Arthur thought, whereupon the little bowler's hand seemed to curl itself around the ball like a twisted claw as he tensed before leaping into a brief springing stride. The ball looped and drifted like a crimson balloon before dropping sharply, right on middle and leg stump and on a good length, drawing the batsman forward into a defensive stoke. It was poetic; beautiful to watch. Arthur's heart leapt into his mouth as the batsman's gloves and bat thrust towards the ball. Knowing the ball need only turn a fraction to catch an edge Arthur felt the little spinner had bowled the perfect delivery for the occasion. But when the ball finally hit the pitch, it spat straight ahead to be met by the bat with a dull thud. It was an anticlimax, although the players all clapped enthusiastically. Arthur heard someone to his rear comment, 'He'd be a great spin bowler . . . if only he could spin the ball.'

The little bowler snapped up the ball and returned to his mark. It was obvious that he was extremely annoyed with himself and wasted no time delivering the last ball of the over, which was another quick one. This time the batsman was wise to him and confidently pulled the ball to the boundary for four.

Arthur decided to stay on to the end of play. The last over was predictably a defensive effort from the batting team, which yielded only a single. However, the little spinner dug deep for the final ball of the day and speared it in fast and short. The batsman set himself for a pull but the ball reared up much too quickly for him and smashed him flush over the earpiece of his helmet as he turned away to avoid it. Stumbling backwards, the batsman only just avoided trampling on his stumps before tripping over in an ungainly fashion. Arthur, who had never seen a spin bowler fell a batsman, watched pensively as the teams returned to the pavilion.

The not out batsman on 94 was clapped off the field by everyone including the fielding side. Arthur sensed a hint of frustration about the engaging little spinner, but his spirit nevertheless shone through as he chatted jokingly with the opposing captain as they left the field.

As was his custom, Arthur hung around for a while instead of rushing home. He waited near the pavilion for a while and was about to go in search of a tap to wash his flask out when the little Indian appeared. He wore a clean shirt and carried his kit bag, still shouting and joking with his team-mates as he prepared to leave.

'I'll see you after work. If you can still stand up, Tom, you drunk.'

'Hey, Chandra. Bring me a samosa!' called an unseen voice as Chandra wandered past Arthur toward the exit. Arthur noticed the man's shirt had a logo emblazoned across the back, which read 'Mogul Curry House'.

After failing to start the car at the first two attempts, Arthur began to wonder if Mrs Cheshire might have tampered with the engine as he sensed she had developed an intense dislike for him after his smiling cat comment. When it finally started, he wound the window down to let some air in as he drove. Unfortunately a light drizzle had started and the shoulder of his overcoat became wet. He wiped some of it on his face to keep himself awake as the heater was making him feel sleepy. Thoughts of the little spin bowler filled his mind as he drove home.

At Charmy Down, he hauled his weary body out of the Renault and tucked his trusty flask under his arm. As he passed the lounge window he saw Jean inside, glass of wine in hand, chatting to Mrs Cheshire. She was ready for dinner judging by the look of her and seemed in good spirits. He took in a few big breaths of the chilly night air and went inside.

'Hi!' he called and poked his head round the corner of the lounge door to acknowledge both women. 'Just popping upstairs to freshen up and we'll go right away.' He winked at Jean.

A cold shower and a stiff scotch later and he was back downstairs.

'Ready to go?' he asked Jean. She quickly said goodbye to Mrs Cheshire, who looked as though she had just bitten hard into a lemon.

Jean chatted non-stop as they drove. As Arthur listened, he thought she would give the Indian spinner a run for his money. Finally he asked, 'What do you fancy to eat?'

Having obviously given it a bit of thought, Jean answered without hesitation, 'Indian.'

The Mogul Curry House advertised itself by way of a magnificent pink sign over the front entrance, under which there was the slogan: 'Don't be in a flurry. You know you want a curry!' written in red and green neon that flashed at passers-by.

They sat at the rear of the restaurant and a friendly waiter brought Arthur a half pint and Jean a gin and tonic. Having just finished telling Jean that he had unfortunately found no one suitable for his scheme, he added that he had witnessed an 'interesting' spin bowler in a turban – at which moment a voice interrupted them.

'I'm glad you found my performance "*interesting*", sir.'

Standing by the table still pouring Arthur's beer into a glass was none other than the little spin bowler from the afternoon's match. Arthur didn't seem overly surprised.

'Chandra Jafar at your service,' he announced, smiling. Before Arthur could get a word, in the man bent down and half whispered, 'I actually prefer it when people use the word "mesmerizing" when describing my performances, but as I only took two wickets today I'll settle for "interesting".' He placed Arthur's beer on the table and headed towards the kitchen, collecting plates and glasses as he went.

A bit later, as Arthur finished his fish curry, he once again sensed a presence beside him.

'Howzat!' Chandra said loudly. Arthur smiled, raising his eyebrows approvingly. 'A little cricketing joke for you. I am asking whether you enjoyed your curry.'

'Yes, I'm aware of that,' said Arthur wiping his mouth. 'Very appealing.'

'Ha Ha! You are my match, sir. Very good indeed.' He waggled his finger approvingly and flashed a wide smile.

'You know, I normally reserve the word "mesmerising" for spin bowlers.'

Chandra put the empty beer bottle down on the table and studied Arthur for a few moments before finally telling him, 'I *am* a spin bowler, sir. Thank you very much.'

Arthur drank the rest of his beer and raised his eyebrows in a questioning fashion. 'So was I,' he told Chandra.

'Really!'

'Yes, and the similarities don't stop there.' Arthur continued. 'I couldn't spin the ball either!'

Chandra's chest rose as his nostrils took in vast quantities of the curry-scented air. A scowl appeared on his slightly sweaty brow, but Arthur seemed to disarm him completely by simply meeting his glare and awaiting his reaction. Chandra looked at Jean, who also seemed keen to hear his response. He grabbed a chair and sat down between them both, saying, 'If I could spin the ball . . . I would be king. I would give anything to be able to do so.' His outstretched hands seemed to be pleading with Arthur as he spoke. 'The gods tease me. They make me love cricket. They make me love spin bowling.' He stopped and gathered himself. 'and then they play a cruel trick on me – no spin!' He looked up helplessly at the ceiling fan. 'Every ball I pray for turn. But no! I bowl that ball straighter than a royal spine. I tell you though, I found my own way of getting wickets.' He held the edge of the table. 'But to spin a ball, to beat the bat with flight and turn–' he swallowed hard for dramatic effect '–I can only dream of it.' Chandra moodily rued his plight.

'You seem to do fine for someone who can't spin the ball,' Arthur pointed out.

'I create my wickets with all manner of tricks. I'm good for one, maybe two top order batsmen, a couple of tail-enders. But once they've seen my stock ball I'm finished!' He made a swift cutting gesture across his neck with his hand. Standing up he concluded by announcing 'As I said . . . if I could spin, I'd be king!' He had Arthur thinking again as he fetched some dishes and retired to the kitchen.

Jean and Arthur finished their meal and with Jean making a quick visit to the ladies' room Arthur watched Chandra busying himself about the restaurant. He pondered the unfortunate spinner's plight. Why couldn't a spin bowler benefit from the principles that he'd applied to Tim's action? This, plus taking his fast ball up a notch were, compelling thoughts. The ideas were coming thick and fast. As he thought about it he could find no reason that a spin bowler's turn could not be improved using the Arthur Jenkins method.

'I hope you enjoyed your meal as much as my bowling this afternoon. That will be thirty two pounds please sir,' Chandra said with a smile, handing Arthur a small silver plate with the bill and two mints on it. Arthur handed him £35 and plus a plain white envelope. Chandra looked at him questioningly.

'Keep the change and open that later,' he instructed Chandra pointing to the envelope.

Chandra scrutinized the envelope then held it up to Arthur as if he were about to open it.

'Later,' Arthur said softly.

Chandra pushed the envelope awkwardly into his back pocket, put the money in the till and gave a wave to Arthur and Jean as they left.

'See you soon.' Arthur called back to him.

As they made for the car, Jean asked Arthur, 'Who was that, dear?'

'I'm not sure. Let's call him "Mr **GUILE**" for now.'

## 15

Waking at an ungodly hour was becoming the norm for Arthur. As the kettle shook and spat, he peered out of the kitchen window at the airfield which was covered in a thick layer of mist. He could almost see the figures of the airmen scrambling for an early morning raid. Pulling a jumper over his head, he crept outside silently. Strolling across the airfield, he discovered there had actually been a triangular network of three runways, which was the norm for the war years, two of which had had the tarmac taken up at some stage, probably to expose the earth underneath for farming purposes. He ignored the heavy dew soaking his shoes and seeping through to his woollen socks as he sniffed in the pleasing smell of cold wet grass.

It was six in the morning. Arthur stood at the end of the runway nearest the control tower having convinced himself there was a lost squadron of Spitfires somewhere out there. He listened for them hoping to see them break through the morning mist at any moment. But the place was silent except for a lark trilling lustily somewhere overhead.

Time for a cup of tea, thought Arthur. On the way back he wondered if the airmen based at Charmy Down had ever enjoyed a game of cricket. Would the former inhabitants appreciate their old aerodrome being used again, this time against a very different opponent?

Arthur felt content as he squeezed a teabag between two teaspoons. Only two more recruits to find, then he could begin on the next phase. Many would have given their right arm to be paid to watch as much cricket as he had over the last weeks – others would have given their right arm not to – but, being industrious by nature, Arthur was restless to get started on the hands-on aspect of his project. He added a little sugar to his tea and stirred it slowly, leaning back against the kitchen sink. At that moment the phone rang. It was Fryer.

'I've just been chatting to Mathew French,' he began.

Arthur could see this was going to be an awkward call. 'Yeeees,' he said slowly.

'He was telling me of all the wonderful offers he has on the table at the moment. Other counties, a couple from overseas. But not one from you.'

'Well I . . .' Arthur started.

'OK, stop right there. I've left it up to you to do the selecting and I've no idea who you've got so far. However, I do insist on one player: Mathew French!' Arthur looked up at the heavens. 'I mean, who else do we have, Arthur? I haven't got a clue.'

'We've got the right people,' Arthur told him.

'Who are they? You've told me nothing,' Fryer's voice was rising in frustration. 'I insist on French . . . do you want to tell him or shall I?'

'I will,' Arthur said quickly, knowing he had no choice.

'Good,' said Fryer. 'See you on Monday.'

And that was that.

Arthur, never one to waste time, got on the phone to French right away. It didn't *feel* right, but then he thought, it probably *was* right. Maybe it was the only right choice so far. It looked as if Fryer had prepped French as there wasn't the usual surprised reaction followed by questions. Arthur later found out that Fryer had even provided French with an excuse to miss the remainder of the county season.

The more he thought about it the more Arthur warmed to French's selection. He was after all an excellent bowler, and having a professional in the group would have its advantages.

Five down. One to go. Taking the well-worn list from his jacket pocket, he pondered French's attributes. Only **WORKHORSE & HEART** were unclaimed. Arthur decided French was neither.

As he contemplated the latest recruit, Arthur spotted a small white envelope propped up against a bowl in the kitchen. It was addressed to him. He picked it up, opened it and was delighted to see that it was from Tim. He'd been meaning to make contact himself but time had run away from him of late.

The contents of the letter were brief. Tim inquired after Arthur's health – Jean's as well, which pleased him – and listed his bowling figures in matches he'd played in recently, including his third hat-trick of the season. It seemed he was progressing well, but was also having to contend with school and a demanding exam schedule. He also mentioned the fact that he'd been approached by a county for a trial the following season. In his concluding paragraph, Tim wrote that his team had made the final, which, if they won, would give the school its first championship for seventeen years.

Arthur was beside himself with the boy's stunning results. Tim was now a true bowling force. Looking back at the boy he'd met in the nets just a year earlier, he felt incredibly proud of his efforts. Tim was a different person, his confidence sky high as a result of all his successes. Arthur decided to watch Tim's cricket final and at the same time fetch some items from home, and visit Ted.

Arthur arrived in Wielding Willow the day before Tim's match and caught up with Ted, but rather than go to the club, they decided have a meal in town. Arthur drank very little that evening and walked the long way home.

The next day walked briskly to the ground where Tim was playing, finding the early mornings and free time an intoxicating mix. He got there well before the match was due to start, knowing that Tim would be warming up as he'd been instructed by Ted and Arthur before him. Tim was delighted to see his mentor as Arthur had not told him of the visit in case sudden commitments got in the way. They had a good hour to catch up before the other players began to arrive.

The first thing Arthur noticed was that the boy had filled out but that certain aspects of his physique weren't quite right. He made a mental note to address this later when talking to both Tim and Ted. Luckily Tim's captain lost the toss, which meant Arthur didn't have to wait to see his protégé bowl. Remembering Good Walloping also had a game that day, he checked his watch, unaware how short an innings could be when Tim was bowling.

True to form, Tim made sure the opposing batsmen never got going. He took another 7 wickets and was even given the honour by his captain of batting right up the order as his team closed in on the other team's paltry total. Showing great composure and concentration Tim was 15 not out when his team passed the 73 runs required for victory. Arthur was fascinated to see that Tim's recent successes with the ball had considerably increased spectator numbers, and he even noticed a small female fan club down by the fence, all of whom seemed to focus their attention on Tim, who was oblivious to it. Arthur stayed long enough to witness an impromptu presentation in which Tim was declared Man of the Match. Not wanting to keep Tim from being with his mates, Arthur gave him his new address in Charmy Down, telling him he was contracted to work there for a year, and said goodbye. It was a lie and he felt bad telling it, especially as he was itching to share his news with Tim, who he felt more than anyone was his true partner in all this.

As he left, he was acutely aware that he would be starting on the Monday with only five bowlers – or maybe less. He could always fall back on Fryer's list but it was not something he wanted to do. Now Arthur was increasingly grateful to have French on board.


It was a home game for Good Walloping and Arthur got there just after the game had resumed after lunch. Their opponents were top of the division, whereas Good Walloping languished at the bottom. As Arthur greeted the club regulars, he noticed that the Good Walloping players were wearing black armbands.

'I hardly dare ask,' Arthur said to Peter Jones – a good wicketkeeper-batsman for the club in his day – as he motioned at the armbands.

'Singleton's father's just passed away,' he told Arthur.

'Terry Singleton. Oh dear,' said Arthur.

He made his way to the boundary and took up his usual seat to watch the session, which passed uneventfully with only a single run-out. When the players came in for tea with their heads down, Arthur wondered why Jim Singleton had not been put on to bowl.

As they made their way back onto the pitch, Arthur surprised himself and everyone else by getting up from his seat as the team passed him and closing the gate just as Ed Morley, Good Walloping's captain, was about to lead them out onto the field.

'What are you playing at, Arthur? Out of my way,' he said, unprepared for what was about to follow.

'What are you playing at, Ed?' Arthur asked him angrily. 'That young man is your best bowler and he's not had a single over. You're meant to be remembering his father. What better way than his son doing him proud at the game he loved?'

'I thought he might want to take it easy first up, that's all,' Morley replied feebly.

'I played cricket with Terry Singleton and the man never turned down a challenge in his life. Why would his son be any different?' Arthur eyeballed Morley, who turned to Singleton.

'You up for it?' he asked. After a moment's hesitation, Morley threw him the ball and Arthur opened the gate again, even giving Singleton a pat on the shoulder as they took to the field.

Arthur waited for the usual bombshells from the big man, but they never came. He waited for the wayward deliveries and the costly no-balls that so often marred Singleton's performances, but they never came either. Singleton's trademark aggression had disappeared. His father, always telling him to slow down and think a bit more, had finally got his way.

There was a time when Jim Singleton let fly with every ball as if it were intended to inflict maximum damage to the batsman, rather than to take his wicket. He had never forgotten what his father had said to him years before: 'Son, most people play this game because they love it, but not you. You play it for a reason I just don't understand.'

For some reason Singleton was not bowling as he normally did that day, replacing his raw aggression with line, length and consistency, each ball laced with desperation. He toiled under a hot sun for two spells, taking three wickets in each one, even though he'd been up all hours the previous night.

But there was no fairy tale ending to the day for Singleton as the visitors scored the 234 runs set by Good Walloping with eight wickets down. It was an excellent performance by the home team, given the quality of the opposition. The team was upset for Jim, as he alone had almost won the match for them – indeed, had he opened the bowling he probably would have! But in the end it was not to be. His father would have been proud of the way he had bowled and Jim knew that. Why couldn't he have done so just once while his father was alive, he wondered.

The players showered, changed and met in the bar to remember Terry Singleton with a couple of ales. Jim Singleton was conspicuous by his absence, and no one knew where he was – all except Arthur, who had a faint idea of where a broken-hearted fast bowler might be.

He found Singleton by the nets, sitting on the grass alone, head hanging low and shoulders shaking. He lifted his head and drew in great gasps of air in between sobs; there were tears running down his face. In his right hand he held a cricket ball. It was clear from the look on his face and the way his hand shook that he was squeezing the ball tightly. His head dropped again and his body shook all over.

Arthur felt he should leave the man to himself and turned to make his way back to the clubhouse – at which moment Singleton rose slowly to his feet. He had still not seen Arthur, who paused at the top of a small knoll to catch his breath. Suddenly there was a shout from the nets. Arthur spun around to see the huge frame of Singleton racing in to bowl, his eyes bulging, his teeth bared like a mad dog. He leapt into his delivery stride as if the devil were on his back and sent down a ball that would shatter steel. Arthur thought the ball would never stop. Never had he seen such a terrifying delivery. Riveted to the spot for a moment, Arthur had to tear himself away from the scene; he was shaken as he returned to the clubhouse. Unable to rid his mind of the image, he felt somewhat dazed.

As Arthur had felt all along, and had told Singleton a year back, the man *was* capable of much better. He could see that his current fitness was well below par, but there was little doubt about the fantastic potential that lay beneath. His height was good too at over 6 ft 5. Arthur was shocked. Was he considering Singleton? Singleton of all people to join his outfit? Was he justifying the selection to himself already? His head swirled as he juggled the possibilities. He struggled with the ramifications of selecting a bowler from his own club; he thought about the incident a year earlier; he considered the sympathy he felt for Singleton at the loss of his father. Did it all fit? Was it right? Could he? He tried to ignore the thought, but it was impossible. Arthur felt himself reach inside his jacket pocket for the last envelope. Then he stopped, knowing he had to approach this particular decision a little more logically and in doing so an equation gradually formed in his mind:

Singleton's performance today + Beast in the nets x Arthur's Method = <u>Intelligent, Absolutely Terrifying, Super-Fast Bowler.</u>

Some time later, feeling empty and weary, Singleton went to shower and change. Inside his locker he found a single white envelope placed neatly on top of his club blazer.

Faced with the drive back to Charmy Down, Arthur decided to stay at the cottage overnight instead. He drove home that night happy in the knowledge that he had completed his entire selection process and had six fine prospects to work with. He put another mental cross through one of the words on his list – **FEAR!** It was the second time he had struck the word from his list. Still, he thought, having two terrifying super-fast bowlers was surely better than one.

Not surprisingly, Singleton's routine Sunday morning hangover was absent the following day. Rising early, he'd arranged to meet up with relatives and some close friends of his father's at 10 o'clock in the village. Some details of his father's funeral were to be discussed followed by an early lunch. The last thing on his mind was the contents of Arthur's envelope, though it had caught him at the right time the previous night and intrigued him sufficiently. On the way to his engagement, Singleton spotted Arthur wandering into the local churchyard. Remembering Arthur's bold intervention the previous day, his conscience got the better of him and, wanting to thank Arthur, he pulled his van into a nearby parking spot. Gratitude not being an emotion Singleton was overly comfortable with, he pondered some possible deliveries as he made for the churchyard running his hand over a thick stubble.

Sliding through the lichgate, Singleton gazed at the plethora of headstones pointing skywards like rows of crooked upturned teeth, before spotting Arthur forty-odd yards away standing at the foot of a grave. Singleton paused then moved closer to the corner of the church where he could easily retreat should he decide his timing might be awkward. Just as Arthur had observed him silently from a distance only the day before, so too did Singleton of Arthur. Arthur stood motionless, slightly stooped, not moving at all. Eventually he bent down and laid something on the grave and after a moment moved off slowly. Singleton, deciding to remain anonymous, wandered slowly around the entire building in order to give Arthur time to leave before returning to his van. Passing the grave where Arthur had been standing, Singleton read the name 'Davey Jenkins' and noticed a crisp new cricket magazine resting on the gravestone, rather than the customary bunch of flowers. Noticing the dates on the headstone, Singleton muttered quietly to himself, 'Seven and a half . . . bloody hell.'

# Part Two

# Charmy Down

## 16

On the day his players were due to arrive, Arthur began to wonder just how many would turn up. After all, the letter had simply stated the recipient had been specially chosen to be part of a 'sporting initiative of national importance'. It didn't even mention the actual sport, although it did guarantee that a weekly salary of £400 would be paid to each player. In typical Arthur Jenkins fashion, there was a simple punchline at the conclusion of the letter, which read: 'If you've ever wanted to do something special in your life, here's your chance.'

Fryer had called to say he would not be there until the following day, so Arthur would have to meet and greet the arrivals himself. He had a light breakfast consisting of toast, a pear and a cup of plum tea, and got busy with some last-minute chores. He was a little nervous about how the day would unfold and hadn't prepared any sort of welcoming speech for his new charges. Yet he had a good idea of what he wanted to say to them having practised in his head for twenty-odd years. Jean could sense he was a little tense anyway having said he'd like to discuss a few points with her at 9.00 a.m. – but at 9.01 a.m., when he found her in the kitchen still finishing her porridge, he got unusually upset that she was running late. She mumbled something under her breath, but not far enough under for Arthur to miss the 'old fuddy-duddy' bit.

He sat in the drawing room waiting patiently for his wife, who arrived at 9.04 a.m. with files, pens and an address book. She moved towards a large armchair which she had made her own since arriving at Charmy Down.

'Best you sit over here,' Arthur informed her in an overbearing tone. Jean, whose bottom was precariously hovering over the comfy chair, stopped just short of dropping into its depths. She shot Arthur a cold look. 'This *is* business. You're not meant to be comfy,' he said, continuing to rustle through some papers as Jean grudgingly moved over to the small table he'd set up; he indicated a small wooden chair for her.

'Right. Inventory!' Arthur barked in a snappy tone, looking up at Jean and beaming at her broadly.

'You go off yours and I'll say "check" to what we have,'

she informed him sternly.

'Right . . . lawnmower,' said Arthur.

'Check!' Jean replied smartly.

'Roller for the pitches,' said Arthur raising his voice somewhat.

'Check!' Jean answered professionally.

This continued for some time and Arthur had to admit that Jean had done a very thorough job. Amongst the items she had procured were bats, balls, stumps, gloves, boxes – she called them 'goolie guards' – thigh pads and helmets. There were indoor and outdoor nets, timing guns, blocks of wood, pulleys, ropes, paint, paint brushes, iron bars, video equipment, a television, indoor synthetic grass, indoor balls, indoor lights and many other bits and bobs. She had had most of the old hangar fitted with lead wiring that Arthur could complete when he had decided where the practice nets would be positioned. When Arthur had exhausted the list, there was only one item Jean had not said 'Check' to, which was 'rubber chicken' – he'd decided to throw that in just to keep her on her toes.

Arthur had put together an information pack for the players, which outlined the rules of the program. Also inside were a confidentiality agreement and a rough training schedule. Their first two weeks would focus on setting up the centre correctly. The most important thing of all was the five practice nets: two indoor and three outdoor. Once these were completed, each member of the group would be allocated his share of pitch duties. Arthur had already selected the location of the outside pitches and had even given them names. As Charmy Down was a historic aerodrome, he had named each pitch after a type of fighter that had flown there at the height of the War. The three grass pitches, which they would rotate in use, were Defiant, Havoc and Whirlwind, and the two indoor pitches were named after bombers: Lancaster and Wellington – even though they had never used the aerodrome. He had also set out a 2.4-mile run around Charmy Down that each player had to complete once a day.

In the days leading up to the recruits' arrival, it had occurred to Arthur that they couldn't *all* use Mrs Cheshire's poor old car for transport when going into town. While Arthur was looking through the local classified ads, Mrs Cheshire mentioned to him that she still had her late husband's old Mk II Jaguar in storage and that he was welcome to commandeer it – if it still ran. It didn't, of course, but Arthur's deft hand soon had the big cat purring like a kitten. The car happened to be in fairly ordinary shape but would fit the bill just nicely.

Of the things Arthur liked the most at Charmy Down was the games room, a massive extension, which Mrs Cheshire had let go somewhat after the death of her husband. It had an open fireplace and a bar complete with a bar tap, which Arthur got to testing as soon as he'd discovered it.

'Butcombe,' he muttered, reading the label on the tap. 'Don't mind if I do.'

After some fiddling around and a phone call or two he had managed to get the tap working and ordered a keg of the same ale to satisfy his curiosity. When the beer arrived some days later Arthur was so taken with it he immediately ordered two more kegs.

It was near 11.00 a.m. and he was bringing the last load of firewood into the games room when Jean came to find him, her voice nervous with excitement.

'There's someone here to see you. I think it's one of the new chaps.'

Arthur put the wood down and dusted his hands off. He pulled down his knitted vest tightly over his ever-decreasing paunch and smoothed his moustache. Rounding the front of the house, he was greeted by the willowy frame of Edwin Roberts sitting astride his beloved bicycle, wearing his flying jacket and hat. Biggles was not in the basket this time but in his arms. Facing him was Mrs Cheshire holding her cat in a similar fashion and shouting at the new arrival.

'There are no dogs at Charmy Down! You'll have to send it away,' she shouted.

Roberts seemed unfazed by the episode as Arthur scuttled over to greet him warmly, ignoring the slight hitch.

'Edwin. Arthur Jenkins. Pleased to meet you, again, and thanks so much for coming.' The two men shook hands firmly as Biggles struggled in Edwin's arms.

'Problem with Biggles?' Roberts asked.

Arthur turned to Mrs Cheshire. 'Problems with pets, Mrs Cheshire?' he asked in an inquisitive fashion.

'Only dogs. They ain't allowed 'ere,' she replied emphatically.

'Presumably because you feel the dog will chase the cat,' Arthur suggested.

'Well, what dog wouldn't?' she asked.

'Actually Biggles here wouldn't,' Arthur explained. 'He's scared of cats. It's obvious.'

They all looked at the dog, which was shaking violently and certainly looked very frightened. Unconvinced, Mrs Cheshire said nothing, her lips at their lemon-squeezing best.

'Besides, Mrs Cheshire, how can you turn a dog named Biggles away from here of all places?' Arthur pleaded to her with open arms.

She relented but not without a parting shot: 'First sign of trouble and he goes, Mr Jenkins.' She strode off back into the house still holding the cat tightly to her breast.

'Mrs Cheshire.' Roberts observed. 'Cheshire cat!'

'She doesn't get it,' replied Arthur dryly. The two men were clearly going to get along fine. Edwin allowed Biggles to jump from his arms onto the gravel driveway.

'Mr Jenkins . . . its about . . .' he started tentatively.

'I know,' replied Arthur. 'I used to have a Staffy when I was young. He shakes when he's excited. Am I right?'

Roberts nodded somewhat sheepishly. 'Biggles will skin that cat if he ever gets it,' he said.

'You wouldn't do that would you, boy?' Arthur asked the dog as he patted the friendly black shadow at his feet. He bent down to acquaint himself with Biggles. 'How about you just leave the cat and eat Mrs Cheshire?' He straightened up and asked Edwin, 'Can you come and help me with something?'

Edwin got off his bike and transferred his duffle bag from his shoulder to the handlebars of his bike. As the two men walked off, Edwin looked around him with interest.

'I can see what sort of place this is, Mr Jenkins. Is what I'm doing here got something to do with the War?'

'More a battle than a war,' said Arthur, 'and do please call me Arthur.'

Chandra Jafar and George Samuels got off the bus and walked to Charmy Down together. Neither had known the other beforehand, but once headed in the same direction down a narrow country lane, both carrying overnight bags, it wasn't long before Chandra called to Samuels who was walking on the other side of the road.

'Does your walking down this road have anything to do a strange little man who came to watch you play cricket, by any chance?'

They talked cordially as they covered the mile to the airfield. Arthur was further relived to see the two arrive and greeted them warmly. He was in the process of introducing them to Edwin when a sleek-looking Mercedes sports drove up, and out stepped Mathew French, looking more like a movie star than a county cricketer. Dressed in a heavily fleeced woollen jacket and square-shaped sunglasses he retrieved a large kitbag from the boot of the car and swung it over his left shoulder.

Chandra recognised French from previous encounters; many of them spiteful.

'Mathew French,' seethed Chandra under his breath.

The female driver of the car, her face partly obscured by the tinted windows, received an air-kiss from French. Before Arthur had time to introduce French to the group, Chandra spoke up.

'Nice of your father to drop you off,' he observed, knowing full well French would not blow his father a kiss.

Smirking knowingly at the sight of his nemesis, French replied, 'Chandra, I can't blame you for wanting to put a bit of spin on that – after all, it's about all you *can* put spin on.'

'Mmm. Good comeback,' Chandra said, earnestly rubbing his chin. 'I can see you've been working on your sledging, must be why other areas of your game have suffered recently.'

French had no answer to that. It was quite clear Chandra and French didn't get along too well.

'You two lovebirds can coo to each other later,' Arthur told them. 'In the meantime, Mathew please meet George Samuels, Edwin Roberts and you obviously know Chandra Jafar.' They all exchanged greetings, with French being rather patronising as he made himself known to the group. All the men fell silent for a moment.

'I'm sure you're all keen for me to tell you what on earth you're all doing here, but we're expecting two more arrivals so it will have to wait.'

'One,' said Edwin, correcting Arthur's mathematics as he nodded towards the front gate where big Jim Singleton was extracting his large frame from an undersized taxi. It was like watching a giraffe give birth as he squeezed himself out and paused to take in his surroundings.

'He looks like a right mean bugger,' George remarked to Chandra, noting Singleton's trademark scowl.

'You should see the next one,' Arthur told George in an ominous tone as Singleton approached the group.

'Great to see you, Jim. Sorry I couldn't be there, but how did last Sunday go?' he asked the big man.

'He did as he was told for once,' replied Singleton in reference to his father's funeral.

Arthur nodded solemnly. 'Don't worry, we'll make him proud here, boy,' Arthur told Singleton in an upbeat tone. 'Meet the others.' Arthur introduced him to the group: 'George Samuels, Edwin Roberts, Chandra Jafar and Mathew French.' Jim exchanged pleasantries without a smile, which caused George to mentally dub him 'Grim Jim'.

'Well, it's as good a time as any to show you your accommodation, so if you'll all fetch your bags and meet me in the entrance hall . . .'

Arthur gave them a tour of the 'Big House', as it was now known, ending with the shared accommodation. French was very put out at having to share with Chandra who, as always, took it in his stride.

'Stop your whingeing, boy. I'll look after you!' he slapped French on the back and winked at him. Other pairings were Edwin with Jim Singleton, and George with Frank Arnold, who had not yet shown up.

George picked the bottom bunk with the words 'I think I'll feel safer on the bottom.'

Not when you see what's above you, thought Arthur.

The house had a good-sized kitchen, which Arthur had told Mrs Cheshire would need to be fully accessible to the guests at all hours. As this was outside the normal rules for guests, she was a little put out, but as Arthur explained to her, it was a more agreeable option than her being available twenty-four hours a day to cater for six hungry athletes. There was a lounge with seating for all and a television. The bare brick walls of the bar and the games room were adorned with old black and white stills of Charmy Down during the war years. There were shots of aircrews seated in their planes ready for take-off, scrambling during a night raid, in the mess-hall, playing cards in their rooms when off-duty, and even one of a group of ground crew playing cricket outside a hangar. At the head of the bar, a roll of honour was mounted listing the names of those who had lost their lives while serving at Charmy Down during the War. Wedged between the bar and the three couches at one end of the games room was a three-quarter-size billiard table.

Faced with another of Mrs Cheshire's longstanding rules of 'No Games after 9 p.m.', Arthur brokered a deal with her which extended the table hours to 10.30 p.m. In return he had had a new felt surface fitted and had polished all the wood and brass fittings.

The guided tour took them up to 5 o'clock whereupon the group gathered in the games room – except for French who was still in his room chatting on his mobile phone to his girlfriend – not wanting to waste time settling in. Chandra was busy chatting to Singleton. In spite of the difference in size between the two men being laughable, Chandra thought it better to be friends with someone Singleton's size and challenged him to a friendly game of pool. His long-winded explanation of the 'House Rules' seemed to be getting under Singleton's skin. Looking on, George thought Chandra was in danger of sustaining a  serious physical injury if he didn't get on with things.

Arthur was wondering why Frank Arnold had not yet turned up when Edwin asked, 'You mentioned there's one more to arrive, Mr Jenkins.'

'I did,' Arthur answered earnestly, 'and I really don't know where he is.' If anyone was going to pull a 'no show', Arthur had expected it to be Frank. Fancy offering a chap who's only played a limited amount of cricket a place in the squad, he mused.  His thoughts moved on to Tim. Where was *he* now and how well was he bowling?

'Mr Jenkins, are we any closer to finding out exactly *why*

we're here?' George asked from behind his pint of ale.

Arthur snapped out of his dream state. 'Why does everyone insist on calling me "Mr Jenkins"?'

Chandra was just about to say something when George cut him off. 'Hey, don't answer him,' he called out to Chandra. 'He hasn't answered *my* question yet!'

Arthur was put on the spot. They all stopped what they were doing and listened intently.

'Patience,' he replied to George succinctly. 'You'll find out soon enough.'

'Is that it?' George cried out.

'Not quite,' Arthur snapped. 'How do you like the ale? He asked motioning to the tap. George sipped his pint and regarded the label on the tap. He announced dramatically. 'Mmm . . I do.'

'Excellent. West Country's finest that is.' Arthur informed him.

Chandra had an easy straight shot on the black ball to win against Jim. Wanting everyone to watch him win, he called out, 'Seven is my lucky number!' He leaned over the table and steadied himself for the shot. 'But eight is luckier still,' he said as he stroked the white ball like a pro.

It was a bad shot. He hit the black off-centre, positioning it very close to the corner pocket, which set up Singleton for an easy win.

'That one moved a bit!' Arthur remarked to no one in particular.

'Did you see that?' Chandra cried angrily. He moved to the part of the table along which the ball had rolled and brushed it with his hand. 'Very suspect playing surface.'

George and Edwin exchanged a knowing look as Singleton moved in for the kill. The moment he struck the white ball there was a loud cough from Chandra. The black ball dropped in the pocket and the two men shook hands.

'OK, I'm warmed up now,' announced Chandra. 'Let's play doubles,' he suggested to George and Edwin.

George declined. 'I'm not moving from here while I've got free beer.'

Singleton meanwhile started to tease Chandra. 'You and I, "Lucky Seven". Why don't you do some ground repairs on that playing surface while I set up?'

Meanwhile, Arthur had noticed that Edwin was constantly looking out of the window across the airfield to the hangar. Suddenly he got up and moved towards the door. 'I'm afraid you can't go over there,' Arthur called out to him.

The others were all ears.

Edwin turned to face Arthur, a slightly perplexed expression on his face. 'I just wanted to have a quick look,' he explained innocently, holding the door ajar.

'Believe me, son. You'll have seen enough of those old hangars to last you a lifetime by the time we're done,' he told Edwin who, not being one to argue, closed the door again and stepped back.

The door swung open again almost immediately and French strode in, looking decidedly cold and a little puffed out. He took in the scene at a glance – the fire, the pool table, everyone with a drink.

'Splendid,' he said, clapping his hands and approaching the bar where George had taken up residency. 'G&T, thanks barman.'

George looked under the bar for a moment then gave French a blank look as he held up an empty pint glass.

'Mmm,' French grimaced, 'not a beer kind of person really.'

George filled the pint anyway.

'Dinner at seven,' Arthur reminded them as he left the room. Chandra leaned over the pool table and called out loudly, 'C'mon, Lucky Seven!' as he struck the pack sending the black straight in, meaning he'd lost . . . again.

Not long after dinner, Arthur and the players headed back to the games room for a quick nightcap. Jean, having met the group at dinner, joined them at Arthur's request. She thought them on the whole very friendly, although she was a little intimidated by Jim Singleton. When she told Arthur this, he replied, 'Good! He's meant to be scary.'

George Samuels, who had seemingly never been offered free beer before, continued to make good use of it. Edwin Roberts tended the fire and refilled people's drinks. Mathew French wandered around slightly ill at ease and talked about himself at every opportunity. Jim Singleton, having not lost yet to Chandra, stalked around the pool table chalking his cue. By now they were all calling Chandra 'Lucky Seven', or just plain 'Seven'. Chandra slightly more subdued that night, played imaginary forward defensive strokes with his pool cue as he waited for his shot.

Arthur, who had slipped away for a few minutes, returned holding a clutch of six brand new cricket bats and a net bag full of balls.

'Bit late for that now,' Chandra joked.

Arthur handed out a bat and ball to each of those not playing pool. 'Give them a good whacking then put some of this on,' he told them, holding up a small bottle of linseed oil. 'Don't hit the edges at ninety degrees. Do it this way.' He demonstrated how to knock in the edges of the bats the correct way.

After a few minutes George asked, 'How long do we have to do this for?'

'About six hours,' Arthur said, to their horror, as he poured himself a pint then found a spare armchair to sink into. The room resounded to the sound of ball on willow. Chandra meanwhile played his imaginary shots with one of the spare bats.

As the fire dimmed, Edwin drew the curtains in order to keep the warmth in. It just so happened that as he did so most of the others were watching him. As he reached up high to unhook the curtains, his body suddenly went rigid as a huge shadow passed in front of the window where he stood. He stepped back, his eyes still transfixed on what he'd seen outside. Biggles, who had been dozing by the fire, came to life and gave a series of loud barks.

'There's something out there,' Edwin told the group nervously. 'It's the size of a house.'

'I saw it too,' George admitted more amazed than scared. They all turned their attention to the second window as the monster passed it. Whatever it was outside, Biggles didn't like the look of it and backed off sheepishly.

'Christ,' said George, 'must be a bear or something.'

The handle of the outside door started to turn.

'A giant bear that can open doors!' George went on, not realising what he'd just said.

As the door opened, a gust of cold air hit the room, closely followed by a giant figure. It was Frank Arnold. All seven feet of him. His barrel chest nearly filled the room, which only a moment ago had seemed quite spacious. Frank immediately noticed all of them speechless, holding dearly to their bats and balls. He looked Arthur for a rationalisation.

'Frank,' Arthur said stepping forward and shaking the man's hand. 'Thought you'd never make it.'

'That Mrs Cheshire told me to come in,' he told Arthur.

'Fine,' Arthur told him still shaking his hand vigorously, so happy he'd shown up. 'Excellent, I want you to meet everyone.' George being the closest was first. 'This is George Samuels.'

George, slightly drunk and totally in awe, looked up at the enormous man. 'You can open doors,' he told Arnold in his inebriated state.

The rest said little as they introduced themselves. Come Chandra's turn he announced boldly, 'We will call you Frank the Tank!' Frank didn't smile as they shook hands.

'Or maybe just Frank.' Chandra added.

When the introductions were complete, Arthur proudly announced, 'Well, here you all are then. Terrific!' He looked around the group, very pleased with himself. 'The six together at last!' Jean clapped delightedly as Arthur smiled affably. 'The Super Six,' he joked. They all looked blankly at him.

'We should have a toast,' Jean said excitedly.

'Excellent idea!' cried Arthur clapping his hands.

George and Edwin got busy handing around drinks. When they all had a drink, Arthur held his high and announced proudly, 'To the Super Six!'

'The Super Six!' they all called out, bewildered by the whole thing, but they lifted their drinks and drank nevertheless.

'What have we done to deserve this?' asked George.

'Nothing,' answered Arthur.

'Well, what are we going to do then?' George continued.

Arthur paused before looking slowly at each one in turn for maximum effect. Then, quite calmly and deliberately, he informed them, 'We're going to win the Ashes!'

## 17

Everyone was finishing breakfast when George arrived announcing that he was starving. The smell of kippers that greeted him almost knocked him off his feet and killed his appetite. He slumped into a seat and dragged a banana from the fruit bowl.

'I played barman all last night; someone make me a cuppa,' he grumbled, then collapsed onto his arms which he folded on the table in front of him. Jean got up and made for the kettle.

'I think that ale's going to be a problem.' Arthur reflected.

'If you take it away, we're all leaving.' George told him without raising his head.

The others were handing their plates to Mrs Cheshire or Jean, who in turn were stacking them in the sink to be washed up. As Edwin and Frank followed Biggles outside, chatting as they went, a figure slipped into the kitchen. It was Bob Fryer.

'Christ Almighty, Arthur! Where did you find him?' Fryer asked incredulously as he looked back at the hulking frame of Frank.

'Bob!' Arthur said getting to his feet. The two men shook hands as Fryer noticed George's lifeless form sprawled across the breakfast table.

'So, when can we have a chat?' Fryer asked hurriedly and without waiting to be introduced to those present, which Arthur considered downright rude.

'After a few introductions,' Arthur told him calmly.

Fryer was clearly impatient to get on with things and after a five-minute chat with Arthur he insisted the squad get together immediately. They duly assembled on a small grassy rise outside the large hangar. The sun was bright and the air was still – a perfect day for flying. Fryer scrutinised the players dubiously as they didn't look quite what he'd imagined. As Arthur prepared to commence his introduction, Fryer took a deep breath of Somerset air and jumped in ahead of him. 'You probably all know me,' he began, 'but for those of you who don't, I'm Bob Fryer, the England coach.' He paused for effect and for a moment there was silence.

'At what sport?' asked Frank Arnold.

Arthur winced as Bob Fryer looked at Frank in amazement.

'Cricket, of course!' he snapped. 'I would have thought that being a cricketer, you might have known. .'

'I ain't no cricketer!'

Fryer turned slowly and looked at Arthur, but just as Arthur was about to say something Fryer turned back to Frank.

'And what might you be then?' he asked.

'A doorman.'

'A what?' Fryer gasped.

'A doorman,' Frank repeated.

Fryer levelled an unimpressed glare at Arthur who flinched slightly.

'Interesting choice for a fast-bowling clinic,' Fryer noted.

Unable to contain himself any longer, Mathew French burst out laughing, whereupon Fryer asked angrily, 'Would you like to share something with us, Mathew?'

'Sorry, Bob. No disrespect. But fast-bowling clinic!' French managed to reply, and looked at Chandra, who seemed a bit uptight. Once more he burst into fits of laughter.

Arthur tried to step in. 'I think we're jumping the gun a bit here,' he said.

But there was no stopping Fryer. 'Would you care to explain yourself, Mathew!' he demanded irritably.

'Well, for a start he's a spin bowler,' he said pointing at Chandra, 'who can't even turn a ball!' Once more French dissolved in fits of laughter.

They all looked at Chandra, who remained surprisingly composed under the circumstances.

'Are you in fact a spinner?' Fryer asked Chandra.

'Yes, sir,' came the proud reply.

Arthur winced again as Fryer stared at the rest of the group with some suspicion. It was all going horribly wrong.

'Arthur, may I have a word?' he asked at last and the two men moved a short distance away from the group.

'You shouldn't have done that, Bob. They're my squad,' Arthur admonished Fryer.

'*I* shouldn't have!' Fryer hissed under his breath, trying hard to restrain himself. 'So far we have a doorman who doesn't play cricket, and a spin bowler who can't spin the ball and one with an atrocious hangover. God knows about the rest. This is not what we agreed on.'

'Not entirely true,' said Arthur. 'The spinner has a lethal fast ball and with—'

'Oh my God,' bleated Fryer.

'And the big fellow played county cricket a few years ago. By all accounts . . .' But Fryer wasn't listening any more.

'Alright, look . . . let's change tack. Just show me the training facility for now. We'll discuss this lot later.'

'Good idea,' Arthur agreed and clapped his hands loudly, trying to get the show back on the road.

'Right then,' he called out, 'let's have a look at where all the magic will happen.'

The men got slowly to their feet, some stretching and yawning. Arthur grasped the large padlock securing the huge hangar doors and fiddled with the key, while Fryer stood with arms crossed, at the back of the group, peering over their heads. At last the padlock swung open and the doors were hauled aside. Arthur hurried inside ahead of the others and as he switched the power on the massive space came to life as the overhead halogen lights flickered momentarily. The hangar was long and wide, while the ceiling seemed enormously high, with all manner of ropes and wooden pulleys dangling from it like long fibrous tentacles. Where the ropes ended there were big wooden blocks of differing sizes on the floor. Other smaller pulley-type devices intersected the main ropes, attached at different angles. Down the middle of the floor were three huge hollow pipes lying on their sides, and about 3 feet high. There were some crude weights toward the rear of the hanger and some more pulley contraptions fixed to the wall. Over to the right-hand side of the hangar were more pulley devices festooned with old rope. The group stood there taking it all in.

Chandra summed it up best. 'Looks like a giant monkey cage.'

Arthur beamed at them proudly as Fryer's jaw dropped lower by the second. French started to laugh again. Like a zombie, Fryer turned and walked towards his car without saying a word. In a state of panic, Arthur ran after him, watched by the others.

'Bob!' Arthur called as he caught up with him. 'Where are you going?'

Fryer stopped and turned to face Arthur, ashen faced. He managed to say only two words: 'You're mad!'

'Oh, everyone says that,' Arthur told him reassuringly as he tried to usher Fryer back towards the hangar.

Fryer waved him away. 'I can't believe I trusted you,' he mumbled as he continued walking towards his car. Arthur placed himself directly in front of Fryer, who reflected softly.

'I should have known.'

'Known what?' asked Arthur.

'I did some research on this place,' Fryer told him. With arms outstretched he spun around.

'Do you know what sort of aircraft flew out of here during the War?' When Arthur said nothing Fryer shouted, 'Bolton Paul Defiants and Whirlwinds.' Arthur was unmoved for it meant nothing to him. Fryer ranted on. 'Two very ordinary fighters. In fact they were near useless.' He moved closer to Arthur. 'Grasp the analogy?' Arthur had but said nothing as Fryer continued, 'I don't want Defiants and Whirlwinds, Arthur. I want Spitfires!' And he pointed at French.

Arthur's world was spinning out of control as he struggled to collect himself. At that moment a hand grasped his shoulder and pulled him back a stride. Edwin stepped forward calmly.

'Actually, Mr Fryer, if you'd done your research correctly, you would've uncovered some other important facts,' he said.

'Is that right?' questioned Fryer.

'Yes. There *were* Defiants and Whirlwinds here. But in July 1941 they were replaced . . . by Hurricanes.' Arthur managed a slight smile as Edwin went on, 'And as you're no doubt aware, although the Spitfire was a fine aircraft, many experts will tell you the Hurricane won us the Battle of Britain not the Spitfire.' Edwin's eyes did not leave Fryer, who smiled mirthlessly.

'All right. I've heard *and seen* enough. I just can't be associated with this . . . with a madman and his Hurricanes.'

Arthur tried again. 'Look, Bob, don't lose faith because of what you've seen in that hangar. We haven't even started yet. As you know, we need to build machines. Special machines. Remember the plan,' he reminded Fryer. 'Trust me, I know what

I'm doing.'

'Trust!' Fryer's voice had gone up an octave. 'You have a doorman who doesn't play cricket, a spin bowler, a war historian . . . God knows who else *and* . . . a bunch of old ropes. You think there are Test players in the making here? I think not! And I'm not hanging round to be proved right.'

So saying, he spun on his heels to leave, but Arthur caught his arm and turned him around. 'Listen. You've had a hell of a lot more than this to work with the last seventeen years and where's it got you?' Arthur reminded him. 'What you've seen is not all there is to it. You can't just up and leave now.'

'Watch me.' Fryer responded coldly. Then, softening slightly, he told Arthur, 'Keep the money, Arthur. Send them home. Then at least you're ahead. I can't help you any more.' Fryer held up his hands and walked away. It was over.


With Fryer gone, Arthur turned to look at the players, and saw Jean standing not too far from him. He looked at her. From somewhere came the words '*Stick to your guns. There's work to be done.*' Arthur looked up at the sky. The sun was shining brighter than ever. He smiled at Jean then, clapping his hands, he rubbed them together vigorously as he walked back over to the squad.

'Right. There's a story I want to tell you.'

Mathew French interrupted him. 'I—'

But Arthur cut him short. 'I know, Mathew. It's all right. Off you go. If you're quick, you might be able to get a lift with Fryer.' With that the young man shot off. Arthur called after him. 'Mathew!' French stopped and turned. 'We'll see you later.'

French turned and ran in Fryer's direction.

Arthur turned back to the squad rubbing his chin. 'Hmm, where do I start?' And he smiled anxiously at the five of them.


A little known fact about Arthur was that he happened to be an excellent storyteller. He knew that the key to storytelling was having an audience eager to hear a story in the first place, especially if it involved them directly. The remaining members of Arthur's squad sat down on the grassy knoll and made themselves comfortable. They were totally confused, having had nothing explained to them so far, other than they were there to win the Ashes. With nothing to lose they were all keen to hear what Arthur had to say. So was Arthur as he was still piecing together a story in his mind.

'Answer this question for me?' he put to them resolutely. 'When a fast bowler bowls, are both sides of his body doing the same thing at the same time?' There was silence before Arthur continued. 'Like a rower pulling back with two hands to perform an even stroke?' Arthur mimicked the action. The men thought about it and shook their heads negatively.

'No,' one or two mumbled.

'Good! You're correct. Many muscles on both sides of the body come into play at different times when you bowl. So why don't we train with this in mind?' He had their interest. 'Why not dissect the entire action, train all the muscles individually, then put it all back together again? Then train them collectively.'

'I hope that doesn't mean you're going to cut us up!' exclaimed George.

'Well, I might be tempted. But I'm speaking metaphorically. Hear me out.' Arthur paced about using his hands to express himself. 'We run and swim and do weights, squats, push-ups and all kinds of other things – all good things, but not good enough. My theory is simple. Isolate the main muscles being used and only train *them*. Pinpoint the deep synergist and fixator muscles and train them individually too. Which is hard to do as they're difficult to isolate. I aim to train these muscles at the exact point where they are needed the most.' He paused and saw he was still holding their attention. 'My theory has a name. I call it Super Specificity Training. Are you with me thus far?' They nodded slowly as Arthur continued.

The group had an interested but dazed look about them as they grappled with Arthur's theory, but they got the gist of it in the end. Arthur suddenly became animated, speaking with real passion. He deconstructed the bowling action and explained how isolated main muscle groups and balancing muscles, when applied to specifically designed strengthening exercises, work the muscles in the correct anatomical manner under which they are required to perform. In other words, he pointed out, why train a muscle that is not going to benefit 100 per cent?

'If we trained your muscles specifically while you perform your bowling actions, faithfully, aiming for maximum exertion, exact action, and do not compromise range of movement . . then amazing results will be achieved.'

He was losing them now as there were some blank expressions. He spelt it out for them.

'I am going to turn you into super bowlers,' he said excitedly. 'as fast as you can possibly be!'

They stared at him disbelievingly. When Chandra raised his hand gingerly, Arthur addressed him dismissively. 'I know you're a spinner. We'll get to you later. Come this way. I want to show you how we're going to do all this,' and with that he hurried off towards the great hangar. The others rose slowly and trailed in after him.

'George, I need your assistance.' Arthur beckoned to him and George moved over to where Arthur stood by one of the huge rope and pulley systems that hung from the ceiling. Arthur positioned George upright but side on as if he were about to bowl. He then hauled over one of the large wooden blocks and positioned it under the pulley.

'Now, if you would be so good as to just pop your front leg up there, and get yourself into a position where you feel you'd like to rip down in order to deliver a ball.'

Arthur reached up to George's lead hand and put a hand grip into it which was attached to the rope that lead up to the pulley.

'Just get a little more side on.' Arthur made a few adjustments to him. 'Does that feel like your normal action?' he asked.

'Well, yeah, pretty much, except that I don't normally have a massive piece of wood under my left foot when I bowl,' George said.

'All right, just tug down on this very evenly until you get to the point where you would normally end this part of the delivery,' instructed Arthur in a very patient tone.

George did so and it immediately became apparent to the others that, using an albeit medieval-looking contraption, the theory behind it was sound as George appeared to be working only a specific part of his body. He laboured slightly under the strain, but performed ten good repetitions of the action.

Arthur addressed the group once more. 'Now, what you all have to bear in mind is that you all have different actions, and that we need to slightly modify these exercises to pinpoint the precise position your muscles need to be in order to maximize the effect of each movement. I had planned that specific machines would be built for this purpose. Alas, we will have to make do for now.'

'I assume Bob Fryer was going to provide the machines?' asked Frank.

'Quite right, but rest assured these contraptions will do very nicely for the time being. I can say that as I've already had some success with them,' he told them. 'Oh, and thanks for reminding me. I want you all to know that despite what he thinks, we have not seen the last of Mr Fryer.' Everyone paid attention now. 'That's a promise.' It was clear Arthur was in his element surrounded by his contraptions. The players saw a purpose and passion they had not even sensed in him before.

Arthur took the grip from George, 'How did that feel?

'Too much like hard work,' replied George, rubbing his left side beneath his shoulder.

'But you could feel it addressing the intended area?' Arthur probed.

'Yeah. Definitely!' replied George, convinced.

'Great. Now, if you'd be so good as to just try the same over here.' Arthur led George over to the wall where another rig was set up. He positioned him facing outwards and George, realising what Arthur was attempting to demonstrate, got himself into the desired position. With one foot up on the blocks and his front arm held high, Arthur put another grip in the hand with which George would normally deliver the ball. 'Alright, George, give it a go. Another ten but slowly,' he said stepping back. All the others watched as George struggled a bit. 'Use your front arm as well,' Arthur shouted. George's whole upper torso remained rigid as he went through the motion of delivering a ball, his face showing the strain as he pulled on the grip which ran over a pulley that was attached to a small weight. They all had a closer look this time before Arthur eventually took the grip from George once the ten were done.

'In a year, I could make you all ten to fifteen per cent faster than you are right now. Maybe more.' He turned to Chandra. 'Same goes for you, but you'll be able to turn the ball a mile.' Chandra flashed an eager smile. 'The only thing is I'll have to modify our plans.' He paused and bit his bottom lip as he thought for a moment. 'The letter I gave you all stated you would be here a year and be paid. I now reckon that with the funds we have we'll only have four or five months. In addition, your monthly allowance may not be quite as much. I'll do some sums and let you know in due course. As I've already said, we'll only have this crude apparatus with which to work. At the end of our time here, however long it is, we shall test ourselves. After that your fate will be decided.'

'What's the test?' Jim asked.

'A test of speed,' Arthur replied. 'If we become fast enough they will have to listen.'

The group stared silently back at him.

'What about that chap Fryer?' Jim asked. 'looks like he doesn't want anything to do with us.'

'Leave him to me,' Arthur advised. 'Right now I need to know who will stay.' He put it to them bluntly. 'May I remind you, gentlemen, we're here to win the Ashes. It *can* be done.' He had the group's full attention and looked each in turn in the eye. It was Frank Arnold who spoke.

'Mr Jenkins, no disrespect, but you've chosen me, a non-cricketer, to come here, leave my job and friends for only four months' pay and you expect me to be up to English Test standard in four months. To top it off, I don't know you from a bar of soap.'

'Well, firstly, Frank, that's not exactly what I'm asking. You'll need to be better than current the English Test standard. I'm telling you, I think we can do it.'

There was still much scepticism amongst the group, until Jim Singleton spoke up. 'Arthur ain't no flash in the pan,' he said to them all. 'He won our club four titles on the trot.'

Frank Arnold, fast becoming the sceptic in the group, folded his arms. 'And what grade might that be?' he asked raising his eyebrows.

Singleton changed tack. 'Where I come from there's a boy.

Weren't much chop in the fast bowling stakes by all accounts. That was until Arthur here got hold of him. Soon that boy's the talk of the town: taking wickets, breaking stumps, put in his school's top team and bagged six wickets or more every match for the entire season. Even took the team on to win the league. I saw him bowl. I know what Arthur can do. I'm staying!'

Arthur gave a Jim a nod of appreciation that belied the emotion behind it. Chandra immediately piped up, 'For a chance to spin a ball, I'm staying.'

'I'll stay for the free beer,' George chipped in.

Just then they were distracted by a commotion near the house as Biggles came tearing around the corner chasing the cat, which ducked under a fence and made its escape. Edwin Roberts made his mind up.

'Biggles likes it here. Be wrong to go now. I'll stay.'

All the attention now turned to Frank Arnold.

'Well, your Super Six is dead. . .So what rhythms with five?'

With that, Arthur clapped his hands as a huge grin appeared on his face. The group let out a cheer. Chandra leapt up and shook Frank's hand. George called out, 'The drinks are on me,' and immediately led the parade to the bar.

'The *fast* five!' shouted Chandra as they moved off. But everyone ignored him.

Although Arthur felt it wasn't quite right to be having a beer at 10.30 in the morning, he also knew that you can't do the right thing all the time, and if you're going to do something wrong, it might as well feel good.

Through the kitchen window Jean watched them file into the games room, delighted that it had all worked out. At that point in time she had even more faith in Arthur than he had himself. If that was possible.

As the rest of the group got better acquainted, Arthur stared into his pint, knowing he'd have to work a lot harder and smarter to achieve his dream now. But there was one thing that needed to sort out immediately.

He found Jean carving ham in the kitchen, with Mrs Cheshire attempting to defrost the freezer in the background.

'Jean, could I have a word in the lounge?' He paused for a

moment, adding, 'and could you leave that knife behind when you come?'

Mrs Cheshire directed a wide-eyed look of surprise at Jean, but she knew it was just Arthur being Arthur.

'Just as well this place is paid for in advance for six months,' she told him once they were in the lounge.

'Yes, quite,' Arthur agreed.

'They're all going to stay, aren't they?' she asked, drying a spoon on her apron.

Wanting to get the whole thing over with, he jumped in straight away. 'Look, I have a four-month plan. Do you want to hear it?'

'I'm sure I'll hear it anyway,' she said. 'You're going to have to give them some money though, Arthur.'

'Of course but according to my calculations, Fryer's kitty will only last six weeks. So some of it's going to have to come from us,' he hesitated. 'you know from our savings . . for the new place.'

'Well, it's not worth having if you're not happy.'

Arthur felt a lump in his throat but kept his emotions in check.

'I have a plan to get it back, you know,' he said convincingly.

'Of course,' Jean said moving over and giving him a kiss. 'With interest!'

## 18

Arthur allowed the players only one pint before lunch. They fed on sandwiches and had a run around the perimeter of Charmy Down to familiarise themselves with its outer limits before he herded them into the hangar for a net session.

The players spent the latter part of the day getting the indoor nets operational, which meant not just the nets, but also the speed guns, the two bowling machines and the video equipment. In the corner of the great hangar Arthur had set up a large workbench, which had a computer, VHS/DVD player, printers and other pieces of equipment, complete with a set of files and a couple of chairs. Next to that there was a mini-fridge and a large couch. This area had been Arthur's office for the last fortnight and would be where he would spend many an hour studying bowling actions and the like. It was also a cool-down area for the players and as the floor was lightly padded they could stretch out and do exercises.

The squad got out all the new equipment and padded up for the first net session. One player assisted Arthur with the video and timing equipment, while the other three bowled and the fifth one batted. Chandra volunteered to bat first while Edwin helped Arthur with the timing guns and results.

'Right, you three,' Arthur called out to George, Frank and Jim, his voice echoing slightly as if they were in a huge tin can – which in a way they were. 'Under NO circumstances are you to bowl at full pace. You're only rolling your arms over. The key here is just to put it on the stumps. Each batsman will be in there thirty-five minutes, so pace yourselves.' He then turned to Edwin and said, 'We're only recording the first twenty-five balls per bowler.' Edwin nodded.

Chandra strode purposely down to the end of the pitch and asked for middle stump, which George duly gave him with a look of disdain.

'I bat at number eight, so don't hold back,' Chandra called out cheerfully to the bowlers.

'Ignore that,' Arthur ordered the bowlers. 'And don't bowl until we call your name.'

'Are you recording our speeds?' George shouted back.

'Yes, but remember just roll your arms over. That's very important.' Then he turned to Singleton, holding the speed gun in his direction. 'Just bowl one, will you, Jim. I need to test this gizmo.'

Singleton ambled in and sent a medium-paced ball down to Chandra, who played and missed. 'Hmm, suspect playing surface,' he mumbled as he wandered down the pitch to carry out some repairs on the faultless synthetic surface.

Arthur and Edwin meanwhile examined the reading on the monitor, which had clocked the delivery at 72.75 m.p.h. Both appeared satisfied that the gun worked as it should.

'Brilliant. Thanks, Jim,' Arthur called, clearing the reading. 'On you go, George.'

Arthur looked at the gun as Edwin aimed it down the pitch. George came in and sent one down as instructed, his action evenly balanced but not fluent. His follow-through was smooth and effortless, but all Arthur could watch was the Afro. Having no answer to the situation, he said nothing and let the proceedings continue – after all, he didn't want to be the bearer of bad news if he could avoid it.

Chandra met the next ball from George with a shaky defensive stroke, playing it safely back down the wicket. Arthur checked the monitor, which read 68.6 m.p.h., and nodded to Edwin, who made a note of the reading. He reset the gun and nodded at Jim. 'You again, Jim.' Singleton delivered another ball at the same speed as before according to the meter. Edwin made another note on his list and Arthur turned to Frank Arnold. 'Right you are, Frank.'

Frank's enormous frame lunged forward awkwardly into his run-up. He was a sight to behold, his hand so large as if it was wrapped around a red golf ball.

Arthur heard Chandra muttering something inaudible as Frank bore down on him. As Chandra tensed, Frank let go a misdirected full toss that hit the side net halfway down.

Frank was extremely embarrassed.

'Not to worry, Frank. It's been a while. Put the next one on the spot. Just slow it down a bit.'

Chandra played the next two deliveries from George and Jim without a problem, the pace of both about the same as their first balls. When Frank bowled again it pitched down leg side but did enough to record an unremarkable 70 m.p.h.

As George bowled what Chandra thought was the last ball, he moved his feet and stroked it a little harder than the others he'd played. Feeling quite cocky, he called to the bowlers as he started to take his gloves off. 'A tidy innings there, I'd say, offering no chances. You'll have to do better than that, boys,' he teased.

'Just one more, Chandra,' Arthur told him. 'Frank. On you go.'

Most people would have seen what was coming a mile off, but not Chandra, who refastened the Velcro wristbands of his gloves and placed the helmet strap back over his chin, oblivious of George nudging Frank and winking at him. Chandra did, however, sense a heightened purpose about the run-up and he could have sworn the footsteps were louder.

The ball pitched short and flew an inch over his head well before he thought to duck. There was a collective gasp from the others at how close the ball had been to him.

'What?' Chandra asked no one in particular.

'Good judgment,' George called to him. Chandra rolled his shoulders and removed his helmet as Frank Arnold smiled at him. Arthur showed Edwin the reading on the monitor – 80.76 m.p.h.

As Chandra began to leave the net, the problem of George's hairstyle continued to nag Arthur. Suddenly he had an answer.

'One more please – from George this time.'

Chandra, normally quite happy to bat, felt there was a conspiracy against him. He whispered under his breath, 'They're trying to kill me already.'

'Would you others please go and stand behind George?' Arthur asked politely. 'Try and see if you can identify what might be hindering George's speed and fluency.'

Edwin, Jim and Frank all positioned themselves against the rear wall to get a good view of George in action, watching carefully as he bowled a decent ball to Chandra.

Arthur looked towards them. 'Well?' he inquired.

Edwin seemed to know, raising his hand in the air like a schoolboy. 'Edwin,' Arthur shouted.

'Would it be his massive Afro?'

Arthur gave a satisfied smile as George patted down his hair and frowned at Edwin.

They celebrated the end of the first day of proper training by cutting George's hair, Edwin being selected as he had spotted the problem in the first place – or so Arthur claimed. It was cut very short using a pair of clippers Mrs Cheshire happened to have that had belonged to her late husband.

Chandra whispered to George, 'Dead man's clippers. Very unlucky.'

George, not enjoying the whole experience, shot Chandra a malevolent glance.

When they finally retired to their rooms for the evening, Arthur returned to the hangar and collated the speeds of each bowler, including Chandra's faster balls, to come up with an average speed per man. On the wall next to the PC, he had a chart of the fastest balls of all time. At the top, highlighted, was the fastest of all time: Shoaib Akhtar, the only man to have broken the 100 m.p.h. barrier, in 2002. Behind Akhtar was Australia's Jeff Thomson in 1976. It was apparent that whereas athletes were going faster, longer and higher, cricket had stagnated for twenty-six years! He felt the so-called experts had a lot to answer for.

### Arthur's Chart:

| S. Akhtar 27/04/02 | 100.04 m.p.h. |
|---|---|
| J. Thompson 1976 | 99.8 m.p.h. |
| A. Roberts – not sure | 97.8 m.p.h. |
| Fastest Englishman D. Gough  13/2/1999 | 93.82 m.p.h. |

Arthur had calculated Fryer's current English attack was averaging 86.65 mph over the last two years. His goal was therefore to surpass this and get as close to the 100 mile an hour figure as possible; he certainly expected one of his bowlers to reach this mark and perhaps beat it.  However, without the specially designed machines they should have had he wasn't so sure any more. At the end of the first full day's speed tests,

Arthur's chart recorded all the players' average speeds:

| J. Arnold | 64.5 m.p.h. |
|---|---|
| Chandra Jafar | 61.8 m.p.h. |
| E. Roberts | 68.4 m.p.h. |
| G. Samuels | 71.1 m.p.h. |
| J. Singleton | 68.5 m.p.h. |

Arthur was well aware that these speeds were nothing more than a starting point, having asked them not to bowl faster for fear of an injury early on in the program. In the days to come, he would ask the players to bowl their fastest balls for timing – from that point on they would not be speed tested for four months, until the true test was upon them.

Other items of interest Arthur had noted during the net session were: Chandra *really* couldn't spin the ball at all; George Samuels was the most accomplished batsman but played too many rash shots; Edwin Roberts would jump off a bridge if asked politely; Jim Singleton's favourite pastime was winding up Chandra about anything he possibly could; and lastly, Frank Arnold was one of the most erratic bowlers Arthur had ever seen – his batting lacked both confidence and technique, but the pleasing thing about him was he was annoyed with himself for being that way. Arthur decided that it would be best to work on his bowling and let the batting come along on its own. It was not panic stations yet.

As he locked up the hangar that night after a long first day, Arthur was in a thoughtful mood, but was getting weary of worrying about the devices he needed to improve Chandra's spin. He had some rough ideas and knew he had to work on them as soon as possible.

After breakfast the next morning, Arthur provided the group with their daily routine: as follows:

| | |
|---|---|
| 6.30 a.m. – 7.00 a.m. | Rise |
| 7.05 a.m. – 7.45 a.m. | Light perimeter run |
| 8.00 a.m. – 9.00 a.m. | Breakfast |
| 9.00 a.m. – 10.00 a.m. | Bowling warm-up |
| 10.00 a.m. – 11.30 a.m. | Hangar time (George-speak for rope regime) |
| 11.40 a.m. – 12.00 p.m. | Cool down and stretch |
| 12.30 p.m. – 1.30 p.m. | Lunch |
| 1.45 p.m. – 3.15 p.m. | Bowling fundamentals, accuracy & technique |
| 3.45 p.m. – 5.00 p.m. | Hangar time Part II |
| 5.05 p.m. – 5.55 p.m. | Stretch and light walk |
| 6.45 p.m. – 7.45 p.m. | Dinner |

Each player was also rostered for ground duty and hangar maintenance. Ground duty consisted of the care of the outside wickets, which were crucial to their practice sessions; hangar maintenance was checking the ropes, oiling the pulleys, sweeping the pitches and powering down the electronic equipment. Once a week, a total security check was performed on the great hangar, Big House, entrance gates to Charmy Down and perimeter fences. So security conscious was the group that the computer password was changed weekly as well. They carried out these tasks during time normally allocated for the 'Light perimeter run' or the 'Stretch and light walk'. No one ever complained about these additional duties after they learnt that Arthur carried out all these duties with them and therefore did four times as much as anyone else.

The only other weekly routine that simply had to be observed was a long-standing Charmy Down tradition that Edwin Roberts had resurrected. Every Sunday evening at sunset, all of them, including Jean and Mrs Cheshire, gathered at the end of the main runway and, with drink in hand, saluted the flag in the name of all those who had served at Charmy Down, past and present. Edwin took this very seriously and none of the others dared miss the ceremony. He always made a little speech as he'd been reading up on the history of the airfield from some books and copies of logs left by Mrs Cheshire's late husband. Each week he gave an account of a story he had uncovered. Truth be known, in time they all looked forward to Edwin's Sunday ritual. Mrs Cheshire noticed that Biggles sat by Edwin's side throughout these readings and thought him incredibly patient and well-behaved, wondering why her cat couldn't do the same.

George commented that Arthur was the busiest person he'd ever known – yet he never actually looked like he did anything! He had a no-fuss way of doing everything and knew exactly what he had to do and when he had to do it by. He had clear goals for all the players and already any of them would have done whatever he asked, without question.

Arthur himself was feeling a growing sense of relief, his high expectations shared now by all five members of the squad, even Jean. Indeed, Fryer's desertion had given him a steel resolve and gritty determination which he drummed into the players every day. He knew exactly what he they had to achieve in just four months' time, for already he had a plan which, if successful, would buy the players an additional seven months' training leading up to the Ashes.

Another crucial task to complete in the first week was videoing each player's action in detail. After that, it was up to Arthur to analyse the actions and alter the devices in the great hangar according to each player's needs. At the same time he was working on the devices for Chandra's action. He had devised four different machines specifically for the little spinner, which he was certain would do the trick, although he knew that he could not do this alone and had enlisted the help of Ted, who was due to visit soon.

After just two weeks at Charmy Down, Arthur gave the squad a weekend off but warned them it was a one-off. They all stayed locally except Chandra, who went to visit members of his family nearby. To his credit, Chandra had been going to remain with the others, but when they all learnt of the proximity of his family, they convinced him that he should be with his family for the break. Jim's relief was tangible.

Jim, George, Edwin and Frank spent two nights in Bath doing much the same as they did at Charmy Down – drinking and playing pool – but they stuck to their fitness regime and ate well. While in a pub one evening, Frank noticed that George kept on slipping out, coming back five minutes later looking bleary eyed and stinking of cigarettes.

'Are you doing that back at Charmy Down?' Frank quietly inquired.

'Been trying to give up,' George told him matter-of-factly.

'All this effort from Arthur and you're still smoking,' Frank said disbelievingly.

'It's not easy, man,' George bemoaned.

'I'll give you a hand,' Frank offered helpfully, putting his arm around George's shoulder.

'Oh yeah, how?' asked George.

'Easy,' Frank chortled. 'If I catch you smoking, I'll haul you up one of them pulleys in the hangar and leave you there to rot.'

'That'd be great Frank. Thanks!'

At the conclusion of an enjoyable evening out the four men walked home to their digs, the towering frames of Jim and Frank an ominous sight lurching through the mist in the ancient streets.

'Are we the famous or fantastic five?' George asked no one in particular.

'The forgetful five,' Edwin answered. 'Oh, actually I just remembered something.'

'What's that?' Frank asked.

'87 Squadron,' Edwin blurted excitedly and turned to face them.

'What of it?' quizzed Frank.

'That was the Hurricane squadron at Charmy Down,' Edwin enthused. 'The most powerful fear me,' he intoned, his head held high.

'What's he on about?' Jim asked Frank.

'What you on about?' demanded Frank.

'The motto of the 87th,' Edwin summed up.

The others caught on, impressed with his knowledge.

'The most powerful fear me,' George repeated in a trance-like state. 'I like it.'

'Not yet they don't' said Jim, spinning Edwin round in the direction of home and helping him on his way with a forceful shove.

## 19

A sorry looking group arrived back at Charmy Down mid-afternoon on Monday after a hair or two of the dog at lunchtime.

'I don't think the *most powerful* would fear us very much right now,' George commented as they pulled up outside the house and got out the car.

Even Chandra had drunk too much and was buzzing around the house like a bumblebee with an attention deficit disorder. Arthur was well aware that the level of alcohol consumption was running too high for a group of supposed athletes, but felt it imperative the group bonded early. Soon there'd be no need to enforce a limit on alcohol for they'd all be too tired to drink.

He took them up to the hangar as they chatted casually amongst themselves. At the large olive building, they were greeted by an impressive scene and as they surveyed what Arthur had been busy with over the weekend, any complacency dissolved. Arthur and Ted had redesigned the entire layout of the place and each bowler now had individual exercises.

An exercise was termed a 'movement'; a succession of 'movements' was called a 'run' which were all labelled individually. There were additional support devices near certain 'movements' ready to be utilised. The blocks of wood had been better shaped and in some cases, two movements could be performed simultaneously. Some pulleys had been welded on at strange angles and had adjustable screws inserted so they were variable. Arthur had also painted targets in the form of wickets at the end of each run so that the bowlers had something to aim at, even though during the movements they did not actually deliver a ball. The most notable addition to all the runs was the huge waist and torso girdles that were installed to hold the bowlers relatively still in the final stage of their deliveries. The girdles' main benefit was to develop improved strength of the abdominals during the phase in which the bowlers ripped down hard on the ball and thrust it into the pitch.

Over to the extreme right-hand side of the hangar was a new run of exercises that belonged to Chandra. It was brightly labelled '7's Run'. Because Chandra was smaller than the rest so too were his devices, and he seemed to have more than the others.

Chandra found himself gaping at a collection of the most bizarre-looking contraptions he'd ever seen. Excitedly he took in the pieces of strange equipment that lay about his run. The others had gathered behind him.

'It feels like I'm looking at medieval implements of torture,' he commented.

'Hopefully they won't be torturing *you* once you're done with them, just batsmen!' The most conspicuous device on show was a Brassard, the arm piece belonging to a suit of armour. Chandra picked it up with difficulty.

Arthur grinned. 'Bloody hard to get hold of that,' he remarked. 'Chap wouldn't give it up without a fight.'

Peering within Chandra checked there wasn't still a limb inside.

'What the hell do I do with this?' he asked, totally bewildered.

'It's a new forearm guard, Seven,' George teased.

Arthur went to help Chandra put it on. There were several leather straps that would hold the device on to its wearer.

'Here we go,' he said helping it onto Chandra's bowling arm. 'Good thing you're right handed,' he joked.

Soon it was fully on.

'Now what?' Chandra asked, totally bemused.

'You roll your arm over very slowly,' Arthur explained patiently. 'And as you do so, just do what you'd normally do – attempt to spin the ball!' He held Chandra's arm and helped him bring it over a couple of times. 'This is specifically designed to strengthen your entire shoulder joint. The shoulder is where the spin starts and it must be strong. Every point after that is an action that is driven by a smaller muscle group, finishing with the fingers, which are the smallest and weakest. It is called "summation of forces".' Arthur took a normal-looking leather gardening glove from a stand and held it up to the group to demonstrate that it had large lead fishing weights sewn onto the end of the fingertips. He slipped it on, fastened a strap tight around his wrist and mimicked the hand and finger motions of a spin bowler. With the weights slowing his movements down, he looked like an Asian dancer performing a mystic routine. It was quite apparent to all of them that over a period this would strengthen the wrist. The group were in awe, especially Chandra.

'Incredible,' he said transfixed.

'Brilliant,' Edwin murmured.

Arthur continued to roll his arm over with great care to perform the action correctly.

'Let me try,' said Chandra excitedly, removing the steel arm. Putting the glove on he started to copy Arthur, going through the motions of rolling his arm over.

At that moment Arthur produced a shiny silver cricket ball from a box on the ground.

'Behold,' he said, holding it up for all to see. 'The great silver ball!' It was a perfect silver replica of a cricket ball complete with seam and stitches and looked extremely heavy. 'If you can spin this, you can spin anything,' He attempted to toss it in the air like a spin bowler, but with little success, almost dropping it, it was so heavy.

The others looked on, fascinated.

'May I?' asked Chandra reaching for the ball with his gloved hand. He attempted to bowl it.

'Actually you're meant to take the glove off first,' Arthur told him. 'This one will strengthen the fingers.'

Chandra attempted to do so with Jim's help. Still holding the ball he examined it closely. 'It's too bloody heavy,' he exclaimed.

Arthur was not perturbed. 'Which is exactly why we have these two as well.' He produced two more balls. 'They're all different weights. You start with this one, then progress to the next one when you're strong enough.'

Chandra was again lost for words.

Arthur went over to two other boxes and removed the lid to reveal twelve shiny red balls. This time he addressed them all. 'These ones are for you lot,' he chirped and held out the box to show them. 'Studies I've carried out have shown that when you bowl with a heavier ball, speed decreases, but strength increases. These look normal enough but have been infused with lead lining inside the leather casings and are twelve and a half per cent heavier than your average cricket ball.'

He offered the box to Frank who was standing at the rear. Each player took a ball and examined it. 'By the time you start using normally weighted balls again, you'll be a minimum of ten per cent faster. You'll all use these balls and nothing but them for the next four months!'

'Arthur, honest to God, you're the last of the great English eccentrics,' George said, still marvelling at the ball and feeling its unfamiliar weight.

Arthur continued. 'Aside from weight the balls also have diminished seams by 6.5 per cent which means they'll be harder to grip initially but when we revert to normal balls you will have additional purchase on the larger seams and should be able to move them a little easier.'

Again the group were suitably impressed. They went over some of Chandra's devices then each moved off towards their own individual runs to take in all the changes Arthur and Ted had made.

'Have a bit of practice with your runs and report to the nets in five minutes, please,' Arthur ordered as he repacked the balls, taking them over to his PC in the corner.

Soon they were all performing on the new devices, then bowling in the nets while he videoed them to provide feedback for the first round of fine-tuning. He worked through the day looking at various angles of each bowler's delivery and chatting to them individually about their actions before making adjustments to the devices to suit individual bowlers, and targeting the muscle groups that would best serve their actions. After the next adjustments to each player's run, no more changes would be made for some time. It wasn't until 10.45 p.m. that Arthur finished replacing a hand grip on Edwin Roberts's front-arm pulley with a small sling that his hand could slip into, to allow him to keep his leading hand cutting sideways as it pulled down, thereby maximising the downwards rip.

He turned to the rest of the group. 'Right, that's it!'

## 20

Surprisingly enough, the weather didn't interrupt any outdoor net sessions during the first week. It was duly noted by all that the heavier balls hit the bat a lot harder than normal ones, and jarred the batsmen's hands, so Arthur ordered some batting inners. During net sessions, the players had engaged in a competition similar to the longest drive in golf, calling it the 'Let's see who can hit a delivery the farthest down the runway' game, which was normally carried out at the end of a net practice. On one occasion, Arthur noticed George was giving Frank some stick, but thought Frank could handle himself.

'Last couple, Frank,' he barked. 'Edwin, pad up.'

Turning his back for a moment as George came in to bowl to Frank, Arthur heard an almighty crack and a curse from the bowler. He turned in time to see George, Jim, Chandra and Edwin all follow a straight-hit lofted drive over their heads and into the wild blue yonder. It was followed by a volley of amazed cries as the ball flew straight over the runway eventually bouncing once or twice in the distance as it rolled completely out of sight.

'Wow!' exclaimed George. 'Good luck finding that one, big man!' It was a massive hit.

'Six on any ground,' Edwin remarked. Arthur frowned at Frank as the ball he had so effectively despatched was one of the limited number of weighted balls to which the players were restricted.

'Was there really any need for that?' George asked.

'Yes, it *was* tripe,' he called out for all to hear. 'Don't worry, I'll fetch it.' he offered to Arthur.

Edwin Roberts bowled the last ball to Frank. It was short and he pulled it into the net with great power. Again there was a resounding crack as he made contact, causing everyone in earshot to flinch as the piercing sound reached them.

'Blimey,' Edwin called out as he put his hands over his ears. It was a pleasing sign for Arthur as Frank's batting had needed improvement and he had demonstrated awesome power. Frank meanwhile was examining the toe of his bat with a concerned look upon his face. He wandered out of the nets and threw the bat on the ground – a long gaping split had travelled up the entire blade to the handle, rendering it totally useless.

'Anything else you'd like to break or lose today?' Chandra asked Frank.

'Only you,' he replied.

Chandra clammed up.

Despite all the work being done to improve speed, Arthur's rule of 'just rolling the arm over' continued. He was constantly urging them to bowl at little more than half pace, watching them like a hawk to make sure the tell-tale grimace of a fast bowler exerting himself did not appear on any of their faces. The only one he'd admonished was Chandra for bowling too fast after Jim had played a lovely straight drive past him down the long runway.

That evening Arthur found himself at the dinner table at the head of a buoyant group. It was a good sign that all was well and would add to their success in the long run. They dined on roast pork with all the trimmings, and the banter was mainly directed at the unfortunate Chandra.

The weeks slipped by with everyone knuckling down to working hard in the nets. For Arthur a highlight was Chandra turning up to training with a generous amount of toilet paper wrapped around his right arm, as his elbow, forearm and wrist had been rubbed raw by his metal sleeve, which now had a small Indian flag painted upon its shoulder piece courtesy of Edwin. However good the excuse, it didn't allow him to escape the 'mummy' jokes – and an unsavoury comment from George. It was very satisfying for Arthur to see Jim Singleton finally laugh, although curiously he still looked scary when happy.

All was going well until, at dinner late one week, Chandra managed to convince Mrs Cheshire to cook a curry. She'd never made one – preferring to eat out when inclined towards Indian – but felt it would be simple enough after listening to Chandra prattle on about it. So, armed with a curry recipe and new-found enthusiasm she set to work.

It wasn't that it tasted bad, it was the after-effects that were the problem, and the speed with which they took hold. The number of toilets in the house couldn't cope with the demand. Frank and Edwin disappeared for over an hour into the cold night air rather than queue for the lavatory. Needless to say, the following day got off to a very slow and tentative start, the bowling delivery strides having shortened considerably. Poor Mrs Cheshire felt quite embarrassed by the whole episode. Only Jean escaped unscathed as she had opted for a light ploughman's. When all was almost said and done, Arthur remarked that 'Out of everything bad, came something good,' and winked at the players. What *that* could possibly be, no one had any idea. It was simply Arthur's way of bringing the curtain down on the unfortunate episode. Soon everyone had knuckled down to work once more.

Blessed with good weather and the longer nights the 'lock-up' and 'perimeter checks' were not something that anyone minded doing so much. Of all the players, Edwin Roberts was the most thorough. Anyone who knew him wouldn't have any trouble believing this. His love for most things flying and his deep admiration for those who fought in the Battle of Britain were not hard to spot. Biggles too was most happy trotting along by his side chasing sticks or looking out for rabbits. Having read up on all aspects of the Charmy Down topography, Edwin always knew where he was and what was what on the site, yet he never let his daydreams get in the way of performing his duties. It was as if he had appointed himself the unspoken custodian of Charmy Down.

One particular evening he confused himself somewhat by unlocking the padlock of the great hangar and leaving the keys hanging out of it. He ventured inside to check the power on all electrical equipment was turned off; upon leaving the building, he shut the door and was about to snap the lock shut when he noticed the keys were gone. He looked on the ground outside, then quickly inside and even checked his pockets. But all the time he was certain he'd left them in the lock. His confusion intensified slightly before a sideways glance revealed the keys lying on a stump of wood just outside the hangar; it was where Arthur sometimes sat and had a cup of tea during short breaks. Locking the doors, he promptly forgot all about the incident.

Edwin treasured his time at the airfield. When he wasn't concentrating on cricket, he allowed his mind to wander. 'Would I have been a good pilot?' or 'How long might I have lasted before being shot down?' What he thought of most though was what sort of plane he'd like to have flown. When he gazed up at the clouds he would imagine the planes weaving and curling in the skies far above. But no one else could. Charmy Down was certainly different through Edwin's eyes – even rabbit holes were craters caused by cannon fire from enemy fighters.

Having started up a fortnightly pool competition that culminated in the winner receiving a mystery prize worth £10, the group had gathered in the games room after dinner. Jean, having recently started playing pool, had beaten Chandra – with some assistance from George – and was bursting with pride. Chandra mumbled as he reset the balls for the next game to a chorus of derision from the others. Edwin and Frank were next on. Frank broke, every single ball rebounding several times off the cushion, such was the force of the stroke. Yet not one was pocketed, leaving Edwin with a number of simple shots, and he finally missed an absolute sitter.

'I'd have my eyes checked if I were you, Edwin,' Jim told him innocently.

'I might just do that after the other day,' Edwin responded.

Arthur was sitting on the couch deep in thought, but when he heard this his ears pricked up.

'Why, what happened the other day?' Jim asked Edwin as Arthur listened.

'One minute the keys were hanging out of the padlock of the hangar doors and the next they were on Arthur's wooden throne. I swear I'm getting forgetful in my old age,' Edwin went on as Frank sank a red ball. Arthur knew Edwin better than Edwin knew himself and one thing he could be certain about was that if Edwin thought he'd left the keys hanging in the padlock, then that's where he left them. Frank could obviously do nothing gently or quietly that day as he cracked a ball loudly. A dull thud followed as the ball cannoned into a pocket nearly demolishing the corner of the table.

Later that evening everyone was sent off to bed by 10.00 p.m. As on most nights there was no loitering around as the players were knackered and looked forward to their sleep, shuffling around in pyjamas and brushing their teeth. No one was more tired than George who had very little stamina once his reserves were at a low ebb.

While Jean sat up in bed reading an Agatha Christie novel, Arthur stood, fully clothed, looking out of the window across the dark runway and into the distance towards the great hangar. Jean could sense something was amiss.

'What are you looking for?' she asked him.

'A shooting star.'

He continued to peer out into the night. Jean was not satisfied with his answer. 'I'm going to turn the light out in a minute,' she informed him in a sly tone, trying another tack.

'Good,' said Arthur. 'It'll be easier to see one when it comes.'

Jean frowned and made a dog-ear on page 127 of her book before closing it and placing it on her bedside table. Arthur glanced at his watch. It was 10.40 p.m. There was a click as the lights went out.

'Goodnight,' said Jean.

'G'night,' Arthur replied, still standing there in total darkness, silhouetted against the night sky. Jean watched his motionless figure. She could just make out one bright star past his right shoulder. Then Arthur moved ever so slightly forward as if he were trying to see something at the end of the runway where the great hangar lay dormant. A light flashed and was gone.

'There he is now,' he said, reaching for his coat and pulling it on.

Jean was quite startled. 'Who?' she asked as Arthur headed for the door.

'I'll tell you shortly,' he informed her as he hurried out of the bedroom, pulling a torch out of his pocket.

Having been dragged from their beds, Frank, Jim, Edwin, a very sleepy George and Chandra were all made to follow Arthur as he left the big house in the direction of the hangar.

'I hope this isn't another of your experiments, Arthur. I don't fancy a net session at this time of night,' grumbled George.

'Ssshhh,' was Arthur's only reply. He held his torch behind him to show the way for the others. Finally, they reached the door of the hangar to discover that the padlock was hanging open from the door. Seeing this, all thoughts of bed and sleep instantly disappeared. Arthur peered through a small gap in the metal

113

sheeting of the enormous door and could just make out a dim light; there was also a strange noise from somewhere deep inside. Arthur signalled to Jim and Frank to open the door as silently as possible and they all filed in, leaving Edwin to guard the only way out should the intruder attempt to escape.

Inside, the group spread out and headed for the source of the noise, approaching from different directions. As they tiptoed forward they began to realise that that the sounds were coming from one of the pulleys being furtively operated. The sound of a weight hitting the floor reverberated around the hangar. As they drew closer Arthur suddenly caught a glimpse of the intruder as he changed to another movement. Again the sound of the pulley system filled the hangar as the ropes wheeled over the squeaking metal disks on the pulleys. Arthur signalled to George to creep around to the right a bit and watched as the intruder examined the exercises designed for Chandra. Although watching him from behind, Arthur thought he recognised the person.

'French!' he hissed under his breath.

At that moment George stumbled over an empty tea mug, alerting the intruder. Startled, the figure took off like a frightened deer with Chandra's tubby little frame in pursuit, but he was too slow and the shape disappeared into the shadows.

Jim and George raced after it. 'He's up this way,' Jim shouted.

Arthur moved to a side door and opened it – it was the perfect escape route. Leaving the door wide open he melted into the shadows of the building. All was quiet for a few moments, then there was a shout from George.

'Here he is!' and the intruder tore past him, heading for the hangar door, but on seeing Edwin blocking his passage he changed direction and ran at right angles towards the side door Arthur had opened. Suddenly a broom was pushed across the floor and caught the intruder mid-stride, causing him to trip over at full speed and land with a heavy thud, face down, outside. He got to his feet almost immediately and would have set off again – but he was going nowhere as Frank had hauled him off his feet and was carrying him back inside, before dropping the limp figure onto the floor in front of Arthur.

It was Tim.

'What on earth are *you* doing here?' Arthur demanded in a state of complete shock.

Tim, still sprawled on the floor, straightened himself up and looked about guiltily. The looming figures of Arthur's men hovered above him like giant trees in a midnight forest. He looked up at Arthur, then told him straight, 'I want to play for England.'

The rest of the group said nothing, sensing this was something between Arthur and the stranger on the floor.

'Tim—' Arthur began to say, but was interrupted as Tim leapt to his feet.

'I'm faster than you think now, Arthur. I've increased the weights and added some exercise of my own.'

Arthur sized up the youngster as he rattled on, noticing that Tim had filled out. His shoulders were rounded but strong and his chest had more depth to it; he even seemed to have grown a bit in height.

'As soon as I saw you with Bob Fryer I figured you'd be helping him with his fast bowlers. When I asked Mr Doyle about where you were, I could tell that he was lying to me, so I tracked you down here when he visited recently.'

'Shouldn't you be at university?' Arthur asked.

'Bollocks to uni!' Tim shot back with a vengeance. 'I know what I want and it's not university,' adding as an afterthought, 'not yet anyway.' The lad seemed to have finished and looked uncertainly at Arthur, who could see that there was resolve and determination in his glare uncommon in one his age.

'Tim I don't know if . . . you're right,' Arthur told him gently.

Tim's face contorted slightly and he looked around at the other players his mentor had recruited for his project.

'You mean I'm not tall enough,' Tim said challenging Arthur to tell him the truth.

Arthur looked sadly at the floor. 'Perhaps,' he said.

Tim looked wildly about him. Spotting a ball under the fold of one of the nets he picked it up. Then, seeing a timing gun, he grabbed it and returned to the group.

'You're trying to train them to be fast, not tall . . . yeah?' he challenged Arthur, who agreed by nodding slightly.

'Right. Let me bowl one ball then.' said Tim, handing

Arthur the timing gun. As there were no objections, he walked to the crease of one of the indoor nets and paced out his run-up. By now the others were intrigued and watched with interest. Arthur moved to the batsman's end of the net, closely followed by the others who lined up to watch Tim's delivery. Arthur flicked on the speed gun and pointed it down the pitch. George yawned but was far from bored. Arthur signalled that he was ready and Tim slowly began his run-up. As he closed in on the crease, his face was full of purpose. He leapt smoothly into his delivery stride, his action more rhythmic and powerful than before, thought Arthur. There was none of the aggression or intimidation that the other bowlers displayed, yet when the ball was released it hurtled down the wicket and, after pitching on a good length, sprang off the deck like a firecracker. All those to the rear of the pitch rocked back as the ball struck the net and it ballooned towards them.

'Good ball!' exclaimed Chandra. 'moved a little.'

Arthur was looking at the reading on the gun with a surprised look.

'I think he's faster than Slim,' George jested with Jim, giving him a poke in the ribs.

The others craned their necks in an attempt to read the speed on the timing gun but Arthur kept it from them. He looked at Tim who had wandered down to the end of the pitch and retrieved the ball. The two regarded each other for a moment but didn't speak. Arthur looked back at the reading on the gun before finally looking up at the others.

'Looks like you're the Super-Six again,' he announced calmly.

This brought no reaction from Tim, who had no idea what the Super-Six meant, so Arthur looked back at Tim and said simply, 'You're in, boy.'

'Yeeeessssss!' came the long-drawn-out cry from Tim that filled every nook and cranny of the great hangar.

The players took Arthur's news in their stride with only amused glances being shared.

'This is Tim Gibson, everyone,' Arthur explained. 'He was the one who put the keys on the tree stump that night after changing the padlock and key.' He looked at Edwin and then back at Tim. 'Am I right?'

Tim grinned enigmatically as he ambled to the end of the net, but due to the net being in between them the others were only able to acknowledge him with nods, mumbles and a yawn or two.

'Welcome aboard,' Edwin said.

'Cheers,' Tim replied from behind a now beaming smile that looked like it would never cease.

'Can we go back to bed?' Chandra asked Arthur.

'I'm ready for a pint now,' George said.

There was a collective groan as they pushed George along towards the door, with Arthur bringing up the rear.

'How fast was it, Arthur?' Chandra pestered.

'Faster than you,' Arthur told him.

They locked the padlock and headed back down the runway to the Big House, chatting as they went. Away in the distance, the low-hanging full moon looked like a planet-sized pearl sitting on the edge of the runway.

'It looks like a big soccer ball,' remarked Edwin.

'Not enough logos for a soccer ball,' Jim replied dryly.

'Mothball,' said Arthur.

'Golf gall,' Frank suggested.

'Marshmallow,' George murmured.

'Snooker ball,' added Jim after a while.

'A big bosom!' exclaimed Chandra.

They all looked at the silly little man who had a wide grin on his face and chuckled like a schoolboy.

'What kind of girls have you been hanging out with, Seven?' Frank inquired. Tim felt at home already.

Arthur turned to him. 'You've filled out,' he remarked.

'Well, I should hope so,' he replied earnestly. 'I'm on performance-enhancing drugs.'

'Naturally,' replied Arthur.

Arthur thought it unusual to be in the company of someone who was nearly his own height. But what Tim lacked in size he made up for with '**HEART**'.

## 21

By morning Arthur had worked out all the particulars of Tim's stay down to the last detail. The two most important things were his weekly allowance and his run of movements, which had to be designed and fitted into the hangar as quickly as possible. Tim's weekly allowance had to come from cutting the others' pay slightly, which they all agreed to. Also, as luck would have it Mrs Cheshire informed Arthur that she had inadvertently overlooked the reimbursement of some money owing to him following Fryer's departure – apparently the food and accommodation had originally been calculated on the basis of nine guests, and now there were only eight. It all helped. When Tim learnt that the money situation was tight, he disappeared one day after practice, came back with some seedlings and soon got to work on a vegetable garden. It was a long-term project but it showed enterprise and willingness. The others occasionally helped him with his allotment and in time 'Tim's Veggie Patch', as it was affectionately known, became a valuable addition to the place.

Arthur was concerned that Tim's parents might not know the whereabouts of their son, but a chat with him soon confirmed that he had told them he'd deferred university and was playing semi-professional cricket in Somerset, and working part-time in a local bar. He didn't feel comfortable deceiving them, any more than Arthur did, but he'd signed a confidentiality clause just like the others at Charmy Down and therefore wasn't in a position to tell the truth.

Tim was first down to breakfast on his first morning, which surprised Mrs Cheshire as she'd never set eyes on him before. Arthur was amazed to find them chatting cordially when he arrived.

He had noticed that Mrs Cheshire's hard exterior had softened somewhat and put it down to her regular exposure to the same group of people, rather than a revolving door of guests who she never really got to know. He therefore decided to involve her a little more in proceedings whenever he could.

Tim soon got the opportunity to re-acquaint himself with all the other players. In the cold light of day, he could make out their features much better. Although he said nothing about it, he was in awe of Frank – the sheer size of the man was almost beyond belief; already the prospect of facing him in the nets was not a pleasant one. Jim too looked a formidable character as he crunched clean through an apple in one bite.

'So, Tim, we've heard of your achievements,' Chandra said. 'Is this man going to take us to the Ashes?' he asked, motioning toward Arthur.

Tim shot Arthur a quick glance. 'Not if you don't believe it,' Tim told Chandra as he finished his cup of tea.

Arthur said nothing. Even Chandra was silent for a moment longer than usual.

'Ah, we have a wise one here . . . too eloquent to be a quick. I'll have to teach him some spin,' Chandra jested.

'Better hurry up and learn some yourself, Seven. You've been spending lots of time in your steel arm but we haven't seen the result yet,' George said to Chandra.

Arthur stepped in before things went too far. 'No, and you won't until he's done a whole month of movements. Now then, let's get out there; we've a busy day ahead.'

It was the first time Arthur had ordered the group in such a tone and they didn't argue.

The day was to be a long one. Arthur was determined to achieve certain things, including Tim being timed, recorded and video-taped. Add to this the adjustment of Tim's run-up, the fine-tuning of his action and the other players' normal daily activities and there was a lot to be done. Edwin did most of the initial rigging for Arthur and then assisted with the fine-tuning, proving he had a keen eye for detail and a good idea of what Arthur was trying to do. It had all been done by the end of the day but there was no visit to the games room that night for refreshments – nor the next two nights either, for Arthur upped the ante on the training front by putting the players through their paces in earnest. His operation was now in full swing and although they didn't know it, their bodies were starting to develop localised concentrations of intense power, which would soon be called upon.

After reading up on the subject, Arthur set Mrs Cheshire the task of cooking a range of healthier meals for the group, although the truth was that he had been forced to cut costs and put some of the savings made on food towards Tim's weekly allowance. Mrs Cheshire rose to the challenge and soon impressed the group with some new vegetarian dishes. After more research on nutrition, Arthur asked that they should all eat one meal per day of uncooked foods, which seemed a bit radical. But having provided Mrs Cheshire with a book on the subject, complete with recipes, she soon preferred the challenge of preparing uncooked meals to cooked ones.

With everyone playing their part and things progressing well, Arthur felt that Mrs Cheshire and Jean needed a break, so he suggested they visit Mrs Cheshire's sister up-country. For weeks Chandra had been suggesting they all visit the Mogul Curry House, which his older brothers owned so this seemed a perfect opportunity.

They couldn't fit all seven of them into the Jaguar so Mrs Cheshire's car was commandeered. As Frank went inside to fetch the key, the others milled about yawning, while Chandra stood on the front lawn of the house casually tossing a ball into the air. Over and over he flipped it. Arthur observed the action of his wrist as he flicked it skyward. Suddenly he missed the ball completely. Spinning furiously it fell to the ground, hit the short grass at his feet, bit like a pit bull terrier and jumped away to his left.

'My God,' Chandra exclaimed looking at Arthur.    'It's working. It spun!'

'You sound surprised,' Arthur said defensively as Jim picked up the ball and tossed it back to Chandra.

'Just a suspect surface, Seven,' Jim declared, drawing smiles from the group as Frank finally appeared holding the keys.

The weeks flew by and now that they were halfway through the program, Arthur sprang another surprise on the players. At training one day he informed them that after a warm-up and stretch they were to bowl at 60 per cent pace, but that they must each hit the stumps ten times in a row. Not until each player had done this could the whole group progress to the 90 per cent pace level.

'Are you going to time them?' asked Chandra with the enthusiasm of a nine year old.

'No, I'm not. And I won't be for a while,' Arthur replied. 'Accuracy levels must be reached and maintained every single day now by each one of you before anyone moves on to the upper pace bracket.'

Edwin got closest with six in a row. The next day it was Edwin again with eight in a row, but it was still not good enough. Finally, on the fourth day of trying, George and Edwin both achieved ten for the first time, but sadly Frank, Jim and Tim only managed six each, so no one was permitted to step up to the faster pace. It was not until eleven days later that George, Jim, Chandra, Tim and Edwin all reached ten in a row. Desperate to bowl at their peak for the first time they all urged Frank on. The anticipation was high as he reached nine and prepared for the tenth. Taking his time and keeping to the same run-up, he came in slightly slower than normal and let one go, bowling to a set of steel stumps. The ball was straight and remarkably fast. It struck the middle stump and sent all three spinning before falling over with a clang. There was a loud cheer from the group as Arthur reached through the net and set the stumps up again. In doing so he noticed a large dent toward the top of the middle stump.

'What about that then, Arthur? Express or what?' George called.

'Bowls faster when he slows down,' Arthur remarked. 'Well done, Frank! That's ten in a row everyone.' He was still looking at the dented stump.

For the final twenty-five minutes of the day's training, the bowlers were permitted to extend their limits. Arthur felt the pace was more than impressive. Chandra's fast ball looked certain to catch some batsmen unawares, though he was still not allowed to attempt to spin the ball. As always, Arthur watched the players like a hawk, constantly warning them never to bowl at top speed. The pinpoint accuracy they had all displayed had dropped off, but the balls seemed to bounce from the synthetic pitch like comets and hit the rear net with considerable force. Tim approached his fellow villager.

'Reckon your bowling twice as fast as at home, Jim.' He could see Jim was pleased to hear it. 'A lot faster!' Tim concluded enthusiastically.

'Hope you're right,' Jim said. 'Keep forgetting these are the heavy balls, an' all. Who knows where we're at.' Jim grasped his shoulder and winced.

'Injury?' inquired Tim.

'No, just this shoulder. It feels–' Jim searched for the right word '–bigger.'

Tim moved behind him and made him stand up straight.

'Put your arms down,' he instructed.

He didn't have to look long. 'That's because it *is* bigger. Not much but definitely bigger.'

Arthur arrived on the scene worried they were discussing an injury problem.

'Something the matter?' he inquired.

'No, fine, we're just looking at Jim's deformed deltoids,' Tim exaggerated. Arthur had a look too, squinting to get a close look.

'Shouldn't get much bigger now,' he said, patting Jim on the back and turning away.


In the games room that night, Mrs Cheshire brought in some old videos she had picked up at a church fête that day, of past Ashes series of the late 1970s and early 1980s. Everyone sat glued to the television and watched the masters of old go through their paces. Jim dubbed the tapes 'The Sideburn Chronicles' and joked of growing an Australian late 1970s handlebar moustache for their first game. Certain players of that era would have been put out by the comments relating to their haircuts. But among all the jesting, they saw some great performances. At one point, Arthur turned to Tim saying, 'Nothing like winning an Ashes series, eh boy?'

Tim looked at him blankly.

'I wouldn't know,' he replied. 'I've never seen us win the Ashes,' he told Arthur, who looked stunned.

'I'm forgetting how long it's been,' Arthur reflected.

'If we win them back it will be the first series win in nearly 14 years,' Chandra informed them all.

'No *ifs* about it,' Arthur corrected him. 'We *will* win them back! You should have all stopped wondering by now.

A more sober atmosphere was detectable in the room. 'It's good you've enjoyed yourselves so far,' Arthur said. 'That's important. But you still have a long way to go and a lot of bloody hard work ahead.' As he spoke an image of David Gower holding up the tiny Ashes urn flashed across the screen.

'Sounds like a lot of work for such a small trophy,' Frank noted, his dry humour breaking the sombre mood. As the group round the television dispersed Edwin and Tim resumed their game of pool. There was a curse from the rear of the room as the beer gun coughed and spluttered the last of the beer.

'We're out of beer.' George called out in a state of panic.

Arthur sauntered across and lifted a rug on the floor of the bar, revealing a trapdoor which he heaved up to reveal three more shiny kegs of Butcombe. Arthur retired early having thoroughly enjoyed looking back at the past series and players, recalling some of the more obscure moments of the game of which none of his charges had heard.

'He certainly loves his cricket does our Arthur,' George announced to all. 'But will that get any of us into the England test side? That's the question.'

He surveyed the room but no one spoke.

'How do we all feel?' he urged them. Suddenly there were some knowing smiles.

'It works,' Tim offered up confidently.

'I know that. I can feel it.' Said George. 'But we can't keep getting bigger, stronger and faster. We have to hit the wall some time. Don't we?' he put to the group.

'Who knows.' offered Jim in an upbeat tone 'We're all still improving. I don't know when it's going to taper off.'

'I don't mind being a guinea pig,' Edwin commented.

'Me neither,' confirmed Chandra enthusiastically.

'I sometimes wonder . . . why us? I mean, who was before you?' George asked Tim.

'Does he have any children he used to coach?'

At the mention of this Jim's heart missed a beat.

'I was wondering the same,' admitted Chandra. 'only one way to find out.'

'Think we would have heard about it by now if he did, Seven,' said Frank dousing the idea. 'That's probably best left alone. And I'd say that's stumps,' he announced as he heaved himself out of his lounge chair and stretched. Jim felt a lot calmer for hearing Frank's comments as he didn't want any old wounds opened. The others made similar movements towards their bedrooms.

'Hey! We should have a wager on who ends up bowling the fastest,' Chandra suggested.

'Why don't we just beat up the slowest?' Frank asked to the others who all nodded.

A month out from Arthur's 'four-month Test' which they all knew would ultimately decide their fate, Arthur thought it was time to fine-tune the shape, strength and endurance of his group. They were all placed on diets tailored to each individual. Frank and Jim were so large of frame that Arthur felt they had to remain trim to avoid injury. They were fed an abundance of fruit and fish, while heavier foods and red meats were eradicated.

Edwin, being very slim, had no problems in the weight department. Arthur thought him in A1 shape and if anything in need of putting on a bit of weight. His frame had become more obviously toned than any of the others, his arms and legs seeming to go on for ever. But they had a strong wiry quality about them now, his veins so prominent it was as if metres of electrical cabling had been inserted under his skin. Even so, Arthur was worried that he might be susceptible to back injury, as many tall, lean bowlers in the past had been, so he sought professional advice and set Edwin a series of specifically designed exercises to address this problem.

Chandra was of less concern and, surprisingly, trained harder than anyone else. Even on the runs and walks he gave it his all. George claimed the morning run was the best part of the day because it was the only time that Chandra actually shut up. Although he still had his paunch, he was noticeably healthier looking and seemed to have more energy than anyone else. His nickname of '7' had stuck, but sometimes they called him '24 by 7' because, as Jim had pointed out, his mouth was never shut.

George and Tim, being the two youngest and in excellent physical shape, were permitted to eat most of what the others had plus some additional pasta dishes. George ate breakfast cereal at any time of the day and would take toast to bed with him, but often woke up in the morning with it uneaten on his bedside table.

For the final two weeks, Arthur increased the weights on the end of the pulleys a fraction, which the players hardly noticed. He also increased their runs to two per day, with no walks. There was a noticeable air of repetitiveness creeping into the training, which at that late stage could have been disastrous, so Arthur sprang a half-day R&R on them and insisted they all went into town to do their own thing.

When they returned that evening, Arthur, Jean and Mrs Cheshire had set up an outside BBQ for them with home-made scrumpy.

Arthur let them have a lie-in until 10.00 a.m. the following day, although Tim used this time to see to his vegetable garden. Arthur then made them do the perimeter run twice in reverse. It was the change they all needed. They seemed brighter and got on with their tasks once more. Unfortunately, the scrumpy caused some sore stomachs but it didn't disrupt their training too much.

After four more days of routine training, Arthur brought out the timing gun and the regulation balls, tossing a new one to each player.

'Let's see where we're at!' he said.

The players were silent. Their moment of truth had arrived. They toyed with the balls nervously, finding their weight almost comical as they warmed up. There was normally a good deal of banter prior to a net session, but all was quiet as Arthur shouted, 'Right, George, pad up!'

George was disappointed at having to bat first, which was unusual, as he normally loved having a bat. He watched his fellow bowlers who had warmed to the idea of cutting loose and were almost salivating at the prospect of tearing into him. It was as if they were suddenly a pack of hungry wolves. He looked worried.

'You probably all think I'm going to let you bowl full pace,' Arthur called out loudly. 'Eighty per cent maximum.'

The players were deflated at hearing this and mumbled to themselves as Arthur calmly went on, 'I just need you to get used to these balls. With any luck on Sunday you'll be playing against a full-strength English batting line-up.'

The players' jaws dropped. There was a stunned silence – immediately followed by a barrage of short sharp questions from everyone. Arthur, not being able to make sense of any of them, held his hands up to quell the row and shouted at the group, 'Listen! I have a plan. I don't want to say too much at present. All right? For now, just bowl . . . at eighty per cent.'

He fiddled with the timing gun as George finished padding up, the rest milling around chatting excitedly among themselves.

'Chandra, I want you to bowl your spin, if you will,' Arthur called up the pitch.

Jumping to attention, the little man suddenly became fidgety. 'Oh boy,' he sighed. 'it's all happening.'

George, who was near to Arthur, asked, 'Why is it he gets to bowl spin but we can't bowl top speed?'

'He needs more practice than you,' was Arthur's frank response.

George pulled on his gloves and walked into the nets. 'If Seven gets me out, I'll never hear the end of it,' he grumbled.

'Great thing, incentive,' Arthur said quietly as George took guard and Chandra readied himself for the big moment. Arthur positioned himself behind the stumps but outside the net at the batsman's end, while all the others stood where the umpire would normally be – single file, shortest to tallest – in order to judge for themselves if the ball spun.

'Don't worry too much if the first one doesn't turn, Seven,' Arthur called out just before Chandra set off.

Chandra bit his lip and gripped the ball in two hands as he started into his run-up. Giving the ball a violent tweak, he flung it into the air with a looping arc. It was a nicely flighted ball that gave George plenty of time before dropping onto the pitch on about leg stump. George played carefully forward with his pads behind the bat as the ball hit the turf and gripped, turning at a savage angle. It touched the edge of his bat, deviated slightly and made its way towards where the slips would have been. Having been waiting for this moment all his life, Chandra was up immediately. The ball meanwhile threaded itself through a tear in the back net and was headed for the back wall when Arthur's right hand flew out instinctively. Lunging sideways, he took a smart catch. Chandra yelled wildly and ran around the back of the net to kiss and hug him.

'Bloody hell!' exclaimed George.

At the bowler's end, Jim remarked to Frank, 'You'd think we'd just won the Ashes.'

'Maybe we have,' Frank reflected.

126

The fast men all had their turn at impressing Arthur. He watched the first couple of balls, particularly noticing that George didn't play them as comfortably as normal. In between balls, Arthur said, 'Well?'

George gave him a quick glance – the look on his face said it all. He was sweating more than usual and looked rattled.

'They're bloody fast,' he admitted, adding with a wink, 'I'd hate to face me.'

He took guard again and faced Frank who came steaming in. The ball pitched short and jumped at George almost vertically, catching him flush on the side of the helmet. He fell to the ground like a sack of spuds. Arthur dropped the gun and ran round the nets, but the others reaching him first and gently removed his helmet.

'George,' Frank said in an urgent tone, 'can you hear me?'

'Good ball!' said Chandra to no one in particular.

Tim came running up with some water just as George moved and gingerly opened his eyes.

'Just take it easy,' Frank told him. Jim and Edwin helped George to lie flat and took his gloves off, putting his helmet to one side.

'Keep your eyes closed and breathe deeply,' Arthur instructed.

'Please tell me Seven didn't bowl that one!' George asked, still groggy. A wave of relieved smiles passed between them as Jim shook his head and stood up. 'Help me get up, will you,' George insisted, already struggling to rise.

'Just take him to the side for a bit,' instructed Arthur.

'Seriously, who bowled that? That bloody hurt, that did!' George moaned, rubbing his head.

The whole episode was, of course, turned into a huge joke. George insisted on batting on as he did not want to become gun-shy, as he put it. Still the balls came at him at a great pace, some of which he played rather well. He was dismissed five times, however, and beaten for pace numerous times. 'They're bloody quick,' he told Arthur when his time was up. 'I've never got out five times in a net session in my life.'

Arthur looked at the speed gun, then cleared it. 'Edwin, pad up!' he shouted.

At the completion of the session, there was a tangible energy about the hangar. The players looked fresh, as if they could have gone on, whereas they were already fifteen minutes past the normal finish time.

'Come on, Arthur. Tell us who was the fastest,' Tim pleaded.

Arthur brought his clipboard under his chin, flipped over a page and took a deep breath. 'Well, George hit the ground faster than anyone actually bowled. Does that count?' Arthur teased them.

'Oi!' George cried.

Arthur moved closer and over his spectacles levelled a promising glare at them all. 'I'll tell you this,' he said producing a small brown card. On it was written '100.04 m.p.h.' 'The fastest ball ever bowled.' He spun the card over to reveal 83.5 m.p.h. and 80.8 m.p.h. '83.5 m.p.h. was the top speed bowled here today and 80.8 the lowest,' he told them.

'So if we're all sticking to eighty per cent then we're looking at . . .' Jim tried to work it out.

'Breaking records,' said Arthur. 'And if that happens, we don't tell a soul,' he reminded them.

'But you can tell *us,* right?' George asked hopefully.

Arthur thought for a moment, then smiled like Mrs Cheshire's namesake. 'Maybe,' he said. There was much heckling from the players as a glove whistled past his left ear.

Jean and Mrs Cheshire appeared at the doorway of the hangar looking incredibly excited. Arthur excused himself to join them. Jean spoke urgently to him. Finally Arthur grinned and patted them both on the back warmly giving each a quick kiss on the cheek. The players watched.

Finally George spoke up. 'Something very strange is going on.'

## 22

The day of the Super Six's first game had arrived but got off to a bad start when the men came down to find there was no breakfast – it seemed Mrs Cheshire and Jean had gone out early to complete some urgent task and had no time to prepare it. This was all the more strange as they'd both been up the previous night cooking and most of them assumed they were in for a treat, which made it doubly disappointing to find there was nothing.

As was always the case, Arthur had the answer. Seeing it was the end of the week and therefore George's turn to do the perimeter check and hangar clean-up, he decided George would cook breakfast instead. He had, after all, told them on many occasions what a useful cook he was – now he had his chance to prove it. Mrs Cheshire had at least prepared the ingredients for a light fry-up and George got stuck in right away. Smaller than normal portions were available as it was a match day, and extra helpings of fruit. Frank still ate twice as much as anyone else.

'Make sure your whites, spikes, plus your kit are all packed straight after breakfast. We'll meet outside at 8.50,' Arthur instructed.

'How on earth did you manage to line up a game against the English team, Arthur?' asked Jim. Arthur was in the process of folding his paper and tucking it under his arm. He removed his glasses and started to clean them.

'I haven't yet. It's not my job,' he told them confusingly. There were blank looks in the kitchen.

'You mean *we* have to do something?' Edwin asked.

'Yes,' Arthur confirmed. 'You have to sit on your backsides until I call you.'

With that, he popped his glasses on his head, slid them up his nose until they were tight against his face and walked out of the room.


The game was to be played in Bristol – a charity match between England and England 'A' – so they didn't have far to travel from Charmy Down. Arriving at the ground at 9.45 a.m., Arthur told everyone to leave their gear and the kitbag in the cars. Each had to pay an entry fee, which they thought was strange as they thought *they* were the players. Having mysteriously advised them to keep their tickets as they might be worth something one day, he then picked a spot for them all, far away from where they had wanted to sit.

'Right, you lot, stay put until I return,' Arthur told them before hurrying off.

'Pint of lager, thanks, Arthur,' George called after him as he hurried off purposely.

Five minutes later he returned.

'Great result. England are bowling,' Arthur told them.

'Why is that a great result?' George asked on behalf of the group.

'Can't tell you, I'm afraid,' he replied, fully focused on the players walking onto the field for a warm-up.

'I thought you said *we* were going to be playing,' Frank pointed out.

'You will. Not just yet though,' said Arthur in a dismissive fashion that was very unlike him. 'All will soon be revealed.'

An air of resentment was growing among the group towards Arthur's strange behaviour. He had never really kept them in the dark about anything like this before and was irritated by their attempts to get him to disclose the details of his plan before he was ready. Now they were all silent which made Arthur feel even more uncomfortable.

'I can imagine how you feel,' he told them, 'but just be patient.'

'I hate watching cricket,' said Frank.

Arthur ignored him.

'Well, well!' said Chandra slowly. 'You were right when you said we would see Mr French again, Arthur.' French was making his English debut that day and Chandra followed his every move out on the field without taking his eyes off him.

'Try not to let him or anyone else see us if possible,' Arthur cautioned. Looking at the enormous frames of his men all huddled together he realised what a stupid comment he'd just made.

The England 'A' team were all out for 223 in 47 overs, with French bowling an above-average spell of 3 for 38 in his ten overs. As the English players began to make their way from the field, Arthur suddenly got up and scuttled off.

'Wait here,' was all he said as he disappeared through the crowd. George, having never been much good at following instructions, sprang to his feet.

'Just popping off to the loo,' he said and followed Arthur who hurried around the back of the clubhouse and disappeared. George hung around for a while but was afraid Arthur might reappear and see him so decided he'd better get back to the others. As he passed the catering tent he saw the English players lining up for lunch through a gap in the side wall of the marquee. The current English captain, Stan 'The Man' Coleman was first in line. Behind him was Bill Fredericks, the No. 1 fast bowler in the team, who was never quite world class but went around acting as if he were. Fredericks was chatting to England's top batsman, 'King' Khan, an Englishman born of Pakistani parents, who was regarded as the finest player in the team, the only one other Test nations feared. He was a large man for a Pakistani and treated any bowling attack with arrogant disdain. 'The harder they bowl, the harder I hit 'em!' was his famous quote after he had mauled South Africa for 196 not out. His feats with the bat were all too often rewarded with the sour taste of defeat, but Khan was a good sportsman and was often found in the dressing room of the opposition sharing a drink after a match. The last player George saw was Harry Winter, the wicketkeeper and the most popular man in the team, who somehow managed to maintain the team's morale. His defiance with the bat had meant some long innings, but his batting prowess was no match for good bowling attacks. Now in the twilight of his career, many felt Winter was good for just one more year as younger men pressed for selection. Mathew French was lined up as well, chatting with Fryer. George felt a swell of anger rise within him as he watched the pair, who had deserted Arthur, joke between themselves. As he moved off, George spotted two dinner ladies who looked remarkably like Jean and Mrs Cheshire serving the players their meals, which struck him as bizarre. He also caught a glimpse of Arthur lurking behind the large white tent, but before he knew it he'd vanished once more.

George made a dash back to the others to report his findings and was in the process of filling them in when they spotted Arthur hurriedly returning through the crowd. Everyone was eager to hear what he had to say.

'Well?' Chandra asked.

'Just have to wait and see now,' Arthur informed them calmly. 'Should work.'

The six of them, still none the wiser, chatted amongst themselves for a while. Frank and Edwin were about to fetch some tea but Arthur warned them to drink only water as they could be on any time now. They returned just as the England 'A' side started out towards the middle, a collection of swinging arms and wiggling heads as they wandered out.

'So we're not playing.' asked Chandra in a deflated tone.

'Ssshh.' Arthur replied dismissively. His unflinching gaze seemed to intensify. He leant forward as if he were almost willing something to happen. All of a sudden, a member of the fielding team stopped, grabbed his stomach, turned and rushed off the field. Then two more made off urgently in the same fashion. A ripple of confusion worked its way round the ground.

'It's working,' Arthur said gleefully. 'Out of everything bad comes something good.'

George jumped up. 'Mrs Cheshire's curry!' he shouted. The others were just starting to catch on as another two players on the fielding side ran off. Baffled, the rest of them walked back towards the boundary fence. Even the English openers had halted their progress towards the middle.

'Right!' said Arthur. 'Go and get changed and bring the kit. Meet me near the clubhouse in fifteen minutes,' and he scurried off once more.

Fryer and the match officials were gathered outside the changing rooms and lavatories, in conference with the captain of the fielding side, discussing how long they could postpone the match. Arthur moved unobtrusively into a position whereby he could overhear their discussion.

'They don't look as if they're going to get back out there for some time,' Ed Cantor, England 'A's' captain, declared.

'What about the other players? Fryer asked him.

'That's the funny thing. Five of us are fine,' Cantor told

him. 'It's mainly my bowlers who are unfit.'

'We can't cancel the match!' stated one particularly important-looking man with a neat navy blazer and thick silver sideburns.

'But where am I going to get six players?' snapped Cantor defending the hopeless position of his team.

'Maybe I can help,' came a loud and unexpected voice from outside the group. They turned to see Arthur standing there, smiling at a startled Fryer. 'Hello, Bob!' he said.

The man with the blazer turned to Fryer and asked him, 'Do you know this chap, Bob?'

As Fryer struggled to think of a reply, Arthur moved forward to join them. 'Bob and I go way back,' he said slapping Fryer on the back, 'don't we, Bob?'

They all watched as Fryer searched for a suitable response, but Arthur answered for him by simply continuing where he had left off. 'It was a brief venture, but it's been most productive.' He glared at Fryer whose eyes widened. 'Anyway,' he continued, 'I came to watch the match with six of my lads. All of them very good players,' he informed his audience. 'They're out there kitted up if you want to continue the match – after all, it is for charity . . .'

The officials and the fielding captain seemed happy and nodded eagerly.

Some reservation was expressed by the navy blazer. 'Any good, these chaps?' he asked. Arthur turned to Fryer. Everyone followed suit. 'What do you think, Bob?' Arthur asked him.

Fryer was beginning to regain his composure as he wondered how Arthur and his players had got on over the last four months. Finally, his curiosity got the better of him.

'Yes, quite good, I suppose,' he answered grudgingly, giving Arthur a suspicious look.

'Excellent! Sort it out, Cantor,' snorted the navy blazer. With instructions issued and the situation saved, he hurried away upstairs to watch the game. Cantor spoke to Arthur in a friendly manner.

'Just send your men in here to get ready and we'll see them out onto the field. Would you be so good as to provide their names to the scorers please, Mr . . .?' Cantor paused as Arthur introduced himself.

'Jenkins. Arthur Jenkins. And I'd be delighted,' Arthur said politely.

'Terrific,' replied Cantor before he turned and jogged back towards the playing area. As an afterthought, he turned, still running and shouted back to Arthur, who was standing with Fryer. 'Got any decent quicks?'

'One or two!' Arthur called back with a smile to Fryer again.

Once Cantor was out of view, Fryer asked Arthur, 'Did you poison those men, Jenkins?'

'Dodgy curry,' Arthur replied.

'I had no idea you were so hell bent,' said Fryer seeing him in a new light.

'Well, that's an improvement on barking mad,' Arthur proclaimed. 'Desperate measures, I'm afraid, Bob, and it *is* a charity match. Can't let the boys down.'

'You've been busy then?' Fryer asked.

In true Arthur style, he completely disarmed Fryer. 'Bob, I should have told you about some of the things I had planned, but you might have had faith in me. You should never have walked out that day. I'm here to pick up where we left off, not rub your nose in it.' Fryer took a step back. 'I want to win the Ashes, that's all, Bob,' concluded Arthur as he held out his hand.

'Rub my nose in it?' Fryer asked him incredulously. 'You don't honestly think you can win?' He was grossly offended.

'Bob, the only way you can win today is if I let you,' Arthur informed him. 'You are mad!' Fryer had never felt so insulted and once more stormed off.

Arthur called after him, 'You need to have faith, Bob!' But Fryer was gone again. 'He's very good at that,' he muttered to himself as he turned to go and update his players.

Arthur was relieved that things had fallen into place exactly the way he'd intended as he had no other plan to fall back on. Breathing a sigh of relief, he sat down and gathered his thoughts as the players began to assemble round him for their final instructions. He thought they all looked supremely fit as a result of the last four months' efforts and felt very proud of them, even though they hadn't even bowled a ball in anger. He didn't have to ask – he knew they were more than ready to have a crack at the England batsmen. There was not a hint of nerves among them.

'We're on,' was all Arthur told them, which produced a loud cheer. They carried out a quick warm-up, which they knew off by heart, as Arthur barked commands. As they did their final stretches Arthur issued his last-minute instructions. 'See this hat?' he told them all pointing to his head. 'When it's on you keep below 90 per cent effort. That's an order,' he insisted. They all nodded. 'When it's off . . . there's no speed limit.' Again they understood. 'And when you hear the signal, I want you to bowl for blood!' He shook his fist in a threatening manner.

'What's the signal?' Frank asked.

'You'll know it when you hear it. There will be two games being played here today. One out there and one back here,' he told them referring to the battle he'd be having with Fryer. 'So I need you to do exactly as I tell you. No matter what you may feel.'

Cantor was calling them onto the field.

'Good luck to you all.' Arthur said. They took the field as the loudspeaker announced the change in the team's line-up, explaining that an unfortunate event had befallen some of the regular players. Funnily enough, Jean and Mrs Cheshire turned up at that very moment.

'Mrs Cheshire, it's a true skill you have there,' Arthur told her.

'We got paid thirty-five pounds each!' Jean gushed excitedly.

Arthur spotted Fryer and immediately began ushering Jean and Mrs Cheshire to their seats. 'There's two seats over there for you – the ones with the red cushions. There are some binoculars under the right-hand one. I must go,' he kissed Jean and Mrs Cheshire, without thinking about it. Mrs Cheshire blushed crimson which Jean thought hilarious, as Arthur headed for Fryer and the dignitaries.

The sizeable crowd settled in as proceedings got under way once more. As the players made their way onto the field it coincided with a busker somewhere outside the ground beating out a slow march on a kettledrum, transforming their walk to the middle into an ominous procession. Out in the middle, Cantor glanced to the outfield as Arthur's men strolled on.

'My God.' he said stunned. 'what have we here?'

Having to select his opening bowlers but faced with the enormous frames of Frank, Jim and Edwin, Cantor was in a quandary about who to pick.

'Where did they find you lot?' he asked in disbelief.

There were smiles all round as Jim told him, 'Best you don't know, skipper.'

Cantor smiled nervously. 'Right, who wants to open?' They all looked at each other.

'I will,' said Chandra eagerly as the others rolled their eyes. Then Jim took the ball from Cantor and gave it to Edwin.

'Edwin here will take the new ball with George if it's all right with you, skipper?' he suggested.

'Fine,' replied Cantor. 'I'll set the field. You change it to suit yourself. All right?' And with that he trotted off issuing instructions to the fielders to get into place. Again Jim spoke in a closed group to the five.

'Listen up. We're all very different bowlers to what we were four months ago. Don't get fooled into old ways of thinking. We're all free to start again. And be better. Let's do it!' With that the group broke and jogged into position.

The entire team cheered and clapped encouragingly as Edwin took the ball and prepared himself. As he carefully marked out his run-up the England openers went about their business. Like two old hens scratching around their coop, they picked small objects from the pitch, throwing them to one side, then kicked some grit away from the crease. They looked round at the field settings and finally one of them took guard. Peter Stiles and Danny Dennis had played sixteen Test matches together and averaged 35.56 and 33.21 respectively, which was well below par, although at county level they both averaged over 55. Needless to say, both fancied their chances against the unknown attack and even though Fryer had sent word to be wary – 'watchful' was the word he used – they had too high an opinion of themselves and believed Fryer was being overcautious. They had both noticed the sizes of Jim and Frank, but neither made any comment to the other.

As Edwin stood watching Stiles take guard, he shot Arthur a quick glance. The hat was on. He felt relieved as he preferred to concentrate on accuracy at this stage rather than speed – which was the exact reason Jim had suggested he bowl first. Edwin's no-fuss way of doing things meant he didn't muck about or get caught in the moment. He just did his best and let the training do the rest. He bowled a rhythmic over of pace that yielded no runs and was notable only for its perfect line and length. When it was complete Edwin had a pleasing grin on his face and gave the 'thumbs up' to George who looked his way. It was a sign to all of them that he felt good. To the spectators it was a thoroughly good opening over. Edwin further reflected on his performance when at the change Jim trotted past and asked, 'How did it feel?'

'Feels different. Really good though,' Edwin replied.

'Good over,' Jim told him and went to his position.

George's over was not so impressive, being more like a bag of crisps: good . . . but not what the doctor ordered. His first ball went down the leg side, followed by a no-ball, then a wide, and then three slower balls to get back on track. Who would have thought the ever-cocky George would be nervous? With two balls left he finally found his rhythm and upped his tempo as the first one moved off the pitch and flew past the outside edge; the last ball was the same. Suddenly the crowd was sitting up and taking notice. Jim gave him a stern look after such an erratic display – he wasn't happy and George knew it. He thought it funny that he had looked to Jim rather than the others on the field for a clue to his performance.

Edwin again bowled five near-perfect balls . . . and a sixth one – but Stiles had made up his mind that he wanted to score off it, no matter what. When Edwin bowled what looked to be a half-volley, Stiles pounced. But Edwin had put a little more effort into the delivery, which hit the pitch sooner than he expected and a tad shorter. Stiles was hurried into his stroke and played a lofted drive to the boundary. Edwin, understanding the mechanics behind the shot and the batsman's mindset, was happy to sacrifice the runs, glaring briefly at the batsman, who turned away. Edwin knew that he'd got the upper hand and that he had a whole over to plot his next move.

Meanwhile, Arthur was watching Fryer who was totally ignoring him, although he was well aware that Arthur was seated just four seats away.

The English batsmen were coasting. George had bowled some ordinary deliveries in his first over and Arthur was beginning to wonder who he should get to bowl the first really fast delivery. George was faster than Edwin most of the time, but Edwin was more accurate. Was it time to gamble and unleash George's great pace? No rush, he thought.

George watched for the hat coming off, but was disappointed so he continued to bowl as close to 90 per cent as he could. The first five balls of his third over were accurate and yielded no runs – to the frustration of the batsmen. Both Edwin and George were bowling a good line and length, but George knew that if something did not change in the next couple of overs, the batsmen would have had a good look at their pace and bounce, and might start scoring runs a little more comfortably. He would have liked to have sounded a warning shot, but restricted to bowling at no more than 90 per cent pace, he needed to be smart about it. He pushed his mid-on and mid-off back a little and brought a man in close to confuse the batsman. As it was the last ball of the over the batsman decided to play safe.

As George ran in, he could feel the thick stitching round the ball underneath his index finger and thumb; his middle finger rested on the seam. The ball hummed its way down the pitch at a good pace but as Stiles went to block it with a forward defensive shot, it hit the deck and cut away sharply. Finding a solid edge, it flew wide to second slip, where England 'A's opening bat Craig Corcoran, took a screamer to loud celebrations by the fielding side. It was a good wicket to have taken. George would have wanted things to be more dramatic but Arthur's original assessment of him held true – he had a sound cricketing brain.

Stiles departed looking very dejected as the supremo of English cricket strode to the crease. Head held high, 'King Khan' twiddled his bat as if it were a toothpick as he looked about him at the non-striker's end.

Fryer had still not acknowledged Arthur or the fine wicket George had taken. Meanwhile, Edwin bowled three balls of good length when Arthur finally lost his patience. Just as Edwin was beginning his run-up for his fourth ball, Jim noticed that Arthur had taken his hat off. He quickly called to Edwin who stopped, looked towards the grandstand and, spotting Arthur hatless, returned to his mark. Everyone, crowd and players alike, were confused, sensing that something was afoot. Edwin picked up the white marker and measured out two massive strides further, then dropped it once more onto the grass. Jim asked for the fielders to come in a yard or two and Cantor obliged. Edwin started on his way, building up to a slightly faster pace as he approached the crease with an air of intent. Putting his all into the delivery, he launched the ball so fast that Dennis went neither forward nor back, but played a pathetic prod, then jerked and froze in shock as something whisked past him faster than he'd ever seen before. The bounce alone would have been enough to terrify most players as it leapt past his elbow and shot past his head. There was a roar of approval from the crowd as the wicketkeeper jumped full stretch to take the ball high above his head, almost unable to stop its progress.

The other five were stunned at the final proof of their efforts – a ball an England batsman couldn't even see! Arthur's heart skipped a beat, while the rest of the fielding side exchanged glances, raised their eyebrows or whistled. Still Fryer was outwardly unmoved.

Edwin's next ball would surely claim a wicket: it was straight at the stumps and fast. Dennis got into an awful mess trying to play it, but somehow managed to hit it over both Edwin's and the umpire's heads, yielding no runs. He didn't even know where it had gone after he'd made contact and spun around looking in the air. The crowd laughed. It was the second unconvincing shot in a row. Edwin's stock was rising rapidly.

Fryer was totally absorbed but dared not look to his left where he knew Arthur to be.

Edwin's last ball of the over was short and flew via the inside edge of Dennis's bat into his stomach, throwing him off his feet so that he ended up sitting unceremoniously on the pitch. The players crowded round him as he struggled for air, having been badly winded. The batsman glared at Edwin, realising that these were no ordinary bowlers. He hauled himself to his feet indignantly, dusted himself off and looked over to where he knew Fryer was seated, thinking a cruel trick was being played on him and his team. Fryer saw the gesture by his player and a hot flush exploded within him. Others about Fryer also noticed the alarm

Dennis had openly displayed. It was game on. Dennis brushed at his trousers and pads while the fielders changed positions for the end of the over.

George now faced the prospect of bowling to 'King Khan'. Khan had calmly watched Edwin's pace, but was not bothered by it. In truth he was looking forward to facing them both. His arrogance was the worst kind of all: the type people possess when they *know* they're the best, rather than just *think* it. To confirm his guard, Khan worked out middle stump from the scratch marks already made by the openers. The umpire nodded and, after a quick glance at the field settings to his rear, Khan was ready.

Arthur's hat was back on, much to George's disappointment. He too had lengthened his run-up – which Khan had noted – but now had to shorten it again. George's first ball to him would have dismissed most batsmen. It was fast, straight and kept low. Khan dug it out with ease and turned it to leg; it reached the boundary in no time. George tried everything but Khan had made up his mind to show the opposition who was boss, the first five balls going for 4, 0, 2, 2, 4. He looked at Arthur before the last ball but the hat was still on. Frustrated, George wondered why he wasn't allowed to bowl fast as Edwin. The last ball was short and almost took Khan's head off, the crowd letting out a huge roar as the ball whistled past the batsman's ear. Although the mighty Khan was impressed with George's bowling, Fryer still did not look in Arthur's direction.

Edwin was permitted to bowl another over flat out at Dennis, who tried everything to get away from the strike. But he couldn't buy a run as Edwin's bowling was tight and straight. Dennis missed two balls that whistled through to the keeper, and could have easily taken an edge had he been a better batsman. Finally, on the fifth ball, he got a thick edge that beat the fieldsmen and allowed a single. Khan then took a bold step down the wicket to the last ball and thumped Edwin over his head to the boundary for six. Arthur felt it was the shot of a man who either wanted to stay off strike or was trying to force a change of bowlers – or both!

The hat was still on at the start of George's fourth over which made him furious and he swore under his breath – but he was still resigned to bowling at only 90 per cent pace as per

Arthur's instructions. The batsmen had a mid-wicket conference, with Khan making some rather strong assertions, gesticulating with his right arm. When George's over commenced, Dennis found little relief and for the first four balls he survived on luck alone. When George dropped the next one slightly shorter and wider he pounced and cut it to the fence over gully's head. The next ball was on middle and leg and Dennis nervously glanced it uppishly square of the wicket. Arthur had never before seen such committed running from Dennis as he scrambled back for a second. He too was trying to avoid the strike for the next over.

Edwin's next over was more varied, but Khan managed to craft a handy 7 runs from it, leaving Dennis to face the last ball. Edwin bowled another short one which caused the batsman to play a defensive stroke on the back foot. The pace, however, didn't give him time to get into position correctly and the movement off the pitch did the rest. The wicketkeeper took a regulation catch to end Dennis's misery and both openers had gone with the score still under 40. Fryer was clearly not happy with Dennis' effort and still no acknowledgement of Arthur.

The next England batsman was Mark Engel. Edwin and George had bowled five overs apiece, with Khan taking five from each of the last two, thereby retaining the strike for the start of the next over from big Frank Arnold. Khan was as cagey as a leopard as he watched the enormous man measure his run-up. Although he normally took the unusual measure of batting well out of his crease, he was back in it now. Arthur's hat was on.

Frank composed himself and as his burly frame rumbled in, he almost blocked out the sightscreen behind before delivering a thunderous delivery that Khan watched through to the keeper. The crowd knew it was fast and let out a howl. Again, Khan watched the next ball through to the keeper.

By now Arthur had had enough and removed his hat. Khan looked as though he'd got his eye in and was heading for a big score. Frank saw the signal but didn't bother to lengthen his run-up – when he wanted to bowl faster he simply put more into it. Khan thought he could feel the footsteps of the huge man reverberate around the pitch as he pounded in. The ball was like lightning and pitched short, shooting up and into Khan like a cannonball, tying him in knots. It was an embarrassingly ugly shot. Hitting the batsman's gloves and forearm, the ball popped up into the air, but dropped in between two close fielders.

The crowd gave out a collective sigh of relief, which was quickly followed by a stunned silence. It wasn't often Khan was made to play such an ungainly shot. An excited buzz rippled round the ground as the incredible speed of the last ball was discussed. Khan was disgusted with himself.

Near to where Arthur sat an elderly man called out to Fryer, 'These boys are giving you a bit of stick, Bob.' Fryer smiled politely not daring to look Arthur's way.

Frank returned to his mark, pounded in and bowled to Khan – who played forward a fraction of a second after his middle stump was uprooted and sent cart wheeling backwards. The crowd was stunned; so was Fryer. Khan's heart missed a beat; he was so shocked at being clean bowled that his feet wouldn't move. The fielders went up with a shout . . . then came the call 'No-ball!' Khan had still not moved but now he brought his front foot back and shook his head to loosen up in readiness for the next ball. His first thought was to hit the next one and break Frank's confidence – shake him up a bit – but people in the crowd might see through that. There was only one thing for it: concentrate. 'Watch the ball and play it on its merits,' he said to himself as he moved back out of his crease, prepared to use his pads to stifle any chance of an LBW. His resolve was rewarded as he batted out the over and lived to fight another day. He even took a single off the last ball and trotted comfortably down the pitch as if he were out for a Sunday stroll – but froze when he saw Jim take the ball: another hulking paceman with a scowl that could kill a cat at twenty yards.

Jim measured his run-up and instead of dropping the white marker ran the spikes of his boot across the ground.

Old school, thought Khan as he sized up his opponent, who resembled an enormous bull stomping at the ground, looking Khan square in the eye as he did so. The crowd was enthralled; the intimidation was almost tangible.

Again, Arthur could hear the banter of the officials sitting with Fryer. 'By jove, Bob, this one looks mean!' said one man. Then, out of the blue, the man in the navy blazer turned to Arthur and said, 'Where on *earth* did you find these lads?'

'What makes you think it was on earth?' he replied, to the

delight of those who had heard the initial query. Arthur and his lads were winning them over on both sides of the boundary. Now Fryer glanced at Arthur who gave him a sly smile.

Meanwhile, out in the middle, Khan was wondering what the next over had in store. Jim approached slow and rhythmic, his run up culminated with a giant leap into the air, his return to terra firma was like a tidal wave breaking. In a flash his ball-carrying arm ticked over and pelted the ball into the pitch. It was short and Khan tried to pull it, but only got a bottom edge onto the inside of his upper thigh, which caused him to crumple painfully to the ground in a most ungainly fashion.

Jim went back to his mark and waited with ball in hand. In all his cricketing life, Khan had never been felled by a ball to the leg! He was madder than a cut snake when he got up, rudely brushing aside any assistance from his fellow batsman and a couple of the fielding side. In considerable pain, he resumed his stance even before the fielders were ready. Bowler and batsman faced each other for a moment before Jim came in once more. Khan made no mistake with the next one, doggedly defending his wicket.

Jim bowled the rest of the over at a great pace, but it was a different pace to Frank's – Jim's balls had less lift and skidded through very fast to the keeper. He also varied his length. Arthur thought that if he bowled like this for Good Walloping they would never lose a match.

Khan rode the storm and reached his fifty without Engel facing a ball. It was a different type of innings to those he normally played, but a good one nevertheless. Arthur kept his hat on for the next ten overs.

Engel and Khan had pushed the score up to over 100 when Tim and Chandra were asked to take over. Khan breathed a sigh of relief. Jim and Frank had bowled well but had taken no wickets. They had both bowled at an average of 85 per cent and had managed to contain the batsmen for the most part.

Arthur watched as the lad he had started training just under eighteen months before took the ball to bowl in a match against England, no less, his mind struggling to come to terms with this amazing feat. Tim caught both batsmen unawares, very nearly getting Engel first ball with an in-swinger that could have taken middle peg, or been adjudged LBW, had it not been for a slight inside edge that the umpire clearly heard.

Chandra, testing his spin for the first time, was a little expensive but considering he hadn't used his stock ball – 'the fast ball' – it was a good performance.

All was going well when suddenly everything changed. Khan and Arthur saw it simultaneously: a huge bank of dark cloud was moving in their direction. It had just begun to edge its nose over the back of the western stand; within the hour it would be over the ground. Arthur knew he had to leave Tim and Chandra on for vital match practice, but he could not take his hat off and permit either to bowl at top speed as they still needed to get their line right. To let them cut loose would spell disaster, but they badly needed to take wickets. Khan on the other hand had a duty to up the tempo, which he did as he and Engel put on 60 more runs during Tim and Chandra's ten overs. With the score at 174 for 2 it looked as though the earlier fireworks from the bowlers were just a spot of luck on the part of the home side. Fryer by now was laughing with other spectators and looking smug and relaxed. Khan was on 99 and looked well set to take his side to victory. At the rate they were scoring it would be over in another twenty minutes or so.

Then Cantor stepped in, taking the unusual step of giving Tim another over when Arthur thought he was about to be removed from the attack. He whipped off his hat. Tim's heart missed a beat, knowing this would be his last over if he did not perform. His first ball flashed past Engel's bat like a comet. The crowd sat up straight once more – it had been a while since such a ball had been bowled. From the non-striker's end Khan thought to himself, 'Here we go again'. Tim's second ball was a repeat of the previous one and hit Engel's boot before rearranging his stumps. He limped off, a sorry sight, with a broken toe.

The England number five was also the captain, Stan 'The Man' Coleman. Khan had a word with him as he walked out but Coleman was always his own man. One of his strengths was assessing the situation for himself. Tim greeted him with three deliveries that flew past the England skipper, who was just trying to survive. He hit the last ball in the air to cover, trying to force the pace. It was an easy catch but George made a meal of it and dropped it. Tim was crushed but downplayed his anguish on George's behalf, while George looked for a big hole to put his head into.

Cantor, sensing a shift in the tempo, put Jim and Frank back on. Arthur decided on one warm-up over for each, then the hat would come off. Khan picked up where he had left off, reaching his 100 off Jim with a back-foot drive through covers. Coleman chipped in too with three unconvincing fours off Frank, who Arthur had realised was more accurate when bowling flat out. After the two warm-up overs England were 193 for 3 with 30 runs needed to win.

With the hat removed from Arthur's head, Jim felt it was time to lift his game. Khan took a single off the first ball of his second over and with Coleman facing, Jim's second ball was a blinder. The England captain had started to push forward but the ball found the gap between his bat and pad and crashed into his stumps. The crowd was suddenly silent as Jim and the rest of the England 'A' team celebrated wildly.

In came England's highly fancied number 6, Mick Franks. A fidgety player with electric footwork, he was an excellent player of spin and always impatient to get on with things. He cracked Jim's first ball to the boundary and guided his fourth ball, a much slower one, wide of third man for two. Jim speared the next one into the ground with everything he had. It was short and Franks, startled by the pace this time, was late onto it with his shot. He looked completely out of control and only managed to pop the ball up into the air. Jim, following through, took a very simple catch and Franks departed, caught and bowled for 6. Meanwhile, the ever-crafty Khan had slipped past Franks as the ball was skied and took strike for the remaining ball of the over in order to protect the lower order from Jim's venomous spell.

Harry Winter strode to the crease. The reliable wicketkeeper and Khan would surely see them through – or so the crowd thought – especially when Khan showed his amazing skill by taking a 3 from the final ball to edge closer to the winning score and retain the strike.

In the following over, Frank's first ball hit Khan's bat so hard he almost lost his grip on it. He shook his hands furiously, trying to restore some feeling in them.

It was then that Arthur saw Fryer shoot a nervous glance sideways. Khan wasted no time at all on Frank's next ball, which was a no-ball. The early call from the umpire allowed him a free swing at it and he sent it a mile into the crowd. It was a magnificent shot. The players all got behind Frank who came in to bowl again. Khan stroked the ball back to the big man who could not get down to field it quickly enough and it escaped his giant paw. Winter spotted the opportunity to scamper through for a single, which was not what Khan had in mind and he only just made it to the non-striker's end before Edwin swooped and fired the ball into the stumps. It was a close thing but the batsmen were safe. Frank's fourth ball gave Winter no hope as the diminutive keeper played all around a ball that took his middle and off stumps right out the ground.

The next man in was Fredericks. Khan issued stern instructions to him. With the score on 208 for 6 the game was in the balance but still tipped in England's favour as long as Khan remained out in the middle.

Three balls remained in the over and Frank was unlucky not to dismiss Fredricks as the ball beat him continuously. If there had been another coat of varnish on the stumps, Frank would have had his second wicket.

Arthur noticed the man next to Fryer had vacated his seat so he made his way over. Before he sat down he ensured that Jim could see where he was. Although he was disappointed that Arthur's hat was on, Jim followed his instructions and bowled accordingly.

'So what do you think, Bob?' Arthur asked Fryer.

'You've been busy,' Fryer admitted, 'but you still have a long way to go.'

'What's it going to take, Bob?' Arthur asked Fryer as Jim bowled to Khan who drove him to the boundary for four. The score moved to 212-6.

'They're still too erratic,' Bob told Arthur.

'They're playing their first game in four months – against England!' Arthur muttered under his breath.

'Look, I'm just telling you. I feel their pace is not very consistent,' replied Fryer.

'Well, that's because my hat is on!' Arthur told him and

146

tapped his head as Jim was hit for four again. Now it was 216-6.

Fryer looked at Arthur in total confusion.

'They only bowl at full pace when my hat is off. Watch,' Arthur explained as he stood up and took his hat off.

Walking back to his mark, Jim had noticed that Arthur was now hatless and added a couple of paces to his run-up, readying himself to bowl at maximum pace. His next ball was hardly visible to the naked eye. Khan played at it and got an edge that flew through the slips to the boundary.

Fryer's was interested but at that moment he got up to leave, showing the true depth of his arrogance. 'I've got to hand it to you, Arthur, they're nippy all right. Just not nippy enough.'

Arthur got to his feet. Reaching deep into his coat pocket he produced a small brass horn.

As Fryer started to trot down the steps, a vibrant blast from behind stopped him in his tracks and he turned to see Arthur removing the horn from his lips. The entire crowd and all the players had heard the sound of the horn and looked in its direction. Arthur sat back down as if nothing had happened, but some of the older spectators were highly amused.

'Going hunting, old boy?' asked one man close to Arthur.

'You could say that,' he replied with a quick glance at Fryer.

Out in the middle, Arthur's men had heard the horn too. George called out, 'Think that might be the sign, Jim?'

Arthur watched as Jim prepared to bowl, then turned to Fryer who was still rooted to the spot on the stairs. 'Mr Fryer, surely you can stay for just four more runs?'

With the eyes of all the officials upon him, Fryer had no choice but to sit down again.

Jim looked at the scoreboard and knew that with Khan on strike there was no room for error. He concentrated all his resources on sending down a formidable delivery that pitched around Khan's feet. It was wickedly fast and most people didn't see the ball, including Khan who played at a vague red blur homing in on his toes. He barely managed to get bat on ball, but in the end kept his defences intact as the ball dribbled to mid-wicket. The next delivery was a waist-high off-cutter; the batsman prudently decided to pull his bat away from the deadly ball as it shot past with frightening speed. Jim's last ball was pitched short and Khan prepared to pull it square. But the pace of it was too great and it flashed past his head as he jerked it out of harm's way in a purely reflex action. Unable to score the winning runs, Khan was kept away from the strike.

Jim had a chat with Cantor and they called on Chandra, who appeared pleasantly surprised. He jumped to it though and hurried in from mid-wicket to take the ball. Chandra warmed up by tossing the ball to Edwin a couple of times and rolling his wrist about, which amused Fryer.

'You choose a spinner at a time like this?' he chortled.

'Who said he's a spinner?' replied Arthur.

Fryer's smile quickly disappeared.

Chandra peered down the pitch at Fredricks before bounding in as if he was hopping from one cloud to another, so light on his feet was he. Fredericks watched him through half-closed eyes as Chandra's arm whizzed past his ear in a blur. His fast ball hit the batsman's front pad before the poor man could move. Chandra was up immediately, appealing to the umpire with supreme confidence. The crowd drew a collective breath as the dreaded finger was raised and Chandra and the team went wild. Fredericks had a long walk back to the pavilion and Barney Talbot marched out with real purpose about him. Alas, it was a walk of false bravado. He was attempting to look confident, but inside his stomach churned like a swirling ocean. He went through the usual motions and took guard after a few words with Khan.

Chandra peered at him as if something were wrong, before finally calling to him, 'Are you sure your bat's the right way round?'

Talbot had a quick look to check but it was only Chandra up to his old tricks. He grinned at Talbot, then at the umpires. Talbot looked duly unimpressed having been made a fool of. The crowd fell silent as Chandra called his slips in.

The next ball was well flighted and sure enough turned a good deal to Chandra's absolute delight. It beat the bat and was taken safely by the keeper. The third ball was tossed high again and Talbot managed to sweep it for two runs.

With little to play with now, the team urged Chandra on. He attempted to bowl a wrong-un which jumped up sharply on Talbot as he pushed forward, hitting high up on the bat's blade and dropping just short of the close-in fieldsman. Chandra pulled in another fieldsman so he had one either side of the batsman.

He came in for his fifth ball and flicked his arm over. It was another of his faster balls, this time pitched short. Completely unprepared, Talbot jumped in a reckless fashion and pulled his head back, trying to raise the bat in front of himself defensively. Taking his eyes off the ball, it hit his gloves and popped up gently, giving the close-in short leg a simple catch. 222 for 8 and Mathew French was striding to the crease. Chandra was almost salivating.

'You'll be pleased to know that I can spin the ball now,' he called to French who tried to ignore him.

The new batsman looked around at the fielders' positions.

Chandra was unable to restrain himself. 'Don't be a hero, Mathew. Last ball of the over,' he called, even trying the umpire's patience.

'Enough!' the umpire warned him.

Chandra returned to his mark with a grin from ear to ear. Flicking the ball from hand to hand, he mumbled something over and over again under his breath, not taking his eyes off French. Finally he skipped in and ripped on the ball, spinning it furiously. French's eyes were as big as saucers as he watched it float harmlessly towards him. His feet shuffled as he danced to meet the pitch of the ball, his back-lift high as he prepared to take an almighty swipe. Dropping a little earlier than he'd anticipated, the ball hit the pitch and deviated. French's flashing blade snicked the red leather as it wafted past, the ball flew wide and the wicketkeeper held the catch, just for good measure whipping the bails off for a stumping as well. A stunned French spun around to ground his bat but it was all too late. Chandra went mad with joy.

'That's one way to get into the record books, Mathew. Caught and stumped!'

French watched as Chandra was engulfed by his team-mates, while up in the stands, Fryer was beginning to feel a little ill. Meanwhile Arthur was having the time of his life, standing and cheering as he waved his hat skywards. Already the thought had entered his head: was it possible he had coached his band of bowlers to victory over the English national team? Only Khan stood in their way.

Arthur could see Jim and Cantor talking again. Who was to bowl the last over? Frank and Jim had troubled Khan the most, but Frank was erratic and Jim had bowled enough already, without any luck. Edwin's pace was not to their level and the responsibility was too great for Tim. So that left George. Jim dropped the ball into George's hand. It was a good choice as he'd not had the chance to bowl fast all day and was gagging for an over of speed – exactly what Arthur had been hoping for.

George limbered up and went through his action slowly. Khan only needed two runs and it was all over. If Khan was nervous, it certainly didn't show as he leant coolly on his bat watching the goings-on around him. Finally, he took strike and the umpire glanced back at George as a means of communicating the fact that all was ready.

With Jean and Mrs Cheshire were squeezing the life out of each other's hands, Arthur did not flinch. Holding his head high, he wondered what was going through George's mind at that moment.

George moved his marker back and gathered his thoughts, thinking only of the spot where the ball must pitch. He knew he had to put everything into the delivery. At last he set off. Lengthening his stride as he approached the wicket, he carried his weight beautifully and his delivery stride was almost casual. It didn't look as if he was about to bowl extremely fast, but George's upper body and back muscles were finely tuned after months of training. His action didn't unfold like the others, but seemed to detonate violently. The delivery hit the pitch and ricocheted off it like a tracer. Khan was halfway though his back lift when he realised the ball was actually cutting back into him and headed towards his chest at speed. Perhaps it was an act of self-preservation that forced such a stroke from Khan as he tried to cut down on the ball desperately. The ball caught an inside edge and sped under his armpit to be taken high by the wicketkeeper. After playing such a wonderful innings, Khan was suddenly made to look like a schoolboy. Fryer wanted to curl up and die.

George jogged down the pitch, his arm high above his head with his forefinger pointing to the sky. The crowd were aghast and rose to their feet as one to applaud the efforts of these complete unknowns. Slowly the victory sank in – Arthur's Super Six had beaten the best England had to offer.

As Arthur stood up and clapped proudly, Fryer, livid with anger and frustration, clenched his fists angrily, knowing his behaviour was on show. He stood waiting for Arthur to stop clapping in order to shake his hand, but others in the immediate vicinity got there first and congratulated him wholeheartedly.

The man in the blue blazer turned to Fryer after a brief chat with Arthur saying, 'Perhaps you two should swap jobs,' which Arthur thought was wonderful.

Wild scenes followed on the field. Khan stayed out there waiting for the celebrations to die down before eventually congratulating all the bowlers and walking off with them.

In the stands, Jean and Mrs Cheshire were acting most unladylike, shouting and hugging each other. The excitement around Arthur had died down a bit, but still Fryer stood by, biting his tongue.

'Congratulations,' he eventually offered dryly. 'I suppose we'd had better have a chat at some stage.'

'Of course, now that you have faith in me again,' agreed Arthur.

Fryer finally allowed himself a smile.

'I still think you're mad,' he said. Arthur obviously knew when to keep quiet and let Fryer finish. 'I'll be in touch.' With that Fryer made his exit to lick his wounds.

Arthur turned his attention back to the field as his players came off. The triumphant band all looked up to him and clapped together in recognition of their coach's efforts. The smiles on their faces were only matched by the joy and immense satisfaction Arthur felt. He clapped back and nodded to them as his mind ticked over, already focusing on the next leg of the journey.

On the way home, as Jean and Mrs Cheshire explained the details of their cunning plot, revelling in the sheer excitement of it, it was agreed that they were the deadliest dinner ladies in the land.

Arriving back at Charmy Down, the players were expecting at least a celebratory drink but they could see Arthur was miles away and as he didn't appear inclined, they too went off the boil. He even suggested they do a run and stretch to end the day, and, although it was near dark, there was no dissension and off they went.

The following morning it was a different story as the kitchen throbbed with energy. No one had much time to talk as liberal amounts of food were shovelled into mouths. Jean busied herself clearing plates and cups, and stacking them by the sink. Edwin picked scraps off some plates and dropped them into Biggles' gaping jaw. Tim and Jim eventually got to washing and drying dishes. Arthur peeled a banana as Chandra tossed an apple in his hand, still talking about his dismissal of French.

'That boy learnt an important lesson yesterday,' he told everyone in the room prepared to listen. 'Humility!' he said almost shouting. 'One should go about one's business in a humble fashion. It's all about respect!' he concluded holding a finger aloft. Although no one was paying attention, they could hardly ignore his ramblings.

'Arthur, when you're finished peeling that thing can you please insert it in his throat,' Frank asked politely.

'Can you imagine the stick Fryer would have copped from his players?' Tim said.

'Ouch,' said George.

'Yeah. They would have felt totally stitched up,' Frank commented.

George, who had his head in a newspaper, looked up incensed. 'Hey! Listen to this!' He stood holding it high up in front of his face as he read, 'The English team's defeat was served to them for lunch as only one of their players was not affected by the mystery virus. Under no circumstances can a player be asked to perform at top level when a hospital bed is more appropriate. The opposition bowlers picked at the hapless batsmen like a vulture would a corpse. The prospect of an England victory was never likely, but due to an incomparable innings by Khan, it became a possibility in the dying stages of the game. Had it not been for a dubious caught behind, a fitting result might have been achieved.' George looked to the others for their reactions. 'I can't believe it!' he said through clenched teeth.

Arthur ate his banana not batting an eyelid as all hell broke loose around him.

'That's bollocks. *They* weren't poisoned. We only poisoned

our own team,' Tim appealed.

'Yeah. We won that fair and square. What the hell?' asked George again, seeing that Arthur was obviously not concerned. He squinted and pointed at the article. 'Have you read this, Arthur?' he asked angrily. Everyone looked towards Arthur for his answer. He sat back in his chair and put the banana skin on his plate.

'We need to play it down – you know, keep it quiet,' he explained, pointing at the paper.

'Why?' Tim asked.

'Think about it! Yesterday was a case of "Mission Accomplished". Gentlemen, we're here for seven more months! Fryer has come to the party!' he informed them casually. They were all stunned. 'Which means we're heading into Phase Two, lads, so we need to downplay yesterday's performance or it could jeopardise longer-term goals. There's no way we want anyone to know what we're up to!' He produced a small replica of the Ashes urn and placed it on the table saying, 'From now on things are going to get interesting!'

# Part Three

## The Tests

## 23

A week after the Super Six's first success, Arthur gave the squad two weeks off at short notice. Tim went home to see his parents then caught up with friends. Chandra spent time with his family, as did Jim Singleton. George wasted no time announcing he was going to France with Edwin and Frank deciding to tag along at the last minute. Arthur had written them all a mini-maintenance program to follow and ordered them to keep off the booze, singling out George. Even Jean and Mrs Cheshire had planned a trip together to see some of Jean's friends and a distant cousin of Mrs Cheshire's who lived in the Midlands. Everyone assumed Arthur would spend time in London with Fryer. But they were wrong.

After their break, George, Frank and Edwin all returned to Charmy Down in the old Jag, which they'd taken to France. Edwin's talent with engines had come in handy on a couple of occasions. Chandra turned up on Edwin's bicycle with Biggles perched in the rear-mounted basket – the minding of Biggles being part of the deal Edwin had struck when lending his bicycle.

It was a cool Monday morning as they regrouped. After Jim and Tim had arrived, the players milled about the front of the house greeting one another and exchanging stories. Presently they made their way inside and were stunned when a young woman in her mid-twenties walked out of the front door right into their midst.

'Hello,' she greeted them familiarly. 'You must be the players. I'm Alice.' The confident young woman briefly shook hands with all six players as they each mumbled their name to her. 'Nice to meet you all,' she said. 'You too,' she told Biggles with a quick scratch behind his ear. Turning and heading in the direction of the hanger, she gave a wave and was off. Slightly shell-shocked, the group looked on as she went. Biggles barked after her.

'Yeah, that's what I was thinking,' said George to the ball of muscle standing next to him.

Some other new arrivals were soon apparent, with all manner of large cardboard boxes tossed in a huge waste bin by the gate of the house. Most unusual of all, however, was the amount of noise coming from the hangar. It was normally a desolate place without the players, but now there was a group of strange people hanging around outside.

'Little man's been busy, ain't he,' Frank commented knowing Arthur would have been behind all the activity. After settling back into their rooms, they joined Tim, who was first down to the games room. They could see he was moving slower than normal.

'Have a good break, did we?' Frank asked. Tim peered up from behind his pint, not looking too good.

'You're hungover,' George announced.

Edwin opened the door for Biggles to run out and play as George poured beers and Frank racked up the pool balls.

'I had a big night at Middlesex Uni,' Tim admitted.

'Girls?' George asked excitedly.

'There were a couple around,' Tim admitted, adding, 'France must have been good. I noticed you're all looking very . . . *healthy*,' Tim joked.

The room became quiet.

'I told you we was eating too much,' Frank grumbled at George.

'D'you think Arthur will notice?' Edwin asked Tim in a worried tone.

Jim entered the room rubbing his hands. 'This place is a circus. Anyone know what's going on round here?' he asked no one in particular. They all looked at each other blankly.

'Well, no doubt Arthur will tell us soon enough.'

There was a crack as Frank sent the white ball into the pack. Chandra prowled about the other end of the table while Edwin peered out of the window towards the great hangar where a group of men had just emerged. He watched as they shook Arthur's hand and shared a quick joke with him before climbing aboard a minivan and departing. The minivan rumbled down the runway past the games room window and out of the front gate. Arthur, Alice and two other men were now heading back towards the Big House. Edwin pulled back from the window. Focusing on his reflection, he patted his hair down, and straightened his shirt and collar.

'I saw that Edwin. D'you fancy her?' George teased.

158

Edwin, embarrassed, took his beer and moved nearer to the fire. Eventually the door opened and Arthur showed his new guests into the room: Alice, Ted Doyle, who they'd already met, and a stranger.

Arthur surveyed his players. Seeing George, Edwin and Frank he asked, 'Who ate all the pies?' much to Tim and Chandra's delight.

Arthur was in a boisterous mood and introduced everyone.

'This is Alice and Jack. Get to know them – they'll be here during the week.'

There were introductions all round with George poking Edwin in the back as he greeted Alice. What Jack and Alice did was still a mystery, however, as Arthur was off sorting out a beer for himself and his guests.

After dinner George inquired. 'So, Arthur, now that you and Fryer are working together again, does that mean French is coming back?'

'He did mention it,' replied Arthur as the others said nothing. 'But I decided against it.'

'Are we going to get on with Fryer?' George asked, slightly concerned.

It was a good question, one Arthur had asked himself several times. 'We won't see him much until May next year,' he told them.

'That wasn't what I asked,' George persisted.

Arthur thought for a moment.

'You lot performing well is the key to getting on with Fryer. He'll be fine, George. I'll make sure of that.'

Then, as if suddenly remembering something, he asked George, 'Did you tell your father?'

'About what?' George asked.

'The game against England, of course.'

'Oh! No, not yet,' George said. 'Thought I'd surprise him in about . . . mmm, seven months' time.'

After a couple of hours of catching up, the men started to filter upstairs and queued for the bathroom. Tim and George still had their drinking hats on and when Arthur left them, it was with the promise they would finish the ones they were on and then lock up.

Weary, Arthur was looking forward to a restful night's sleep. Being last out of the bathroom, he flicked off the light and closed the door. As he made his way towards his room, he noticed a light flickering outside and heard a car engine.

Gripping the wheel tightly, Tim kept his eyes fixed ahead but couldn't help looking behind occasionally. Some 10 metres behind the car George swayed in and out of view. Standing on a skateboard he held a rope that was tied to the rear of the Jag, as he glided from one side of the runway to the other.

On the return run Tim made out a figure in the middle of the runway. If cars could creep that's what it did until stopping in front of Arthur, who walked slowly down the side of the car, hands clasped behind his back.

Back at the house an audience had gathered upstairs watching the distant figures through a hallway window. Alice joined the group.

'What's going on,' she asked.

'We're watching Arthur. He's about to kill George.'

Passing the driver's window, Arthur ignored Tim who shrank back behind the wheel. Calmly approaching George, Arthur looked down at the oversized skateboard then up at him.

At the house they could see Arthur was now having words with George. A door opened and Jean appeared.

'What's all this fuss?' she asked as they made room for her to join the gallery. When they turned their attention back to the scene on the runway the three were almost out of view. Everyone watched as the car rolled slowly along the runway with Arthur teetering behind it on the skateboard and George jogging beside him, holding his arm for support.

# 24

The weather at Charmy Down had changed for the worse as a late October chill set in, making it much harder for them all to get out of bed in the mornings. The breakfast menu changed again with the addition of porridge and a noticeable reduction in the fried foods on offer. Bacon and sausages were now a once-a-week special on Saturday mornings; fruit every other morning became compulsory. Jean had acquired some recipes for high-energy juices, which Arthur thought a good idea, and made them in a noisy juicer.

Ted set off home on the Tuesday after they had all returned, while the rest of them made their way to the hangar straight after breakfast. It had been a long while since the players had trained in the hangar, considering it had always been a daily occurrence.

'Now you lot might notice some changes,' Arthur told them as he retrieved the key to the door from his pocket. 'We will be doing things a little differently from now on.' Arthur and Frank pulled the heavy door open allowing Tim to dart inside and flick on the power. It was still gloomy but when the massive halogen lights flickered and came alive with a burst, everyone stood speechless. Gone were the maze of ropes and pulleys, the large blocks of wood and old-fashioned free weights. In their place was a collection of huge steel structures. The stale smell of ropes and the old world had gone; instead there was the stench of grease and burnt metal. No one spoke as they took in their new facility and its ominous-looking equipment. It was Edwin who ventured in first, the others following slowly.

'He's going to turn us into Borgs,' George stated.

Seeing Arthur's confusion, Alice explained. 'Half-man, half-computer,' she whispered.

'Oh,' huffed Arthur.

'What the hell are these, Arthur?' Jim asked in awe of the enormous machines.

'This was what I wanted to build back at Good Walloping all those years ago,' he said for Jim's benefit. Jim's eyes bulged as he rounded a corner and saw his name on one of the huge things.

'I don't think we had the budget,' he murmured. 'No wonder they binned you,' quickly adding, 'No disrespect.'

Chandra was running around looking for something with his name on it, having figured there would be one designed to suit him.

'Are these all designed for us individually?' Jim asked.

'Three each to be precise, each one designed to do much what the ropes and pulleys did, but having been specially designed for each of you, they can isolate your muscle groups in a far more precise manner. The machines can be configured accurately and have the load increased or decreased with ease,' Arthur explained.

The others had had a quick look at the set-up and were milling around Arthur, who was still inspecting the machines as he went on, 'These will make you a little faster. Not much, only a little. The old gear got us started, but this will give us the edge.'

'Your own personal fast-bowling gymnasium, boys,' Alice announced proudly.

'Crikey, we really roughed it for *four* months,' George commented.

Frank looked at Alice and Jack, and asked, 'So, what are you two then?'

'Biomechanics and Exercise Physiology,' Alice said simply.

'I make things,' was all Jack offered.

Frank nodded in appreciation of their no-frills replies.

They were all eager to start.

'Right, who wants to go first?' George asked unnecessarily and they all followed Chandra to his corner of the hangar. His steel arm hung from a hook that in turn hung from a long rope that trailed down from the roof. The glove was mounted on an old plaster hand that Edwin had found in a box on the floor of the Jag. The silver balls were all placed in their original box inside a wooden container. Right against the back wall was a small machine no taller than Chandra himself.

'Is this it?' he asked Arthur. When Arthur didn't reply, he turned to Alice and Jack. 'This *is* it?' he wanted to know but neither Alice nor Jack made any comment.

'We ran out of money,' Arthur explained, upsetting Chandra. 'When we looked at everything you already had, it was pretty much all you needed.'

'That's right. Arthur's gear was actually doing a great job

mechanically. We just needed one more thing to maximize the strengthening phase,' Alice clarified.

Chandra reflected for a moment as the others tried not to laugh. 'OK, so it's a lot smaller but will it work?' he asked, not realising what he'd just said.

Arthur looked down at the floor as the others giggled.

The apparatuses were lined up in rows, each of which had one of the players' names marked on it. Arthur decided to give a demonstration of the new equipment and Frank was selected to be the guinea pig. Jack nodded towards the largest of the three machines and as Frank stepped forward he was assisted by Alice and Jack into the frame of the metal beast. He was still very visible to the others as the open design allowed observers to see through the framework. Once inside he was instructed to position his body at a side-on angle, at the point in his delivery when his back foot hit the ground and he started bringing his upper body into the equation. His posture was reminiscent of a giant starfish and allowed the others to identify four major muscle groups that came into play at different times. The machine Frank was encased within had been designed so that each movement could be worked on in isolation as others were locked off. When all the exercises had been completed one at a time, the apparatus could be unlocked again. Before all the movements could be brought together to work in unison, the subject had to stabilise himself by wearing a torso brace, which gave him the impression of floating in a free state while inside the machine. Working together with added resistance the effect was incredible, as bowler and machine seemed to come alive together, almost suspended in time, yet performing part of the bowler's action without actually moving forward. Frank got the hang of the whole concept quite quickly with Alice and Jack's instruction. The remainder of the players looked on in awe.

'I can see why no one has thought of this before,' Tim offered to no one in particular. 'They're amazing, Arthur!'

Arthur was full of pride.

Jack Kennard tinkered with an adjuster as he told the group, 'Arthur was right. Despite their impressive appearance, these machines will only improve your current speed marginally. The old system you were using has really laid the foundations for you all, but these new ones will give you the edge. I actually think one of you might break records.'

The others watched as Frank came to the end of his routine, and Arthur continued where Jack had left off. 'Alice and Jack carried out a risk assessment on these machines and found that unless correctly trained and calibrated a serious injury could occur. So they will be staying with us for a while to ensure good practice is established. We are going to take you all through this individually this morning. Each of you has to learn and understand everyone else's machines, so you'll have to sit through the whole thing. It's going to be a long morning, I'm afraid.' Arthur looked at Frank strapped into his apparatus and declared, 'May as well start with muggins here.'

Alice returned from Arthur's desk in the corner of the hangar with a set of charts for her and Jack. The others all sat down next to the machine as she addressed the group. 'Now first we'll run over the basic principles that all the machines have in common,' she said, assuming an air of authority.

But Frank brought her up short by putting his hand up awkwardly. 'Can you just hold off a minute? I have to go to the little boy's room,' he told her.

The next day the training was over by about 3.00 p.m. and every player had confirmed that they had sufficient knowledge of all the machines to be able to assist one another with training. Weight-load guides had to be followed and before a weight load could be increased, either Alice or Jack had to be consulted. To stop a complete muscular imbalance occurring, a program was designed to train the non-active muscle groups on the opposite side of the body. This way the likelihood of injury was minimised and total harmony was guaranteed.

The following day it was down to work and life around Charmy Down settled into the familiar routine that had been in place for the first four months. The players had a long seven-month haul ahead of them until the first Test against Australia. Arthur, meanwhile, was constantly trying to come up with ways to break the monotony, although it was sometimes the players who provided distractions. George often used to steer their evening runs away from the neighbouring farmland and into the nearby forest. Often they would run along a ridge which sat high above a small farm on the eastern flank of the airfield. The farm's owner, Bert McCabe, was an elderly gent but his eyesight was perfect. He became accustomed to seeing six ghostly silhouettes lurching across the ridge against the evening sky – Tim usually out in the front, followed by four large black shadows and a short stout frame bringing up the rear.

Chandra too kept everyone entertained, though not always intentionally. Having always fancied himself as a bit of an all-rounder, he took his batting quite seriously. In facing as much fast bowling as they had over the last four to five months, everyone's batting had obviously improved. When quizzed by Chandra about whose batting was the best, Arthur's only response was, 'George is handy and that's about it!' But Chandra's initiative had to be admired four weeks later when his name was called out to bat – he got ready eagerly and waited for Edwin to finish his session. It was then Arthur noticed something unusual attached to the back of Chandra's bat.

'What on earth's that?' he asked.

Chandra calmly explained. 'I've been thinking too, you know and have applied your own principles to my batting!' Arthur said nothing but at least looked interested. 'You see, if this bat is too heavy for me but I continue to use it, then when I go back to using a correctly weighted bat I will have more time to play the ball.' Arthur was looking reasonably impressed. 'But wait!' Chandra told him, 'There's more.' Now he had Arthur's complete attention. Chandra pulled out a pair of very old thick-rimmed glasses and held them up to Arthur who could see they were very strong indeed. 'If I wear these and therefore make it extremely hard to see the ball . . . then when I take them off the ball will appear as big as a basketball you see and easy to hit!'

Arthur thought about it. 'Right, Edwin, out now please,' Arthur told him.

'What do you think?' Chandra pestered him.

'Well, I'm not sure–' Arthur started, but before he could finish, Chandra butted in.

'It'll be fine. I'll show you.' Chandra shuffled off down to the end of the net.

Jim was the next to bowl as Chandra took guard, holding his hand up for Jim to wait before commencing his run-up. By now everyone's attention was focused on Chandra who was putting on the glasses, which made his eyes seem enormous; he squinted down the pitch and took strike as everyone watched in disbelief.

'Give me your best shot, Slim!' Chandra called out to Jim, who was laughing as he ran in to bowl. His spikes, however, accidentally caught the ground near the crease causing him to stumble slightly as he delivered the ball. The upshot was that he bowled a little shorter than he'd intended. Chandra, blind as a bat, didn't move an inch, the ball cracked him hard, flush on the helmet, and he collapsed in a lifeless heap. Everyone ran to his aid. Once they had established he wasn't hurt at all they had a long laugh at his expense. In no time seven was up again shaking his head and rubbing his temple.

'I think maybe I will leave Arthur to do the thinking,' was his only comment.

Rattled a little, he carried on batting after ditching the glasses and bat, later blaming the incident on 'a very suspect playing surface'.

Although everyone took to Alice immediately, most of them felt Jack Kennard was a different kettle of fish. A seemingly intelligent character he appeared fastidious and stand-offish, preferring to keep to himself. He had a clean-cut, no-nonsense look about him, ate like a sparrow, must have been in his late thirties and always had his head in a book. His dedication to the machines was beyond question – if not tinkering with them he was questioning the players, sometimes even jumping into the machines to test a particular movement. Alice had boundless energy, a genuine willingness to get involved and brought much-needed spark to the place. She restructured the players' fitness regime and maintenance programme, as well as adding some yoga to the stretching class.

After seven weeks with the new machines Christmas was suddenly upon them and a night of festivities was planned before everyone returned to their families for a week. Mrs Cheshire was going to travel back to Wielding Willow with Arthur, Jean, Tim and Jim. It was also the night the group bid farewell to Alice and Jack, although they would be returning sporadically in the New Year. Speeches were made, gifts exchanged and a good time was had by all. As all nights ended in the games room, this one was no exception other than the fact that they arrived there much later than usual. Edwin, knowing Alice was to leave the next day, was trying to pluck up the courage to say something nice to her. When he finally made his move, Alice made hers too. He saw her slip a piece of paper into George's hand and give him a quick kiss on the cheek. Caught unawares, George happened to glance at Edwin, who looked absolutely crestfallen, made a beeline for his pint and took a big swig from it. Moments later there was someone standing next to him. Edwin froze. It was George, who held his arm tightly.

'Edwin, I didn't know,' George whispered.

'What – that I liked her or that she liked you?' Edwin asked.

'That she was going to do that!' George said earnestly.

'It's OK, George,' Edwin said finding it hard to look his mate in the eye.

'No mate, it's not OK,' George said. 'Not if you're feeling crap.'

'I shouldn't get my hopes up. I always do this. It's because I've never had a proper girl. They know.' Edwin said.

George didn't have to think too hard for something to say. 'Edwin, you of all people *should* get your hopes up. One day you *will* meet someone.'

'Yeah, well, no offence, but I hope *you* ain't going to be around then,' Edwin said. George was cheered by the fact Edwin still had his sense of humour intact. 'George, it's fine really. You'd better go and chat with her or she'll know what's going on,' Edwin suggested. George put his hand on Edwin's shoulder and smiled.

Arthur tapped his glass and called out, 'Last orders.' So saying he held up his glass. 'And here's to the next twenty-eight.'

'The next twenty-eight what?' Jim asked.

'Number of weeks before the Ashes,' he announced, tossing a nice looking wrong 'un out the back of his hand.

167

## 25

Arthur weighed everyone before going on holiday, warning them that anyone more than a kilo overweight returning from leave would be subjected to a horrendous punishment. It was stupid of him to have weighed himself at the same time, for when everyone came in under the kilo on returning to Charmy Down, Frank asked Arthur to step on the scales. He was horrified to see that he'd put *on* 1.2 kilos.

'Right then, what was the punishment, Arthur?' Frank asked.

Arthur scratched his head. 'Hadn't really figured one out,' he admitted.

'If you had to do what we do every day you wouldn't have put it on in the first place,' Chandra pointed out.

'That's it!' Tim shouted. 'You'll have to do what we do.'

'That's ridiculous – I'm sixty years old. How can I possibly bowl fast? Besides, I wouldn't fit into those monstrosities,' Arthur said, referring to the machines and duly resting his case.

'He'd fit into Chandra's,' Tim noted.

Arthur gave him a deadly stare.

Chandra took up the argument. 'Indeed. You told me once you wanted to spin a ball. Let *me* teach *you*,' Chandra pleaded.

Arthur made a mental note to exclude himself from any bets, challenges or games for the next five months.

They got back to work right away with Arthur more involved than ever – literally! He walked, he ran as much as he could, he bowled awkwardly, he batted – playing and missing a lot and wearing every piece of protective equipment available – he did fielding drills and even wore the 'arm of amour', the 'spin glove', and used the 'silver bollocks'.

When the time for his weigh-in came two weeks later, Arthur passed with flying colours having lost 2.1 kilos. Jean had commented on how good he was looking but he assumed she was just teasing him.

He made a habit of staying in touch with the players thereafter by continuing to do many of the activities with them, particularly enjoying Chandra's exercises, even though he couldn't spin the ball yet. He was unable to develop the right muscles in his ageing body but every now and then he beat the bat anyway, thereby convincing himself it had moved - though deep down he knew it hadn't at all. Everyone admired Arthur's willingness to get into the nets and have a go, telling the bowlers still to bowl at 70-80 per cent to him. Frank bowled him four times in a row one morning, and George hit him a heavy blow on the forearm that shook the bat from his grip and a cuss from his lips.

Arthur had Fryer send a fielding coach down for a fortnight to dust away any cobwebs in that department.

It was obvious that George was spending more time than normal on the phone in the evenings rather than topping up pints. As a result there was much leg pulling about there being a girl, but the only one who knew the truth was Edwin, and he soon noticed that George's attitude was falling off. Edwin tried in vain to cheer him up on occasions, but eventually George had to face facts, telling Edwin in a dejected tone, 'I'm pathetic. I've been bitten by the love bug.'

The next day while training, Edwin became increasingly concerned about his machine. He told Arthur it wasn't running smoothly and he felt that his body should be set at a better angle. Arthur immediately got on the phone to Alice and the next day, George got the surprise of his life. When he learnt the reason for her being summoned he felt immense gratitude towards Edwin.

Alice found that certain settings on the machines were actually in need of minor adjustments as they had all settled a bit after so much use, and ended up staying a week. Arthur felt it was a worthwhile trip and heaped praise on Edwin for being so in tune with his physical requirements.

Edwin often volunteered to do extra perimeter duties as Arthur had voiced concern over security. It was on one such check early one morning that Edwin spotted a figure in a nearby field with what looked like a pair of binoculars. Hurrying into an adjoining paddock, Edwin outflanked the man. Closing in on him slowly it became apparent the man was quite elderly and dressed casually in the manner of a local. Edwin got the impression very quickly it was an inquisitive neighbour and decided upon a friendly approach. It was Bert McCabe, whose curiosity had finally got the better of him.

Edwin and he had a long chat with Edwin careful not to give too much away. He told the old man what he had witnessed was simply a new training camp involved with cricket and asked him not mention it to any other folk for a couple of months. Further conversation revealed that Bert's father had been a pilot at Charmy Down who had sadly died in 1945 five months before Bert was born. Naturally this interested Edwin enormously and he extended an invitation to Bert to have a drink with the group one evening.

April's arrival surprised everyone. They had all been working so hard that no one even made plans for any April Fool pranks. Fryer had been down twice in recent months and wanted to bring Khan with him to face the bowlers in order to test their competence. When Arthur refused, Fryer wanted to time the deliveries instead, but again Arthur refused – as he pointed out, it had been agreed that in May the players would be released to play some games for their old clubs in order to gain valuable match practice. But even then their speeds would be capped. His plan was to include them in the England squad only a week before the first Test, and Fryer could pick the bowlers from there. Secretly, as part of the deal he had struck with Fryer, Arthur had the rights to selection – it was on a handshake that Fryer would not overrule him. Overall, Fryer was very satisfied with the speed of the players. In addition to the fielding coach, Fryer sent a fast-bowling coach, and a spin coach for Chandra. All the players found these sessions were beneficial and their opinion of Fryer improved after that. The fast bowling coach reported back favourably to Fryer and as his faith in them grew, so too did theirs in him.

In the background all the while was the master puppeteer, Arthur, pulling the strings, making suggestions, offering encouragement and guiding his ship with a deft hand towards its destination. He worked them harder then ever before and they gave him their all. The nightly ritual of a pint or two after a hard day remained a constant.

When he entered the games room one night, Arthur found it strangely empty. Searching the Big House he found them all in the lounge asleep in front of the television. It was quite a sight to see Frank pinning Mrs Cheshire to the sofa with his massive head flopped over to one side, and Jean sandwiched between an unconscious George and Jim, unable to move.

Late in April, Fryer spent a night at Charmy Down and got a taste of what it had been like for the players for the last nine months. He was impressed with the rapport Arthur had built up among them. After the visit, Arthur saw a noticeable difference in Fryer's attitude – he was wholeheartedly involved in the project and no longer distanced himself from them. Yet Arthur remained on guard when it came to Fryer. He had separated 'faith and trust' in Fryer's case. He had to for he had seen Fryer turn his back on the group once before and needed to protect his players and all they'd worked for. If there was one thing Arthur knew about people in high places, it was that they disliked falling from them.

The players continued to train incredibly hard as they closed in on the summer ahead. The results came as their human framework took on a new look that Jack once described as 'reedy'. During the long spells on the apparatus, the players would sometimes talk among themselves, mainly during the warm-up sets. Once the weights were increased, the effort required often made talking impossible. The time spent on the apparatus was quite short really, but was often long enough to lose oneself in thoughts of other things. When this happened they each dreamed of different things. Of all the bowlers, only Tim regularly thought of nothing else but bowling, or playing cricket, or winning matches, or holding the Ashes high. In his mind, Tim had already played 100 Tests for England. Jim thought of cricket too, and his father. He desperately wanted to make up for lost time. There had been too many days spent being angry at the world and Jim knew he'd wasted the best part of his youth ignoring what people had been telling him all along about using his abilities. This was his last chance to be the best he could be. After this chapter of his life was over, Jim couldn't imagine doing anything else other spending more time with his family.

Chandra dreamt of the copy of *Wisden* kept on display in the family restaurant turned to the page that outlined his career stats and in which he was described as a 'mesmerizing' spin bowler with several 'five fors' to his name. George just thought of Alice. If he did think of cricket, it was always in the bar having a beer after a day's training. Frank's fear had much to do with letting his mates and Arthur down; his devastating county season was some years back and all but forgotten. Strangely, Frank feared his bowling wouldn't be up to scratch, constantly worrying about the press finding out he wasn't a regular player, so that Arthur's decision to select him in the first place would seem foolhardy. This, together with his fear of bowling too many wides and no-balls, meant that even in the game against England, he had never attempted to bowl at full pace. If anyone had their head in the clouds, though, it was Edwin. Whenever Edwin was lost in thought, he was probably in the cockpit of an imaginary Hurricane, hot on the tail of a Messerschmitt. It was Edwin's ambition to grow old quickly and get a job at Duxford Air Museum. He could picture himself talking to visitors about great air battles – but he was also determined now to have some fun before he got old. Someone had once told him he wasn't very good at having fun and since then he'd rather given up trying. His time at Charmy Down had changed things and he knew he was going to be sad when it all ended.

When the pain all got too much the players turned their minds to the warm-down, which was more or less a series of stretching exercises in which other less-emphasized anatomical areas were worked on. The players found it relaxing in contrast to the explosive nature of the machine workouts.

By the time May had begun, an ominous and noticeable metamorphosis had taken place. Gone were the excess kilos on Jim, Frank and, to a lesser extent, Chandra. Jim resembled a massive oak tree – his back was broader, his legs were much stronger and his neck was thicker. Frank's chest, due to his front-on action, had rounded out and his tummy had flattened. His enormous legs were able to carry his huge frame in limited bursts for his relatively short run-up. Everyone still thought he resembled a gigantic beer keg on legs. Where Edwin and George had been shapeless and rangy nine months ago, now they had developed strong sinewy limbs, and hulking shoulders on top of their powerful torsos.

Tim had remained the truest to his original physique with the addition of a few kilos. This was intentional as Arthur, Alice

172

and Jack had decided not to burden his frame with excess bulk in his early years, as it might hamper his long-term prospects and possibly lead to injuries. It was a clever approach. Tim's range of movement had been less impaired than anyone else's and his delivery was the most fluent to watch. His wiry frame delivered a whip-like action that generated fantastic speeds, which meant he would be pushing for selection right from the start.

One thing they were all acutely aware of was the changes to their physicality and the fact that some parts of their bodies were out of proportion, being either larger or more powerful than their opposing anatomical parts. Even to the untrained eye they looked out of place, something that was illustrated during a day trip to a local market town in order to fetch provisions. It was as if six beings from outer space had descended upon the town, with passers-by rooted to the spot as the massive forms approached. All were acutely aware of the stares and whispers from the townsfolk.

Fryer returned after an absence of over three weeks, just after all weights had been increased by 5.5 per cent – the last time it would happen. He was absolutely amazed. The speed they were now bowling at was faster than he'd ever seen. He pleaded with Arthur to carry out some time trials but Arthur steadfastly refused for he didn't want the players becoming complacent from any reaction that Fryer might show. Arthur had a plan and he was going to stick with it! Fryer not unreasonably continued to plead with Arthur to allow the current English batsmen to come down to Charmy Down and face the new boys as he felt facing such fast bowling would better prepare them to face the Australians. Still Arthur refused, telling Fryer that when he announced that their names were included in the squad to play the Australians they would be available for net sessions, and not before.

In mid-May, Alice and Jack returned to examine the players and carry out some tests. They felt everyone was in peak physical condition and that the final two weeks before the announcement of the English squad should be a maintenance only period. The players' confidence was sky high.

The practice games Arthur had planned were all cancelled as no injuries could be afforded. Stretching sessions were increased and weights dropped slightly. Arthur insisted on 90 per cent speed and 100 per cent accuracy during the net sessions in the final weeks. The normally relaxed atmosphere became slightly tense as the Ashes series drew nearer. Nerves were starting to creep in and Arthur pulled the reins a little tighter to compensate. Arthur spent more time with Frank than anyone during this period as the big man had become much less vocal around the players and looked as though he was fretting about some aspects of his game. Arthur had him concentrate on accuracy and asked Alice to recalibrate his machine. Reducing the weights and increasing Frank's repetitions ensured he didn't add to his bulk. Arthur and Alice decided to cut two machine workouts from both Frank and Jim's weekly schedule and replace them with net sessions and stretching. A final speed test showed a slight increase for them both. A pleasing nod from Arthur was all they needed to know they were ready.

Their time together at Charmy Down was whittled down to one last day and, although no one admitted it, they all felt a degree of sadness. Arthur had toyed with the idea of doing something different but when it dawned on him that it could be the last time they would all be together there, he only wanted one thing: the last day, which happened to be a Sunday, had to be just like all the others. Fryer had been down the day before and had told them the England squad was bigger than normal – all the present bowlers would be included.

'Members of your squad will have to earn their places in the Test team just like any player ever has,' Fryer told Arthur at his last meeting. 'There will be no free rides.'

The squad was due to be finalised by 4.00 p.m. in London, with the 6.00 p.m. evening news carrying the announcement to the nation. Followers of international cricket were bound to be in for a few shocks if six completely unknown names were to be included.

Edwin was in the games room with Bert McCabe examining some documents they had recently found relating to missions flown from the airfield, when the rest of the group drifted in.

'Let's go to a pub and watch it,' George insisted. 'I'd love to hear the comments when our names are read out. Frank who?

174

Tim who? George who?'

'Assuming Fryer selects you,' Arthur told him with a deadpan expression on his face. George's head snapped up to glare at Arthur, who raised his eyebrows.

'Evening Bert,' chirped the group as they noticed their guest. They all slumped heavily into the couches and armchairs as George headed for the bar. Looking at his watch, Edwin announced, 'Time to pay our respects.' They rose slowly to their feet again and filtered outside. Mrs Cheshire, whose timing was immaculate, was outside waiting with a drink for all.

They stood together on the runway watching the sun slip westward, their stiff Scotches helping as buffers against a bitter wind that whipped across the runway and rattled the hangar. Edwin's words swirled. After his normal respects were paid and a short story was told, he summed up by telling them, 'When you think about it this runway, which so many took off from, is actually still in action.' He looked earnestly at all of them. 'But this time perhaps we're the ones taking off.' He held his drink aloft. 'Good luck, boys. Tally ho!' he shouted. And with that they knocked back their drinks and held their glasses skyward shouting.

'Tally ho.'

After a slightly early tea the lounge buzzed with excitement as the 6 o'clock news got under way. Jean was bustling around at the back of the room getting champagne glasses out for the celebrations. Bert McCabe was still there happily oblivious to the events about to unfold, and happily drinking champagne.

'Should I ring my old man?' George asked Arthur.

'You mean warn him?' Arthur replied.

'Have any of you told anyone . . . you know . . . what's going on?' George appealed to everyone.

Frank answered him in a condescending manner. 'We all signed confidentiality agreements, George.'

'Yeah, but did you not tell *anyone* to watch the telly?' George continued. Judging by the looks on everyone's faces they had not. Then they looked at Chandra, who had a guilty look on his face.

'Seven!' George shouted.

'I just asked them to watch the news. So what?' he exclaimed, proclaiming his innocence. 'And maybe record it,' he added.

A hail of cushions rained down on him along with jeers and some elbowing for good measure. Mrs Cheshire rushed in and closed the door behind her. The mood was at fever pitch as the sports news began.

'Here we go,' Arthur called and turned the sound up.

The television presenter launched into the item. '*First, cricket. And as the Ashes series looms, the England selectors have announced an enlarged squad that contains an unprecedented number of new players, mainly bowlers. England's head coach, Bob Fryer, had this to say . . .*' The news item cut to a clip of Fryer dressed in his standard England tracksuit and baseball cap.

'*It's true we've added some new names to the squad, mainly to bolster the bowling ranks. These new players will be given every opportunity to press for selection. The selectors have gone for this approach in order to introduce some newcomers to the next level a little earlier than we normally do. We're in a rebuilding phase and it simply makes good sense in terms of where we're at right now with the squad as a whole,*' he commented in an official manner.

There were all sorts of cheers and whistles from Arthur's players.

The picture cut back to the television presenter who launched into a roll call of the squad's names. As he called them out the entire squad, was listed on screen. In summing up, he read out the new additions last: '*Jim Singleton, Edwin Roberts, George Samuels, Tim Gibson and Frank Arnold. Here's hoping for a successful Test series!*' he concluded. The room went wild and there were congratulations all round. Bert McCabe was stunned to be in the midst of such goings on, but at least all the pieces had fallen into place for him now. But two people were not celebrating: Arthur, who had walked to the back of the room, was angrily punching numbers into his mobile phone; and Chandra, who was sitting silently on the floor staring at the television. The others quickly realised something was horribly amiss when they saw Chandra's dejected figure struggling to come to terms with his omission.

'It's probably a mistake, mate,' George told him.

'I'm not so sure, boys. But hey–' Chandra was on his feet now and started shaking their hands '–you all made it. Man, you're in the England squad all of you. Come on!' Chandra shouted enthusiastically at them all.

'It ain't right,' said Frank in a dour tone. 'I'm out of it.' With that Frank turned to face the others. 'I never liked that Fryer – it should be all of us or none.'

They all agreed.

'Don't worry, boys. Come on, let's celebrate,' cried Chandra. There was a moment's silence as they all looked toward Arthur.

'Bob, Arthur. What the hell are you up to?' he demanded. Everyone waited as Arthur listened to Fryer's response.

'Look, Arthur, when we looked at the make-up of the—' Fryer started but was savagely cut off by Arthur.

'I'll tell you what we'll be looking at, Bob: the eight a.m. news tomorrow with my other bowler's name added to the squad. And, if we're not, then come August you'll be looking at the Australians holding up the Ashes!' Arthur advised him. 'I've just been told it's *all or none*, Bob.'

Fryer was adamant. 'Arthur, there's no going back. There's no funding for a sixth. And that's final.'

'You heard the deal, Bob.' With that Arthur ended the call. Snapping his phone shut, he turned to face the players. 'Minor setback,' he told them confidently.

The others were not so confident as Jim spoke up. 'I'm with Frank; Fryer's a tosser. He needs all of us. And if it ain't all of us . . . he can take a hike. Sorry, Arthur.'

'I understand, but I suggest we withdraw to the games room for a chat then retire for the evening.'

But no one was keen to move; they all just milled around. One or two looked at Chandra, who eventually sprang to his feet.

'Come on, Jim. I'll kick your arse at pool; that'll cheer me up,' he said as he headed the pack to the door.

Frank was unmoved. 'To be honest, I don't want to hang around tomorrow if the news is bad. I'd rather just get on with packing if it's all the same.' The others echoed Frank's sentiments in subdued tones.

'Yes. It seems again Fryer's rained on our parade. Not to worry, there's always Plan C!' said Arthur. Judging by the looks on the players' faces, Plan C wasn't something they wanted to hear about.

'Night, Arthur,' said Frank and Edwin. The others mumbled their inaudible farewells and traipsed off up the stairs to their rooms. Arthur remained pensive and unmoved for some time before doing the same himself.

First up in the morning, Arthur soon heard the stairs taking a pounding as the six filtered downstairs. Mrs Cheshire and Jean were prepared and started pouring teas and one coffee. Arthur did most of the talking, trying to keep the subject from turning to the matter of cricket, which was strange considering five of them had just been selected for England. Jean popped her head around the corner from the hallway.

'Tim, your father called. I've taken a message.' Tim nodded.

Suddenly Arthur's phone rang. He looked at the screen. 'Here we go,' he announced to everyone.

'Bob!' he said and then listened. 'Right . . . well, that's it then. Fine. Great. No, we won't bother. Bye.' He snapped his phone closed and rubbed his eyes. The pressure was telling.

'Well?' demanded Jim.

'Are you all sure you don't want to hear Plan C?' Arthur asked them.

'So, we'll be getting our bags then?' asked Frank.

Jean and Mrs Cheshire who were listening in were dumbstruck. Arthur hung his head low.

'Talk some sense into them, Arthur,' Chandra appealed to him. 'You're jumping the gun; we can work something out.' Feverishly he attempted to change their minds. 'I'll tell you what!' he announced. 'If all of you were left out, I'd still play! What do you think about that, eh?' he demanded. Jim and Frank simply turned toward the staircase. Still he didn't give up.

'Plan C, Arthur. Let's hear it, shall we? Come on, what's Plan C?'

Arthur looked up and announced with a smile on his face, 'Plan C for Chandra is . . . proceed as normal. He's selected.'

Frank and Jim turned around excitedly. Edwin grabbed Chandra and shook his hand wildly as the others all whacked him on the back. Arthur looked at his watch.

'Ssshh!' he called and reached for the radio. Turning it on he caught the end of the 8.00 a.m. news and sport. The familiar tone of the BBC announcer was heard once more. '*Jim Singleton, Edwin Roberts, George Samuels, Tim Gibson and Frank Arnold. Chandra Jafar is a late addition.*' In the Jafar household, as Chandra's brother Kersi sat listening to the radio, his partial paralysis gave way only to a quivering bottom lip. A roar went up at Charmy Down.

'Don't worry,' Arthur told them all. 'I wouldn't have let you go.' Edwin and George smiled at each other. 'Well done,' Arthur said to his spinner with a heavy slap on the back. 'Right! We need a "what happens now?" meeting.'

For Arthur it was another tick in the box and it was fair to say that much of his role had been played out. But as with all endings, a new beginning was about to dawn.

## 26

It was a sorry-looking group that hobbled, limped or tripped out of the house for the last time after a final drink the night before. George opened the boot of the Jag as Jim and Frank dropped their bags in. Mrs Cheshire approached Edwin who was topping up the water in the radiator.

'We'll bring her back in about two weeks if that's OK?' Jim shouted at her from the rear of the car. She held out her hand to Edwin and dropped the keys into his.

'Keep it. You'll be doing me a favour,' she said. Edwin was lost for words. 'Just you all come back and visit. You're always welcome here,' she told them. Biggles jumped into the car and made himself at home on the front passenger seat. Mrs Cheshire clapped her hands at him. 'Come here.' The sturdy little fellow jumped down and waddled over to her.

'I'll bring you back something,' Edwin told him with a firm pat on the head.

Jean was saying her goodbyes to Jim, Frank, Chandra and George as Tim and Arthur squeezed into Mrs Cheshire's car.

'Who's going to bring this car back to Mrs C?' Tim asked.

'I am!' said Jean as she lumped herself into the front seat.

'While I'm in London with you lot, Jean's going to come back and give Mrs Cheshire a hand here for a bit,' Arthur told them as he wriggled into his seat and fastened his seatbelt. With that, the two cars were started up and slowly pulled away from Charmy Down, leaving the great hangar and runway behind. Mrs Cheshire waved as they went. A host of arms protruded from the windows as the cars disappeared down the road.

Half an hour out from London, Tim asked, 'If we're in the squad, shouldn't there be contracts and wages and match payments? If we make the team that is!'

Arthur was surprised no one had asked the question before.

'Your manager will look after all that,' he said very matter-of-factly. Tim sat to attention, said nothing for a moment then sat back in his seat. He caught Arthur's eye in the rear-view mirror.

'I don't suppose you have any idea who that might be, do you?' Tim asked.

'Well, you can choose anyone you like. That person could look after all of you until the Test series is over, then it would be up to each of you to find someone more suitable.'

Arthur said nothing more but Tim had got the message.

When they pulled up to the team hotel the cars were taken away by members of staff. Arthur and the others strode into the foyer. It was fitting that the first person they should encounter was Bill Fredericks, the current top ranked bowler. Like all modern-day cricketers his sunglasses appeared to be mounted in a fixed position on top of his head in a seemingly cool manner. He took one look at them and sighed.

'Not you lot again.'

With that he marched off in the direction of the lifts. Everyone was amused by his behaviour, knowing that their inclusion in the squad would have ruffled a few feathers. The next few weeks were going to be awkward. Chandra spotted French in a corner of the lobby talking to two team mates. All three looked disapprovingly towards Arthur's entourage as Chandra flashed a smile and waved.

Not long after checking in, there was a knock on Arthur's hotel room door. He opened the door to be greeted by all his players who were looking serious. Jim spoke first.

'Tim's mentioned about a manager; if it's all the same to you we'd like you to take care of that for us . . . if it's all the same to you?' he reiterated politely. The others backed him up with a good deal of nodding and mumbling.

'Never thought you'd ask,' replied Arthur. 'I'd be happy to.'

With that, Jim suddenly changed his tone. 'Brilliant, because we've had a meeting and there's a few things we need.' He handed Arthur a long list. The six turned away and disappeared through the door, leaving Arthur examining the list feeling slightly shocked.

Later that afternoon, Fryer addressed the players, briefly introducing the six new members of the squad. There was still a clear division between Arthur's six and the rest. Fryer told his current players that the new members were from a fast bowling developmental program – French had put this slightly differently to his fellow bowlers, giving a full account of the first day at Charmy Down – and explained that Arthur would be assisting the entire squad for the duration of the series. This rather surprised Arthur as he assumed Fryer would attempt to shut him out of the proceedings, hence his desire to manage the players. Fryer went on to outline some of the expectations of the England team management and covered the itinerary of the season's fixtures, team protocol and endorsement rules, commitments and so on.

'We're all here to win the Ashes,' he told them. 'I know the news of the enlarged squad is a surprise to most of you, but life is full of them. If I detect any intentional disharmony, I will seek out the culprit and remove him from the squad.' Fryer glared at them all. 'Any questions?' There were none. 'Right, see you all in an hour.'

Arthur was pleased this message had been put over as it demonstrated that Fryer's end goal was the same as his own. When he'd finished, Fryer called Arthur and the six over to him. He wasted no time. 'As agreed, Arthur,' he said handing each player a neat brown envelope. Inside was the balance of the money they were due as a result of Fryer's 'walk-out' on day one. 'I understand from Arthur that he paid you a weekly wage, so you can all pay him back what you owe him. The balance is a sign-on fee to the England squad.' Fryer never mentioned his decision to part company with the group over a year earlier, preferring to forge ahead dogmatically. After settling with Arthur, each player had roughly £7,000, which naturally pleased them.

The machine behind the England team kicked into gear. Arthur had organised equipment manufacturers to meet his players prior to their first net session. No outright sponsorship deals were offered at that stage, just discounts on gear, or in one case unlimited cricket shoes for the duration of the Ashes series. However, the owner of a small independent firm in Bristol had the foresight to offer free kit to Arthur's players in return for the first right of negotiations after the conclusion of the Ashes. Arthur admired one of the handmade bats as he chatted with the proprietor.

'English or Kashmir?' Arthur asked of the willow. The man

dipped an eyebrow at Arthur, who smiled knowingly. Then, noticing the brand name, Phoenix, he examined the logo of a charcoal bird rising out a flame.

'Ashes to Ashes,' said the man.

'Indeed,' Arthur reflected thoughtfully.

The men shook on the deal there and then. Arthur was comfortable with the arrangement especially as it allowed the players to concentrate their thoughts on cricket for the duration of the summer.


French had other ideas however. Upon entering the change-rooms he came across a core group of the batsmen readying their kits for a net session.

'Be interesting to see what these chaps are like today,' remarked one of the openers as he wiped the inside of his helmet.

French gave him a cold stare as he dropped his bag.

'Hope you lot have all had a chat,' said French.

A bemused look came over most of the batsmen's faces.

'What do you mean?' one asked.

'Well,' started French, 'we have a strong team, which we've been building for two years. These blokes just come along and . . . well, who knows.' French put his bat down, and faced the batsmen. 'All I'm saying is cricket is a team sport, and we have a core of good players who perform well together. We just beat the Windies, didn't we? I don't think anything radical is called for. I just don't know what these guys are doing here. A lot of what happens now is in your hands as batsmen. We should be looking after our own – those bowlers out there, who have been doing the job, and working towards this series all their lives, not six hacks who have taken part in some mad scheme devised by a bored old man.'

French paused to gauge their feelings. No one spoke but they were listening.

'I just think Bob is panicking. He's getting on a bit and maybe this is his last shot at the urn. What's that old saying? Divide and conquer.' French picked some turf from the bottom of his spikes and flicked it on the floor. 'I just feel we should stand firm. Not do them any favours.' With that he stamped his feet hard on the concrete floor to loosen more dried dirt from the bottom of his shoes, and picked up his bat and kitbag. The others still said nothing but he had them thinking as a voice sounded from the end of the locker room.

'Messing things up already, French?'

It was Khan. He strode toward them slowly.

'Sorry?' asked French in a state of panic.

Khan pointed to the bits of dried mud and grass that had come from French's shoes which now littered the floor.

'Oh.' said French as he scuffed the mess towards the lockers with the side of his foot. 'Well, best I get out there then,' he added, relieved Khan hadn't meant what he'd first thought. But Khan was not just a skilful batsman; as it happened he was a very good listener as well.

Before they knew it, Arthur's six were tying up their bootlaces and rolling their shoulders in preparation for their own personal campaigns for selection. Arthur decided to take a back seat for this session, but told them all 90 per cent as usual. Most of the England batsmen from the old squad had introduced themselves and had a brief chat to the new members. The incumbent England bowlers were obviously feeling threatened by their presence, but, as Fryer had suggested in his briefing, were trying to lift their own games.

The session was just as Arthur had hoped. His bowlers held their own against the batsmen and looked to be on a par with the rest of the England bowlers. Where the current bowlers had the advantage was in the amount of match practice they had had. Arthur noticed that his players appeared not to be bowling at 90 per cent speed, preferring to vary their speed, line and length in order to test the batsmen. They were all glad to be performing well and knowing they had an extra 10 per cent up their sleeves helped. It was also obvious they were using the practice to try out new things on the batsmen and didn't mind getting some stick. Fryer eventually came to stand by Arthur.

'Well, you made it this far, old boy,' he said with a wry smile.

Arthur held his emotions in check and rocked back on his heels as he shot Fryer a sly sideways glance. 'Did you doubt I would?' he asked.

Fryer chose not to answer, instead saying, 'You've done a good job. Samuels looks the part. So does Singleton.' Arthur watched as at that moment Jim thumped a ball into the pitch that caught the batsman full on the gloves, causing him to drop his bat and hop about like he were dancing on hot coals. Fryer went on, 'I'm not so keen on Jafar or Seven or whatever you call him, as you're no doubt aware.'

They watched him bowl a ball, which was smashed by Winter with complete contempt.

'He's the partnership breaker. He'll win you a Test. Maybe a series. He can turn the tide,' Arthur told him.

Fryer pondered Arthur's comments then commented, 'I hear you'll be taking care of their affairs.'

'Yes, it's short-term only. When we've won I'm off!' Arthur told him.

Fryer was amused by his self-assuredness.

'I think it's a good arrangement. Actually, after this session I'd like them to meet team management to go over additional series details, match payments and the like.'

The two men continued to observe the session in each other's company, as Chandra was unceremoniously carted out of the nets. French's words' had hit their mark. Against Arthur's men, the batsmen were sure not to play any rash shots and their body language appeared casual, whereas against the incumbent bowlers they seemed more focused. If a loose ball was bowled by one of Arthur's six, the batmen punished it rather than leave it. It was a subtle campaign but Khan was watching and biding his time.

During one net session Khan paid the ultimate compliment by disposing of his cap in favour of a helmet when George was brought on to bowl. Of course Khan had waited to ensure Fryer was watching. Khan had never made a secret of the fact that he thought the English bowling attack was well below par. On one occasion, after an appalling test defeat against Sri Lanka, he had mauled his own bowlers so savagely in the nets that he was eventually removed by the coach. Khan's demonstration of respect for George's bowling had the desired effect, cementing Fryer's thoughts – George was as good as in the team as there was no way of denying him his dues.

The batsmen were quick to acknowledge a good ball from a current team mate but never offered encouragement to Arthur's men. Despite this Fryer could see the potential with his own eyes he just needed some more convincing sessions.

French was forever on their case. He batted doggedly against them and gave him plenty of lip. During one session it became too much as French dealt with some good deliveries from Edwin harshly then called out.

'Hate to see what a real batsman would do to you.'

Edwin walked back to his mark, noticing Arthur standing arms crossed, some way back from the net. For a moment Edwin thought he saw Arthur nod in his direction and looked more intently; again it came. He also detected an almost devilish glint in Arthur's eyes. Edwin knew what to do. He thumped one in, fast and short. French wasn't prepared as the ball pitched short and blasted off the pitch. He pulled his head and shoulders out the way so fast it upset his balance and he found himself mid-pitch upon his rear. Khan in the next net commented.

'Hate to see you face a real bowler Mathew.'

French was livid.

'What do you expect these surfaces are so bloody uneven.'

Edwin looked at Arthur and to his surprise got another nod.'

This time the ball hit French an inch away the Adams apple as he tried to hook. As everyone crowed around French as he gulped for air, Khan found a moment to set the record straight with the other batsmen in the squad.

'By the way, best you all ignore Mathew's words of wisdom from the other day. These boys obviously have something up their sleeves. Who knows, you might even learn something.' Khan said, as he returned to his net. 'But. . . ' he said calling back to them. 'I do agree with him on one point.' he offered. 'Divide and conquer. You lot are doing the dividing now though.'

Tim impressed everyone with his attitude and application. There seemed to be no one who worked on all aspects of their game so hard. Fryer would have preferred him to have been two years older and an inch or two taller. On current form he was not in contention for a place in the team.

Jim, on the other hand, was superb but tended to lose concentration at times as he seemed too concerned with watching the other five. Intimidation being a great weapon in his armoury, he did not like to show it during net sessions with his team-mates. Fryer and Arthur were both acutely aware of this.

Edwin was more consistent, his angle and lift making him very hard to score off, but he seemed too nice to Fryer.

This left Frank. Both Arthur and Fryer felt he looked awkward as if something was troubling him. He had become very good at swinging the ball at slower speeds but tended to be inaccurate at pace. Arthur held off talking to him for reasons he couldn't quite understand – perhaps he hoped Frank would just come right. Fryer reserved judgment on Frank's performances, though of all the bowlers he could produce the most astonishing pace.

On the batting side, all were 'very ordinary' as Fryer put it, with only George showing any promise. Fryer commented that if they were all as good as Chandra *thought* he was, everyone would be averaging over a hundred! Towards the end of a solid net session, Arthur noticed some of his bowlers having a laugh with the other players. Wanting to get in on the act, he sauntered over casually as one of the England openers, Stiles, was speaking.

'An envelope?' Stiles asked Edwin in disbelief.

'Aye, he's cricket's answer to Willy Wonka, is our Arthur,' Edwin commented to the delight of the small crowd, causing Arthur to blush.

The Australians arrived on 20 June led by the respected long-standing Australian captain Steve Moore. Although still suffering from a recent injury, his chances of playing in the first Test were reported to be promising. As usual the British media mauled the England team before even the Australians had a chance. The Australian squad included several well-established players at the peak of their powers, making them firm favourites to win the best of five series by a margin of 4-0, the '4' not being a '5' due to an almost mandatory rain-affected draw somewhere in the scheme of things. So as not to allow the Australians too much match practice the ODIs were being played after the Test series and the normal order of rotation for the Test grounds had controversially been rearranged. As many insisted the first Test had to be played in London, it became a two horse race, and playing at the ground which most improved the chances of a first up victory for the home team made sense. With this in mind, the first Test this year was to be played at the Oval. The Australian bowling line-up included two players with over 400 Test wickets apiece, as well as the current fastest bowler in international cricket. Add to this a wicketkeeper who had bettered every English batsman other than Khan, and two of the latest 'top five' *Wisden* batsmen of the year, and the prospects for England looked bleak. It was safe to say there wasn't much interest in the series from 'Joe Public'. Only true cricketing diehards – which of course included the Barmy Army – were getting into the spirit of the fast-approaching series. In the first two county matches the Australians, fielding a below-strength side, managed to brush aside their opponents by an innings and some wickets in both cases. Already their tour was following an all-too-familiar pattern and a typical build-up to a Test series England style was in full swing. Recent tours didn't give much hope for loyal supporters. Hope as always ran high but realistic expectations were grim. The press were busy sharpening knives as the first day of the series drew closer.

Arthur noted a change had come over some of his players. There was a hardened resolve as they pushed for selection, their speeds increased and looks of concern were seen on the faces of the batsmen facing Arthur's men – while similar looks of concern could be seen on the faces of the bowlers they were attempting to oust. Timing is everything and it looked as if Arthur had his just right. Neither Fryer nor Arthur had given any indication of the team line-up thus far, although they had all but settled on Jim and George and had two other new players in mind.

When Kent played a one-dayer at Somerset the players used it as a chance to get back to Charmy Down for the weekend and get into the machines once more – and watch some cricket too. Little did they know that Arthur and Fryer had registered Frank and Chandra for the Somerset squad, the first they knew of this being when they arrived at the ground and Arthur said, 'You two had better hurry up; it starts in half an hour.' With that he pointed out the Somerset captain talking to Fryer, who was calling them over. Before they did so he instructed Chandra not to bowl any fast balls. This worried him as those were once his stock wicket-taking balls.

The sight of Chandra and Frank stepping out to play for the county was an incredible moment for Arthur and his group, and there was a great roar as they took the field. The regular Somerset pacemen took the new ball and were duly carted about the field by the two Kent openers. With 13 overs and 96 runs on the board the day's play was looking decidedly lopsided.

Eventually, the Somerset captain, Eugene Powell, tossed Frank the ball and said, 'Do your worst . . . damage, that is!'

Frank started badly with two wides. A chill went down Arthur's spine as he'd witnessed Frank have some very erratic net practices and things could turn ugly quickly.

Chandra watched closely as Frank and the other new bowler fed Kent all the fruit they could handle. With the score on 157 after 24 overs, Frank had one over left prior to lunch and hadn't threatened either batsman thus far.

Chandra tossed the ball to him calling out, 'Frank, I'm not sure we've done all this training to be smacked around like schoolboys. Mrs Cheshire could hit some of your rubbish.' He then scuttled off faster than a bomb disposal chap who'd just snipped the red wire instead of the blue.

From the sidelines, Arthur had seen there had been some sort of verbal exchange. 'Oh no! What's he said?'

Frank's body language changed. His face had hardened and his shoulders seemed to have tensed up. It was obvious he was not a happy camper.

'I think Frank is turning into the incredible hulk!' commented George.

Frank took a longer run-up and rolled his shoulder. It was like watching a volcano approaching an eruption. The batsman too had noted a change in tempo as Frank steamed in, faster than before, his speed over the turf impressive for a big man. He speared the ball into the pitch angrily. The batsman, completely unprepared for the level of pace, took the ball on the point of the elbow, dropped his bat and stomped about the wicket doubled up with pain. He was eventually taken from the field unable to continue.

Chandra did not go over to congratulate his team-mate. However, just before Frank bowled his next delivery, he called out, 'He'll be back, Frank. You'd better get some of them out before he does.'

Frank glared at Chandra, who completely ignored him, then came in at the new batsman with equal ferocity, the ball promptly removing the off stump as he played all round it and about half a second too late. It was a blistering ball. Arthur noticed that Chandra still didn't go in to join the celebrations at the fall of this wicket.

As Frank prepared to bowl his next delivery, there was nothing from Chandra this time. Frank then bowled three perfect balls, which were defended well.

As Frank prepared to bowl the last over before lunch, Chandra trotted up and said to him, 'Try getting a wicket with your brain this time,' before running off somewhat faster to his position in the field.

Frank was seething but forced himself to calm down as he studied the batsman closely. Then he called a man in close up on the leg side in a catching position and also asked for a man to be brought round deeper on the square-leg fence. Frank thundered in and pitched it short but held back on pace. Too late, the batsman rushed his shot – and the ball hit the toe of the bat, popping up into the hands of the close fielder. There were wild celebrations as the players left the field for lunch, although Chandra kept well away from Frank.

In the end, Kent reached 266. Frank took four wickets, but was taken off after seven overs so that he wasn't overexposed. Chandra took one – the stumping of a tail ender in three tidy overs. Somerset reached 202 after a poor batting display. Frank and Chandra batted at 10 and 11 and scored 1 and 0 not out respectively. If nothing else, it proved Arthur's men could hold their own against decent opposition.

George had arranged to meet Alice and some of her friends for drinks after the match, no longer feeling he had to keep their relationship a secret – with her friends tagging along, something was sure to slip out anyway. Edwin wondered why George insisted they both get a haircut that evening, and buy new shirts together.

'George, are you sure you're not confusing me with your girlfriend?' he moaned as George threw another shirt over the top of the changing room doors for Edwin to try on.

'You need clothing advice, pal,' called George. 'You've got to look your best as an emerging international cricketer. Besides, some of Alice's friends are coming.'

Edwin's head popped over the top of the changing-room doors looking agitated.

'You're not setting me up, are you?' he demanded to know.

George appeared shocked at the thought. 'Yes, Edwin. I've found a gorgeous twenty-five year old going on seventy-five, who dresses like a "Waafy" and builds model planes.'

'Just as well,' said Edwin, coming out of the changing room wearing a very loud shirt. George gave him the thumbs up.


The post-match analysis was well under way as the first drinks arrived. Chandra had still not gone within ten feet of Frank who continued to blank him. Alice had introduced Edwin to one of her friends Jane, a small, quiet-looking girl who realised, 'Oh, you're the one with the dog!'

Edwin looked over at George, who smiled back.

'I have a girl Staffy,' she enlightened. 'that's why Alice mentioned you.'

She had caught Edwin's attention now. 'Oh yes,' he said.

'Her name's Bunty,' mentioned the girl and beamed. Edwin noticed she had a friendly smile.

'Biggles and Bunty,' he sighed, unaware of the implications that could be drawn from his slip. Standing nearby, Frank and Jim could scarcely believe what they were witnessing.

'He's a real womaniser that Edwin,' Frank remarked to Jim, who coughed into his beer. Next to them Chandra heard them laugh and looked over, catching Frank's stare. Chandra's heart beat a little faster as he prepared to run, but he need not have worried as Frank raised his glass to the little spinner, who smiled and started to move toward him for a chat. Frank held up his hand signalling he hadn't completely forgotten the afternoon's events. Chandra halted in his steps. Jim listened as Arthur leant towards Frank to enquire, 'Indeed, what pearls of wisdom did he bestow upon you to get that fantastic result, Frank?'

The big man took a deep breath. 'Let's just say among other things something to do with Mrs Cheshire's batting prowess.'

After a few rounds Arthur stepped forward and cleared his throat, announcing to all, 'I'd like to say that, before next week takes over our lives, how grateful I am. Firstly, that you all stuck with me.' Then he looked at Tim. 'Tim, I'd like to thank you for giving me my first assignment. Then making it a success.' They all cheered Tim. 'Well done all of you thus far. I think I did well selecting you,' he told them, 'but now it's up to you. I can no longer tell you to bowl only at ninety per cent, or when to unleash whatever it is you have now. The gloves are off and hopefully you'll know when to use what I've shown you. More importantly, use what you've had all along,' he said, tapping the side of his head. 'Help each other out there. Back each other up. Above all, have faith. Lastly . .' he paused and raised his glass. 'Win the Ashes!' With that they all charged their glasses and shouted to the heavens.

Arthur watched the group enjoying themselves and slipped out just after 10.00 p.m., unnoticed by everyone except George. They managed not to overindulge themselves, calling it quits about half an hour later. Come the morning all were fit to train, putting in a solid session on the machines, which they were well and truly accustomed to by now. For the first time in weeks Edwin didn't have his mind on *war*birds!

## 27

Arthur observed the behaviour of the current England bowlers with interest. Their disdain gave way to intrigue, before becoming trepidation then turning to awe. Some of them felt as though they'd been cheated as Arthur's men hit their straps with vengeance. During the England team net practices it was obvious some of the 'old guard' *were* going to be replaced for the first Test. To their credit some tried to keep up with Arthur's boys. Geoff King was first to give way to the furious tide that was sweeping their ranks – he approached Fryer one morning and quit the squad, at the same time offering to stay on and assist in any way he could. It was a smart move and King became invaluable in his advice and friendly manner towards the new bowlers. It put another England quick, Tony Hunter, in an awkward spot. When he finally realised he was fighting a losing battle he too sought out Fryer and offered his assistance, but all too late. Hunter soon withdrew his services and wanted to announce his retirement from international cricket. Fryer asked him to keep the news quiet for it would sound a warning shot to the Australians. Hunter remained with the squad but subsequently faded into obscurity after thirteen unconvincing Tests. Bill Fredericks and the improving Mathew French were now the only fast bowlers pushing Arthur's boys all the way.

Fredericks mostly kept his own counsel and tried not to pay much attention to the others. His seemingly frosty demeanour and total focus in training told all comers that he was not going to relinquish his Test position without a fight. It was therefore a shock to Arthur when one day Fredericks appeared by his side and, without a hint of emotion, informed him, 'I'm *not* going to roll over for your boys, Arthur,' adding as he turned away, 'but that lad Samuels's head should be a bit steadier during his delivery.' Arthur immediately went to watch George and noticed that to his credit Fredricks was absolutely correct. He was suddenly glad the man was still around.

As for the spinners, Stewart Kenny was new to the team and yet to cement his place. He got good turn and was very accurate, but was a true batting bunny. Determined to a fault, he had his nose in front of Chandra for the spinner's spot. Always willing to help, George regularly tried to face Kenny in the nets and took him to pieces at every chance he got. The team's batsmen had all been getting as much practice as possible against Arthur's quicks, as they felt it would sharpen their skills for the upcoming series. Deep down the common goal kept everyone focused and pulling in the same direction as an air of confidence grew within the squad.

One day Khan was in a particularly brash mood, giving all the bowlers hell no matter what they dished up. Chandra called to George for help in a good-natured way, 'Hey, Georgey boy! Come and teach this man a lesson for me.'

Everyone watched as George declined, waving Chandra away, whereupon Khan called out, 'Come on, Georgey boy. Do as you're told.'

George then proceeded to roll Khan over twice in as many balls to the surprise of all those watching. When Khan removed his helmet to reveal a bewildered smile, and patted George on the back, everyone knew something special was in the air. Khan had never been dismissed twice in consecutive balls. Arthur saw what he'd hoped for all along: a gleam so bright it would dull diamonds that flickered in Fryer's eyes. It spoke volumes about how George was coming along.

When the final session in the nets finished, everyone relaxed as Tim removed his pads. 'Reckon I might make the team as a batsman after that last shot,' he joked with Frank who was covered in beads of sweat.

'Nothing to do now but wait,' George reflected as the group fell silent.

'Think you're at the end of the road, do you, George?' Jim asked as he got up stiffly. 'Let's hope not.'

While the selectors met early that evening to decide the make-up of the team to contest the first Test, the players had a light fielding practice. Bob Fryer was the last selector to arrive in the oversized room which housed an undersized table at which three men already sat. No one acknowledged Fryer until he actually sat down, then came muffled greetings. Fryer felt for the piece of paper in his inside pocket that Arthur had given him a few minutes earlier, and placed it face down upon the table. Next to it was a pad of blank paper on which he wrote after much deliberation:

> George Samuels
> Jim Singleton
> Bill Fredricks
> Frank Arnold
> Edwin Roberts

He scrutinised what he had just written for a few moments and then turned over the other piece of paper to reveal Arthur's selection. It was uncanny. The only difference was that Arthur had preferred Edwin to Frank as the fourth bowler, probably due to Frank's tendency to bouts of waywardness at times.

> George Samuels
> Jim Singleton
> Bill Fredricks
> Edwin Roberts
> Frank Arnold

Fryer smiled a smile of relief and put the bits of paper back in his pocket as one of the other selectors rose and headed for the drinks cupboard asking, 'What's your poison, gents?'

'OJ, thanks Mike,' said one man as another agreed.

'Two OJs and . . .?' he asked looking at Fryer.

'Better make that vodkas all round,' Fryer replied.

'Oh, like that, is it, Bob?' Mike exclaimed.

'Doubles,' added Fryer.

The other three selectors, having watched many training sessions and being acutely aware of the pace of the new arrivals, thought it was only a question of experience that was up for debate. But Fryer wanted to go into the Test with five fast bowlers, which surprised the other three, who huffed and puffed their disagreement. Fryer argued that it was time for bold moves and sweeping changes, delivering his message with obvious enthusiasm, arguing that the initiative had been handed to them and must be grasped. When the inclusion of Mathew French or a spinner was suggested instead of Frank Arnold, Fryer's only response was swift.

'Brian, you're nearly seventy. Do you want to see the Ashes back in England again before you die? This may be your last chance.' The man looked stunned. 'Don't blow it!'

Meanwhile, Arthur was seated halfway down the end of a long empty corridor, from where he could hear raised voices. His gaze was fixed upon the large double doors that hid Fryer and the others from his view. A small strip of daylight was visible at the base of the heavy-looking doors, which finally clicked open in a rush, flooding the hallway with light. Dust particles rose as Fryer hurried out and made his way towards Arthur smiling broadly. Arthur twitched and fumbled with his cap on his lap.

'We're going in with five,' Fryer barked. 'You got the four you wanted,' he added, which was enough to send Arthur leaping to his feet. He grabbed Fryer by the shoulders and shook him excitedly, then turned and scampered off down the corridor.

The Six were summoned to Arthur's room, arriving all at once as they had been together waiting for the call when it came. Not wanting to waste time, Arthur composed himself.

'Now, you all know it's a long series. And if you have been omitted from this Test there are others on different surfaces. This time, Tim and Seven, I'm very sorry.'

With that, Tim, Chandra and Arthur all faced England's newest players. Jim, Edwin, Frank and George were stunned but were quickly bombarded with handshakes, slaps on the back and bear-hugs. When the congratulations died down a couple of them had to sit down and relax. George had his head in his hands and Edwin was walking around, taking in very deep breaths and running his hands through his hair.

Arthur stood back a little and watched. 'Well done all of you. And I do mean *all* of you.' He noticed Tim was still shaking Jim's hand vigorously and Chandra was helping Edwin with his breathing. 'George,' Arthur called. He looked at Arthur, who had opened the fridge door to reveal seven cans of beer. George smiled and got up to do the honours in keeping with the role he had relished for the past year, but even as he stood up, Tim pushed him back in his seat, saying, 'You rest your legs, mate. I'll do the honours this time.'

Arthur meanwhile ducked into the bathroom and came back with a magnum of champagne. The others all crowded round him before picking him up, together with the magnum, and shook them vigorously as one. Frank fiddled with the wire cork guard as the group cheered and sang.

'Careful, this was expensive stuff,' Arthur pleaded. 'I'd rather not wear it.'

With that the bottle exploded and they were covered in a fountain of 1998 Veuve Clicquot. Chandra went about handing out cups.

'We will settle for the *brink* of test selection for now,' he told Arthur, motioning to Tim who topped up Arthur's cup. 'But not for ever.'

## 28

Enormous, metallic and forever synonymous with cricket, the looming Oval gasholder had Arthur and his bowlers feeling strangely at ease.

'Something about it makes you want to roll up your sleeves and just get on with it.' remarked Jim as they arrived early on the morning of the first test.

'This is the pitch to do it.' Arthur told him. Always a more suitable venue for the quicks, Arthur well remembered Devon Malcolm taking 9 wickets in 1994 on the former cabbage patch of the late 1700's.

The ground was a hive of activity, with Jim, George, Edwin and Frank caught up in team matters upon arrival. Alice paid George an early morning visit to give him a present, knowing she wouldn't be able to see him after breakfast.

'What's this?' he asked looking down at a small silver nut threaded by a string of leather. Taking it out of his hand, she slipped the necklace over his head.

'It's from one of your machines at Charmy Down,' she said. 'It fell off on the last day.'

'Cool,' he replied, placing a kiss on her forehead as he slid the link to the rear of his neck.

Arthur had other matters to attend to before keeping an appointment with Carl Thompson to go over some points for an article he was developing for Fryer. Tim and Chandra, though omitted from the team, still went for their normal morning run, then did stretches and went through all their other exercises, finishing up with a brief net session of which Arthur managed to catch the latter part. For a moment it seemed like it was business as usual, except for Fryer who was the most nervous of them all, wondering if he'd made the right selection – omitting French had started to nag him already. He knew only to well if this bid for the Ashes failed his head was going to roll.

Tim nipped out to a chemist to fetch some strapping for his right ankle which was causing him some pain. Ambling back to the ground, he allowed himself to be swept away by the crowds who were flowing down the streets to the Oval. Feeling more like a mere spectator again caused him to reflect on how close he had come to being among the men these people now flocked to watch. He felt a tinge of disappointment.

Tim noticed the pubs were slowly filling up too. There was a certain feeling in the air – a feeling of anticipation that went with the beginning of summer. Tim thought about the bitter taste of defeat that all English fans knew only too well, and the hollow emptiness that accompanied it. How he wanted it to be different this year. Spotting a small park, he left the river of bodies and sat on a bench with his shoe off, preparing to bind up his ankle. As he did so, he watched an elderly man leading his young grandson by the hand. The small boy wore an oversized cricket jumper and carried a small backpack ready for the long day ahead.

'Daddy says cricket's boring,' he moaned to his grandfather.

'He's right,' said the old man, 'but it's the best boring game in the world.'

Still smiling, Tim jogged back to get settled for the start of proceedings, sensing the heightened expectation that stemmed from the wholesale changes to the English team. It might also have had a lot to do with the announcement that Australia's captain and premier batsman, Steve Moore, was to be rested due to the rib injury that had failed to heal satisfactorily. This was a major bonus for England.

Passing through the grounds main entrance into the players, area to join Chandra and Arthur, Tim saw another player out of the corner of his eye, but when he backed up a couple of paces he realised that it was actually his own reflection which he'd caught a glimpse in a mirror. He found himself looking back at himself, all decked out in an English tracksuit, his country's emblem over his breast. He felt ashamed remembering how he'd thought Arthur mad after their first meeting and recalling how close he'd come to telling Arthur he wasn't interested in getting involved. Only politeness had stopped him from refusing initially. Tim pondered where he'd be if Arthur hadn't stumbled upon him that day? Tim was well aware he could have ambled toward mediocrity in his cricketing life, and perhaps even life itself.

As a lift bell sounded, a pair of elevator doors hissed open. Inside, Arthur shook hands with a stranger who bustled through the doors past Tim. It was Lloyd Samuels. As it happened, Arthur had just supplied Lloyd with tickets for the first two days' play, allowing entry for the entire Samuels clan. As Arthur and Lloyd exchanged pleasantries and parted, Arthur noticed Tim.

'How's that ankle, boy?'

Tim smiled and joined Arthur in the lift.

'Going down?' he asked Tim.

'Actually, it's probably thanks to you that I'm not.'

The players readied themselves in the dressing rooms. Arthur had wedged himself in a corner of the room and was putting tape on the bottom of his players' bats where the grip met the willow so it didn't ride up the handles. Tim and Chandra sat to the rear familiarising themselves with pre-game goings-on at Test match level.

'I'm more nervous sitting here doing nothing,' Chandra whispered, standing up. 'I might go and give Frank a gee-up.'

'Better nervous than snapped in two,' Tim told Chandra, who looked at Frank and sat down.

Fryer had already had brief words with the new players; now Fredricks was saying his piece: 'You lot forget about that crowd until they're cheering you off. Understand?'

Stan Coleman entered the dressing room having completed the toss and singled out the pair of Stiles and Dennis.

'Pad up, lads.' With that the whole team sprang into action except for George, Jim, Frank and Edwin. The washing machines residing in their stomachs ended their cycles. Breathing a sigh of relief, they made their way to their seats overlooking the ground.

Out in the middle, Fryer was being interviewed by a slick-looking individual in an immaculate blazer. They were discussing the team's make-up and the inclusion of the new bowlers who'd thrown 'the cat amongst the pigeons' as he put it.

The commentator pressed for details. 'There is an air of great uncertainty tinged with a hint of intrigue at this ground right now, given the wholesale changes the selectors have announced today. Can you tell us anything about these new inclusions, Bob?' he asked Fryer who was looking very composed.

'They're players we've had our eye on for a while. Sure, they're green, but I think we'll let their performances in this Test do the talking,' responded Fryer.

'Just two of these players have limited county experience, which is unheard of! Can you understand the grave concern most English supporters have right now, considering the opposition we face? This is a best-of-five series and still I think some people right now will be thinking whitewash!'

'I can understand their concern, but I think they need to show a bit of faith in the selection process. After all we are in a rebuilding phase and these changes are for the future as well.'

'How fast the future has arrived indeed.' was the reporter's curt reply. 'Well, Bob Fryer, the very best of luck and thanks for talking to us today. You've certainly added some spice to the first morning of the Ashes series and, my goodness, won't the tongues be wagging all over the country today with the inclusion of four debutants in the England side to face Australia, the current world champions in this, the first Ashes Test here at the Oval, of all places, where play is due to commence in only a few minutes' time. Bob Fryer, again, good luck and thank you.'

'Thanks, Clive,' responded Fryer cordially.

The two men shook hands and Fryer wandered off.

'We're going to get done!' the commentator informed his cameraman.

In the dressing room, final instructions were issued. Soon the English openers made their way out to the middle and the stands burst out in applause. Conditions were perfect with the faintest of breezes detectable. As play got underway the openers made what could only be described as an inauspicious start to the series amassing a score of 35 before Danny Dennis was beaten all ends up by a ball that cut enough to beat the bat and tickle the off-stump. It was a superb first wicket by the Australians who didn't get overly excited about the dismissal as they knew who was on his way in to replace the hapless Dennis. Chants of 'King, King, King' went up around the ground as Khan strode to the crease. In true Khan style, he watched the first three balls sail by without offering a shot. When the Aussies threw him a bone in the shape of a wide half volley, he reached forward and almost kneeling slashed ferociously at the ball, sending it square and flat to the boundary. He did not move to run but got up slowly and was heard to say 'Thank you' to someone, presumably the bowler. With the home side's score on 70, Stiles poked forward to a straight ball but lazily left a gap between bat and pad. Like a pinball the ball hit both middle and off stumps. The commentators were already talking about England making silly mistakes and the Australians capitalising on every one of them.

Coleman strode to the crease and had a quick chat with Khan. By the time he left, given out LBW to the Australian spinner, Martin Nash, he had scored 43 and they had lifted the score to 163. Khan was moving along confidently when Engle came to the crease and played shots from the outset. He and Khan hit a purple patch and scored runs effortlessly for over an hour.

Arthur glanced at the scoreboard and thought that 273 for 3 was a healthy score

. . . an hour later, George walked out for his first innings in Test cricket, the last three batsmen having gone for 36 runs. Joining the ever-reliable Khan with the score on 309, George's advice from Khan was simple.

'These guys are going to try and rush you back in there. You have all the time in the world. Take it!'

George checked the fielding positions as Arthur studied George's family through his binoculars. They were on the edge of their seats and bursting with pride. He noticed George's father shaking his head in disbelief whilst slowly clapping. When George played his first shot in Test cricket, a glance off his hip to deep fine leg for a single, his father carried on as if he'd scored a century. It was the final ball of the day's play and George had survived.

By the time George arrived at the crease the next day to resume his innings he had played a thousand shots already – all in his head. He'd slept poorly during the night but the funny thing was he didn't feel in the least bit tired. Somehow he felt confident as he took the field with Khan.

As the two of them settled in, Khan spoke to George less than any other batsman he had shared partnerships with so far in the innings. His tactics were sound, with George remaining patient and playing within himself. When he mistimed a rash drive, Khan met him mid-pitch. 'They getting to you?'

Khan was tiger-like in more ways than one, sensing that George was losing concentration after about an hour and so, given the lack of batting talent to come, Khan decided to cut loose. He carted the attack around the ground for a few overs then, chancing his arm once too often, he was caught off a mistimed hook shot that flew to gully of all places. His innings of 167 was a fine start to the series.

Soon George found himself mid-pitch with Jim.

'It's weird being out here, isn't it?' George said.

'Aren't you meant to tell me what to do?' Jim reminded him.

'Yeah, right, Jim. And you'll listen to me!' George said. Jim huffed and made for his crease. They both scratched around before Jim finally thumped a ball straight down the ground for four. In between a near run-out and some thick edges, there were a couple of runs. Finally the number one Australian fast bowler got Jim with one that he played over. His stumps rearranged, he trudged off. Big Frank was hit on the pads repeatedly by the quicks in the first over he faced, but he survived. He then swatted away at Nash, but failed to connect. Luck more than anything saw him gather the same amount of runs as Jim before a top spinner failed to bounce and skidded off the deck right into his pads for a plumb LBW.

Edwin made his way out to the middle much faster than the others. He was taking in short sharp breaths when he greeted George.

'You OK?' George asked.

'Fine.'

'Come on, pal. Get it together. I think Jane may be watching,' George told him.

Edwin breathed even faster now. Facing up, he defended resolutely, his gritty determination counting for more than his technique. Eventually he turned a ball off his pads and the pace took it to the boundary. The crowd applauded his correct choice of shot, not to mention its execution. George too put some more runs on the board, running the total up to 385 before his lanky Australian counterpart got one to rise sharply. It hit the bottom of Edwin's gloves and down onto the stumps to dislodge a single bail unconvincingly – a rather lacklustre ending to the innings. The end of the innings and George's relatively handy performance of 27 not out were congratulated warmly by the crowd.

As Edwin and George left the field, Arthur joined in the applause before reaching for his binoculars in order to locate George's father, who stood clapping his son off.

There was a good deal of banter in the dressing rooms as the turnaround took place. Arthur caught a moment with his bowlers after they had just completed some warm-ups with Alice. It was outside normal team protocol, but as Fryer was not keen on any injuries he allowed it.

'Not sure what to say really, boys. Test cricket now. Bigger than any game you'll ever know. The important thing now is sustained effort during the entire match. You must never give up . . . never give up. You can come back from the dead or lose when you've won. Good luck, lads.'

They filtered out slowly. Their spikes crackled on the tiled floor.

'Tally Ho!' cried Arthur holding his fist high in the air as they disappeared down the steps. Trotting down the stark stairway, George asked Edwin within earshot of the others, 'What does "Tally Ho" actually mean?'

Edwin looked at him quite shocked.

'Attack!' he replied with a grin.

As they strode onto the ground, they shared some fleeting sideways glances with one another. For a second Arthur thought he saw Jim shake his head a little. Perhaps it was pure disbelief on Jim's part? Taking the new ball, as he was accustomed to, was Bill Fredricks. Coleman set a regulation field with Fredricks making the required adjustments. The first over to the Aussie opener Crocket was like a warm-up for both batsman and bowler.

Then George was tossed the ball. He marked out his run-up precisely and re-checked it. The second Aussie opener, Paul Haynes, did a double take as he noticed how far back the slips were standing – surely it was a joke of some kind, he thought to himself. George sailed in for his first ball in Test cricket, letting go of a very safe, very straight, predictable ball that was played in similar fashion. When he had sent down two no-nonsense balls, he thought there'd be no harm in firing a warning shot – they were here to win, after all. Feeling rhythmic and powerful as he bore down on the batsman, all the elements of his action came together as he jumped high and rocked back. His back and abdominal muscles helped rip his torso earthward as he released the ball. The delivery was like a shot from hell, even surprising George how powerful his action had become. The ball pitched short and headed directly for the batsman's head. At the last moment, Haynes ripped his head out of the line of fire. As he did so he saw the ball flash past his helmet's visor. On the big-screen replays Haynes's eyes were seen to be as big as saucers as the ball flew past. It had clearly rocked him though he did not watch the replay. The crowd gasped and looked to the scoreboard to see the speed of the ball – 98.9 m.p.h.! A great roar went up. George was shocked. Sensing something unusual had transpired, Haynes looked at the scoreboard then at his partner at the other end.

From behind the stumps Winter called out, 'All right George, enough mucking about. Let one go!'

The speed recorders were being checked for a malfunction as George returned to the top of his mark and began his run-up once more. He was very wound up this time and gave it his all. To him it was all a flash of white clothing and green turf as he hurled the ball down. To Haynes there was nothing to see. He got to perform a nice back-lift but that was about it. Seeing just a blur, he panicked and rushed a shot at a fast-approaching reddish streak. It was a good guess but his timing was out. There came a loud crack as the ball hit his off-stump and split it right down the middle. Time seemed to freeze as for the second time in as many minutes the batsman looked behind him in disbelief at the smashed stump protruding from the ground. A chill went through the Australian dressing room as Haynes came to terms with his demise and started back to the pavilion. Then came the cries and cheers of the England players as they converged on George. They were soon drowned out by the roar of the crowd as the picture of destruction became apparent to them as well. The players all turned to the scoreboard to view the replay as the speed flashed up. 100.06 m.p.h – the fastest ball in cricketing history! The speed guns were rechecked again but eventually the speed was confirmed over the loudspeakers round the ground. The context of the series had suddenly been changed by one ball. The entire ground came alive as reporters typed, photographers scrambled, commentators enthused and the crowd buzzed. Back on the England balcony, Arthur was relatively calm, remarking to Tim, 'Thought it might have been a shade quicker.' Tim looked at his mentor incredulously, but said nothing as he pondered Arthur's composure.

'He's bowled that fast before, hasn't he?' asked Tim.

'Mmm,' was all he got from Arthur.

Back in the middle the celebrations had died down. The umpire was making his way to the stands with the two halves of the stump as the new batsman entered carrying a replacement. It was a good-natured gesture not lost on the crowd for as the incoming batsman held it high they all cheered. George eventually returned to his mark, already trying to drive thoughts of record speeds and low scores from his mind. Each ball was a potential boundary if he didn't direct them correctly. The fifth ball was just as quick but the batsman played it well, getting forward early. Then the England team were reminded of the downside of super-fast bowling as the new batsman, Ken Barnes, got a thick edge playing a square cut. The ball flew away over the slips and the boundary for a spectacular 6. Barnes was amazed at George's pace, so much so that when the umpire called over, he felt an enormous amount of relief.

A few overs later, the two batsmen had taken the total to 35 and George was beginning to wonder if his first wicket was a fluke. There were moments of panic and uncertainty due to his pace, but no wickets. He remembered Arthur's words and knuckled back down, bowling a superb over with five of the six balls right on the stumps. Fredricks meanwhile was having runs scored off him and looked to be running out of steam in his seventh over. Coleman had Jim start to warm up to replace him and told George he was going to give him three more, which suited him. Next over he bowled a slower bouncer and completely fooled Crocket, who went back and spooned a catch to short leg that was well taken. It was embarrassing for the opener but George felt all his previous thunderbolts had softened him up. But he showed his true cunning when he then bowled three balls of average speed at Ken Barnes before slipping in another 100 m.p.h.

one that surprised the batsman and forced him onto the back foot. The ball ripped past his hastily constructed defences and tickled the bat en route to Harry Winter who gloved a simple chance. Wild celebrations took place again as the total dominance of the English bowlers was confirmed. Across the land the name George Samuels was forcing its way into the record books and Arthur's bizarre methods were finally being vindicated.

However, at 35 for 3 the Australians didn't appear concerned. Each man heading out to the middle seemed determined to stem the flow of wickets but keep the scoreboard ticking over as well.

When Jim's second ball beat the edge of the Aussie number five, Greg Church, and the speed gun clocked over 99.9 m.p.h., England had two of the top three fastest bowlers in history operating from either end of the ground, a fact that was picked up straight away by the statisticians and passed to the commentators. Soon the word had spread like wildfire and the hype surrounding the game had built to an unimaginable level.

As the wickets tumbled, someone in the Australian dressing room asked the inevitable question: 'Who are these guys?'

The frustrated Church managed to plunder some quick runs for the Aussies until Jim broke through with a ball that was slower but cut back savagely, giving Harry Winter another simple take behind the stumps: 68-4. The most productive partnership of the match came leading up to tea.

After the break the batsmen were fresh. Mark Moore and Doug Dyson raised the score to 126 before Moore was caught plumb LBW by the last ball of Jim's last over of his first spell. George had broken the back of the Australian batting line-up with his first three wickets. At the other end, Jim had kept the momentum going with two further wickets, one of which ended a vital Australian partnership by claiming the wicket of Moore.

Jim, being the oldest in the group, was tired and lacking in match fitness but of course, not wanting to say anything, he carried on. This was where Coleman was an excellent leader for he had spotted that Jim was flagging. With a wealth of riches to choose from, he had been watching Frank Arnold lumbering around for some time on the boundary. Thinking it must take a lot of energy to keep a big frame like that moving around, he felt he'd better use him before the big man toppled over – after all, it was their first full day of cricket for a very long time. He paired him up with Edwin and set them loose on the Aussie tail.

Edwin was only bowling at 90 per cent pace but the additional bounce he was getting off the pitch was too prodigious for the Aussies and he bagged three relatively cheap wickets in no time at all. For a while it looked as though Edwin was going to go right through the remaining batsmen and claim the first five-wicket haul of the series, but Doug Dyson was still in, had a well-earned 53 under his belt and did not seem troubled.

Somewhere in Leicestershire the Major was huffing and puffing excitedly as he saw the massive frame of Frank Arnold readying himself to bowl his third over – he had missed the first two as he'd been busy telling another story.

'It's him, that chap from Plymouth!' The Major spluttered through his Scotch to his fellow onlookers.

'I thought 'e 'ad a wooden leg,' said someone nearby.

The sight of Frank on TV screens in pubs brought cheers from fans every time he readied himself to bowl. One could almost sense the fear in the batsmen. There was some good swing for Frank and he was happy to keep his pace down to about 85 per cent, which was still up around the 85 m.p.h. mark on the scoreboard. The sheer force of one of his deliveries split Dyson's bat and he had to call for another. Then Coleman asked Frank to really turn on the pace. His next ball was an unintentional in-swinger that swung so sharply it seemed to have taken a 90° right turn somewhere near the end of the pitch. It darted in behind Dyson's pads as he moved to cover it and rearranged his stumps. Frank celebrated outwardly, but inside he felt enormous relief. It was probably the most satisfying wicket of the day for Arthur as Frank was the biggest gamble he'd taken. It was the final nail in the coffin for the Aussie innings and the follow-on was now a distinct possibility as they teetered on the verge of disaster at 167 for 9. The crowd was at fever pitch; the singing was almost deafening. A sea of St George crosses and Union Jacks waved in the stands like seaweed swaying in an undercurrent of national pride. The run of play was definitely going England's way.

Facing the last batsman, Frank's scowl was enough to claim the wicket for itself. Ben Weir, the last Australian batsman, was not noted for his prowess with the bat. Frank ploughed into a stiff breeze as he approached the crease. Weir, having decided what he was going to do well before the ball was bowled, had a wild swipe at what looked like it might be a good length to hit, but ended up as a fine yorker that beat him completely. Once again the uprooted stumps told the story of an innings in disarray. Frank stood mid-pitch with his mighty arm thrust skywards as the players converged on him. Come his first ball of the next innings, Frank would be on a hat-trick, which again sent the statisticians scurrying off to bury their heads in the record books.

It turned out to be a day to relish for the broadcasters' analysts. From an operations centre crammed full of PCs and monitors a small team had been crunching numbers, collating images, working angles and unearthing all sorts of relevant statistics for the television audience. All these facts and figures gave armchair viewers a better understanding of all aspects of the game.

'Well, today was the day English cricket has been waiting for, for a long, long time.' enthused the commentator. 'Pure, unadulterated pace bowling at its very best. It has bewildered the best batsmen in the world and, we have a new world record bowling speed set by not just one but two bowlers. Yes two! We also have four bowlers bowling consistently above 95 mph and the most remarkable aspect of all this is that none of them have ever played in a Test match before. It's freakish. It's fantastic, and if they keep this up we'll be looking at five-nil . . . That is, if the weather can hold up! In fact, perhaps for the first time in the last twenty-odd years, it might not be the *English* fans praying for rain.' The commentator was beaming as he went on clearly relishing his role. 'Let's look at it from a stats point of view. The speeds being reached are about fifteen per cent faster than these batsmen are used to. This means the batsmen have a lot less time to play the ball.'

A screen was shown to television audiences showing a digital 3-dimensional image of a cricket pitch.

'We are seeing a differential of nearly three yards compared to an average fast bowler's delivery.'

A red line appeared over the image running from crease to crease, then next to it a shorter blue line appeared.

'The red line represents today's incredible average speed and when these deliveries get to the batsmen we can look and see where a normal delivery would be, which is about three yards behind, or about point two of a second behind, these deliveries today. Astounding! It may not sound like much to us but it's a big difference to the batsmen. On top of this, these bowlers are enormous, and the steep bounce they are generating is causing no end of trouble. Let's compare the trajectory of these new bowlers to that of the other English bowler out there, Fredricks.' Another screen was shown which compared new angles in red and Fredricks in blue. 'Look at these deliveries in red compared to Fredricks's in blue. Now, Bill Fredricks is about average in the fast bowling height stakes at about six foot three inches tall, so the bounce he would generate would be about the norm. But these new bowlers, the red lines, are showing an amazing amount of bounce, much steeper. It's proving just too much to ask the batsmen to compensate for these massive increases in speed and bounce in one innings. But beware! These are top-shelf batsmen and they will know where they are going wrong. Whether or not they can get back on top of these giants is going to be the question on everyone's lips. I'm Simon Hughes and I'll be back to you during the course of the next innings.'

In their first effort, Arthur's attack had conquered the world champions, bundling them out for 172 and forcing the follow on. There would now be another forty-five minutes remaining for the second day's play once the Aussies came back out after a short break. Arthur and Fryer were already deep in discussion about the innings. One thing they were sure about was the Australians' ability to bounce back. They would therefore use the break to regroup and come back stronger in the second innings, the element of surprise having been sprung in the first innings – or so both teams thought. Fryer gathered his troops and went behind closed doors.

Arthur meanwhile had decided to pay Mr Samuels a visit. Alice, hearing where he was headed, decided to go along too, in spite of the fact that they wouldn't know who she was. There was jubilation as the family welcomed Arthur. When Mr Samuels began asking questions about George's meteoric rise to Test cricket status, Arthur simply explained to him that he was a talent scout and had merely spotted George. It was not until much later that George's father learnt the whole truth about the route his son had taken and what Arthur had done with the players. As for Alice, she chatted away with the family, telling them she was part of the support crew and left it at that. George's mother didn't have to ask too much to know who or what she was – Alice was beaming from ear to ear as they chatted away.

Back in the dressing room, Fryer was painting an optimistic picture of the current situation for the players, his tone upbeat and belligerent. The players were then left alone for a short period. When they made their way to the middle their resolve had hardened.

Fryer could say all he liked, but his words were not backed up by his own actions for he advocated that Fredricks should open the bowling once more, which annoyed Arthur no end. As the Australian innings got under way in dim light, Fredricks bowled poorly and avoided eye contact with his bowling partners as he allowed the Australians to accumulate runs. For the first time in his Test career he felt completely outgunned by other bowlers in his own team. He even toyed with the idea of throwing the ball to one of them, but he was bowling for England. He toiled away but failed to make an impression.

George on the other hand was superb and the five overs he bowled yielded only 3 runs, the Australians making it to the close without loss. For the entire evening the tourists discussed the mistakes of the first innings and plotted their resurgence in the second and subsequent Tests. It was a low-key evening for the England team.


The next day the sun had come out and dried the wicket somewhat, but there was promise of some extra bounce in the slowly cracking surface of the Oval pitch. It was a sleeveless pullover kind of day as the batsmen stretched and curled their backs and shoulders.

Fredricks opened the proceedings with a maiden,

whereupon George's first three deliveries shot past the outside edge of the bat, each one closer than the last. Then, with the score on 29, George struck. Having tested Crocket with some short-pitched balls that were getting ever slower, he slipped in a very quick one which hit just about everything and bobbed back to him for a simple caught and bowled.

Minutes later Fredricks was removed from the attack and Coleman nodded to Frank, who missed his hat-trick but earned himself a split helmet as he cracked open Haynes's like a rotten walnut.

By the time the Aussies had reached 50 they had lost two wickets. Modest 10 or 15 run partnerships were put together along the way but Coleman rotated his bowlers well. Jim came on to replace George after another fine spell and took two quick wickets just as he'd done in the first innings. By the time the Aussies reached 100 they were five down. Edwin's bounce was once more excellent. Even though the ball had lost its shine, he managed to extract prodigious lift and picked off a couple of batsmen. With the job all but done and the Australians' fight-back having completely failed, Coleman looked to someone who could finish the job in quick time. Fredricks felt he might be given the chance to gain some respectability, even if it was mopping up the tail, but Coleman called up a well-rested George as he wanted to see the innings over as quickly as possible. Fredricks felt humiliated. After all his years of service to his country, he realised the writing was on the wall. The Aussies tried to rally one last time, knowing that only the weather or a cricketing miracle could save them. George removed two tail-enders, with Edwin having the honour of bowling the last batsman for an emphatic win.

Jubilant mid-pitch celebrations included the grabbing of the stumps and the formation of a cluster of bodies for the mandatory 'group hug'. Arthur slapped his hands and clenched his fists after the final wicket had tumbled. Tim and Chandra embraced. Still crowing and whooping, they made their way down to greet their mates.

Arthur trotted down the stairs last of all, holding the rail as he puffed along. A little ahead of him, Alice could hear him shouting and singing and could have sworn she heard him mumble something as he reached the bottom of the stairs where he did a little jig – something about a 'supercoach', she thought.

As expected the mood in the dressing room was euphoric. The resounding victory was all the more astonishing when one considered the winning margin: an innings and 77 runs! It was a phenomenal first-up win. Arthur's expectations had been overwhelmed as he came to grips with the magnitude of what his players had achieved.

The celebrations were mostly confined to the dressing room where beer and champagne were in plentiful supply. In true cricketing tradition, the players did most of the celebrating in their whites, not bothering to get changed.

When George was named Man-of-the-Match the dressing room came alive and the party reached fever pitch, particularly when Alice brought George's father in to meet the players, along with the rest of his family. Jim and Edwin had already spoken on the phone to their nearest and dearest.

Frank didn't call his mother who was all he had left for family. She was more into gardening than sports, and in any case was as deaf as a post, he told Arthur, who couldn't help but feel a bit sorry for him. But Frank seemed happy just to be part of it all. Finally he got a call from the staff at The Belfry, who had seemingly all arrived at work and switched on the bar televisions, only to discover their old colleague was rolling his arm over for England, no less.

Chandra and Tim milled about the big room topping up drinks and talking to the other players. Khan was in a cheery mood and for the first time began to ask Tim questions about what exactly had gone on at Charmy Down. They sat down and chatted. When Tim had finished his whole story, Khan was dumbstruck. He spotted Arthur across the room chatting to Fryer.

'Respect,' he said under his breath, as much in awe of Arthur's methods as the achievement.

Fryer clapped his hands. 'Listen up, chaps!' he shouted. 'I'll see you all at the restaurant in a couple of hours and remember, no comments to the press,' he warned. 'Don't forget. We have to do it all again next Thursday, so don't wreck yourselves.'

There was a loud knock on the door. Steve Moore the injured Australian captain and his stand-in captain for this Test match entered the room. Moore appeared both humble and friendly as he congratulated each and every member in the room, smiling as he chatted to them. Fryer soon made his departure but Arthur watched the Aussie captain work the room like a politician. Seeing Moore heading George's way he decided the interests of the team would be better served if George didn't meet the Aussie captain prior to the next test, in which Moore would no doubt be fit to play. As he moved across to cut Moore off he needn't have bothered. Chandra introduced himself and gave an instamatic camera to Tim, before putting his arm round Moore and smiling broadly as Tim fiddled with the camera. The Australian skipper was accustomed to having his picture taken, but not in such a forthright manner.

'Watch the duck!' Chandra jested to Moore's chagrin.

Having finally escaped Chandra's clutches, Moore spoke with Coleman for a while, apparently genuinely happy for his opponent in his moment of victory. After a good half hour or so, Moore finally made his exit, giving a clap to the team and a wave that managed to include everyone at once. But as he slipped through the door, he turned just enough to see everyone in the room, and in that instant his eyes swept across the entire dressing-room, capturing the attention of every player and momentarily holding their attention. They all thought he would give them a parting smile and be gone, yet all they got was a second's worth of pure granite. Come the second Test, Moore would be back and they knew better than anyone what that meant.

England v. Australia
The Oval
First Test Match July 21st, 22nd, 23rd, 24th and 25th
England won by an innings and 77 runs
Man of the match – George Samuels

England
1st Innings

| | | | |
|---|---|---|---|
| 1 - | D. Dennis | b Rogers ................16 | |
| 2 - | P. Stilles | b Rogers................31 | |
| 3 - | R. Khan | c Dyson b Patterson...167 | |
| 4 - | S. Coleman* | lbw Nash.................43 | |
| 5 - | M. Engle | c Nash...................60 | |
| 6 - | H. Winter † | b Weir ....................3 | |
| 7 - | B Fredricks | lbw Rogers.............15 | |
| 8 - | G. Samuels | not out...................27 | |
| 9 - | J. Singleton | b Rogers .................5 | |
| 10 - | F. Arnold | lbw Nash ................5 | |
| 11 - | E. Roberts | b Weir....................4 | |
| | | Extras.................... 9 | |
| | | Total...................385 | |

FALL OF WICKETS
First Innings:      35-1 70-2 163-3 273-4 280-5 309-6 364-7 370-8 378-9

| Bowler | Overs | Mdn | Runs | Wkts |
|---|---|---|---|---|
| Rogers | 32 | 5 | 95 | 4 |
| Nash | 27 | 6 | 87 | 3 |
| Weir | 22.4 | 1 | 81 | 2 |
| Patterson | 21 | 0 | 82 | 1 |
| Church | 7 | 0 | 35 | 0 |

* Denotes Captain
† Denotes Keeper

Australia

| | | 1st Innings | 2nd Innings |
|---|---|---|---|
| 1 - | D. Crocket | b Samuels ................5 | c&b Samuels................25 |
| 2 - | P. Haynes | c Coleman b Samuels...12 | lbw Samuels.................17 |
| 3 - | K. Barnes | c Winter b Samuels......19 | c Samuels...................16 |
| 4 - | M Moore* | lbw Singleton............. 24 | b Singleton...................3 |
| 5 - | G. Church | c Winter b Singleton ...20 | lbw Arnold ................ 4 |
| 6 - | D. Dyson | b Arnold....................53 | c Singleton.................19 |
| 7 - | W. Talbot † | b Roberts.................. 18 | c Roberts.....................3 |
| 8 - | C. Rogers | c Roberts....................7 | not out.......................11 |
| 9 - | G. Patterson | lbw Roberts.................3 | b Samuels...................10 |
| 10 - | M. Nash | not out.........................5 | c Samuels...................17 |
| 11 - | B Weir | b Arnold....................0 | lbw Roberts..................4 |
| | | Extras.......................6 | Extras.........................7 |
| | | Total....................172 | Total.......................136 |

FALL OF WICKETS
First Innings:       17-1 35-2 35-3 68-4 126-5 126-6 155-7 159-8 167-9
Second innings:    29-1 50-2 59-3 69-4 76-5 91-6 98-7 114-8 126-9

| Bowlers | Overs | Mdn | Runs | Wkts | | Bowlers | Overs | Mdn | Runs | Wkts |
|---|---|---|---|---|---|---|---|---|---|---|
| Fredricks | 14 | 0 | 71 | 0 | | Fredricks | 10 | 0 | 44 | 0 |
| Samuels | 13 | 3 | 43 | 3 | | Samuels | 19 | 3 | 38 | 5 |
| Singleton | 12 | 3 | 42 | 2 | | Singleton | 7 | 3 | 8 | 2 |
| Roberts | 3 | 3 | 13 | 3 | | Roberts | 6.2 | 3 | 26 | 2 |
| Arnold | 2.2 | 1 | 2 | 2 | | Arnold | 4 | 3 | 19 | 1 |

* Denotes Captain
† Denotes Keeper
Umpires:  Mike Petruchelli & Tim Huggins

215

## 29

Trent Bridge was a sell-out and had attracted unprecedented interest and a sizeable crowd. Outside hopefuls had gathered to gain entry any way they could. In the days between the Tests, Arthur thought the press had been too optimistic in their assessments of how the season might unfold from this point on. He couldn't believe that some had written off the Aussies already, which was a dangerous thing to do.

'Don't they realise they are just giving them *more* reasons for winning now?' Fryer lamented as he scanned the papers in the hotel breakfast room.

Arthur didn't answer him. He was livid with Fryer for not having selected Chandra for the Test, opting again for Fredricks and the part-time spin of the opener, Stiles. It was weak of Fryer. Deep down even Fredricks knew that if he did not perform things could become very uncomfortable during the Test. Chandra took the news better than Arthur had hoped and went down to the nets to practise with Tim as the team prepared to do battle.

Coleman had a surprise waiting for him as he went to confirm the make up of the team. The Australian team had a familiar name pencilled in to play. Wayne Horn, the long retired world record holding spin bowler had been called back into the team. The charismatic spinner who had been single handily responsible for winning many a match and series had been coaxed out of retirement at the age of 44. Perhaps not as potent as he once was Horn was still playing state cricket and taking wickets when the call came. It would be an opportunity he would relish and already his inclusion had had the desired effect as Steve Moore observed the look upon Coleman's face. Moments later the announcement was made over the ground's public address system. The crowd were stunned into submission.

The toss went against England with the Aussies deciding to bat first. Moore would be hoping to build a large first innings total to make England bat second with a lot of runs to chase, which was of course a supposed weakness of the team.

At the end of the day it was honours even as the Australians reached a higher total than they had in either innings in London, although had it not been for the talent of Steve Moore, the total would have been an embarrassment. Scoring an unbeaten 122 runs he saved face for the tourists.

Once more Arthur's bowlers had done exceptionally well. George had opened and had taken four devastating wickets when disaster struck. Having destroyed the top order, it looked like they would be dismissed for under 100 when George, pushing for extra pace, rolled his ankle on a softer than normal run-up. With the score on 35 for 4 he took no further part in the day's proceedings, With George gone, Frank had immediately removed Doug Dyson for 0 and at 35-5 the Aussies should have been dead and buried. This gave Fredricks an opportunity to rise to the occasion. He could have saved his career and country with a good performance, but sadly for the English stalwart of sixty-six Tests it was not to be and his pace couldn't compete with that of the new breed he was bowling alongside. He simply looked pedestrian in comparison. Moore flogged him unceremoniously until he was finally removed from the attack, a forlorn figure. Moore was given valuable assistance by the lower order and built useful partnerships with Talbot, who scored 49, Rogers 10 and Horn who chipped in with a precious 28. Jim and Edwin, doing most of the bowling to Moore, took some stick but performed admirably. When Frank came back for a short spell, he again did the damage with two wickets. Stiles bowled a few overs of spin but was ineffective. With Fryer's dual gamble with Fredricks and Stiles was a complete failure, Coleman once more resorted to Edwin and Jim. A rejuvenated Edwin took two vital wickets and Jim speared in a savage last ball to end the innings with another broken stump, leaving the unbeaten Aussie captain defending a paltry total in the first innings. For the Aussies to reach 240 runs after being 35 for 4 was remarkable; for the English to have let them off the hook was unforgivable! Though the final flurry was a good sign for England, the attack without George was sadly lacking and everyone watching knew it.

The England innings was steady in that almost everyone got a start. It was also consistent in that once a batsman had played himself in he was soon dismissed. What hurt most was Khan's early dismissal. The familiar form of Wayne Horn stepped in to take up the attack. Sporting a close shaved head and a healthy tan Horn was obviously still match fit. A fully figure now but strong looking he flipped the ball from a leathery hand. Savouring the moment, Horn smirked and waved to the crowd as it cheered and booed simultaneously. The soft underbelly of the England middle and late order had been exposed and Horn exploited the situation dismissing Engle and Coleman after a brief period of resistance. Thereafter succession of England batsmen trudged reluctantly back to the pavilion. The England captain was top scorer with 31 in a total of 147, which put them 93 runs in arrears. Despite taking only 3 wickets, an average performance by his standards, Horn's inclusion had unquestionably lifted the tourists. Things were suddenly going wrong for England. A superhuman effort was required in the field, but being a bowler down made it almost impossible.

Arthur felt powerless to do anything but he need not have worried, Jim and Frank got stuck in from the first ball. Jim's level of intimidation was monumental. His deliveries spat and reared up from the pitch like meteors bouncing off metal. The sound of them thumping into the rib cages of the batsmen was sickening, chest guards or not. From the other end, Frank was firing missiles too and there were near-hysterical scenes from the crowd as the Australian openers were both removed with only one run on the board. At one point, Moore had taken two savage blows on the shoulder and chest, but like a true champion he concentrated on staying put and scoring runs. However, he was powerless to prevent the dismissal of batsmen at the other end, which prompted one commentator to liken the debacle to scenes at a shooting gallery at a local fair ground. When Frank bowled Mark Moore, the ball somehow removed all three stumps completely out the ground. It was as if Lillee & Thomson had been unleashed upon a team of schoolboys, such was the carnage. Edwin and Fredricks were only asked to bowl towards the end of the innings when Frank and Jim were exhausted, by which time the score was 104 for 9. Once again the Australian captain had resisted to the end, but this time no one was able to stay with him and the innings ended on 106, with Moore on 61 not out. Jim had taken 6 for 36 runs, earning immense respect for the way he'd taken it upon himself to fill George's shoes. Frank had bagged 3 for 58 in a great supporting performance and Edwin had claimed the last wicket.

In the papers the next day, Jim's performance was described as 'ruthless' and 'demonic'. Arthur's prediction of Jim's talent had at last been realised. At Good Walloping, Jim's miraculous performance was reason enough for free beer all day instead of the end-of-season trip to the Caribbean.

England were therefore left with exactly 200 runs for victory, which would give them a two-nil lead in the series.

It was day three and there was an hour left before lunch when the English openers made their way out to the middle under clear blue skies in pursuit of their target. They hadn't enjoyed much success in recent times when it came to building decent partnerships, but now their drought ended. Try as they might, the Australian bowlers could not separate the two as they nudged, nurdled and occasionally drove the ball around the field. The England camp was delighted at being 57 without loss at the interval. Arthur, Tim and Chandra were seated with Jean and Mrs Cheshire some distance away from the others so as not to distract them. Biggles sat by Mrs Cheshire. Too short to see out the windows to the middle, he looked up a television mounted in the corner of the room. There was the usual banter from most of them except for Arthur, who just wanted to get on with things and secure another victory.

With the score on 120 without loss the game looked as if it were England's, but a bowling change secured the wicket of Danny Dennis. No sooner had that wicket been taken than another bowling change was made and Horn was brought into the attack. When Stiles joined his opening partner in the pavilion, the wily spinner was grinning like an axeman about to behead his victim. And swing his axe he did. Once the tail went up in this Australian team it stayed up. Though no one dared use the word panic, some of the England team were deeply concerned at the fall of wickets as Horn masterfully worked his way through the England batsmen like a hot knife through butter. The middle order was now officially 'a worry'. When Harry Winter was met in the middle by George, who was forced to bat with Stiles as his runner, it looked like they might bring the English home as a useful partnership developed. Alas, with the total on 185, just 15 runs short of the target, any pressure they'd built on the Aussies was released as both men were dismissed in quick succession. Shell-shocked would best describe the mood of the England supporters, who by now were on the edge of their seats. A hush had descended on the crowd with every run being cheered as if it was the winning run itself. Not a radio in the land played music.

Still in with a relatively good chance, the odds were lengthened when Jim was subjected to a barrage of vicious fast bowling from the Aussie bowlers. He took two nasty blows on the body but battled on courageously, before being completely confounded by a clever flipper from Horn that jumped up at him ferociously and hit his gloves before flying to the wicketkeeper via his shoulder.

Frank and Edwin, the last two batsmen, were aware of the task at hand. They immediately found themselves in all sorts of bother but managed to claw their way closer to the total with the help of some undisciplined no-balls and a bold boundary from Frank as he pulled a short ball from Rogers square into one of the radio commentary boxes. Striking the window with such force it shattered the entire pane. The commentators within were scattered but regained their composure quickly enough to comment, 'Well, that was a *cracking good* shot from Arnold.'

With victory only six runs away it seemed all England was focused on just two men – Frank and Edwin – who were having a quick chat in the middle as millions of fingernails were whittled away.

Horn took the ball from the umpire and wiped it as Frank returned to the non strikers end.

'You know I didn't pick you for a slogger.' remarked the spinner to Frank who ignored the comment.

Edwin glanced Horn's first ball for a quick single leaving Frank on strike and just five for victory. Most observers felt the advantage might have turned. Frank being very careful prodded forward to most balls on offer, but was watching for a short one too. Finally Horn sent down what looked as if it were a slower ball and there to be hit. As it floated in, Frank decided to get forward and stroke it with some controlled force but it dipped deceptively early and his foot wasn't quite there. A smaller, more nimble man might have been able to adjust his footwork, but fleet of foot Frank was not. With his weight firmly anchored to the pitch, the ball turned, caught the edge of his bat and a low quick chance flew towards second slip. Frank's heart stopped and a hot flush tore through him as the ball flew obediently into the waiting hands of Mark Moore. It was all the Australians needed. It took Frank a moment to realise it was all over.

The leaping, dancing, all-hugging Australians had clawed their way back from the brink of defeat in a memorable Test. The gamble on Horn had worked, for he had turned in a match winning performance. The crowd left the ground totally devastated. When the masses departed, it was akin to a huge funeral procession drifting out of the ground. How apt the word 'gutted' seemed just then as they flowed out of the gates, a sea of zombies.

Edwin tried to console Frank, but the big man had plunged into the depths of despair, feeling he had cost his team the Test match. Arthur was more certain – and 100 per cent correct – in his opinion of who had been more responsible for the loss, and that person was not a player.

The scene in the dressing room was sombre. Fryer thought it best to leave them alone for a while before addressing them. When he finally stood and called the team to order, another man moved purposefully behind him, put his hand on Fryer's shoulder and stepped forward to speak. It was Bill Fredricks. 'Just a minute, Bob. I'm sure this will come as no surprise to any of you, but . . . I'm done. Just thought I'd let you know. That's me finished. Cheers, lads,' he said with a smile and a wave. 'Do carry on, Bob,' he instructed Fryer and stepped back.

There was a moment's stunned silence then Fryer turned to speak to Fredricks, but was quickly stopped in his tracks. 'Don't say nothing, Bob. Mind's made up. You keep on learning in this game, and if there's one thing I've learnt in this match it's that you'll all have a better chance in the series if I step down. Frank, I know what you must be feeling right now, but it ain't your fault.'

The silence was deafening as Fryer was ushered forward once more by Fredricks.

Tim suddenly shouted out, 'Three cheers for Bill Fredricks! Hip hip . . .'

'Hooray, hooray, hooray!' They all stood and clapped.

Fredricks merely nodded his appreciation.

'Good luck boys,' Fredricks called out.

They all sat down as Fryer began again. 'Well, as Bill said, you keep on learning. We've all learnt something from this. We're going to change some things and we're going to work hard leading up to the next match.' He looked at George. 'Bad luck there for George didn't help our cause. You make sure you mend quickly.' Fryer then took a deep breath. 'I'm incredibly proud of our performance. To have got them out for 106 was a monumental effort.' He turned to Jim. 'Well bowled there, Jim. I dare say they'll be talking that one up for some time to come.' He then addressed the team as a whole once more. 'We have some work to do in the batting department. That's something we've got to work on. I'll have more to say in the days to come, but right now that's about it. Anything to add, Stan?' he asked Stan Coleman.

'Yes, got any batsmen in your bag of tricks?' he asked Arthur. But Arthur barely smiled.

The door to the change room opened. It was Horn wearing a huge grin.

'You blokes coming for a drink?'

**England V. Australia**
Trent Bridge - Nottingham
Second Test Match July 28th, 29th, 30th, 31st & 1st August
Australia won by 5 runs
Man of the Match – Wayne Horn

### Australia

| | | 1st Innings | 2nd Innings |
|---|---|---|---|
| 1 - | D. Crocket | b Samuels ................5 | b Singleton....................0 |
| 2 - | P. Haynes | b Samuels................10 | b Singleton.…..............0 |
| 3 - | S. Moore* | not out..................122 | not out......................61 |
| 4 - | M Moore | lbw Samuels...............3 | c Khan b Arnold...........4 |
| 5 - | G. Church | c & b Samuels ...........2 | c & b Singleton ...........3 |
| 6 - | D. Dyson | b Arnold....................0 | c Winter b Singleton......4 |
| 7 - | W. Talbot † | b Arnold..................49 | b Singleton...............19 |
| 8 - | C. Rogers | c Arnold..................10 | c Engle b Arnold...........0 |
| 9 - | W. Horn | lbw Roberts.............28 | b Arnold…….…... ......6 |
| 10 - | G. Patterson | b Roberts...................6 | lbw Singleton..............5 |
| 11 – | G Weir | c Singleton................1 | b Roberts....................1 |
| | | Extras.......................4 | Extras.......................3 |
| | | Total.....................240 | Total....................106 |

**FALL OF WICKETS**

| | | |
|---|---|---|
| First Innings: | 7-1 20-2 25-3 35-4 35-5 | 136-6 215-7 223-8 232-9 |
| Second innings: | 1-0-1 1-1 8-3 18-4 32-5 | 87-6 88-7 96-8 102-9 |

| Bowlers | Overs | Mdn | Runs | Wkts | Bowlers | Overs | Mdn | Runs | Wkts |
|---|---|---|---|---|---|---|---|---|---|
| Samuels | 7 | 3 | 18 | 4 | Samuels | DNB | | | |
| Fredericks | 7 | 0 | 34 | 0 | Fredericks | 2 | 0 | 7 | 0 |
| Singleton | 19.1 | 3 | 71 | 1 | Singleton | 17 | 4 | 36 | 6 |
| Roberts | 18 | 6 | 40 | 2 | Roberts | 1.2 | 1 | 4 | 1 |
| Arnold | 16 | 3 | 50 | 3 | Arnold | 17 | 4 | 58 | 3 |
| Stilles | 4 | 0 | 24 | 0 | | | | | |

\* Denotes Captain
† Denotes Keeper

### England

| | | 1st Innings | 2nd Innings |
|---|---|---|---|
| 1 - | D. Dennis | b Rogers............ .....16 | c Church b Weir..........60 |
| 2 - | P. Stilles | b Rogers................10 | b Horn......................73 |
| 3 - | R. Khan | lbw Rogers ............ ...8 | c Crocket b Horn...........0 |
| 4 - | S. Coleman* | lbw Horn........ ........31 | lbw Weir…..…...........8 |
| 5 - | M. Engle | c Horn...................20 | b Horn......................0 |
| 6 - | H. Winter† | b Weir ...................12 | lbw Rogers...........21 |
| 7 - | B Fredericks | lbw Rogers.............14 | b Horn......................3 |
| 8 - | G. Samuels | not out...................14 | c Talbot b Patterson......13 |
| 9 - | J. Singleton | c Talbot b Church........9 | c Talbot b Horn............0 |
| 10 - | F. Arnold | lbw Horn .................3 | c Talbot b Horn...........4 |
| 11 - | E. Roberts | c Moore b Patterson ......0 | not out......................3 |
| | | Extras...................10 | Extras......................11 |
| | | Total...................147 | Total ....................194 |

**FALL OF WICKETS**

| | | |
|---|---|---|
| First Innings: | 22-1 33-2 58-3 84-4 112-4 | 127-6 138-7 140-8 147-9 |
| Second Innings: | 120-1 133-2 133-3 142-4 | 144 -5 152-6 185-7 186-8 186-9 |

| Bowler | Overs | Mdn | Runs | Wkts | Bowler | Overs | Mdn | Runs | Wkts |
|---|---|---|---|---|---|---|---|---|---|
| Rogers | 12 | 5 | 33 | 4 | Rogers | 14 | 2 | 39 | 1 |
| Patterson | 14.4 | 3 | 45 | 1 | Patterson | 16 | 3 | 45 | 1 |
| Horn | 7 | 2 | 23 | 3 | Horn | 14.5 | 1 | 32 | 6 |
| Weir | 9 | 1 | 32 | 1 | Weir | 16 | 0 | 64 | 2 |
| Church | 3 | 0 | 12 | 1 | Church | DNB | | | |

\* Denotes Captain
† Denotes Keeper

Umpires: Daniel Parry & Ian McGregor

## 30

The main thing to be worked on prior to the third Test was a repair job to the team's shattered morale. Arthur sustained a heightened level of enthusiasm that bordered on frenzy. He was everywhere during the week, cajoling, encouraging, imploring and at times begging the players to rise to the occasion. In the end he dragged them out of the mire of self-doubt and reinstalled an abundance of confidence in themselves. His enthusiasm extended to the other squad members, which was advantageous to all concerned. He felt strongly that for the players it should never be about all the peripheral trappings that go with being an international sportsman – Arthur's philosophy was about enjoying the game first and foremost; then came ensuring his players did the best for their country and team-mates. He managed to get this message across without ever broaching the subject head on and never spoke of his love for the game per se – that was something everyone accepted. Just as a broken bone heals stronger, the England team had healed and healed stronger thanks to Arthur's guidance.

But Fryer never understood this and pushed them even harder.

'Don't overcook them,' Arthur warned him and to his credit Fryer eased off slightly. Not that he ever acknowledged his gratitude to Arthur.

With the make-up of the team being carefully considered, Chandra still had his work cut out for him. Throughout all the practice sessions he had remained determined to hone his new craft, refusing to use his fast ball. His battle with French continued and Fryer still needed a lot of convincing, however, he'd won over Harry Winter with his dogged attitude and sense of humour. After claiming Winter's wicket with a slow leg-cutter he joked that his next ball would be faster than lightning and that he should do all his blinking in advance. Winter was amused but even more impressed when Chandra's next ball sent his stumps flying with a medium-paced inswinger. After those two wickets, Chandra succeeded in pinning the batsman down for the remainder of the session causing Winter to doubt whether he would have scored another run off the remaining deliveries. French witnessed the episode, taking note of Chandra's growing bond with the players, and set about unsettling his nemesis as he headed into the net for a bat. With Fryer watching, the time was right. Arthur sent Chandra a message via George – the sight of French having to thump his middle stump back into the ground after consecutive deliveries from Chandra, was immensely satisfying for all to watch. Fryer was in awe, thinking, a spinner who could generate such pace had to be worth a gamble. Try as he might to keep Chandra out of the team, French had ironically ended up being instrumental in his inclusion.

Edgbaston, the baby of the six regular test grounds, was described a tricky little strip at times. There is no doubt it would take some swing but the inclusion of Chandra, to the delight of the team, meant a new dimension had been added to the contest and the anticipation had gone up a notch. His fast ball was now officially the team's secret weapon. George had mended well and returned to the squad full of confidence. French was furious at his continued omission - which pleased a few. But credit where its due, French worked like a demon to gain selection and had now set his sights on keeping the ever-improving Tim out of the equation.

Everyone seemed to be fine, except for Frank. Arthur had noticed a change in him since the loss of the second Test. He'd become sullen and almost morose at times, despite words of encouragement from all his teammates. Sometimes it was as if he didn't want to be there any more.

They all made a trip to Charmy Down and worked on the machines for three days to regain some strength. While there Frank trained like a man possessed but still his mind wandered. As Arthur watched him train he suddenly recalled the reason the Major had given for Frank's departure from Northants: 'A woman,' he'd said. Arthur's mind went into overdrive and when the session ended he was onto something but even he wasn't sure what.

'Frank,' he said calmly as he helped him out the machine. 'Your mother,' he continued, 'she lives in . . .?'

Exhausted, Frank climbed out the machine. 'Tavistock,' he puffed.

'Ah, near Plymouth of course. And your father, I think you've told me,' he went on.

'Died three years back,' replied Frank.

'That's right,' replied Arthur vacantly.

Frank looked at him. 'That'd be you working out why sometimes I don't feel I should be here,' he suggested.

'It would be, Frank, yes,' said Arthur.

'Like I said, me mum's deaf as a post. Don't even watch TV. I have a cousin and a mate checking on her but . . ' Frank shrugged.

Arthur appeared pensive. 'So she hasn't seen you play?' he asked.

Frank wiped the sweat from his brow with a towel.

'And you won't get her out of Tavvy in a pink fit Arthur, if that's what you're thinking,' Frank made clear.

'Blimey! Read me like a book, you can,' Arthur admitted.

The next day, a wonderful new TV, complete with instructions on when to watch what, and on which channel, was delivered and installed for Mrs Arnold of Tavistock. The delivery slip informed the confused lady that it was courtesy of 'Uncle Arthur'.

The stage had been set for a tense rematch, the Australians having cruised to another easy victory in a county match. The batting genius Steve Moore had hit another winning century and still hadn't been dismissed on the tour. The England team was fully fit, finely tuned and as ready as they would ever be. Fans everywhere had been whipped into a frenzy by the ever–reliable media, and the country braced itself for round three. Another sell-out crowd was ready to cheer them on. In next to no time the sun was reflecting brightly from a silver coin spinning high in a warm breeze.

'Heads,' called Moore as the coin hit the turf.

'We'll have a hit,' Coleman told Moore. They shook hands and parted company after wishing each other luck.

Stiles and Dennis began slowly in a dour start to the day's play, although it was a better display from England in that it was controlled and measured. The Aussie sledging started early. Every

226

time Stiles played a false shot there were plenty around to tell him it wasn't *Stylish* at all! Finally he went for 24 when his feet didn't move quite to the pitch of a regulation off-cutter from Rogers. As he made his way towards the pavilion he heard someone call, 'Now *that's* Stylish!'

The Khan and Dennis partnership lasted as long as a Hollywood marriage – nine minutes for 8 runs, but by the time Coleman and Khan had added 116 for the third wicket things were looking healthier at 171 for 3. Sixty runs later Khan was unlucky to be dismissed when his glove clipped the top of his pad as he played a defensive stroke, causing his bat to lag behind his hands in meeting a sharply turning ball, resulting in a close-in catch for Crocket off Horn. Once again he had reached three figures, but after his dismissal the innings began to fall apart. Three scores of 0 and some token runs from the tail and England struggled to reach 301.

Coleman still managed to find positives in their batting performance, but Fryer was considering an additional batsman for the next Test and dropping down to four strike bowlers. The task now was simply to keep the Aussies under 300 as they took the field on the morning of the second day's play.

As was becoming very predictable, George took an early wicket – and just as predictable was the stubborn Australian captain. As if following his captain's lead, Haynes batted well and together they hauled the total up to 170 for the loss of just the one wicket. All the bowlers, bar Chandra, had had a crack and thus far in the series had been unable to dislodge Moore, who had now accumulated over 250 runs and had played no false shots.

Arthur was champing at the bit up in the stands as he knew that Chandra had the ball to unsettle Moore. When the Aussie captain clubbed two disrespectful boundaries from Edwin it looked like there was no stopping him as he closed in on another century.

Finally, Coleman called upon Chandra. Coming on for his first over in Test cricket, Chandra relished the occasion. First he smiled at Moore, then wasted a bit of time by moving his fielders around while tossing the ball about to warm up. Again he smiled and apologised to Moore. Somewhere inside Moore a little coil was being wound up ever so slightly as Chandra drew out proceedings. Eventually he started off with his gentle spin. Arthur knew it was only a matter of time before he unleashed a fast ball, and waited impatiently. Tim too was filled with anticipation.

'What's he waiting for?' Tim asked impatiently.

'I believe this is his idea of fun,' came Arthur's response.

'He's losing his opportunity,' said Tim, increasingly frustrated as the Aussie skipper stroked another 2 runs as if he were stirring a cup of tea.

'I don't think it will be too long now,' said Arthur, as he watched Chandra joking with Moore about something or other. 'It's normally a good sign when he starts to chat.'

Chandra walked back to his mark then for the first time looked up towards Arthur and Tim. Springing to the crease like a gazelle, he didn't bowl his fast one as expected but ripped forcefully at the ball as it was flung from his grip. Looping gently in flight, it hit the deck and popped up, surprising Moore, who barely managed to keep it down as he moved back just in time. The next ball seemed identical, pitching the same length after sailing through the air twirling at high speed. This time Moore moved onto his back foot a fraction earlier, but the ball hit the pitch and, without getting up more than an inch, shot forward like a rocket and rapped Moore on the pad. He looked plumb LBW. Chandra appealed confidently to the umpire then clapped his hands together mid-pitch as the dreaded finger was slowly raised. Moore was rocked to the core having been beaten by such a cunning ball on 98.

Chandra went wild and his teammates, who had watched him spin his web at close hand, mobbed him enthusiastically on his first Test wicket. He pointed to Arthur in the stands, then clapped. In his next over, Chandra extracted Haynes with a savage ball that cut across the face of the bat and was taken wide in first slip. Looking every bit a Test-class spinner, Chandra was having the time of his life. The Aussies had gone from 178 for 1 to 183 for 3. Having done the job, Chandra was whipped out of the attack and George put back on. He and Jim proceeded to bowl out the Aussies in rapid succession, with Edwin and Chandra being brought back late, getting one more each to clean up the tail and bundle the tourists out for 231. England therefore found themselves with a handy 70-run lead as, full of commitment, they began their second innings.

But if Test cricket were an animal it would surely be a snake – twisting, meandering, sometimes moving fast, sometimes slow, sometimes not moving at all.

England went in to bat having tamed the snake, but perhaps they blinked once too often and soon the snake had wrapped itself around England's neck; at 40 for 6 its grip was rapidly tightening. If it continued, strangulation would occur within a matter of overs. The situation was absolutely desperate.

It was at this dire stage that George and Jim found themselves at the wicket. All the hours facing each other at Charmy Down finally counted for something as they bore the brunt of the Australian bowling attack for twenty overs of pure defiance, taking the score to over 90. George seemed quite comfortable in the middle and played the more correct shots. The crowd had a collective heart palpitation when he shaped up to hook Rogers, only to leave the ball in the end. He resisted chasing all short-pitched bowling until Jim was hit under the armpit. The next ball George faced he flat-batted it back over not only the bowler's head, but his father's too as George had given his family guest passes for the five days. Lloyd Samuels stood upright arms aloft as it sailed 20 rows back then sitting back down turned to the woman seated next to him saying. 'That's my boy.'

Meanwhile, Jim's towering height didn't allow him to get forward enough to a ball from Rogers and he gave an easy catch to the wicketkeeper.

Next in was Chandra, who hit his first two balls for four and was then quickly beaten by a ball from Horn that spun low and bowled him. Edwin and Frank offered little resistance and the innings ended disappointingly on 115. Frank's only scoring shot was another six that he pulled into the stands before departing, leaving George stranded on an invaluable 50 not out.

Arthur, looking for positives, calculated that his bowlers had scored 67 per cent of the team's runs and was very proud of this, but the overall total was still appalling. In all likelihood it would cost them the match which would mean a 2-1 series lead for the Australians – and if there was even a draw from that point on the Ashes were gone.

In the England dressing room, Coleman became incensed

when he saw that the heads of his batsmen were down. 'Is that what you think they need now?' he said pointing at the bowlers. 'You lot are feeling sorry for yourselves at a time when they need to feed off your energy.' Coleman pointed to Arthur's men again. 'Sort yourselves out,' he snapped angrily.

Getting a grip of themselves, they greeted George and his first ever half century in Test cricket with a rousing reception as he entered the dressing room, cheering with gusto and patting him on the back. Tim was there in the thick of it, geeing everyone up. If ever there was an unselfish bench-warmer, it was him.

Needing a mere 186 runs for victory, the Australian team felt optimistic as they prepared to get on with the task at hand. As Jim passed Arthur on his way out to the field, Arthur shook his hand and wished him luck.

'Keep your eye on him, will you?' he asked Jim, nodding in Frank's direction. Though Frank had taken some valuable wickets in the first innings, he was obviously still having trouble forgetting his costly dismissal in the second Test. Jim understood Arthur perfectly.

Edwin and George toiled away on an unusually hot and humid day. Their accuracy was below their usual standard as their energy had been sapped by the abnormal heat. George was frustrated, having not had his customary early break-through – and it showed. It was Edwin who took the first two wickets this time but once more it was the tenacious Australian skipper who stood in their way, having found a rock-solid partner in his brother Mark. Despite all efforts, the pair scored freely and the game slowly ebbed away from England. With the score on 155 for 2 it would be fair to say that the thought of defeat had crossed all of the England players' minds. But they'd all promised Arthur they would never give up, so they did plenty of talking and remained positive in the face of adversity. Jim had had a bowl too, but was unable to remove the barnacle that was Steve Moore, when Coleman told both Frank and Chandra to warm up.

'You and me, Big Man,' said Chandra to Frank as they passed each other changing ends. He was rubbing his hands together excitedly, apparently not daunted by the task. Once again Chandra was about to bowl at Steve Moore, who would surely not be tricked again by his smiling assassin. He looked around him at the field placings. Arthur could see that Chandra was chatting away again, this time throwing the ball up in the air as he prepared to bowl. Arthur said to Tim, 'Five pounds he gets 'im this ball.' Tim thought Arthur was mad but after a moment's hesitation he replied, 'I'll make it ten if you want!'

Whereupon they shook on it.

Some of the England officials had started chatting in the dressing room and were not really paying much attention to the drama unfolding outside. There was mention of the fourth Test already as Chandra ran in. He was about to bowl when he pulled up short, looked at his field again and brought two players in close. An innovative fielding change was all it took to get everyone's interest again and the officials got back to watching cricket. Moore on the other hand smiled under his helmet, and shook his head. Satisfied, Chandra went back to his mark. He danced in once more and, as Arthur had guessed, his arm flew over like a catapult. But the ball was well pitched up, and fired directly towards Moore's leg stump – full, straight and fast. It slipped under Moore's bat, over the toe of his back foot and past leg stump. In doing so it shaved the base of the stump ever so slightly, sending a vibration rippling upwards. When it reached the top the bail popped off like a champagne cork. Harry Winter was first to rush over and congratulate Chandra; the rest followed.

'Should have made it twenty pounds,' said Arthur as he and Tim celebrated the key breakthrough.

Moore was stunned as he made his way to the pavilion. As he passed Dyson on the way back he growled, 'Watch him.'

Chandra completed a wicket maiden.

Now it was Frank's turn. Jim ran in and handed him the ball.

'I know you worry about your accuracy, mate, but don't let's die wondering. Give 'em hell.'

He returned to his position as Frank made some minor alterations to the field, paced out his long run-up, stretched his shoulders and slowly arched his back. He'd decided it was time to see what Arthur's training had really done for him and wasted no time after a quick warm-up before he set off with great intent, the chants of the crowd ringing in his ears.

Mark Moore was an elegant batsman, known for his stylish

strokes and uncomplicated defence. Nevertheless, Frank's first ball struck the batsman so hard on the pad that it unbalanced him completely and he trod on his stumps. To the delight of the crowd the replay appeared on the big screen over and over again. The England players too marvelled at the raw speed that could force such a dismissal. It was a sign of things to come.

The new batsman, Church, was wary having seen the result of the previous ball. But his was a short stay too. Frank's next ball gave him no chance of getting his bat on it. It was just too fast and hit Church in the ribs. He clutched at himself, staggered away from the wicket, lay down and was eventually carried off looking the worse for wear.

On it went for the next two overs as Frank managed to work himself into a state of fury. He struck the splice of Doug Dyson's bat handle like a sledgehammer and Dyson pulled his lower hand away just in time. With the handle of the bat held limply from his left hand, the blade came away from the handle and lay useless on the pitch, blasted loose by Frank's thunderbolt. For the second time in as many Tests, Dyson called for another bat while facing Frank. The next ball was short and virtually invisible to the batsman. It caught a faint inside edge and flew to the keeper for a straightforward catch. Chandra pointed to the speed on the scoreboard: 106.50 m.p.h. –a new record had been set.

Bowling like a man possessed, Frank took two more cheap wickets and the tourists were on the ropes at 160 for 7, plus one retired hurt. Although Frank's energy reserves were dwindling fast and the scoreboard showed that his pace was dropping off, Coleman kept him on, with Chandra operating the other end.

The Aussies mounted a defiant last-ditch stand. A desperate partnership between Horn and Patterson yielded some valuable runs. When a ball flew off the edge of Horn's bat and went untouched by the slips, it brought the visitors four runs. The two tailenders had now added ten each and the score had crept up to the point where Australia were only two runs from victory with three wickets in hand.

At this point Chandra once more justified his selection with another fast-ball wicket on the last ball of his fifth over. The vast crowd was brought to its feet as slim hopes were kept alive.

In the members' stand nerves were frayed, as handkerchiefs

worked overtime dabbing down glistening brows. The commentators revelled in the closeness of the contest and whipped their audiences into a frenzy. Never had back-to-back Tests been so closely contested. Arthur, Tim, Jean and Mrs Cheshire were almost sitting on top of one another. Alice, who was now a permanent fixture at the Samuels's clan gatherings, kept putting her head in her hands, not wanting to watch. George's father kept pulling her hands away playfully so she had no choice.

Chandra had kept them in the contest but still the odds were in the Australians' favour. With two batsmen still to come the slow-moving figure of the injured Greg Church made his way out into the middle to resume his innings, the general opinion in the Australian camp being that an injured Church was worth more than a fully fit Weir. Church was in great pain but needing only two more runs there was really never any doubt that he would return if required. Stan Coleman, Frank and Jim had a mini conference about how to handle the situation, and brought a fielder in close.

'Look, Frank, I know you might not want to bowl short to an injured man but—' started Coleman.

'You must be joking!' Frank spat. 'I'll put him six feet under if I have to,' he said and stormed back to his mark.

'Right, OK,' Coleman said, quite shocked at Frank's outburst. 'So much for the gentle giant.'

Frank came in with a good head of steam. His back bent ever backwards, he leapt high before the crease then cocked himself like the hammer of a gun. The ball hurtled towards the batsman but was pitching harmlessly outside off stump. Church played forward and looked to push it firmly to mid-off hoping for a couple of easy runs, but the ball had other ideas. Swinging very late, it pitched and shot through the batsman's defences, still angling inwards. Once past his bat and pads the ball, as if locked onto a target, proceeded to knock back the middle and leg stumps. The entire England team appealed wildly and unnecessarily, before converging on Frank. Church surveyed the damage again as the square leg umpire walked towards the stumps to carry out much-needed repairs.

It was hard to know whether to feel sorry for the incoming batsman or not. On the one hand, Ben Weir was about to face perhaps the most ferocious spell of fast bowling in a Test match. The crowd had been constantly looking at the speeds being flashed up on the scoreboard, and so far Frank had bowled at a freakish top speed of 106.9 m.p.h. They had decided to ignore the screen in the Australian dressing room. On the other hand, Weir only needed to get a bit of bat on ball and the chances were it would race away for a couple of runs at least.

Weir stood tall and appeared relaxed as he took guard. He had obviously adopted the frame of mind that he might as well have a go, but did not appear to be in a rush as he glanced around the ground. The roar of the crowd pumped Frank to new heights as he leant into his stride. Weir's eyes were wide open now he was facing the moment of truth. Frank prayed he would not let the team down again as he came to earth. His enormous weight unsettled the bails at the non-striker's end as his front foot thumped down like a tree falling in a forest. Frank released the ball but during his follow through he stumbled awkwardly and as he fell there came a most unusual sound, like the snapping of a stick.

Weir meanwhile had to contend with a fast approaching blur of red. He had indeed made his mind up to go down swinging, but his swing was way too late. His back-lift became an abbreviated semi-swat as the ball swept past him flattening the stumps and propelling England to a 2-1 lead in the series.

The players ran to Frank sprawled on the turf, struggling to half sit up, shaking his fist defiantly. He was engulfed by men in white reaching down to embrace him. The crowd was already on its feet yelling and singing passionately. The pubs too had exploded. Arthur and Tim hugged each other and shouted. They were back on top.

Jim and George went to help Frank from the ground but he shook his head and winced, pointing down at his ankle. They all stopped celebrating as Jim knelt down and looked tentatively under the turn-up of Frank's trouser leg. A stunned silence came over the team as Jim rose quickly and signalled urgently for a stretcher.

**England V. Australia**
Edgebaston - Birmingham
Third Test Match  August 11th, 12th, 13th, 14th & 15th
England won by 1 run
Man of the Match – Frank Arnold

### England

| | | 1st Innings | | 2nd Innings |
|---|---|---|---|---|
| 1 - | D. Dennis | run out ................. 28 | | c Church b Moore.......14 |
| 2 - | P. Stilles | c Talbot b Rogers.......24 | | run out .....................6 |
| 3 - | R. Khan | c & b Horn ............111 | | c Rogers b Moore.........2 |
| 4 - | S. Coleman* | lbw Patterson............53 | | run out......................4 |
| 5 - | M. Engle | c Horn...................31 | | lbw Horn...................9 |
| 6 - | H Winter† | b Weir .................17 | | c & b Horn.................0 |
| 7 - | G. Samuels | lbw Weir..................0 | | not out....................50 |
| 8 - | J. Singleton | run out ...................0 | | c Talbot b Rogers........13 |
| 9 - | C. Jafar | c Dyson b Patterson.....0 | | b Weir.......................8 |
| 10 - | F. Arnold | lbw Horn ..............18 | | c Talbot b Weir............1 |
| 11 - | E. Roberts | not out...................6 | | b Patterson.................6 |
| | | Extras...................13 | | Extras.......................2 |
| | | Total...................301 | | Total....................115 |

FALL OF WICKETS

First Innings:  47 -1  55-2  171-3  231-4  273-5  276-6  276-7  277-8  285-9
Second Innings:  17-1  21-2  25-3  33-4  35-5  40-6  98-7  102-8  107-9

| Bowlers | Overs | Mdn | Runs | Wkts | | Bowler | Overs | Mdn | Runs | Wkts |
|---|---|---|---|---|---|---|---|---|---|---|
| Rogers | 32 | 5 | 98 | 1 | | Rogers | 6 | 2 | 24 | 1 |
| Weir | 26 | 1 | 83 | 2 | | Weir | 5 | 1 | 18 | 2 |
| Horn | 24 | 6 | 77 | 3 | | Horn | 9 | 4 | 22 | 2 |
| Patterson | 17 | 0 | 32 | 2 | | Patterson | 6 | 0 | 16 | 1 |
| M. Moore | DNB | | | | | M. Moore | 7 | 2 | 28 | 2 |

\* Denotes Captain
† Denotes Keeper

### Australia

| | | 1st Innings | | 2nd Innings |
|---|---|---|---|---|
| 1 - | D. Crocket | b Samuels ...............2 | | b Roberts................40 |
| 2 - | P. Haynes | b Jafar..................76 | | lbw Roberts.................28 |
| 3 - | S. Moore* | lbw Jafar.................98 | | b Jafar.......................65 |
| 4 - | M Moore | b Samuels.................2 | | b Arnold ....................22 |
| 5 - | G. Church | lbw Samuels.............4 | | lbw Arnold ..................0 |
| 6 - | D. Dyson | b Arnold................19 | | c Arnold......................0 |
| 7 - | W. Talbot† | b Arnold.................0 | | b Arnold......................1 |
| 8 - | C. Rogers | c Chandra b Arnold.....3 | | b Arnold......................1 |
| 9 - | G. Patterson | lbw Roberts............7 | | b Jafar.......................10 |
| 10 – | W. Horn | not out.................21 | | not out......................11 |
| 11 – | G Weir | c Jafar......................0 | | b Arnold.....................1 |
| | | Extras.....................9 | | Extras........................7 |
| | | Total................. ..231 | | Total........................184 |

FALL OF WICKETS

First Innings:  4-1  280-2  183-3  198-4 199-5  205-6  210-7  229-8  230-9
Second innings:  56-1  70-2  155-3  155-4  155-5  155-6  159-7 160-8 182-9

| Bowler | Overs | Mdn | Runs | Wkts | | Bowlers | Overs | mdns | Runs | Wkts |
|---|---|---|---|---|---|---|---|---|---|---|
| Samuels | 21 | 5 | 79 | 3 | | Samuels | 15 | 1 | 57 | 0 |
| Singleton | 12 | 0 | 52 | 0 | | Singleton | 16 | 4 | 48 | 0 |
| Roberts | 5 | 0 | 23 | 1 | | Roberts | 15 | 0 | 42 | 2 |
| Arnold | 15 | 1 | 48 | 3 | | Arnold | 6.5 | 0 | 13 | 6 |
| Jafar | 6 | 1 | 24 | 3 | | Jafar | 3 | 3 | 17 | 2 |

\* Denotes Captain
† Denotes Keeper

Umpires: Howie Pedersen & Paul Ryan

## 31

Frank's incredible performance elevated him to national hero status. His efforts with the ball at Edgbaston were made all the more surreal as they culminated in the breaking of his fibula– the small bone in his lower leg and a long crack in his tibia. Sadly, his Test series was finished. His heroics had put England one up again, a vital lead. Already Frank had been operated on by the best surgeons in the country – all mad keen cricket supporters who wanted him back on the park as soon as possible. Frank hobbled about on crutches with the large cast covering the lower half of his leg already covered in signatures, witticisms, graffiti and a recipe for samosas from Chandra. Frank had bowled near perfectly in the third Test and, strangely enough, more accurately than ever before, all the while maintaining his top speed. Everyone was amazed how keen he was to get back to bowling again.

Meanwhile, the rest of the team were looking ahead to Headingley, where the series could be wrapped up with another victory. The main topic of debate was who would replace Frank.

In between the team practice sessions and other commitments there were a couple of pleasant outings. While relaxing on a boat trip one day, Coleman chatted with Khan about the pitch at Lord's, it being the venue of the last Test of the series this year. Overhearing them, Fryer heard Stiles make an 'off-the-cuff' remark to Coleman. 'If we win at Headingley, we won't *need* to play Lords.' It was good they were so confident and he was in a good spirits too, relaxing with a couple of well-earned ales. He added for fun, shouting at Stiles, 'If we win at Headingley . . . I'll even let Arthur play at Lords!'

There were cheers and jeers from the group. Arthur was a little embarrassed but didn't mind the jibe at his expense.

The subject of taking an additional batsman into the Test and dropping to four bowlers was raised, but the selectors stayed true to the form players in the squad: Arthur's men. It had also been duly noted that as the bowlers were expending enormous amounts of explosive energy in short bursts, their bowling spells were shorter than most, so the need to rotate them was imperative, which made the fifth bowler crucial. Tim had been training well, but it was still widely felt he had nowhere near enough experience for a Test match. Mathew French had been improving as well and it was thought he had his nose in front to replace Frank for the fourth Test match. Arthur and the team were behind Tim all the way, offering as much advice and support as they could, but in the end, French was given the nod. Everyone in the squad was disappointed for Tim but none could fault the team that went into the fourth Test. Had the players been picked on their enthusiasm, Tim would have been a clear winner.

The Australians took an unchanged team into the match, having once more convincingly defeated a county team during the period in between the Tests. The Australians had rested some key players and rumour had it the team's batsmen had been practising in the nets on shortened pitches to counter the speed of the English quicks. Of course, this was not true as it would have meant the deliveries they were facing would not have been of the correct bounce. What they *had* done was increase the amount of indoor training sessions using bowling machines, in order that they could practise facing deliveries at the unaccustomed speeds they were subjected to in the Tests.

On the first day of the fourth Test match, the weather was overcast, which is always a dangerous sign at Headingley for the swing can be wild. The pitch, no stranger to big individual scores, had seen three triple test centuries in years gone by and looked a belter again. The ghosts of Botham and Willis's triumph in '81 still lingered but the Australians had nevertheless been installed as favourites to win. The prospect of a clear day was good as the cloud cover was breaking up rapidly, courtesy of a strong wind. The toss went the visitors' way and the Australians once more chose to bat. With history on their doorstep and a fresh speech from Fryer ringing in their ears, England took to the field with the prayers of 50 million people behind them.

George and Jim bowled without luck and when they didn't take any early wickets, this was left to Edwin, who had been given a boost by Arthur that morning. Whilst the players were getting changed, Arthur wondered out loud how many Second World War veterans would witness just one more Ashes victory for their beloved England before they went to 'the big hangar' in the sky.

Edwin carried this thought onto the ground with him as though he were brandishing a Bren gun – and sprayed the Aussies with some formidable deliveries. He didn't celebrate his wickets, he simply marched back to his mark and waited for the next batsman. Mrs Cheshire and Jean gave Biggles a rev up with every wicket Edwin took and he howled loudly much to the delight of all in the vicinity. The obstinate Moore stood firm once again, accumulating runs as he moved remorselessly towards another century. Edwin finally claimed the Australian captain after he had swatted, stroked, steered and swept his way to 131 in quick time. The commentators were running thin on superlatives to describe the dazzling array of shots that were on display. One of them likened it to watching a fragmented fireworks display for you never knew in which direction the next explosion would head. George took some much-needed wickets in the middle order for a change, and Jim and Mathew French mopped up the tail with French's first and only wicket in the innings – a catch to Chandra, which was quite ironic really. The firepower of the English attack was still formidable without Frank but the crowd and Barmy Army missed him, chanting, 'Bring back Frank. Then they're sank!'

It was obvious that French was a misfit in the team who'd not helped himself by failing to offer thanks to Chandra for taking a difficult catch off his bowling to give him his only wicket.

The Aussie total of 340 runs was what the series had made everyone expect by now: low scores and short Test matches. When the English batting line-up managed a total of 276, a little worry crept into the equation. Although one of the openers, Stiles, had at last scored a century, and Khan another valuable fifty, the English tail generally failed. The spectre of Horn was looming. Despite only three wickets, one suspected something special was just around the corner. If it had not been for 47 minutes of defiance from Jim and Edwin, which yielded a further 28 runs, England would have ended up less than 250. Coleman and his team had hoped to go back out to bowl with a lead for a change, but once again they had a deficit to deal with. Chandra's third innings in Test cricket had lasted just four balls for no runs – his second duck of the series. It was perhaps the most valuable duck in Test cricket. Being so disgusted by his performances, he asked Tim to help him in the nets and in two marathon sessions before

England batted again, Chandra worked feverishly on his batting technique.

An enormous media blitz had caused a groundswell of anticipation regarding the outcome of this Test match. Again the England players carried the weight of the nation's hopes upon their shoulders. Shoulders Arthur had fashioned with his machines. Shoulders made to carry a lot of weight.

It was the moment of truth for the English bowlers: bowl well and the Ashes series was there for the taking. But Australia held a lead of 64 runs.

As the innings got under way, George's spark had seemingly returned. Suddenly he was unplayable again and took two quick wickets. Edwin picked up where he had left off with one of the best balls of the series that drew Moore forward as it drifted in front of his body. Then, on a whim, it seemed to flirt with the edge of his bat. Moore made a late adjustment to the shot and in doing so managed to get a slightly thicker edge pushing it wider. Flying low to third slip Coleman dived full to his right and slightly forward taking a freakish one-handed catch low to the ground. Coleman was more surprised than any as he was not the youngest in the team and certainly not the most agile. He was grateful to his rangy frame for getting him to the ball. Moore nodded to Edwin as he departed. For every bit he was a fine batsman, he was a good sport too. Edwin had claimed his wicket twice in this Test, which was a telling contribution.

After a short rest, George was back and kept the Australians guessing with superb variation in speed and movement. Never was any batsman allowed to get into a rhythm. Just when it looked as though two of the middle order had settled in, George removed both of them and was then involved in a run-out. Chandra once again proved his worth, breaking the most threatening partnership the Aussies had built with a wonderfully fast ball. Dyson tried to hook but only managed to help the ball on its way to the keeper.

Jim picked off the last batsman like a towering bird of prey. Never fully capitulating, but never in control, the Australian innings was one in which they failed to capitalise. The Australians had only reached 202, thus leaving England 267 for victory in the Ashes. George ended up with a 6 for, with Edwin, Jim and Chandra taking a wicket apiece.

Arthur sat back and reflected on the choice of Jim. Originally he thought Jim might have turned out as a much more aggressive type of bowler; though he certainly delivered a fearsome spell at Trent Bridge. Yet over time he'd assumed an anchor-type role and beat the bat more often than any other bowler. Jim had transformed himself into an indispensable breed and finally fitted the tag of 'Workhorse'. Where others strove for pace and wickets, Jim bowled more consistently than the rest and his no-frills approach complemented all his bowling partners. He was a rare find and completely unselfish.

The winning target was neither easy nor hard. England's batting was suspect at times and the nation looked on with trepidation as Stiles and Dennis made their way out and made a solid start with a 50-run opening partnership before Dennis lost his wicket, which brought Khan to the crease. He seemed to be playing well within himself but soon lost Stiles who played a loose shot and was caught behind. Coleman, however, set the pace and raced towards the required total, until he tripped over – literally – and was disastrously run out going for a quick single for 51, after looking better than he had in the entire series.

The Australians applied the blowtorch. Khan held fast as Engle and Winter departed for 13 and 2 respectively, but England looked to be expiring slowly at 141 for the loss of 5 wickets. Khan was the wild card. If he went, England were lost. He did what he could to retain the strike but even he found the going tough against the savage onslaught being dished up by the smart Aussie attack. George, who had done well with the bat in the past, continued where he had left off, and defended stoutly for over forty minutes, playing his shots as best he could. Alas, having scored 7, the spin of Horn was too classy for him and he was drawn into playing a false sweep shot. 'Why a sweep?' he cursed over and over to himself as he lurched off. He'd never played one before in his life, so why now? In a Test! George was disgusted with himself. Mathew French had the dubious honour of joining the ranks of debutants who scored first-ball ducks when he was knocked over by Rogers. When Jim was bamboozled by a Horn wrong-un for 2, hope turned to despair and England wobbled horribly on the brink. Once more, Fryer's thoughts turned to the team line-up for the fifth Test, and an additional batsman.

Khan was joined by Chandra. It was a curious sight indeed, an irony not lost on many keen observers: both English-born, one to Indian parents and the other Pakistani. They had never said too much to each other at practice, but Khan liked the way Chandra varied his deliveries and talked a lot, never dropping his head. Chandra on the other hand admired Khan's arrogance and coveted his leg-side shots.

Chandra never minced words. 'What's wrong with you today?' he asked as Khan came to meet him.

'Surely you of all people know about lulling the opposition into a false sense of security,' Khan replied.

'And are they lulled now?' asked Chandra.

Khan flashed him a smile. The score was 188 for 8 and he was one run short of another Test fifty, with England needing a further 79 runs for victory and the Ashes. The Australians at that point must have felt victory was a mere formality, but it was a crucial time as their two main strike bowlers tiring and in need of a rest. Moore on the other hand felt he should persist with them.

Like a shark smelling blood in the water, Khan read the situation well and wore them down. In Weir's final over, his pace had dropped off noticeably and Khan pounced on three loose balls sending all to the boundary. It was a warning shot to Moore, who took both bowlers off. Khan once more sized up the situation as Horn was brought on.

'He's slow to warm up these days, so hit him for a couple early if you can,' he told Chandra. Chandra wondered if Khan had actually seen him bat before, or if he was confusing him with someone else. Still, if Khan thought it was a good idea, then it was best to follow orders. Chandra skipped down the pitch to the first ball of Horn's over and hit it high over mid-on for six. The next ball he flayed to the square boundary for four. Having completed a run before the boundary was signalled brought Chandra face to face with Horn.

'He told me to do that,' Chandra explained, motioning to Khan. 'I have the utmost respect for your bowling.'

Khan had to give him a sign to calm down a little as they walked back to their respective ends. However, the next ball was there to be hit too and Chandra pulled it savagely so high that it brought another six. Chandra wisely avoided Horn's stare.

Following the ball's progress over the boundary, Chandra noticed a small group of supporters going wild. A young girl held up a banner that read *Sandra 4 Chandra!*

The two batsmen meet mid pitch as the bowlers changed ends. Chandra was buzzing.

'Look, I have a fan club,' he said pointing to the boundary.

'Great. Just ignore them.' replied Khan tersely and returned to his crease.

The two batsmen ground out a nail-biting 42 runs in the next hour and twenty-seven minutes, quite slow considering the first 28 of their partnership had taken just eleven minutes.

Soon Khan noticed that Chandra was tiring mentally. With 9 runs left to get for the ultimate prize, he decided to change tack and began playing with restraint, nudging and nurdling the ball around, much to the frustration of the Australian quicks. Khan was now clearly protecting his partner from the strike as he gathered another four singles all from the last balls of the over. With the target looming closer and England needing just 5 runs for victory, the great spinner Horn was given the task of saving the Ashes series.

Chandra was feeling nervous now and wondered why he hadn't been at the start of his innings – probably because in the back of his mind he had thought that 79 runs were impossible? Shaking the doubts from his head, he looked to the heavens and twirled his bat, urging himself to concentrate. Now they were so close his gut churned. Even Khan was wrestling with his natural instincts.

The beer was flowing in the pubs once more. Victory looked distinctly probable and some were celebrating already. All around the country, offices and businesses had virtually ground to a halt in the last hour as the pair edged England closer. The pubs were still packing them in. In Good Walloping, Ted Doyle was wishing he'd paced himself better as he squinted to focus on the TV screen.

Edwin was padded up in the dressing room, praying that his services wouldn't be called for. Jean and Mrs Cheshire were behind Arthur, having their glasses topped up for the celebration as they told each other they had never had any doubts about their boys bringing the bacon home.

The brilliance of Khan was enough to keep him alive for a whole over, but as he tried to turn a leg-side delivery away for another last-ball single, it popped a little. He dropped his hands and took the ball on the hip. It fell away harmlessly, but left Chandra stuck on strike to Rogers, the most dangerous Aussie quick, who was coming back fresh from a break. He played the first four balls of the over cautiously – all dot balls. When Rogers pitched one in short and wide on the off side, Chandra instinctively rocked back onto his back foot and cut it hard towards the boundary, but the ball reached the fieldsman so fast the batsmen only managed a single. Khan, facing the last ball, was handed the game on a platter. He leant into a straight drive and thumped it powerfully wide of the mid-off fieldsman, who dived in spectacular fashion. All of England held its breath as the fielder deflected the red streak thus taking the pace off the ball and saving a certain boundary. Taking two runs meant Chandra was on strike to Horn for the first ball of the new over, requiring two more runs for the Ashes.

The nation held its breath. Spinner vs. spinner. Most would have preferred a faster bowler bowling to Chandra for he appeared more comfortable facing the quicks. Chandra's head was spinning. He knew not to stretch the moment out too long and took guard. Back in the dressing room, Arthur looked at Edwin who was ashen faced.

'What on earth are you worried about?' he asked Edwin bluntly. 'D'you really think he's going to give you a shot at all the glory?'

Jim and Tim heard the comment and thought 'How true!' But Edwin could still not relax.

As the over began, Chandra padded up to the first ball and got well forward to the second. He let another two go past the bat wide to be gloved by the keeper. Then he was rapped on the pad after an indecisive shuffle out of his crease. There was a blood-curdling yell from the bowler and Chandra froze. Edwin's heart skipped a beat. All the onlookers were transfixed with apprehension.

'Not out,' came the call from the umpire as he shook his head. From the crowd came a collective sigh that could have taken the roofs off several houses.

The last ball was a full toss on leg with two men out deep. Horn was hoping for a bold match-winning swipe. At first Chandra was shocked to see it floating towards him. A gift! In the end he swept it square and they ran a single. Khan was already wondering if they'd missed their chance for victory, thinking Chandra should have selected a different shot.

Again Chandra was on strike to Rogers, who was fired up and looked menacing as he flew in like a banshee. The first ball was short and Chandra ducked under it unconvincingly. The next was speared in at leg stump. Chandra rushed the shot as he half-swiped and dug it out, relieved when it made contact with the bat and trickled to leg. No run. The third ball was short again, very quick and sat up for Chandra. Everyone watching the game drew a sharp breath as his body language suggested he was shaping to play a back-foot drive. An outside edge beckoned. Chandra moved back, stood tall and flashed at the rising ball. Making firm contact, he carved it square. The ball screwed its way towards the boundary and thumped into the fence without a hand being laid on it. Having no doubt about the outcome of the shot, Chandra had run forward his arms raised triumphantly in the air. The umpire signalled four as Khan and Chandra came together mid-pitch and rejoiced. It was done, the Ashes were won. So long coming; so quickly over.

All England rose to its feet and proclaimed the Ashes victory.

The rest of the England team sprinted madly out of the dressing room towards the pitch. Arthur, who had been sitting with Frank and Tim, jumped up and down with the big man. Tim embraced them both and they all remained in a huddle until the result began to sink in. Frank's plaster cast thumped on the ground loudly as they all shouted. The team officials who were on hand, congratulated Arthur and embraced him euphorically. Never had he been hugged so much. He looked around for Jean, who was standing back letting him have his moment. He made his way towards her, slowly rubbing the back of his neck. Jean was smiling madly at her husband; she took his hand and kissed his cheek.

'That wasn't so hard,' he quipped.

Mrs Cheshire smiled, blushed then screamed as Frank

picked her up and spun her around. Alice celebrated boisterously with George's family and kept an eye out for him as the other players ran onto the field. Jim and Tim hauled Arthur back onto the balcony to cheer the batsmen in.

Out on the field Khan and Chandra were butting helmets like two old rams as they jogged back to the pavilion holding a couple of stumps each. Chandra made a slight diversion in the direction of his small group of supporters and shook his fist and bat triumphantly at them as they cheered back at him. The Australians patted their backs as the two batsmen scurried past and there were handshakes of sorts. The crowd began to rush to the middle and were met by police officers and stewards as the rest of the England team ran onto the ground to congratulate Khan and Chandra. Jim finally rallied the whole team to head back inside where they found Arthur, Frank and Tim.

'There he is!' they all shouted.

Arthur turned and held his hands high, fists clenched, as they all swarmed around him. Soon he was seated on the broadest shoulders in the land. His dream had vanished. In its place there was nothing but irreversible history.

At the awards ceremony, Coleman got to say his piece and finally everyone in the country heard about the man who had plotted the resurrection of English cricket – Arthur Jenkins.

As Steve Moore listened to the speeches he recalled seeing Arthur here there and everywhere over the last month but hadn't a clue who he was. Now it all made sense. Moore was impressed with the tale of Arthur's men. Incredible that one ordinary man's desire could overthrow the most gifted and skilled sportsmen in the world. It was a lesson to be learned by everyone. Thompson's exclusive article documenting the rise of Arthur's men was prepared for the press already, and they took it to all corners of the world. In time Arthur was lauded as the saviour of English cricket.

As the day wore on into the evening Arthur and the team got completely carried away with things, as they deserved. After a long while at the ground they were taken to a suitable venue towards midnight and celebrated with the people of Leeds. It was a proud night for Arthur. He had achieved the unimaginable – the Ashes were back home, his country reigned supreme once more and his faith in himself and his players had been justified. Still

something was not right.  Looking about he saw Tim in the thick
of things but somehow . . . not.

England V. Australia
At Headingly - Leeds
Fourth Test Match 18<sup>th</sup>, 19<sup>th</sup>, 20<sup>th</sup>, 21<sup>st</sup> & 22<sup>nd</sup> August
England won by 2 wickets
Man of the Match George Samuels

## Australia

| | 1st Innings | | 2nd Innings | |
|---|---|---|---|---|
| 1 - D. Crocket | b Roberts | 51 | b Samuels | 9 |
| 2 - P. Haynes | b Roberts | 19 | lbw Samuels | 2 |
| 3 - S. Moore* | Roberts | 131 | c Roberts | 21 |
| 4 - M Moore | lbw Samuels | 21 | b Samuels | 46 |
| 5 - G. Church | c & b Samuels | 40 | lbw Roberts | 13 |
| 6 - D. Dyson | b Samuels | 36 | c Samuels | 19 |
| 7 - W. Talbot † | b Roberts | 0 | c Samuels | 28 |
| 8 - C. Rogers | c Roberts | 3 | run out | 11 |
| 9 - G. Patterson | not out | 17 | b Jafar | 20 |
| 10 – W. Horn | b French | 0 | b Singleton | 19 |
| 11 – G. Weir | c Singleton | 7 | not out | 14 |
| | Extras | 15 | Extras | 10 |
| | Total | 340 | Total | 202 |

## FALL OF WICKETS

First Innings    49-1   94-2  139-3  249-4 251-5   298-6  305-7  331-8  333-9
Second innings:  2-1  220-2  35-3  61-4  97-5  144-6  172-7  183-8  184-9

| Bowlers | Overs | Mdn | Runs | Wkts | | Bowlers | Overs | Mdn | Runs | Wkts |
|---|---|---|---|---|---|---|---|---|---|---|
| Samuels | 23 | 5 | 93 | 3 | | Samuels | 14 | 4 | 36 | 5 |
| Singleton | 22 | 6 | 88 | 1 | | Singleton | 15 | 5 | 55 | 1 |
| Roberts | 20 | 6 | 73 | 5 | | Roberts | 12 | 1 | 57 | 2 |
| Jafar | 1 | 2 | 31 | 0 | | Jafar | 7 | 2 | 19 | 1 |
| French | 8 | 1 | 47 | 1 | | French | 6 | 0 | 30 | 0 |

* Denotes Captain
† Denotes Keeper

## England

| | 1st Innings | | 2nd Innings | |
|---|---|---|---|---|
| 1 - D. Dennis | b Rogers | 29 | c Weir bPatterson | 33 |
| 2 - P. Stilles | b Rogers | 102 | c Patterson b Weir | 25 |
| 3 - R. Khan | c & b Horn | 59 | not out | 87 |
| 4 - S. Coleman* | lbw Patterson | 14 | run out | 51 |
| 5 - M. Engle | c Horn | 26 | b M. Moore | 13 |
| 6 - H. Winter† | b Weir | 7 | c&b Horn | 2 |
| 7 - G. Samuels | lbw Rogers | 8 | c Moore b Horn | 7 |
| 8 - M. French | b Rogers | 0 | b Weir | 0 |
| 9 - J. Singleton | not out | 20 | lbw Rogers | 2 |
| 10 – C. Jafar | lbw Horn | 0 | not out | 42 |
| 11 - E. Roberts | b Weir | 8 | DNB | |
| | Extras | 3 | Extras | 8 |
| | Total | 276 | Total | 270 |

## FALL OF WICKETS

First Innings    46-1   163-2   188-3  211-4  234-5  237-6  239-7  245-8  248-9
Second Innings   50 -1  74-2   149-3  167-4  5-173-5  174-6  177-7  188-8

| Bowler | Overs | Mdn | Runs | Wkts | | Bowler | Overs | Mdn | Runs | Wkts |
|---|---|---|---|---|---|---|---|---|---|---|
| Rogers | 32 | 5 | 100 | 4 | | Rogers | 16 | 3 | 72 | 1 |
| Patterson | 11 | 0 | 60 | 1 | | Patterson | 15 | 4 | 50 | 1 |
| Horn | 27 | 6 | 104 | 3 | | Horn | 19 | 0 | 75 | 2 |
| Weir | 16 | 1 | 89 | 2 | | Weir | 14 | 1 | 49 | 2 |
| M. Moore | DNB | | | | | M. Moore | 6 | 0 | 21 | 1 |

* Denotes Captain
† Denotes Keeper

Umpires: Martin Saunders & Bob Moore

## 32

In the days that followed, there were celebrations and ceremonies all over the country. Arthur's picture was in all the papers and he could go nowhere without being mobbed. It was a wonderful time for him. He experienced a sensation of immense satisfaction and pride that comes to few.

The players were hard to hold back given the last match was a dead rubber. A plethora of gala nights, ceremonies and parties to welcome the Ashes home were scheduled to take place after the last Test. George seemed to be in most of the papers and Frank was still featuring prominently as well. The man who had supplied Arthur's men with their training apparatus had held off talks until after the final Test, as agreed. However, a large sports goods manufacturer had offered a generous sum to buy his business in order to access the first rights of negotiation, a deal which he rejected as it was not in keeping with the ethos of the business founded by his father.

The Lords Test took a backseat to the overall achievement of the team, but as it drew closer, Fryer insisted the festivities be kept to a minimum. A couple of days before the start of the Test there was a lull in the frenzied activity around the England camp.

On the eve of the final Test, as Arthur wandered the deserted corridors of Lord's alone, he witnessed a most curious thing: Jim Singleton, dressed in his team blazer and looking very sombre was being led by Fryer and a small group of officials into a committee room. Arthur's heart skipped a beat. As they disappeared, Fryer moved to pull the doors closed behind him. Arthur started cautiously towards the room but as he did so, Fryer noticed him. Nothing was said as their eyes met, then Fryer shut the doors.

To Arthur it was an awful shock. His mind was reeling. Jim didn't look happy at all. Was there something he did not know about him? Did Jim harbour resentment towards Arthur, born from their dispute all that time ago at Good Walloping? Surely not, he thought.

If Arthur had not been due to meet Tim and his parents that evening, he would have stayed around until the business in the room had concluded. It bothered him the entire night and when he tried to track down Jim and Fryer after his meal engagement with the Gibsons, both were said to be uncontactable. Something ominous must have happened.

The team breakfast was set for 8.00 a.m. and for the first time Arthur was on time rather than early. When he got to the dining room he found it empty.

'Arthur,' came a voice from behind him. He spun around. It was Fryer. He waved Arthur over. Arthur was past being concerned now and was positively beside himself with worry. Had something happened to one of the players? He was ushered into a room where all the team were dressed in their blazers. Fryer turned to face him. There was a serious look about him.

'What's going on?' Arthur demanded. He felt drained.

'We've decided on a change to the line-up for this match,' Fryer told him plainly.

'Yes . . . and?' asked Arthur.

'We've decided to choose another spinner for the twelve,' Fryer explained.

Arthur looked at Chandra. Chandra smiled and held his hands up as if he had no problem with the selection. Arthur was just about to speak his mind when Fryer stepped forward and held out an English blazer to him. A round of applause broke out as the meaning of the gesture began to dawn on Arthur. He was unable to move to take the blazer so Fryer took a couple of paces towards him. Arthur struggled to come to terms with the ridiculous selection process of the English management.

'I . . . I can't possibly play,' he muttered.

'Don't be daft – you're only twelfth man,' Fryer told him as the players burst out laughing.

'This is ludicrous, I just can't accept this.' Arthur protested but Fryer cut him off.

'Arthur, we've all spoken about this. We have the Ashes and you were the one who made it possible. There *is* no one more deserving. This game of ours has been about winning for too long now. It's time we gave it something back. It's what they all want.' Fryer gestured to the team who all nodded their heads. Fryer and Jim helped Arthur into the blazer.

'Pull your belly in, Pops,' Jim told Arthur as he did a button up.

As it finally settled on his stout frame, they all clapped enthusiastically once more and moved in to shake Arthur's hand to the point that it almost dropped off. Looking more like he'd been kicked by a mule rather than having been selected to play for England, he soon began to feel comfortable in the blazer.

'All right, lads, time to start getting ready!' The commotion around Arthur finally cleared and there was more backslapping as the players filtered out. When the room had cleared, Tim stood alone facing his friend.

'World's gone mad,' Arthur told him, struggling to comprehend the situation. 'I was having fun until a few minutes ago.'

Tim smiled and put his arm around Arthur, steering him slowly toward the door. Tim's smile hid bitter disappointment at having missed all the Tests for the summer, but as they walked down the long corridor, Arthur said softly, 'Your time will come, boy, if that's what you're thinking.'

'Yeah. Maybe. But I've just been kept out by a sixty year old,' Tim lamented.

'I hear he's pretty good though,' Arthur told him.

Jean had to have it spelt out to her twice by Frank and Mrs Cheshire that Arthur had been capped, but only as twelfth man, struggling to understand what it meant.

'Well, I'm very proud of course, but . . .' She paused.

'But what?' asked Frank, amazed at her hesitancy to celebrate.

'Well, it's just silly!' she said. 'The team's just getting back on track and they go and choose him.'

Frank gave up.


It certainly felt unusual for all involved with the match, being at Lords, the spiritual home of cricket, at the wrong end of the season. And to be holding the Ashes already? It was altogether inconceivable. The glow of expectation was noticeably absent and the swelling crowd seemed sombre in comparison to previous years. Arthur, Frank and Edwin stood out the front of the terracotta-coloured pavilion watching the groundsmen busy themselves as the spectators slowly filtered in.

'There'll be some empty seats today.' Arthur remarked.

'No. Just because it's decided! I don't think so.' Frank disagreed.

'Not talking about that,' Arthur said. 'Fryer said some of the members have refused to turn up as the normal order of venues was changed. It's a tradition thing.'

'Bloody hell. We give 'em what they want and they can't even turn up.' Frank moaned.

'Out of everything good comes something bad,' Arthur remarked. 'Cricket is linked with tradition. It is tradition alone though. I think some people just get way too caught up in the whole thing. It becomes about something other than the game for some.'

They looked in the stands and behind them as a party took their seats. The forlorn faces of the spectators were telling indeed.

'You know, I've been to Test days here before.' Edwin told them. 'It's doesn't feel like it normally does.'

'No. It does feel a bit stale,' Arthur said in agreement. 'But this is Lords,' he reminded them, 'and I don't want you to walk off *this,* of all grounds, without a win. And neither does he.' Arthur pointed to a spectator settling into a seat next to Mrs Cheshire and Jean. It was Bert McCabe. He waved a rolled-up newspaper to Edwin who beamed back at him and gave a thumbs-up.

Stan Coleman ventured to the middle for the toss whereupon it was announced that Arthur Jenkins would be making his Test match debut. After a moment of bewildered silence, the crowd erupted and gave him a standing ovation. The Barmy Army was, as always, strong in voice and called his name endlessly. Back at Good Walloping, Ted Doyle was being revived with smelling salts.

Although Steve Moore thought it an amazing gesture on the part of the England administration to select Arthur, he felt it lacked respect for his own team and the competition overall.

'You're having a laugh, aren't you?' he asked Coleman at the toss.

'Not at all, old chap!' replied Coleman.

'Could come back to bite you,' Moore said, a worrying glint

in his eye. Coleman felt a faint pulse of apprehension flicker in his mind as he flipped the coin in the air. Moore called, 'Her Majesty.' mockingly.

It was tails and Coleman elected to bat.

Soon Stiles and Dennis were out in the middle while back in the dressing room, Coleman approached Arthur. Both stood silently for a moment. Arthur could tell something was bothering Coleman.

'Something the matter?' Arthur asked him.

Coleman said nothing for a moment but was clearly preoccupied.

'They're up to something,' he hissed eventually. 'Just not sure what.'

The first delivery of the day was played safely enough. It was Khan who noticed first. Watching from the players' balcony he stood up and shouted to the others, 'They're coming off.'

'Bloody rain,' cursed someone.

'It's not raining!' Khan informed them.

What followed was an emergency meeting of the International Cricket Council, even though one ball of the match had been bowled. They summoned Fryer, Coleman and Mathew French to the meeting. Twenty minutes later Fryer and Coleman emerged looking distraught and called a team meeting. Fryer addressed the group.

'I won't beat around the bush. The Ashes are still up for grabs!'

There came a gasp of horror from the team, followed quickly by a flurry of questions. Fryer tried to calm them. 'Listen, please,' he appealed to them. 'It seems Mathew French has not made himself eligible for England selection in the correct manner. It's partly the management's fault. Apparently he's still a Kiwi national. He's played here for twenty odd years but still failed to mention he was born there! Seems his county team also completed some forms incorrectly and to top it off his British passport expired a month ago. It's a right mess.'

'What now?' asked Peter Stiles.

'We have been advised that the fourth Test was handed to

Australia under the ICC rules, which is the case in situations such as this. So it's two tests apiece.'

The seriousness of the situation was starting to sink in as the team's morale went into freefall.

'Which means we have another fight on our hands,' Fryer admitted.

'Come on, snap out of it. We've beaten them before; we'll beat them again,' Coleman said.

There were some muffled shouts as the team tried to lift their spirits.

Coleman had not finished though. 'Here's what we do. As far as this Test is concerned, we can replace French with someone else, but the rest of the team can't be altered. Which means you're still twelfth man, Arthur.' Coleman then looked at Tim. 'Gibson here will make his debut.'

Tim was dumbfounded as he was engulfed by well-wishers, which of course included Arthur. Coleman got ready to leave, adding, 'I have to hand them the new team list immediately. We're due back out there in five minutes.'

'Welcome, Mr Gibson,' said Fryer coolly, 'and good luck.' He shook Tim's hand, then turned immediately to follow Coleman.

The congratulations for Tim carried on until a team official took him away to complete some administrative formalities. Everyone returned to the viewing area except Stiles and Dennis, who made their way back out to the middle, after Arthur and Khan had had a few words with them in the absence of Fryer.

When Tim joined everyone on the balcony a few minutes later, Arthur was the first to address him. 'They say be careful what you wish for, don't they, boy!' he told Tim.

Tim shook his head in disbelief.

Arthur looked over to Edwin who was also looking his way.

'Not feeling stale anymore?' Edwin offered dryly.

'No. Just like old times.' responded Arthur.

## 33

When play resumed, the Australians had a renewed spring in their step as they went about setting the field. The ground announcer informed the crowd of recent developments thus causing over 35,000 heart attacks. All across England, television reports carried the news of the 'Ashes Debacle', as it was now referred to, and that the series was alive once more. Where interest had dropped off after the *supposed* victory in the fourth Test, it was now not only rekindled, but increased. The incident and therefore the Test became the talk of the nation. Radios and television sets were tuned back on and once again cricket enthusiasts headed for pubs to watch the match. Any MCC members who had boycotted the match were on buses or in taxis now heading for the ground at breakneck speed.

It was sleeveless pullover weather. Stiles and Dennis were in the thick of it once more, constantly chatting between overs and geeing each other up. England knew their bowling ranks were slightly depleted for the Test with the inclusion of a debutant, so had to make amends for it with runs. Fryer had given his batsmen the task of reaching 400, pointing out that if the match was a draw, the Australians would retain the Ashes – they simply *had* to win. Dennis was first to go with the score on 60. As Khan took guard, the nation prayed for one of his typical obstinate performances but this time it wasn't to be for he was dismissed within half an hour to a wide ball from Horn which he chopped onto his stumps.

Many thought that was the end there and then, particularly as Stan Coleman had always been a better captain and ambassador than a batsman. Though averaging around 40, his Test 100s had all come against weaker Test nations – something the press was always happy to point out when the team was under the cosh for underperforming.

Stiles was carving out what looked to be a handy half-century for himself when he fell on 47 to a slower ball from Rogers. The manner in which the ball was returned to the bowler for a simple return catch seemed almost obliging. Coleman was still there and going slowly when Engle passed his score, stroking the ball nicely and apparently in no bother at all – until Horn sent down a ball that spun behind his legs and somehow took his leg stump. The situation had become precarious as play approached tea on the first day with England having slumped to 192 for 4. Horn was a massive danger. Every time he was thrown the ball the crowd had palpitations. Horn's ball prior to the lunch break was short and fast catching Coleman unawares, it missed the bat's edge by a whisker as it flew through to the keeper chest high. Horn sneered at Coleman and cursed his bad luck as a familiar cry came from behind the stumps.

'Bowled Horny.'

After tea, Coleman found an ally in Harry Winter, who helped take the score past 200 before he too fell victim to the classy Australian spinner. The Australians were talking it up in the field knowing they had only to dismiss Coleman to be into the English tail.

George adopted Coleman's blunt tactics and for the remainder of the day the pair of them denied the Australian attack another wicket. Coleman was approaching an unexpected century and hopes were high as England neared 300.

The overnight rest served the Australians better than the home side on day two. Coleman added five to his overnight total before being dismissed for 94 with the score 290 for 5. Jim, try as he might, couldn't stop a ball from Weir wrecking his stumps. Chandra did little better, going for a first-ball duck, which brought Tim to the crease, having been elevated over Edwin for his debut.

Tim's determination was obvious but there was no denying the nerves he was suffering as he went neither forward nor back for his first ball. It looked like the Australian openers would be padding up very soon. However, the second ball Tim faced was a different story altogether as he drove it smartly back past the bowler to the fence. The following delivery was short and designed to intimidate, but Tim, fuelled by youthful exuberance, swung into it with vigour and to the amazement of all present hooked the ball stylishly for six.

The crowd went quite mad and the singing from the stands rose to another level. George joined in and showing little regard for anything dished up, they spanked, slashed, bludgeoned and murdered for 60 further runs. Tim was finally caught at gully after an enterprising debut innings of 31 wonderful runs, leaving the field to a standing ovation.

Edwin joined George in the middle for all of three balls. Then Horn got one to rear up at him which he popped up so that any one of three fieldsmen could have taken the simple catch. Down the other end, George was on his way back to the pavilion well before the call 'Mine!' came.

George had excelled with the bat, racking up a respectable 60, the crowd gave him a good reception and the overall score of 344 was a reasonable result.

The Australians were now accustomed to the extra pace of the England bowlers and Fryer pointed this out in their briefing.

'Bowling must be accurate and clever!' he stressed to them, emphasising that the Australian first innings total must be kept below the English score.

The innings opened with a dropped catch off the very first ball. Danny Dennis spilt a chance from Crocket off George's bowling and he made England pay, going on to score 69 runs and figuring in two good partnerships for the Aussies. George toiled harder than he had in the entire series to get the first two wickets.

The Test was being played in unusually intense sunshine so that, although the bowlers were made to toil, the dryer track had some extra pace for them. When Tim was finally given his chance to perform, he bowled both no-balls and wides, despite showing good pace initially. He was carted about the park by Steve Moore, so he concentrated on line and length rather than speed to stop the run flow. The result was a below-par performance, which was disappointing for both himself and Arthur.

The Moore brothers were charting their team's passage through the day's proceedings like true mariners and were well in command as play closed at 286 for 2. Some were writing off England already as the Aussies only trailed by 58 runs with 8 wickets in hand.

The players were not required at any official team dinner or event that night as Fryer felt a good rest was the best thing for them. Arthur spent the evening dining with Jean and Mrs Cheshire. Jean made jokes about dining with her husband the Test cricketer, and her 'international sporting' husband, but Arthur's thoughts were elsewhere. The likelihood of losing the Ashes now was unthinkable, yet fate had intervened. Arthur wondered what else fate might dish up. Eventually their thoughts turned towards Charmy Down as they were all missing it greatly. When asked about her long terms plans Mrs Cheshire was vague. It was clear she did not have any and probably didn't want to think further than the next four days. Arthur had thought to mention that the players' machines would no doubt be moved but decided against bringing it up until the Tests were over. What he did mention was that now Edwin was a fully fledged international cricketer, Biggles was in need of a full-time minder, which she seemed very happy about.

The following day the English tabloids wrote about England's lost opportunity and harped on about the folly of selecting Arthur. As people all over the country read their morning papers, most felt as though they were destined to watch the Ashes campaign crumble before their very eyes. It was frustrating, unforgivable and somehow seemed incredibly unjust as for the best part of the summer they had had the measure of the Australians well and truly. One paper carried the headline 'Mid-Summer's Nightmare.'

Undaunted, Fryer and Arthur sent their men out on the third morning having emphasized the need for maximum effort all the time when playing cricket, and citing examples of teams coming back from hopeless positions to record stirring victories.

The ever-reliable George quickly took the wicket of Mark Moore with a howling fast ball that had him LBW. However, this galvanized his brother, Steve, who plundered the attack almost until lunch, reaching 149. Jim, Edwin and Chandra all had a crack at him, but to no avail. Moore had even carted Chandra about the park, forcing Coleman to take him off before too much damage was done. Coleman, looking at his watch, knew he had time to bring George back for one more over before lunch at the opposite end. If he did not remove Moore soon, the game would surely slip beyond their reach. In the meantime, he had to fill in with a quick over of spin.

'Chandra,' he called.

Soon Chandra was measuring out a hasty run-up as time was of the essence. It was so close to lunch, the Aussie captain would surely not be tempted into a false shot. Moore noted the absence of chit-chat – it was apparent this was just a fill-in over to get George on for one more.

Chandra's first five balls were dot balls, which he was pleased with. It was as he prepared to come in for the final ball that Greg Church, the Aussie non-striker made a monumental error of judgment.

'Can't you get wickets if you're not shooting off your mouth, mate?'

No one was more annoyed than Moore, who stepped back from the crease and gave his batting partner what could only be described as a filthy look.

To his credit Chandra said nothing. It was the most appropriate time he'd ever known to keep his mouth shut, but the narrowing of his eyes spoke volumes. He scurried in for the last ball and let fly with what appeared to be a decent length off-spinner. He ripped it brutally as it left his hand. It almost buzzed as it looped down the wicket. Moore pushed forward to smother it with a defensive push, but it dipped slightly quicker than its predecessors, landing further from Moore's blade than he intended. Fearing the worst, he tried to make amends by shuffling out a tad to play it to the on-side. The ball came off the pitch incredibly slowly and in the end it was scooped up by the Aussie skipper, who'd played too early. Chandra was already on his way down the wicket and dived at full length to take a spectacular catch mid-pitch. The England team went wild.

With both Moores removed England scented a revival. As they watched the replay on the big screen, Chandra was filled with pride.

'Gazelle like,' he remarked.

A wind of change had indeed been signalled. A palpable doggedness crept into the England team's play. George's last over before lunch contained a delivery of such velocity that after striking the middle of Greg Church's stump it sent it into the air to be caught by Harry Winter. Anyone watching could sense the tone of the game had shifted back in favour of the home side. The Aussie team went to lunch at 340 for 5, still four runs in arrears and with five wickets in hand.

It was not an easy task to remove the last five wickets. Coleman was tempted to bowl Chandra again but resisted, much to the disappointment of the crowd and Chandra's small fan club. He stuck with George and Jim. Dyson and Talbot were putting a dangerous partnership together and nearing the 400 run mark. Coleman was thinking about a bowling change when Edwin had a quick word with him. Edwin came on and in two overs promptly removed both obstacles. Dyson was lured into playing a hook that sailed to Jim at a more square than usual deep fine leg and Talbot was bowled by a slow ball. Coleman put Jim back on and it was all over 10 runs later as they wrapped up the innings for 403, a lead of 59 to the tourists. George took another five-wicket haul and was having a great match. But Edwin's double strike was the pivotal moment of the innings. Though the Australians only had a moderate lead, Fryer had hoped for less going into the second innings.

England's second effort was meant to be the innings of their lives, but the England batting misfired once more. The pitch had broken up a touch. There was some movement for the quicks but, more importantly, plenty of turn for Horn. Khan and Coleman had the most productive partnership and took the score to 126 for 2. A good score still looked possible, but the magnitude of the occasion provided Horn – the perfect villain – with a fitting backdrop and he turned the ball sharply from the outset. Cloaking his concentration and determination with a seemingly happy-go-lucky attitude, Horn ripped out four batsmen without breaking a sweat. When Tim was joined by Edwin with the score on 199, many of the true believers were lining up to change their faith. Edwin met Tim mid pitch for a chat before facing up.

'Fancy meeting you here!' he said smiling. Tim's grin was only partly visible behind the wire faceguard and the shadows it cast.

'Any point me trying to build an innings?' asked Edwin.

'We have to give it a shot. There's runs left out here.' Tim told him. Edwin nodded and they punched gloves for luck.

'Good luck,' Edwin said earnestly as he turned to go back to his crease.

'And you.' Tim replied as he did the same.

Tim showed amazing contempt for the Australian attack and was clearly batting lower in the order than he should have, playing some outlandish shots to carry the score to 217. Edwin on the other hand was at least involved in a partnership this time, loping like a giraffe between the wickets when Tim called him for a run.

'Foot to the ball and swing. Don't die wondering!' was Edwin's mantra. George had told him about mantras in the dressing room before he went out to bat and Edwin rather liked the idea, even though he'd thought they were a type of stingray. He repeated it over and over to himself as the intimidating Rogers bore down on him. The first ball was widish but full. Edwin had a good swing at it and his feet moved but not quite enough. He managed to get a very thick edge on the up and the ball skewed away like a bullet over the head of the mid-wicket fielder and into the square boundary. It was as though the Ashes were won judging by the crowd's reaction. Edwin meanwhile leant nonchalantly on his bat as the ball was returned. Rogers bowled the next ball short and, like a pro, he let it fizz by harmlessly. He then resettled into his crease and went through the motion of playing a forward defensive shot. Making a slight feint towards the off-side as the ball was released, Edwin felt sure the ball would be pitched short and duly swatted at it as it passed him. Finding the toe of the bat it went wide and towards the boundary, to be chased long and hard by Church, as Edwin and Tim ran two easily. There could well have been steam coming from Rogers' ears at that point. Edwin pushed the last ball past mid-off and took a single to retain the strike.

Facing Horn again, Edwin swatted at the first ball and got a leg bye. Tim sent the next ball into the stands for a huge six. Chancing his arm once too often, Tim holed out to a man at mid-on and the innings was closed on 230. Horn had claimed another 5-wicket haul to take his tally to 28 for the series, making him the top wicket taker for the side. Moore's captaincy had been faultless and the team's fielding sharp – all worrying signs for England, as the series looked to be firmly in favour of the tourists.

Edwin and Tim walked back to the dressing rooms having made the second highest partnership of the innings.

'We're only defending 171!' said Tim despondently.

'Better than chasing it!' remarked Edwin dourly.

It was after lunch on the fourth day of the Test match. The atmosphere could not have been more tense. The fans and MCC members were now well in favour of the final test being played at Lords and were hoping for the second Ashes celebration in within the week. Fryer's nerves were frayed though he hid it well. A minority of the crowd felt that for England to have got this far and still have a chance of winning the Ashes against this Australian side was a victory in itself. The general feeling amongst cricketing enthusiasts was that the Australians would prevail. Perhaps it was all too good to be true. On the other hand the average man on the street was full of bold expectation and hope. None demonstrated this better than the Barmy Army, who were still belting out the songs. As the England team emerged, it was to a deafening roar.

When Arthur arrived on the balcony with a can of beer to settle his nerves, Fryer whipped it off him and tapped the emblem on his jumper.

'Oh heavens. Forgot about that.'

Fryer shook his head and smiled.

The Australians got about their business in a workmanlike fashion playing no-nonsense cricket. There were no rash shots for the first 40 runs, then a mini-explosion of free scoring was unleashed. Coleman was frustrated as all his bowlers were bowling tight and didn't deserve such disrespect. But, as they say, who dares wins and it was the way the Aussies played the game. Chances went begging as balls dropped just out of reach or edges flew wide of the slip cordon. The day was shaping up as a luckless one for England. As the Australians closed in on 100, Coleman had to make a bowling change fast as George and Jim would soon be out on their feet. He called upon Tim.

Jim, remembering Tim's performance in the first innings, had some settling words for him as he warmed up. 'Wouldn't bother about them scoring runs, lad,' he said. 'You need to put them back in the pavilion. Get them out!'

Jim returned to his place on the boundary while Tim was bending this way and that, and shaking loose all his limbs as the batsmen finally got ready. Tim collected his thoughts and sped in mustering all the energy he had. He unleashed the ball slightly off balance as he was not fully warmed up and overly keen. The delivery was wide and hit for four by Haynes to bring up his fifty.

Tim knew that, whilst he was bowling flat out, he also had to be smart, and decided that a barrage of well-pitched balls that were hard to score off would be a good place to start. He managed what was almost a yorker with the next ball and Haynes rushed to dig it out as it was bang on target. The bat clipped the ground then followed through late. Getting a thick leading edge, the ball shot back towards Tim, only an inch from the ground and fast. He stopped, slipped over and stuck out his left hand. 96 for 1. The England players rallied round Tim and congratulated him madly. It had been a slightly lucky wicket but no one seemed to mind.

The Australian captain, brimming with confidence, strode out quickly and, obviously wanting to get on with the job, took guard. Tim was prepared to gamble on his prized scalp and decided that offering him a chance at his beloved back-foot drive so early in the innings might undo him. But first he would slow it down. He bowled a couple of balls at 80 per cent pace that were defended well as Moore carefully played himself in – or so he thought. When the next ball was offered it was short but delivered by express mail. Moore saw it pitch short early and set himself up for his favourite shot by moving onto his back foot. Even as he did so, the ball grew large much too fast and his shot was rash, not calculated. Normally this would have meant a boundary anyway, but Tim had rolled his fingers down the inside of the seam and as the ball drew close to the bat, it swung in late and kept coming. Moore brought his hands down, trying to kill the ball but a thick edge sent it at a sharp angle down upon his stumps. Winter and the slips jumped for joy. The Australian captain turned to survey his shattered stumps and began the long walk back to the famous old pavilion. The spectators were in an uproar.

Tim's third wicket came with a scintillating ball and the captain's brother was joining him in the dressing room after being clean bowled for a first-ball duck. The crowd were euphoric.

Crocket could do nothing but watch as his team crumbled hopelessly at the other end. When he had completed his first over Tim had taken 3 wickets for 4 runs, a remarkable statistic.

At the other end Edwin was spurred on fervently by his team mates. Minutes later Crocket was given instructions on how to find the dressing room after a slow half volley enticed a drive to deep mid off. England were well on top and with four top-order

Aussie batsmen gone the game had become interesting to say the least. Dyson and Church should have been worried, but they batted with confidence and stemmed the flow of wickets. Neither Australian nor English fans could relax as the game unfolded.

Coleman decided to do short rotations of his bowlers in order to upset the batsmen's rhythm and when Jim and George were brought back on, the change had the desired effect. Jim took the wickets of first Dyson, then Church, both bowled. Church's wicket seemed to be an act of will on the part of the ball as it bludgeoned its way through what seemed to be a perfectly constructed defence. Only by watching the replays could one see that as the ball squeezed between bat and pad, its velocity caused Church's leg to buckle slightly.

The second ball of the following over saw a double tragedy for England. Winter dived to take a catch but only managed to deflect the ball into the hands of second slip, Engle, whose middle finger was split as he spilt the chance.

Arthur was watching the replay when it was brought to his attention. 'You're on, Pops,' Frank whispered at close range into his ear. Arthur stood to attention, completely startled.

'Right,' he said nervously. 'Oh Lord, what do I need?'

'Nothing, Arthur, you're all set.'

Frank stood up, placed Arthur's cap on his head for him and, putting his arm around his shoulders, started to walk with him towards the players' exit, talking as he went. Everyone in the vicinity shouted encouragement and clapped Arthur out.

'You have everything you need. Just go out there and do your best,' Frank said limping alongside his friend. 'Stan will greet you; just keep walking down that way.' Frank pointed down the steps. Arthur shuffled off but looked back at Frank, who just pointed and waved.

'Bloody hell,' Frank sighed.

Arthur passed Engle who was being escorted by a trainer, nursing his hand.

'Best of luck, Arthur,' he said as they crossed paths.

Arthur looked down to see a faint trail of blood, which he followed until he emerged from the building to a tremendous reception. Arthur could feel the chants of the crowd reverberate within him. He resisted the temptation to wave and made a beeline for the huddle of players in the middle, who clapped him on. As they watched Arthur waddle towards them, the England players smiled and laughed despite the seriousness of their situation.

'Where can we hide him, Stan?' Khan asked.

The players welcomed him warmly then Coleman scattered them with a flick of his hand.

There were ominous clouds coming in from the north. Coleman had seen the following day's weather forecast which warned of heavy showers. Time was running out. However, with no specialist batsmen left in the Australian line-up the seemingly impossible was also in sight for England.

'Where do you want me?' asked Arthur.

'Deep fine leg, please, Arthur,' said Coleman.

'Thought you might say that,' replied Arthur and off he trotted. Once settled in on the boundary, he noticed Tim was at mid-wicket and looking his way. Arthur tipped his cap a little and Tim replied the same. The remaining balls were all dot balls from George, although the last ball drew a gasp from the crowd as it narrowly missed the batsman's outside edge.

Coleman relieved George and Jim from the attack as quickly as he had brought them in. Hoping the short break was enough for Tim to have recuperated, he paired him up with Chandra. The score was on 165 for 6 with the end of the day's play due in just ten minutes. Chandra rattled off instructions to his field, calling to Arthur to move squarer and then pulling him in five metres from the boundary. Having placed a short mid-on close up to the batsman, he skipped in and sent down a superb short-pitched delivery. The batsman, Rogers, shaped to pull it, but finally wisely employed evasive action and ducked under it with no time to spare. Hopping in again Chandra repeated the same ball but pitched it shorter, giving it his all, hoping the batsman would pop it up close, trying to defend. But, as it was angled more down the leg side, Rogers swung into the ball with gusto. Had not been for the extra pace he would have sent it into the stands, as it was it caught a top edge and flew sky high . . . towards Arthur!

'Catch it!' came the cry from all. The entire ground froze. Arthur froze. As the ball swirled in the grey sky, he sprang to life, hearing the second more urgent 'Catch it!' from Chandra. Arthur started off but slowed to assess where the ball was headed. Then, realising it was going to be short if anything, he sped up and headed to his left. There were cries from the crowd but they went unregistered. As the ball started its descent, Arthur stepped up his pace, his legs went like short stumpy pistons. A lot of people thought he would get there too late but others with a better angle could see that he and the ball were on a collision course. With no time to position himself under the ball and no need to dive he just stuck his arms out full stretch and motored into the path of the ball like a steam train. The ball dropped into his hands and stuck. Arthur kept on running, holding the ball aloft for all to see as the crowd went berserk. Chandra clapped his hands and sprinted towards him. Arthur's progress was eventually halted by George and Tim simultaneously. He was soon enveloped by the rest of the team and brought down like a wounded buffalo. The cluster of bodies writhed on the grass. There was no sign of Arthur. Jean was beginning to wonder if he'd ever see the light of day again when out popped an arm at the top of the huddle defiantly holding the ball aloft.

The new batsman took his time coming out and carefully played out Chandra's over. At the end of it the Australians started to walk from the field, only to be called back by the umpires as there was time for one, maybe two more overs that day. Despite the cloud, the light wasn't a problem. The umpires warned Coleman that at the first sign of steady rain they were off, but if a result looked likely they might be able to add an extra over. Arthur had always been a fan of independent umpiring and now he knew why. This Test had seen the pairing of a long-standing West Indian umpire named Anton Guishard, and a Kiwi named Valentine Seabrook, who had both played Test level. As the batsmen conferred before facing the next over, Seabrook felt some light raindrops on the back of his hand. This, together with the fact they were slightly over time already, meant that the 'fair ruling' was beginning to be stretched – and if they stretched it too far, the Australians might have grounds for complaint. Both umpires were aware of Moore standing up at the front of the balcony watching proceedings like a hawk. His presence alone demanded that the next over be the last throw of the dice for both sides that day. If it was a washout the following day the Ashes were gone. Everyone knew Moore would be more than happy to take the draw and retain the Ashes.

After a brief chat with Guishard, Seabrook informed Coleman, 'Last over, Stan.'

Coleman cursed under his breath. Tim was about to be handed a ridiculous assignment: three wickets in six balls for victory. The Australians needed just 7 runs to win, or a draw, to retain the Ashes.

There was a hush around the ground, then singing from the Barmy Army started up again. Tim did not have the luxury of taking his time, but at least he was bowling to Talbot, who was no great shakes with the bat. Ball one was a wasted delivery that drifted down leg as the batsman watched it speed by innocuously. Tim jogged back to his mark and sent down a ball that had the seam angled away from the batsman. Tim, being a left-hander, drifted it out after committing Talbot to playing at it. At the moment Talbot could have let it go, he went even wider. Almost unable to leave it alone, it caught his edge and obediently flew high to a deep second slip. Khan jumped full reach as the ball hit the tips of his top three fingers and ballooned high into the air behind him. Not taking his eye off the ball Khan landed evenly balanced, spun around, ran two paces, then dived for the ball, taking a memorable catch. The crowd came alive as the ground erupted once more. Tim ran down the wicket, his arm raised triumphantly as Talbot began to walk, amazed at his own stupidity. The players closed ranks and tried to remain composed.

'England . . . England,' was the chant all around the ground as the new batsman approached the crease. Tim was ready and wanted to get on with the over – which was quite the opposite of what the new Australian batsman, Wayne Horn, had in mind. Hoping the rain would bucket down any minute, he tried to slow things down, ignoring the fact that you should never irritate a fast bowler, especially one as fast as Tim, whose fastest delivery that day had been over 98 m.p.h. But, judging by his manner, Horn appeared to be in control of the situation.

Tim came racing in for the third ball of the over, having decided he would aim it at the batsman's body. Horn jolted into a fully upright stance, his feet leaving the turf as he thrust the bat out in front of him and ripped his head back. The ball came off the pitch with blistering speed, taking a very slight inside edge as it thudded into Horn's sternum. Stiles, who was positioned at silly point, later swore blind that Horn was driven back mid-air by the speed of the ball. Others were of the opinion that his movement backwards had begun with the defensive shot he played. Whatever the truth, Horn was sent reeling backwards, his legs forced into the stumps, he then collapsed. There was no need for an appeal. A couple of the England players rushed to the winded batsman's assistance and helped him to his feet. When he regained his composure he looked at Tim incredulously, then at his ruined stumps, before trudging from the field in a complete daze. The England players barely celebrated the wicket as they were so busy discussing the situation. Horn got an enormously appreciative send off as he departed international cricket for the last time. Back on the England balcony, Frank and Engle watched replays of the previous ball from every angle, each one causing both to grimace uncomfortably as the ball thumped into Horn's chest.

The last batsman, Weir, was well liked by the England team for his no-nonsense approach and good humour – but now all he got was the silent treatment.  Tim knew that no shots would be played as Weir was the type to take any short deliveries on his body, leave any wide ones and resist all stroke play. It was well known Weir couldn't score a run to save his life but he had been known to hang around.

Tim didn't need a miracle ball but a plan and asked to bowl around the wicket before settling himself to start his run-up. He tore in at breakneck speed and delivered a straight fast ball on off stump which Weir defended well. The next ball Tim returned to over the wicket and bowled an in-swinger at roughly 85 per cent speed. For a moment it looked as if the batsman had been trapped LBW as it thumped into his pads. There was a huge appeal but umpire Seabrook was unmoved.

Suddenly it was 'do or die': the last ball of the day. It was announced by a loud crack of thunder from afar. What Tim did next was pure brilliance. As he had some runs to play with, he decided to gamble and bowled another 85 per cent delivery way down the leg side – a wide. But as he released the ball, Weir advanced forward almost side-on, covering his wickets entirely with his pads, and offered a token loose shot as the ball sped by. It was clever ploy. Had the ball been straight and hit his pads when he was well advanced, it would have made an LBW highly unlikely, meant a dot-ball and the end of the day's play. Weir had shown his hand to Tim, who in turn had bowled another slower ball, which would have impaired Weir's judgment.

Again it was the last ball and Tim bowled an intentional no-ball which was slow, short and way over Weir's head, with no chance of a shot. But the 'No Ball!' call had come early and Weir had a wild flash at the ball as it streaked way overhead.

'Bit jumpy?' Tim asked Weir with sadistic intent.

'Nuh.' Weir replied.

But Weir looked nervous as he berated himself for almost playing a rash shot. Tim had him precisely where he wanted him: thinking – something fast bowers shouldn't do when batting. Weir decided the best thing to do was defend – which was exactly what Tim wanted. He knew a straight ball would demand a defensive shot. Unbeknownst to the batsman, Tim lengthened his run-up. As he prepared to bowl he looked over at the chubby figure of Arthur, clapping his hands and talking it up.

Tim's run-up was steady, strong and fast, his eyes transfixed upon the exact spot on the pitch he needed to hit. Bowling as close to the stumps as he possibly could, Tim fired down a brutally fast delivery that pitched a perfect length on leg stump. Weir was committed. He'd pre-planned a short back-lift for his defensive stroke to counter the ball's speed and punched forward firmly with total confidence but when the ball pitched, it subtly cut away to the offside and completely flattened his off-stump. Tim must have leapt 20 feet into the air and seemed to hang from a cloud before returning to terra firma. Arthur dissolved into the moment as the roar of victory descended upon them.

The Ashes had returned to England. Again!

The elated England players ran to each other as the crowd jumped to their feet to cheer and clap like they had not done for many years. All of England rejoiced as their victorious team celebrated ecstatically on the hallowed turf with an outpouring of relief. The mass of bodies clothed in white stood in the centre clutching one another for what seemed an eternity. Arthur had to fight through his team-mates to get to Tim, who was smiling from ear to ear.

'Well done, boy,' he shouted as he shook Tim excitedly.

He could barely see him through all the bodies.

'We did it!' Tim screamed ferociously. 'We bloody won!' Arthur shook his hand as George appeared and embraced Arthur wildly.

The range of emotions the tiny urn's return evoked was incredible.

The Australian team, although shattered, couldn't simply hide away in the dressing room. They made their way down to the boundary fence to greet the victors when they eventually came off the pitch. There was no stopping the predictable pitch invasion but the crowd, after much back-slapping, eventually hoisted each England player onto an assortment of shoulders and marched them off the ground. All except for Arthur, who was taken on a lap of honour high on the shoulders of England's Barmy Army, who proudly presented him to those still in the stands chanting:

> *He's old, he's fat, but he bloody won 'em back.*
> *He's old enough to be your father:*
> *But he's not, he's our King Arthur!*

Outside the members' stand Arthur waved to Jean who couldn't stop herself from shedding a tear of happiness for him. As the celebrations cooled off, the team congratulated each other and were swept around the ground once more and into the pages of history. Alice assisted Frank down the stairs towards the ground.

'Poor sods!' he reflected.

'What do you mean poor sods?' she asked incredulously as Frank hobbled down the last step.

'They have to celebrate all over again, don't they.' he said.

'You mean *we* have to celebrate all over again.' she told him enthusiastically.

Not many people noticed that the speed of Tim's last ball was 102.7 m.p.h. Incredibly, George, Tim, Frank and Jim all ended up bowling faster than 100 mph, testimony to Arthur's great vision and dedication to the cause. Poor Edwin was the only one of Arthur's quicks who never reached the magic number. Whenever George wanted to get under Edwin's skin, he'd call him 'the snail'. Edwin normally took it very well as his fastest ball was equal to Jeff Thomson's old mark of 99.8 m.p.h., and he was perfectly happy with that.

Arthur's bowlers had taken all the wickets in the series except for two runs-outs and French's wicket in the fourth Test. George led the way with 28 wickets in total, then came Edwin 21, Frank 18, Jim 17, Chandra 8, and Tim 6. French's single wicket was struck from the record books for ever. Chandra's record of 8 wickets from just twenty overs was outstanding and his 11 run average per wicket almost unheard of.

George was stunned to be named joint Man of the Series with Steve Moore. George's father and Alice were bursting with pride. Forgetting no one in his interviews with the media, George told an entertaining account of a strange little man who liked to collect giant bowlers. He ended by saying to the interviewer, 'Thinking about how I almost gave the game away sends a chill down my spine.' He looked off camera to where Arthur and his team-mates were all watching him, raised his glass to Arthur and was joined by all those nearby. 'Cheers, Arthur.' There was a loud chorus of cheers.

'To Arthur!'

Alice patiently waited until George had had a few minutes with both his father and Arthur before she got her slice of George's moment. Tim meanwhile was named Man of the Match. He too struggled with what had transpired over the last two years and made a wonderful speech which again featured Arthur heavily. At eighteen, Tim now had the world at his feet and he celebrated in style.

Beer-soaked dressing-room scenes followed the great win and some more short speeches were made by Coleman, Fryer and finally Arthur. Steve Moore also made a short but pleasant speech for the losing side, not failing to mention how surprisingly good the English quicks were. Having made a brief reference to Arthur, he also made a very humorous remark about the Australian Cricket Board getting in touch with him soon regarding his services for the next Ashes campaign.

Lords turned out to be a wonderful place to celebrate an Ashes victory as the sun arrived in time for the celebrations. The pavilion glowed as Coleman showed the Ashes urn to the crowd still waiting patiently on the ground. Arthur stood shoulder to shoulder with Tim, who leant into him saying. 'It's just not real. The whole thing, start to finish.'

Arthur laughed. 'No. Extraordinary isn't it.'

Each player held the tiny brown trophy, most giving it an obligatory kiss for the photo album. When Arthur's turn came the crowd became increasingly vocal. He held the small urn regarding it strangely. He took the top off and peered inside. Holding it up to the crowd, he turned it upside down and shook it theatrically. The crowd jeered as Arthur then put the top back on, kissed it and held it up high, smiling broadly, before giving a wave and handing the urn on to Fryer.

Arthur stayed until he'd absorbed enough of the occasion and went in search of Jean, who was celebrating inside with Mrs Cheshire and Bert McCabe. Biggles waited patiently by Mrs Cheshire's side.

'He's out there,' said Arthur to the dog, pointing outside. Biggles took off like a shot for the balcony. Arthur had a sheepish look about him as he approached Jean, who held out her arms warmly.

'We're very proud of you.' she said.

'Yes. Well done.' said Mrs Cheshire not knowing exactly who Jean had meant when she said 'We'.

Arthur smiled and hugged his wife without so much as a word. Then, pulling back, a quizzical look came over him until he appeared quite grumpy.

'Cheer up, you old fuddy-duddy,' Mrs Cheshire told him as Bert slapped him on the back and thrust a glass of champagne into his hand.

'Cheer up!' he shouted incredulously. 'I've probably just been dropped from the national squad,' he said taking a sip from his glass. 'My Test career's over.'

Jean rolled her eyes.

'Maybe our footballers need a hand,' Mrs Cheshire suggested, drawing a stern look from Jean.

# 34

Arthur clasped a rolled-up magazine as he slid through the lichgate of the church in Wielding Willow. Standing at the foot of Davey's grave, he noticed he hadn't been the first visitor to pay his respects. A copy of the same magazine he'd bought, as well as three other cricketing magazines and copies of all the major newspapers were placed upon the gravestone. Most had pictures of Arthur and the victorious English team splashed across the front covers. Arthur was touched and thought what a great friend he had in Ted Doyle – though Ted *was* a good friend, this act was not his doing.

Some weeks later at a specially convened celebratory cricket match at Good Walloping, Arthur and Jim were presented with life memberships of the club, and Ted was chosen to unveil two honorary plaques celebrating the feats of Good Walloping's only two Test players, Jim and Arthur. There was a wonderful mounted picture of Jim launching into his terrifying delivery stride at Edgbaston. Alongside it was another framed picture of a huddle of bodies from which an arm protruded, holding a ball. Arthur looked over at Ted who shrugged innocently. Many of the club's older members still found it hard to comprehend Arthur's amazing feats.

For Arthur it seemed as though the last few weeks had been a constant flow of clapping, back slapping, streamers, handshakes and speeches.

'You do this one, Jim,' Arthur said wearily. Jim happily obliged and got up on a chair with a microphone and a pint. Looking down at the crowd gathered around him, then at Arthur, he smiled, held his chin high and shouted to them all, 'Ladies and gentlemen: Arthur Jenkins . . . supercoach!'

The End

**England V. Australia**
Lord's
Fifth Test Match – 1<sup>st</sup>, 2<sup>nd</sup>, 3<sup>rd</sup>, 4<sup>th</sup> & 5<sup>th</sup> September
England won by 5 runs
Man of the Match Tim Gibson
Man of the Series: George Samuels & Steve Moore

England
|  |  | 1st Innings | 2nd Innings |
|---|---|---|---|
| 1 - | D. Dennis | b Rogers ...............36 | lbw Rogers...............17 |
| 2 - | P. Stilles | c & b Rogers...........47 | c Horn b Patterson........14 |
| 3 - | R. Khan | b Horn ...................14 | run out....................40 |
| 4 - | S. Coleman* | lbw Patterson............94 | c Talbot b Rogers........54 |
| 5 - | M. Engle | c Horn....................23 | c & b Horn................28 |
| 6 - | H Winter† | c Dyson b Patterson....27 | c Haynes b Horn..........10 |
| 8 - | G. Samuels | not out..................60 | c Haynes b Horn..........12 |
| 9 - | J. Singleton | b Weir ...................2 | c Talbot b Horn............0 |
| 7 - | C. Jafar | lbw Rogers...............0 | lbw Weir...................21 |
| 10 – | T. Gibson | c Dyson b Horn.........31 | c Rogers b Horn ..........24 |
| 11 – | E. Roberts | c Church  b Horn........0 | not out.......................7 |
|  |  | Extras....................10 | Extras.........................3 |
|  |  | Total...................344 | Total......................230 |

**FALL OF WICKETS**

First Innings:     60-1   74-2   140-3   199-4   290-5   294-6   297-7   301-8   344-9
Second Innings:   27-1   32-2   126-3   134-4   155-5   160-6   168-7   171-8   199-9

| Bowler | Overs | Mdn | Runs | Wkts | Bowler | Overs | Mdn | Runs | Wkts |
|---|---|---|---|---|---|---|---|---|---|
| Rogers | 30 | 5 | 72 | 3 | Rogers | 16 | 3 | 57 | 2 |
| Patterson | 24 | 4 | 68 | 2 | Patterson | 10 | 4 | 37 | 1 |
| Horn | 27 | 5 | 94 | 4 | Horn | 14 | 3 | 58 | 5 |
| Weir | 25 | 3 | 101 | 1 | Weir | 18 | 2 | 75 | 1 |

\* Denotes Captain
† Denotes Keeper

Australia
|  |  | 1st Innings | 2nd Innings |
|---|---|---|---|
| 1 - | D. Crocket | b Samuels ................69 | c Khan b Roberts..........45 |
| 2 - | P. Haynes | b Samuels................19 | c & b Gibson.............51 |
| 3 - | S. Moore* | c Jafar ..................149 | c Winter Gibson............0 |
| 4 - | M Moore | lbw Samuels..............63 | b Gibson.....................0 |
| 5 - | G. Church | b Samuels ...............7 | b Singleton.................27 |
| 6 - | D. Dyson | c Roberts.................45 | b Singleton.................31 |
| 7 - | W. Talbot† | b Roberts.................19 | c Gibson.....................1 |
| 8 - | C. Rogers | c Singleton................6 | not out.......................0 |
| 9 - | G. Patterson | lbw Samuels..............6 | b Gibson.....................0 |
| 10 – | W. Horn | b Singleton.................5 | ht wkt Gibson...............0 |
| 11 – | G Weir | not out....................4 | Bowled........................0 |
|  |  | Extras....................11 | Extras..................... 10 |
|  |  | Total...................403 | Total......................167 |

**FALL OF WICKETS**

First Innings:     44-1  286-2   290-3   291-4 340-5   6-382-6   393-7   396-8   397-9
Second innings:   96-1   97-2   97-3   97-4   157-5   163-6   165-7   165-8 165-9

| Bowler | Overs | Mdn | Runs | Wkts | Bowler | Overs | Mdn | Runs | Wkts |
|---|---|---|---|---|---|---|---|---|---|
| Samuels | 42 | 8 | 127 | 5 | Samuels | 11 | 0 | 44 | 1 |
| Singleton | 34 | 11 | 119 | 2 | Singleton | 8 | 1 | 38 | 2 |
| Roberts | 35 | 7 | 128 | 2 | Roberts | 10 | 2 | 55 | 1 |
| Gibson | 4 | 0 | 23 | 0 | Gibson | 6 | 2 | 20 | 6 |
| Jafar | 1 | 1 | 0 | 1 | Jafar | 1 | 1 | 0 | 1 |

\* Denotes Captain
† Denotes Keeper

Umpires: Valentine Seabrook & Anton Guishard

# Ashes Series Averages

## England – Batting

|  | M | I | NO | R | HS | Avge |
|---|---|---|---|---|---|---|
| R. Khan | 5 | 9 | 1 | 488 | 167 | 61.0 |
| S. Coleman | 5 | 9 | 0 | 352 | 94 | 39.1 |
| G. Samuels | 5 | 9 | 4 | 191 | 60 | 38.2 |
| G. Stiles | 5 | 9 | 0 | 332 | 102 | 33.2 |
| D. Dennis | 5 | 9 | 0 | 249 | 60 | 27.6 |
| T. Gibson | 1 | 2 | 0 | 55 | 31 | 27.5 |
| M. Engle | 5 | 9 | 0 | 210 | 60 | 23.3 |
| C. Jafar | 2 | 4 | 1 | 50 | 42 | 16.6 |
| H. Winter | 5 | 9 | 0 | 99 | 27 | 11.0 |
| B. Fredericks | 2 | 3 | 0 | 32 | 15 | 10.6 |
| E. Roberts | 5 | 8 | 2 | 48 | 21 | 8.0 |
| F. Arnold | 3 | 5 | 0 | 31 | 18 | 6.2 |
| J. Singleton | 5 | 9 | 0 | 51 | 20 | 5.6 |
| M. French | 1 | 2 | 0 | 0 | 0 | 0 |

## Australia – Batting

|  | M | I | NO | R | HS | Avge |
|---|---|---|---|---|---|---|
| S. Moore | 4 | 8 | 2 | 647 | 149 | 107.8 |
| D. Crocket | 5 | 10 | 0 | 251 | 69 | 25.1 |
| P. Haynes | 5 | 10 | 0 | 234 | 76 | 23.4 |
| D Dyson | 5 | 10 | 0 | 226 | 53 | 22.6 |
| M. Moore | 5 | 10 |  | 188 | 63 | 18.8 |
| K. Barnes | 1 | 2 | 0 | 35 | 19 | 17.5 |
| D. Talbot | 5 | 10 | 0 | 138 | 49 | 13.8 |
| W. Horn | 5 | 10 | 3 | 89 | 21 | 12.7 |
| G. Church | 5 | 10 | 0 | 120 | 40 | 12.0 |
| G. Patterson | 5 | 10 | 1 | 107 | 28 | 11.8 |
| C. Rogers | 5 | 10 | 1 | 52 | 11 | 5.7 |
| G. Weir | 5 | 10 | 3 | 32 | 14 | 4.5 |

## England – Bowling

|  | O | M | R | W | Avge |
|---|---|---|---|---|---|
| T. Gibson | 10 | 2 | 43 | 6 | 7.16 |
| F. Arnold | 60.7 | 12 | 200 | 18 | 11.1 |
| C. Jafar | 18 | 8 | 91 | 8 | 13.0 |
| G. Samuels | 197 | 53 | 535 | 28 | 19.11 |
| E. Roberts | 125.4 | 29 | 461 | 21 | 21.95 |
| J. Singleton | 162.1 | 40 | 557 | 17 | 32.76 |
| M. French | 11 | 1 | 77 | 1 | 77.0 |
| B.Fredricks | 33 | 0 | 156 | 0 | 0 |

## Australia – Bowling

|  | O | M | R | W | Avge |
|---|---|---|---|---|---|
| W. Horn | 127.5 | 24 | 420 | 28 | 15.0 |
| M Moore | 13 | 2 | 49 | 3 | 16.33 |
| C. Rogers | 154 | 30 | 461 | 20 | 23.05 |
| G. Weir | 96 | 9 | 370 | 15 | 24.66 |
| G. Patterson | 98.4 | 8 | 371 | 11 | 33.72 |
| G. Church | 10 | 0 | 47 | 1 | 47.00 |

# The Wash-up

**Frank Arnold**: Frank celebrated his return to cricket by scoring a stunning 19 ball 54 run dig and taking 9 wickets in one innings in India. After 16 more Test matches, played in India, Australia, the West Indies and England, he returned to Devon and bought a pub on the moors. He married subsequently and became the father of three 'big' girls.

**Jim Singleton**: Toured only once, playing four more Tests on the subcontinent and three more in England. After two ankle injuries he eventually bought into his uncle's trucking business. He continued to play for Good Walloping and became club president later in life. He and Arthur remained on the best of terms for ever more.

**Edwin Roberts**: Played thirty-one Tests and negotiated the purchase of Charmy Down from Mrs Cheshire, who stayed on until she passed away. Edwin and Jane and set up a Super-Six cricketing museum in the great hangar and a Fighter Base museum, restoring all Charmy Down's buildings to their original state. Bert McCabe became a permanent fixture around Charmy Down and a great mate of Edwin's. Both businesses provided a suitable income for Edwin and his family. Charmy Down was the venue for many a Super-Six reunion. Biggles lived to a ripe old age and when his time came he managed to make his way into the basket of Edwin's old bicycle one last time.

**Chandra Jafar**: Over a six-year period he played twenty seven more Tests for England and five more full county seasons at the top level with Somerset. He and his family expanded their Curry House and renamed it 'Lucky 7's' curry house. Within its walls was an exclusive dining room filled with his cricketing memorabilia and copy of Wisden in which he was described as very being '*very chatty*'. All customers were treated to an audience with Lucky 7 – whether they wanted it or not.

**George Samuels**: Played thirty-two Test matches and took over 200 test wickets for England. Edwin and he retired from international cricket during the same Test. He married Alice Feldon and upon retirement from Test cricket grew his Afro again, bought into a organic brewery, fathered a boy & girl and headed north again.

**Tim Gibson**: Played seventy-three Test matches for England. He claimed over 350 Test wickets, and scored two Test centuries and thirteen half-centuries. He retired relatively young in his cricketing career to study winemaking, eventually buying a vineyard and ski lodge in France where he lived for some years. He received a steady flow of guests each year, with George not leaving for six months at one stage. Tim named one of his eldest sons Arthur.

**Arthur Jenkins**: Never returned to full-time work after the Lord's victory, turning his hand to event speaking, charity work, youth cricket programs and coaching. Arthur received numerous awards and accolades from both the cricketing world and his countrymen. He continued his involvement with Good Walloping, assisted by Ted and Jim. Jean assisted Arthur and Carl Thompson with the production of a best-selling book called *King Arthur and the Super-Six*. She regularly visited Mrs Cheshire and Edwin at Charmy Down. Tim and Arthur remained firm friends for life. At the age of seventy-four, Arthur's ageing knees had one last assignment, this time nearly buckling as the sword of the Sovereign lightly touched his shoulders. Sir Arthur never got his century in years but was pleased with his final score.

My sincerest thanks go out to Mike Petrucchelli, Duncan Hickman, Dave Groves, Laurens Taylor, Swift Horse, Bobby Gainher, David & James of Two Associates.

Special thanks to Mo Kerwood, Miles Orchard, Miss P, Pete McRae, Ben Smith, Angus MacDonald and Katie Wheeler who *all* went the extra distance for me.

Top billing plus love & kisses to Sarah and my girls who pushed me along all the way. This is for you.